A POTENTIAL INTERNATIONAL BEST SELLER

THE GOLDEN SPARROW

A NOVEL
BY ASHOK MALHOTRA

A story set during the waning days of the British Rule in India, World War II, the partition of India and the carnage that followed.... it entraps the reader

Printed by

Createspace,
an Amazon.com company

The Golden Sparrow

Copyright © 2013 by Ashok Malhotra

All rights reserved. No part of this book may be reproduced in any form or by any means, electronic, mechanical, photocopying, recording or otherwise, without the prior written permission of the author. The author can be contacted at amalhotra@rogers.com.

Publication services provided by Createspace–an Amazon company

ISBN: 1491082275
ISBN 13: 9781491082270
Library of Congress Control Number: 2013919906
CreateSpace Independent Publishing Platform,
North Charleston, SC

This is a work of fiction. All incidents and dialogue, and all characters, with the exception of well known historical and public figures and well known historical incidents, are product of the author's imagination and are not real. Any resemblance to persons living or dead is entirely coincidental. Where real, historical or public figures, incidents, situations, books, scriptures and institutions appear in the story, they are used for reference only, and any situations, dialogue or incidents ascribed to them are fictional in character.

*This may be a work of fiction, but in the realm of imagination…
everything is real.*

ASHOK MALHOTRA

TABLE OF CONTENTS

Prologue vii

1	Shakespearewala	1
2	*Dahej*–Dowry	15
3	War	25
4	Marriage	31
5	Intrigue	39
6	The Householder	45
7	I am born	55
8	Health is Wealth	67
9	Paradise on Earth	75
10	The Dream	89
11	Third Life	95
12	1945: The Bomb	103
13	1946-47: Communal Conflagration	113
14	Lahore: July 1947; Train to Simla	127
15	Lahore: August 1947; Bequeathed	139
16	Simla: August–September, 1947; Dawn of Independence ..	143
17	Delhi: September 1947; New Beginnings	167
18	Delhi: January 1948; Assassination	177
19	Horsing Around	183
20	Plane to Lahore	189
21	April 1948; Accommodations	197
22	Delhi: May 1948; Ray of Hope	209
23	June 1948; Close Quarters	223
24	Interview: The New East India Company	229
25	July 1948; My School	239
26	A Thread That Binds	247
27	October 1948; Adoption	257
28	1949: Galaxy of Stars	265
29	Motorcycle	273
30	New Arrival	281
31	Growing up	289
32	Delhi 1950: House Building	295

33	Thought Provoking	303
34	House Warming	307
35	Abduction	311
36	Epilogue	321

    Acknowledgements and Musings 323

PROLOGUE
Lahore: 1947

Sometimes I feel that I have always existed. I do not have any memory of not existing. My experiences are a journey of my consciousness through time. Some experiences that leave an imprint on our mind become our memories, and some experiences leave deeper imprints than others. A few of my early experiences are so traumatic that their vividness still lives with me. The one that follows stays with me. Always.

It is a moonless, dark and hot night in May 1947. I am five years old. I am trying to sleep under the open sky on the roof top, tossing and turning on a *charpoy*—a bed made of a wooden frame with strings of jute strung across—fitted with a net to keep the mosquitoes[1] away.

Karan *chacha* and Dilip *chacha*, my two uncles, my father's younger brothers, are standing on the roof top. They are stacking bricks on top of the parapet. The bricks are stacked three or four high, practically all around the perimeter of the terrace.

"Hit one brick over the other; break it into two and, when they come to attack us, hit them on their heads with the bricks," says Karan *Chacha* to Dilip *Chacha*.

My grandfather has his double barrel gun open and is loading yellow cylindrical cartridges into each barrel, while inspecting the perimeter of the terrace. My father, Surinder, is downstairs checking that the doors and windows are secure and is bringing upstairs several boxes of gun cartridges that are kept hidden in the secret compartments in the ceiling of the house.

---

1 Mosquitoes: Type of flies that travel freely between Hindus, Muslims, Sikhs, Jews and Christians and know no difference between their bloods.

They are preparing against a suspected attack, on our Hindu locality of Prem Nagar, by Muslims of a neighboring locality, Rajgarh, in Lahore. Fighting has erupted between Hindus and Muslims upon declaration that the British government has decided to partition India into two parts, one Hindu, the other Muslim.

All the window openings are blocked up with brick masonry to prevent the attackers from throwing fire torches inside the house. The wooden window shutters and doors are painted with fire retardant paints. Setting fire to houses is the favorite offensive weapon of both Muslims and Hindus. A hand pump is ready and tested to make sure it can pump water to the roof top, in case fire lit torches are thrown on the roof. Every night, my father and his two brothers are on duty taking turns to look out for attackers.

Wails of *"Allahu Akbar"* are filling the distant air brought over by a gentle warm breeze of the hot May evening from the Muslim locality of Rajgarh. In reply, shouts of *"Jai Bajrang Bali"* are filling the air from the Hindu neighborhood of Krishan Nagar. I am afraid and shivering with fear. I am lying in bed with my hand between my legs. I get out of my bed by removing the side of the mosquito net and walk over to my grandfather who has just clicked the gun barrel shut and is moving his hands over the two barrels as if he is caressing a pet. It is a while before he realizes that I am standing near him. He still keeps moving his hands up and down the barrels of the gun, deep in thought.

As he senses my presence, he looks up and asks, "Son, what is the matter?" He can see that I am shivering. I address him as *Pitaji;* same as his sons do.

I reply, *"Pitaji, Pitaji,"* clinging to his legs, "are they going to kill us?" He places the gun against the wall, picks me up and sits me on his lap and then gently moves his hands over my head to calm me down. After a minute or so, he picks me up again, gets up and takes me into one of the *Barsaaties*. This is a room we move into if it starts to rain when we sleep on the roof terrace.

In the background, a man's voice announces in mixed Hindi and Urdu, "I am speaking from the Lahore Studio of the All India Radio. There have been a few incidents of killing and looting."

As soon as I hear these words on the radio, my teeth start chattering. At this instant, *Pitaji,* my grandfather, switches off the radio and makes me sit on the bed nearby. He stands up and bends down gently, holds me by my shoulders and says, "I am *Khan Baba*. I am not afraid of anybody. People are full of fear when they see *me*. See that gun over there? We have three more like that. When I am here nobody can harm us. Do not ever be afraid of anybody or anything."

He picks me up and takes me to my bed, lifts the mosquito net and makes me lie down. I pull the sheet over my head; as if to protect myself from all that is going on around me. I turn on my side and pull my legs up in a fetal position.

"Vikram Kumar, what is the matter *beta?*"... my mother's voice.

My grandfather moves away.

My mother lifts the mosquito net. She sits on the bed and puts me in her *goddi* or lap and hugs me close to her. I am in the hands of *my Janani*, my creator.

Nobody can harm me now. I am safe.

Or am I?

As soon as my father comes up on the roof with a gun in hand, I jump out of my mother's lap and shout pointing towards the parapet, "Daddyji, ... Daddyji, they are coming up."

He runs to the parapet, points his gun towards the ground and fires.

A gun shot reverberates through the air. My bed is wet. I become aware of the liquidity of fear; it is there everywhere.

"Vikram, how did you know somebody was on the ground?" my grandfather asks.

I cling to my mother.

My grandmother, who is standing nearby, says, "I think, like Surinder, Vikram also has the Sixth Sense."

• • •

Some time in the middle of the night.

Jimmy, our dog, is standing outside the mosquito net of my bed sniffing, trying to get attention. I am up; everybody else is asleep. He appears uneasy. He is trying to lift the mosquito net and get his head in. Unsuccessful, he walks away towards the parapet of the roof. He stands up resting his paws on the parapet, sniffs and is back again, groaning. Mummyji wakes up. She gets out of the mosquito net and wakes up my father. All the family is now up.

My father has sensed movement on the ground just outside our house. He crouches on the floor and moves towards the parapet and looks down the peephole.

There is loud banging on the front door. "Get out all of you; we will burn you all to death," they are shouting from the ground.

The guns are out again. "Don't shoot at them, there are too many of them," my father says, "I have an idea."

He cups his hands around his mouth and starts to speak loudly in an English accent. "I am Colonel Bradshaw, commander of the Punjab Boundary Force. You are surrounded by my forces. If you don't clear this area within five minutes, we are going to arrest you all."

The voices outside our house slowly die down and the attackers disappear.

My grandfather, putting his arms around my father's shoulders says, "Surinder, what a brilliant idea. We are all proud of you; you saved our lives today."

My father replies, "Pitaji, you should thank Mrs. Wilson. She is the one who taught me to speak like this."

As he has finished talking, he goes to the parapet and looks down the peephole. "Pitaji, he says calling his father, "the attackers are standing under the street light. Oh, my God, I know these boys. I see Jaggi Johnson; he is a gang leader of *Lashkar-e-Shaitaan*, the Army of Devil. His gang is for hire. Why would he be attacking us? He has Hindus, Muslims and Anglo-Indians in his gang. Somebody must be paying his gang to attack us."

Pitaji says, "Oh, now I see what is going on. Dawar is right. He was telling me that the attacks on Hindu and Muslim neighbourhoods are organized by some interested parties, who want to drive a wedge between, the otherwise, friendly Hindu and Muslim communities."

I
SHAKESPEAREWALA

Some are my memories and some are those of others, but now have become mine. Does it really matter? Memories are memories. They are always there. We just have to dig them out.

This is a story woven together like a tapestry from the threads of the memories of many a people. They are not all of the same colour but of different colours, different textures, different weaves... a colour here, a colour there; a thread of cotton here, one of silk there, and another one of wool over there. Oh, and, now and then, a few gems have been woven in–not gemstones but gems of wisdom-some from my grandfather, some from my father, some from my grandmother, and some collected from the lap of my mother. As the story unfolds, you may find a strand here, a strand there not quite knotted yet, but, in the end, when it is all said and done... you will see a tapestry of blazing shades of rich culture, history, politics and plain every day trials and tribulations of the colorful people of India.

And now the story begins.

My grandfather, Yodh Raj Mehra, a Permanent Way Inspector (PWI) in the North Western Indian Railways, is riding the rails on a *Thella* to inspect the railway tracks. It is being pushed by two men running bare foot on the hot rails with perspiration running down their necks. He is on his way home after a grueling day in the June heat.

As he reaches home, he is greeted by, his son, Surinder, "Pitaji, look at this; Mrs. Wilson gave me this leather bound volume of the Merchant of Venice. I stood first in the English class. It was our prize distribution function today."

My grandfather looks, touches the book softly, as if it is an untouchable and says, "Surinder, this will not get you anywhere. Shakespeare is not going to feed you when you grow up; you have to learn a skill that is in demand. You should aspire to be an officer in the Indian Railways. Look at Rajinder Singh; he is only 30 years old, and he is already an Executive Engineer. You should have selected science subjects and gone on to become a civil engineer."

After this lecture from my grandfather, Surinder goes to his room with a long face, sits down on the edge of his bed, caressing the leather on the Merchant of Venice and determined as ever to continue with his love of English literature.

As soon as he sees that my grandfather has finished tea and appears to be talking cheerfully to my grandmother, he goes to him and says, "Pitaji, I want to join Forman Christian College. Mrs. Wilson thinks I may be able to get a scholarship."

My grandfather retorts back, "If you can get a scholarship, well and good; otherwise, you should give up your dream of becoming a professor of English. I am near retirement, and our house is under construction; I don't have money to pay your fees. I can get you a job as an apprentice technician in the railways, and, with hard work, you will also retire like me as a PWI with life time of pension and free first class tickets."

As Surinder is sitting in his room brooding, he gets a premonition: He should go to the Wilson residence.

Later in the evening, he walks over to the Wilson residence. As he reaches there, he finds a number of English couples sitting in the front lawn being served by uniformed bearers. He just stands there trying to decide what to do. As luck would have it, Mrs. Wilson notices him and sends a servant to call him in. When he notices the servant walking towards the front gate, he starts to walk away; the servant catches up with him and says, "*Memsahib* wants you to come in."

Surinder turns around and walks in with confidence. Mrs. Wilson asks, "Surinder, what brings you here?"

"Good evening Mrs. Wilson, I just wanted to talk to you for a minute, but I will come back another time," he says in an upper class British accent—some of it he has picked up over the last two years that he has been a student of Mrs. Wilson, and some is a put-on. But, it draws the attention of the others sitting there.

She then introduces him to other guests, saying, "Surinder is the best student in my class; he received the William S. Shakespeare Prize this year, and, for that, his friends call him *Shakespearewala*."

An Englishman sitting nearby says, "This word *Shakespearewala* is rather amusing. Young man, you should join us at Forman Christian College. We need bright young men like you."

Gordon Wilson, Mrs. Wilson's husband, who was inside the house, comes out and says, "Hello Surinder, nice to see you here. What is this? I hear John tempting you to Forman Christian College? Your father wants you go to study at Thomason College of Civil Engineering at Roorkee and become a civil engineer like Rajinder Singh." Gordon Wilson is the Chief Engineer of the North Western Indian Railway and my grandfather's superior.

Mrs. Wilson says, "Gordon, let him be what he wants to be and not what his father wants him to be. John, tell us, are you prepared to offer him a scholarship?"

"I am sure we could work something out; after all, he does come highly recommended by you." And he gets up from his chair, walks up to Surinder and introduces himself, "I am John Hughes, and this is my wife, Lynda."

Surinder extends his hand confidently and says, "I am honoured to meet you, sir," and bows, respectfully, towards Lynda Hughes."

Surinder walks out of the Wilson residence in high spirits. As he reaches home, my grandfather is sitting in the front lawn going through the mail. As Surinder approaches, he looks up affectionately and says, "Come, *beta,* sit here with me for a while."

Surinder is not the one to let an opportunity like this pass by; his father is usually not home at this time of the day, and when he is home, he is so tired and irritable that he seldom talks to his sons.

"Pitaji, I was just visiting the Wilson bungalow. I met Professor John Hughes of Forman Christian College there. He is sure that I will be offered a scholarship. He even stood up and shook hands with me," Surinder says, hoping to get a favourable response.

My grandfather says, "*Beta*, I am really proud of you. But, I wish you would also give attention to Indian scriptures and literature."

Surinder says, "All right, Pitaji, I promise to read, our holy book, Bhagavad Gita, regularly."

My grandfather gets up and says, "Surinder, let me give you a copy of Bhagavad Gita right now." And they go in the house. My grandfather takes out a book from the shelf and hands it over to him. Surinder leafs through it and says, "Pitaji, this is in Hindi. Do you have the English version?

This really sets the fuse off in my grandfather and he says, "Young men like you are the future of India. You must know your own languages before you master the foreign languages. It is not that I do not like the British, or I do not like the English language; I have good relations with the British; it is the British *Raj* I hate. You know, once upon a time, India used to be known as the **Golden Sparrow**; it was one of the richest nations in the world. And look what we have become now. The British ruling class has kept aloof, exclusive and in a world of their own, quite apart from millions of Indians. In the land of the caste system that is India, the British have built a caste system of their own – 'exclusive'. Not only the British, but all Europeans are members of this 'exclusive class'. Railway carriages, railway station waiting rooms, benches in the parks are marked 'For Europeans only'. "

Surinder says calmly, "Pitaji, they are always very nice to *me*."

My grandfather says, "I think you must be British in your previous birth." And they both laugh. And then, my grandfather says placing his right hand on Surinder's shoulder, "Son, whatever you do, our blessings are always with you. Go conquer the world, but make sure that the Sun never sets on it like the British Empire." And they laugh again.

• • •

At Forman Christian College, Lahore, he shines the brightest, goes on to become the head of the debating society and, eventually, completes his M.A. in English literature with honors. Brimming with profound wisdom of the East and the West, he takes up a teaching job in a private college.

Surinder is six feet tall, slim, wears glasses and has a penchant for Western clothes—a true son of the British Empire. His friends tease him that God gave him birth in India by mistake; he should have been born in Britain.

They could all see it coming: Surinder will not be the one to be satisfied with an ordinary station in life.

• • •

After retiring in 1939, my grandfather and my grandmother build a small house in Prem Nagar locality of Lahore, a city about 500 kilometers northwest of Delhi, the capital of India. Surinder, along with his other two brothers, Dilip and Karan, lives in the parents' house. His eldest brother, Shyam Nath, is a lawyer and lives with his family in the Gawaal Mundi area of Lahore.

Daulat Ram Suri is a prominent and an influential businessman in Lahore. He represents British and other foreign firms in India. He has a large house, not too far from where my grandfather lives and drives a Morris car, a luxury that very few people enjoy. With his six foot frame, fair complexion and broad chest, he has a commanding presence. My grandfather and Daulat Ram go for their morning walk in the same park and many times walk together and have started exchanging small talk about their respective families. Daulat Ram is about ten years younger than my grandfather, but they address each other with due respect. My grandfather addresses him as Suri sahib—sahib means sir or master. Daulat Ram addresses him as Lalaji—a respectful term for an elderly man.

...

On a warm summer day, during the early morning walk—the sun just hugging the curvature of the earth—Daulat Ram says to my grandfather, "Lalaji, I have a younger sister, Kamla, who is a teacher in *Mahila Maha Vidyalaya,* a girl's high school; we are looking for a suitable match for her. Please let me know if you have a suitable boy in your sight."

My grandfather immediately thinks of his number two son and replies, "Certainly Suri Sahib, I will."

As soon as my grandfather reaches home, he, excitedly, seeks out my grandmother, whom he never addresses by name, but by saying, "Where are you, did you hear me?"

She is busy in the kitchen and replies loud enough for him to hear, "Listen, I am here." In turn she also does not address him by his name. It is a custom of the time where husband and wife tactfully gloss over using each other's names as a sign of respect.

He walks over to the kitchen, where my grandmother is sitting on the kitchen floor peeling onions, with tears floating down her cheeks. He takes his shoes off—as is the custom in Hindu homes to keep the cooking area clean—and walks into the kitchen and goes and stands beside her. She is sitting on the floor on the *patra*—a wooden stool about one foot wide by two feet long and about 6 inches off the floor. He pulls up another *patra* and sits beside her. He says to her, "Oh, remember, I have told you about Daulat Ram Suri, who I see in the park sometimes; he has a younger sister; he talked to me about finding a matrimonial match for her."

She, wiping her eyes of onion tears, looks up at him and says, "How about Surinder?"

"I am thinking the same way. I will talk to Suri next time I see him."

For several days, Daulat Ram does not go for his morning walk, being busy with some early business appointments.

A few days later, my grandmother asks my grandfather, "So, did you talk to Suri?"

My grandfather replies, "No, not yet, Suri has not been coming to the park for morning walk, but I will go to his house this evening and see if I can meet him."

Later in the evening on his way to attend the *Katha,* the mass prayers, in a nearby temple, my grandfather sees Daulat Ram standing in the front lawn of his residence. He looks towards Daulat Ram and just stands there for a while hoping that Daulat Ram sees him.

At the same time, Daulat Ram walks towards the entrance gate and happens to see my grandfather and says, "Lalaji, so nice to see you. What brings you here?"

"I am on my way to attend the *Katha* at the Temple." My grandfather clears his throat as a way of gaining some time in order to find the right opportunity to bring up the topic, and he continues, "You remember, Suri Sahib, last time we met… you talked about your sister."

"Yes, of course, I remember," replies Daulat Ram.

"Well, my son, Surinder, is 25, and we are looking for a suitable match for him."

"That is very interesting! What is he currently doing?" Daulat Ram enquires.

My Grandfather replies, "He has completed his M.A. in English literature from Forman Christian College and is now working as a professor in J.N. Chatterji College."

Daulat Ram is very interested in this proposal and says, "How about you and your wife visiting us, next Sunday, to meet our family and have lunch with us; and do bring your son along."

• • •

My grandfather dresses in a suit without a tie. He wears a *Pagari on a Kulla*—a white well starched turban wrapped on a stiff cap—with the *Turra,* the one end of the turban, rising a foot above his head, and the other end hanging a few feet down his back. At six feet three inches tall, with blue eyes and fair skin, he portrays a commanding presence. Surinder looks dapper, dressed in a well tailored suit with a tie. My grandmother dresses in the traditional Punjabi *Shalwaar and Kameeze.* On Sunday afternoon, my grandfather, grandmother and their son,

Surinder, arrive at the Suri residence at the appointed time. They are greeted by Daulat Ram and his wife Nirmala and are invited into the *baithak,* the sitting room. After the pleasantries are over, Nirmala goes away and, a little while later, walks in followed by Kamla, Daulat Ram's younger sister. My grandmother lovingly asks Kamla to sit beside her on the sofa. Kamla is short like my grandmother, has fair complexion and is wearing a dark blue sari with a light blue blouse with the *pallu,* the end of the sari, covering her head. She demurely walks over and sits down beside my grandmother. My grandmother asks, addressing her as a daughter, "*Beti,* how long have you been teaching?"

Kamla replies, "For about two years, *auntyji.*"

What my grandmother really wants to find out is, first of all, if her possible future daughter-in-law can speak and hear, and secondly, if she can cook or not. My grandmother is the only one who does all the cooking at home, and she wants to make sure that her future daughter-in-law will share her burden.

In the meantime, Nirmala says, "Kamla, go and bring some cold drinks for the guests." Kamla gets up and goes to the kitchen.

Meanwhile, Nirmala continues talking, while looking at my grandmother and doing her best to bring forth all of Kamla's qualities and says, addressing my grandmother as respected sister, "*Behenji,* Kamla is very good in cooking and household chores. She even teaches Home Science in school."

After a little while, Kamla walks in with six glasses of *Shakanjavi,* homemade lemonade, on a silver tray.

Daulat Ram is also trying to strike a conversation with Surinder and is trying to find out if the boy is normal and what his future prospects are. He asks, "Surinder, when did you complete your M.A.?"

"Last year," he replies.

"Do you plan to continue working in a private college, or do you plan to take up a job in a government aided college?" Daulat Ram asks.

"I want to work in a private college and work towards becoming a partner," Surinder replies.

"Tell me more about how private colleges operate. I don't know much about them. They seem to be mushrooming everywhere," Daulat Ram says.

Surinder describes his association with the college, "The College, I am teaching in, is J.N. Chatterjee College. This is a private college that prepares students for appearing in exams for the Faculty of Arts (F.A) and for the Bachelor of Arts (B.A) designations. I teach English literature. One has to spend two years to complete F.A. after passing Matric, and spend two more years thereafter, to complete the B.A. Degree. The students who attend the private colleges are, generally, those who cannot get admission in regular colleges, but are still permitted by the Punjab University to appear in university exams."

"I did not know that one can complete a university degree studying in a private college," interrupts Daulat Ram.

Surinder continues, "Since most of the students are not good in studies, they depend on the professors to tutor them in a way that they can just pass the exams. All of us teaching there have acquired the art of tutoring the students in such a way that a high percentage of the students get through the exams. We are also experts in "guessing" the questions for upcoming exams, and then preparing answers to those questions and sell the answers for a price, which the students are happy to pay."

"That is interesting—education as a business! Who is the owner?" Daulat Ram asks.

"Professor S.L. Soni is the owner, and he also teaches mathematics. He was a student of J.N. Chatterjee, who was a well known Professor of mathematics. S.L. Soni established the college in 1931 and named it after his esteemed teacher," Surinder replies.

While the conversation is going on, the ladies are setting the table for lunch. The fact that Daulat Ram likes good food is apparent from the exotic dishes that are being set on the table. There is *Rogan Josh, Tandoori Murgha, Buhuna Gosht and Briyani* adorning the table. Everybody is starting to sit around the dining table.

My grandmother asks, "Did you cook all this, Kamla?"

She looks shyly at the floor and before she can say anything, Nirmala replies, "She has cooked *Rogan Josh and Briyani*."

My grandmother smiles approvingly, but does not say anything. As the lunch starts, tall brass tumblers full of *Lassi* or butter milk are brought to the table.

My grandfather is a connoisseur of meat dishes, having been born and brought up in the North-West Frontier Provinces. He says, "Suri Sahib, this is the best meat I have eaten in a long time." Things appear to be moving in the right direction. Surinder seems to have made a favorable impression on Daulat Ram, and my grandmother is doting over Kamla. There is no direct conversation between Kamla and Surinder, but they do steal glances at each other, as they know that this is their only chance before they are asked to make a decision about their future.

Langra mangoes are brought to the table in a bucket of cold water that has been kept outdoors at night to keep it cool, in the absence of availability of ice. Daulat Ram takes pride in serving the best food to his guests.

He puts his hand in the bucket and brings up mangoes, one at a time, and appraises each by pressing with his fingers and taking in their fragrance and remarks, "See Lalaji, I think you will like this one."

He picks up a knife and begins to slice the mango by taking slices off the two sides and leaving the seed, thus slicing the mango in three parts and offers it to my grandfather with pride in his eyes. My grandfather picks up the piece with the seed, as that is his favorite part of the mango.

As soon as the dessert and tea is done, my grandfather gets up and says, "Suri Sahib, this has been a memorable meal. Please share a meal with us also at our humble home one day."

Daulat Ram looks at his wife, Nirmala, for approval, which she gives tacitly by nodding, and he replies, "Lalaji, anytime you command, we will be there." They decide to get together at my grandfather's house the following Sunday, also for lunch."

· · ·

When they reach home, my grandfather and grandmother sit down in the *Baithak* and ask Surinder to join them. They ask him, "Surinder, what do you think of Kamla?"

It appears that he has already made up his mind. He replies without hesitation, "I think I like her."

My grandmother starts preparations for the lunch for coming Sunday. After some discussion, they settle the menu.

Daulat Ram informs my grandfather during one of their morning walks, "Lalaji, I just want to let you know that Kamla will not be joining us for lunch on Sunday. I hope you understand. It is our custom that the girl does not visit the boy's home during matrimonial negotiations. Also, I would like you to know that we like Surinder; and therefore, I took the liberty of informing our parents, who live in Gurdaspur. They replied back that they are also interested in meeting Surinder."

My grandfather replies, "We also like Kamla; in fact, my wife can't stop talking about her. Please invite your parents on our behalf to join us for lunch on Sunday."

· · ·

On Sunday, the Suri family comes over for lunch in their Morris car. The neighborhood urchins gather all around the car, as Suri's are getting out. My grandfather and Surinder go out to receive the guests. Daulat Ram introduces his father, Salig Ram, to my grandfather and to Surinder. They all step inside and are directed to the *Baithak*. My grandfather's house is not as big as Daulat Ram's. There are four rooms on the ground floor and two on the roof terrace. There is *Vehra* —a courtyard in the centre of the house —a kitchen and two bathrooms. One of the rooms is used as a *Biathak* and the others are bedrooms. There is no formal dining room. Daily meals are partaken in the kitchen while seated on the floor. For this occasion, a table has been set up in the courtyard to be used as a dining table. As soon as everybody is seated, my grandfather asks the guests for drinks. He announces that either *Sharbat or Lassi* is the choice.

At that time, Daulat Ram's mother, Melan Devi, gets up and goes out of the room to the kitchen to join my grandmother. Both the mothers are getting familiar with each other and are also putting forth the best qualities of their respective son or daughter. Melan Devi is also using this occasion to look around the possible future home of her daughter. In the meantime, Karan, the youngest son of my grandparents, walks into the house and is introduced to the guests and is promptly asked by my grandfather to bring in the drinks that are being prepared in the kitchen. While men are sipping drinks, women are in the kitchen getting the food ready. Daulat Ram's father is older than my grandfather, but they both address each other as *Bhai Sahib*—respected brother.

Daulat Ram's father asks my grandfather, "*Bhai Sahib,* where does your family hail from?"

My grandfather responds, "We are from district Jhelum in the province of Punjab, and for your information, Surinder was born in Jhelum City. And, *Bhai Sahib,* how long has your family lived in Gurdaspur?"

Daulat Ram's father replies "We have lived in Gurdaspur for two generations. I have a small electrical contracting business."

Soon thereafter, my grandmother comes in and requests everybody to come over to the dining table in the courtyard.

A white table cloth covers the round table that my grandfather had brought with him, when he retired. Chairs are set up around the table.

"Lalaji, this looks like a round table conference," Daulat Ram jokes, making reference to the round table conferences that had taken place in early thirties between the Indian freedom fighters and the British Government.

Surinder adds half jokingly, "I have read that the tables were not round at all; they were oblong with rounded ends."

It is a sumptuous lunch with curries of lentils, vegetables and chicken along with home cooked *Roti* and Rice *Pullao*. The Suri's enjoy the simplicity of the dishes and pay suitable complements to my grandmother's cooking style. For dessert, there is *Kheer,* the rice pudding, and mangoes. Mangoes have already been peeled and served in a brass plate. Daulat Ram likes to eat his mango pieces mixed with *Kheer*. My grandfather picks up his favorite part of the mango, the *Gittuck*, and peels the skin and eats with the juice dripping on his plate. The two ladies have their meal in the kitchen, while they exchange small talk about their families. After lunch is finished, the Suri family departs with promise to get in touch soon.

After the Suri family reaches home, they decide to sleep on the matter for a few days. Daulat Ram makes some inquiries about Surinder and his family through his contacts at Forman Christian College. His contact confirms that Surinder is a Formanite, an alumnus, and that he has completed his studies with distinction in English Literature. Kamla has already left the matter of the approval of family and background of the boy in the hands of her elder brother, Daulat Ram, and her parents.

When Daulat Ram and my grandfather meet at the park during their morning walk after a few days, Daulat Ram says with folded hands, "Lalaji, we are placing the honor of our family in your hands. Our family will be honored to have Surinder as our son-in-law."

My grandfather and his family have already come to a similar conclusion. He replies with equal respect and humbleness, "Suri Sahib, God is great. We are blessed to welcome an accomplished and noble young lady like Kamla to our family."

When my grandfather reaches home after his walk, he announces the good news. My grandmother is delighted. Surinder is just about to leave for work when he hears the news. He shows some indifference to the announcement, as if he did not hear it. As he is placing his books in the cane rack clipped to the bicycle handle bars, my grandfather gets hold of him, physically, and asks him with a smile on his face, "Surinder, did you hear what I said?"

"Yes, Pitaji," he replies shyly, and bikes away to the College to teach his class.

• • •

As he is riding his bicycle, he is thinking of Kamla, and how she will change his life. He remembers the day he first saw her and felt that she was the girl for him;

the day when he went to the school where she teaches, without telling anybody, to catch a glimpse of her while she is getting out of the school to go home; and how, one day, he musters enough courage to meet her outside the school to talk to her. Daydreaming of his future with Kamla, he arrives at the College. He leaves his bicycle at the bicycle-stand and enters the Professors' room. He comes face to face with his Principal, S.L. Soni.

The Principal asks jokingly, "What is the matter Professor, you seem lost?"

Surinder has a few minutes before the start of the class, and he asks S.L. Soni, "May I speak to you alone, please?"

They go into S.L. Soni's office, and Surinder tells him the whole story about his matrimonial goings on.

S.L. Soni is delighted and congratulates him and reminds him mischievously, "Don't forget to invite your friends from the College to the marriage ceremony. We are the ones going to be dancing the *Bhangra* in front of the *Baraat*."

Surinder gets up with a smile on his face and goes to teach his class. This is an English literature class that is attended by both boys and girls studying towards their B.A. One of Shakespeare's plays, Romeo and Juliet, is the subject of study that day. Surinder has the book in hand, but he is reciting from memory in an oratorical style. In fact, he remembers most works of Shakespeare by heart. The students affectionately call him Shakespearewala. Literal translation: The one who is Shakespeare's keeper. He recites a number of well known romantic passages from different acts and scenes and explains their meaning in detail. There are a few that are receiving special attention from him. One of them is:

What's in a name? That which we call a rose
By any other name would smell as sweet.

Some boys and girls, sitting in the rear of the class, start to giggle and start teasing each other. One of the boys whispers to the other, while pointing slyly to one of the girls with a sharp tongue, "What if the rose has a thorn, how sweet will that smell?"

And the other:

See how she leans her cheek upon her Hand!
O that I were a glove upon that hand,
That I might touch that cheek!

One of the girls in the class raises her hand as if to ask a question, but says instead, "Professor, sir, I am sitting with my cheek on my hand, I hope nobody is thinking of touching it!"

The whole class breaks into laughter. Surinder realizes that in the euphoria of his forthcoming engagement, he got carried away with romanticizing the play. He steers the attention of the class to more mundane passages.

Surinder knows that most of the students are not interested in the intricacies of Shakespearean romantic tragedy, but, rather, they are there to pass the examinations so that the boys can get jobs and the girls' parents can tell the prospective grooms that the girl has completed her B.A. in English literature.

2
DAHEJ–DOWRY

Both sides consult their respective Pundits and the dates for the formal engagement and marriage of Kamla and Surinder are set. The engagement is in two months time on Sunday, July 28, 1940 and the marriage on Sunday, December 15, 1940. Setting dates is the easier part of a wedding in India. The issues of "give and take", *Dahej,* the Dowry, also have to be settled. The "give" is generally from one side—the bride's.

A week or so later, Daulat Ram and my grandfather meet in the park during their morning walk. Daulat Ram brings up the topic of dowry and asks, "Lalaji, please forgive me. May I ask, if you have any special demands?" This is a way of asking, how much Dowry do you want? My grandfather is the most principled man you can find. He himself, having gone through the weddings of his two daughters, is dead against the system of groom's family asking dowry from the bride's family.

He replies, "Suri Sahib, please do not embarrass me by asking this question. We do not have any demands. You may conduct the wedding any way you wish."

The matter does not end there.

When my grandfather reaches home, he tells my grandmother, "Suri asked me about *Dahej,* and I told him that we do not need anything."

My grandmother is not pleased to hear this. She says, "I have married off two daughters, and I gave a reasonable amount of dowry. Every boy's mother has aspirations. We are going to have all the relatives around at the time of the marriage. They will all talk about it. It is not that I want anything for myself; it is just that the relatives are going to embarrass me by making odd comments."

He replies, "Listen, and don't get upset. Suri is a well-to-do man. After all, he will do things that are in keeping with his status. Let us not talk about this any more. I am not going to talk to Suri about this topic again."

The matter is not talked about, but thought about a lot over the next several months.

For reasons that will become apparent later, my grandfather has kept his eldest son, Shyam Nath, and daughter-in-law, Sona Devi, out of the initial matrimonial discussions. Once the matter is settled, he sends a message to them inviting them for lunch on Sunday. Shyam Nath has a horse drawn Victorian buggy, with a coachman, that he utilizes for his and his family's travelling convenience. It is aristocratic in design with all the bells and whistles. On Sunday at about noon, they announce their arrival with the coachman jingling the bells by the side of the buggy and the horse coming to an abrupt stop with a loud neighing. Everybody in the house knows that Shyam Nath and family have arrived. Both Shyam Nath and Sona Devi do *Peri Penna* by bowing down and touching my grandparents' feet.

After they are seated in the *Baithak*, my grandfather tells them, "I want to give you good news. It happened very suddenly." He is trying to lay the ground work for releasing the news gradually, because, in his heart, he knows that he should have involved them in the process, but he did not do so in order to keep the decision making to as few a people as possible. He continues, "You know Daulat Ram. I have told you about him a few times. One day, he brought a proposal of his sister's for marriage to Surinder. We met them. Surinder liked Kamla, and they have decided to get engaged."

Shyam Nath is a lawyer and is of a calm demeanor, and he says, "This is very good news, Pitaji. I know Daulat Ram. He is a very prominent man of Lahore. Surinder has made a very good choice. We are very happy for him."

His wife Sona Devi, who is also sitting nearby, is not so diplomatic. Whenever she is in the presence of my grandfather, as a mark of respect, she covers her head with the end of her Sari; using it as a veil. Otherwise, she is somewhat domineering and outspoken. As soon as she hears the news, she realizes that she has been deliberately left out. She likes to be consulted in matters, such as this, that affect the whole family. It was because of her aforementioned nature that my grandfather did not involve her in the discussions related to the match-making.

As soon as her husband, Shyam Nath, has finished speaking, she says in a sarcastic tone, "I am sure you have made the right decision, but I would have liked to have seen and approved my *Devrani*—my dear younger sister-in-law... Where is Surinder? I want to complain to him." Fortunately for him, Surinder is not home at the time.

• • •

The day of the engagement, the whole family is at the house. Surinder's sisters and their families have also arrived the previous night. Preparations are underway to receive the engagement party from the Suri family, who are expected to arrive at about 4 P.M. with the *Shagan*—a collection of "auspicious offerings" for the groom's family. Although the matter is not talked about, there is anticipation in the air about the "auspicious offerings". Depending on the status of the bride's family, the "auspicious offerings" may include gifts for a wide range of relatives. Finally, the suspense is over and the Suri family arrives accompanied by a few relatives and friends and bearing baskets of fruits and red boxes of, as yet unknown, goodies. Kamla is not part of the party. The Suri family is treated to light snacks and tea. After that, the Priest carries out a brief ceremony by applying a saffron mark on Surinder's forehead and reciting sacred hymns in Sanskrit. At the conclusion of the religious ceremony, Kamla's father offers gifts to Surinder, my grandparents and other relatives. The whole function is over in about ninety minutes, and the Suri party departs. The Suris have hardly left the house when the ladies of the house rush to open their gifts and start talking to each other comparing their respective "auspicious offerings". The smiles on their faces show that Suris have looked after everybody adequately. My grandfather is not pleased with what he sees, but, for the time being, he decides to keep his feelings to himself.

The engagement ceremony is only half complete. The groom's family is supposed to pay a return visit to the bride's house to perform the *Chunni* ceremony—formal presentation of a set of ceremonial clothes to the bride.

My grandfather announces, "I want everybody to be ready to depart for the bride's house in one half hour."

Items that are to be transported to the Suri residence, in order to conduct the ceremony, are distributed to different members of the family to be carried by hand. The groom's side is not supposed to bring any "auspicious offerings" for the relatives of the bride; therefore, the "offering" from the groom's family is rather thin. The only items that are carried are a Sari, blouse, jewelry and some items of make-up for Kamla and some sweets. Relatives and friends, led by my grandfather and including Surinder, the Groom, arrive at the Suri residence, which is within walking distance. It is a hot, humid and a cloudy day. Some members of the party are carrying umbrellas in case it begins to rain. The party is greeted at the gate by Kamla's father, Salig Ram, and her brother, Daulat Ram. Everybody is invited to move to the front lawn. The men folk make themselves comfortable on the chairs. Being a hot and humid day and after a long walk, they welcome cold drinks of Rose and Orange Squash, very popular non-alcoholic drinks of the day. Assorted sweets, such as *Burfee* and *Jalebies*, are also being served.

The women are invited to come into the house. My grandmother hands over the ceremonial clothes and jewelry she has brought for Kamla to Kamla's mother. She takes the clothes into one of the bedrooms situated on one side of the sitting room. After about fifteen minutes, Kamla, escorted by her two sisters, walks into the sitting room wearing the clothes and jewelry that had been brought by the groom's family. The original plan was to hold the engagement ceremony outdoors, but because of the overcast sky it is moved indoors. The men folk, who are seated out in the front lawn, are also requested to move indoors. Surinder and Kamla are asked to sit on the sofa. This is the first time that most members of my grandfather's family have seen Kamla. Therefore, they gather close to the sofa to have a look, especially Surinder's sister-in-law, Sona Devi, and sisters, Chanda and Kanta. The three of them make eyes at each other with smiles on their faces, signifying approval; not that it made any difference now. After the priest has completed the religious ceremony, rings are exchanged, and Surinder and Kamla are engaged. The newly engaged couple accepts blessings from everyone.

A light drizzle has started. People stand in the verandah and enjoy a welcome relief from the heat. A slow cool breeze is blowing and some young girls break out in a chorus and start singing a folk song of the Punjab state about *Suhana Sawan Da Maheena*—the fragrant month of Sawan of the Hindu calendar during which the Monsoon rains are in full swing, and people celebrate respite from heat by hanging swings on the trees and singing songs of joy.

"It is a very good omen to have rain on the day of engagement or marriage." the priest declares.

As the rain abates, people say thanks and good bye to the hosts. My grandfather and his family walk back home.

• • •

When the guests have left and the family is together, my grandfather brings up the subject of dowry. It has been bothering him ever since he has seen gifts brought by Suri family being greedily opened by his family.

"This system is really a shame on society." He says angrily, as he is walking up and down the sitting room. Everybody is taken aback by his outburst.

My grandmother tries to calm him down. She says "This has been a tradition for centuries. How is it that you never brought this subject up when your own daughters were getting married? We did whatever the tradition demanded at that time."

"I feel embarrassed to accept so much from a family that is about to become a part of us. I wonder how this ugly tradition started," my grandfather retorts.

Shyam Nath, his eldest son, who is a lawyer, gets up from his chair as if he is about to address a judge in court and says mockingly, but with respect, "My Lord, may I have the court's indulgence?" My grandfather is amused by this act, and Shyam Nath goes on, "According to the Hindu law, a female has no right on the assets of her parents. The original purpose of the dowry was to give the bride a share of assets of her family. Over a period of time, it has taken the form of a "price" that bride's parents have to pay to the groom's family to have their daughter accepted as part of the family. It is unfortunate that it is becoming worse with time. This is going to have terrible consequences for our society. A day may come when people will shun the birth of a girl."

After this exchange, some family members get up, one at a time, and go to their respective rooms and Shyam Nath and his family also take leave and depart for their home.

Overnight, all members of the family have had time to reflect upon the subject of dowry. In the morning, Surinder goes over to my grandfather and tells him, "Pitaji, please talk to Suri Sahib to make sure that he understands that we have no demands for dowry. They need not give any gifts to any of our relatives at the time of the marriage ceremony."

My grandfather says, "It is a very sensitive topic. I will see what I can do."

• • •

As soon as Surinder enters his class the day after his engagement, he is mobbed by his students, especially the girls.

"Sir, we have heard that you got engaged yesterday. Congratulations!" He is taken aback and begins to blush.

He is thinking: *How on earth did the students find out about it—must be principal, S.L. Soni, who had also attended the engagement party.*

A few of the girls ask him, "How about showing us her photograph."

He has a photo in his wallet but decides not to show it to any of the students. He wants to keep his personal life separate from his professional life.

The girls are not giving up, "Sir, no wonder you have been narrating romantic passages from Romeo and Juliet."

He just keeps smiling and says as little as possible and, gradually, walks into the professors' lounge for refuge.

A few days later, my grandfather goes for his morning walk, hoping to see Daulat Ram in the park. The route to the park passes in front of Daulat Ram's residence. As he is approaching Daulat Ram's residence, Daulat Ram's car is pulling out of the driveway. Their eyes lock.

Daulat Ram asks his driver to stop the car and comes out to greet my grandfather. "Good morning Lalaji. I have to pick up some important papers from Mall Road so I thought that I will stop on the way and have the pleasure of morning walk in Lawrence Gardens. I will be honored if you join me."

My grandfather hesitates, and then decides to accompany Daulat Ram, hoping that this will give him the opportunity to talk to Daulat Ram about some matters that have been uppermost in his mind.

The driver parks the car, and both Daulat Ram and my grandfather set out for a leisurely stroll through one of India's finest gardens. This is my grandfather's first visit to Lawrence Gardens. Daulat Ram is one of the few Indian members of the Lahore Gymkhana Club located there; therefore, he is familiar with the history and the facilities. As the two of them are enjoying the fresh morning breeze, Daulat Ram begins to relate to my grandfather the history of the gardens, possibly to inform him or maybe to impress him, "The gardens were established in 1862 on about 112 acres. Thousands of saplings were brought in from different parts of the British Empire, where the sun never sets. The gardens were named after Sir John Lawrence–late 19th century British Viceroy of India. In the middle of the Lawrence Gardens, buildings were built to house the Lahore Gymkhana. Even a cricket ground was laid with the best turf in the country, and the cricket pitch that was second to none in the world."

"Suri Sahib, I used to think that only *Sahibs and Memsahibs*–the British gentry–are allowed in these gardens," my grandfather adds.

"Well, Lalaji, things have changed after all the pressure that Gandhi and others have put on the British. There have been so many Round Table Conferences that the British are going in circles," he says in jest. "Gardens are now open to everybody, but there are restrictions to membership in the Gymkhana Club. The day is not far off when India will be free of the British rule and everybody will be treated as equal."

My grandfather gives a sarcastic laugh and says, "We Indians don't even treat our fellow Indians as equal, so why blame the British. Look at our own class system. The people who perform tasks such as cleaning our homes and toilets are termed *Achoote*—the untouchables. We treat our servants as slaves. Do you think this will change after the British leave India? I don't think it will."

"You are right, Lalaji. We Indians have developed a habit of blaming all our problems on the British rule or on our Stars. We must look into our conscience and ask ourselves what we can do for our fellow Indians and stop blaming the rest of the world."

My grandfather continues passionately "Well, Suri Sahib, as far as my understanding goes, there are three classes of Indians. The visible minority, and by that I mean the rich and the well to do, who are in a minority but are the most visible or get the most attention. Then comes the invisible majority, and by that I mean the very poor and the downtrodden, who are in majority but do not get noticed at all, and that is why I call them invisible. In between are people like us, the bulging middle class, who are neither here nor there—the forgotten ones. At least Gandhi is standing up for the poor untouchables. Middle class is the orphan class; which has nobody looking after its interest."

Daulat Ram is scratching his head, while he is listening, "I must say that I have never looked at it that way."

"The problem is that we people get so used to being served by the poor that, either sub-consciously or unconsciously, we do not want the poor to come out of the trap…" realizing that this is neither the time nor the place for this type of conversation, he says, "Suri Sahib, please forgive me. I don't want to ruin your morning walk with this kind of talk."

My grandfather leads Daulat Ram towards a tree with shade. It is getting pretty hot and humid and my grandfather is looking around to see if he can find some shade and water. Daulat Ram senses this and invites him to the Gymkhana Club that is located in the centre of the gardens. Both of them walk over to the club and Daulat Ram finds a table in one corner of the verandah and hails, "*Bera, come hea*". This is how the English people pronounce *Bearer, come here; the R being silent*. The, so called, upper class Indians have picked up on the way the English pronounce the words ending with R and some other words such as *Hour, Power* and pronounce these *as Arr and Paar*.

Now, Daulat Ram is trying to impress me with his English accent, but he does not know that I have worked all my life with the English colleagues, my grandfather is thinking.

As the bearer walks over to their table, my grandfather asks for a glass of water, but Daulat Ram insists that he have some other drink, such as Orange Squash or Lime Cordial. He politely insists on having water. Daulat Ram orders Orange Squash, a drink made from orange syrup mixed with water. My grandfather has not taken to the fancy drinks. He prefers the Indian drinks, such as *Shakanjabi,* made with fresh lime squeezed into water with some sugar added, and *Lassi* made with curd swirled with a handheld wooden mixer. While they are enjoying their drink on this hot morning, a very British voice loudly calls out for my grandfather, "Yodh Raj, jolly good to see you again." He immediately turns around to look, and is pleasantly surprised to see Gordon Wilson the Chief Engineer of the Northern Western Railway. He was his boss just prior to retirement.

Both Daulat Ram and my grandfather get up, and there are hand shakes all around. My grandfather asks, "Gordon Sahib, how are Mrs. Wilson and the children?"

Gordon Wilson asks in return, "How is your family, and how is *Shakespearewala?*"

"He is fine and engaged to be married soon." My grandfather says looking at Daulat Ram and then he introduces Daulat Ram. Daulat Ram, being a salesman, sees an opportunity to make a connection for future business. He invites Gordon Wilson to join them for a drink. Three of them sit down for a while. Daulat Ram gives his business card to him. Gordon Wilson looks at the card and is very intrigued to notice that Daulat Ram represents top British manufacturers of machines.

"The Railway Board has decided on a major expansion of the railway network; who knows we might do some business with these firms," Gordon Wilson says. After finishing his drink, Gordon Wilson takes their leave. My grandfather and Daulat Ram also get up and leave the club and walk over to the waiting car.

Daulat Ram asks the driver to take them to Mall Road first and then back home. As the driver turns on to Mall Road, Daulat Ram directs him to one of the side streets and asks him to stop the car in front of a house. He whispers to my grandfather, "I will be back in a minute," as he gets out of the car and goes into the house. My grandfather notices several boys dressed in the *Sangh* uniform in and around the house. *Sangh* is a volunteer group established in 1925, whose objective is to organize the Hindus in a disciplined group for the protection of the Hindus. My grandfather is very wary of belonging to or identified with any particular political organization, be it Hindu or Muslim. He is a secular kind of person.

He is thinking: *what if Daulat Ram and his family are involved with the Sangh.* And while he is absorbed in his thoughts, Daulat Ram enters the car and takes the seat beside him at the rear of the car. "Suri Sahib, do you know these people?" My grandfather asks.

From the tone of his voice, Daulat Ram senses that my grandfather is uncomfortable with the situation, and he replies, "I have been involved with the *Sangh* for the last five years but only as supplier of materials for the organization. I have attended a few of their *Shakhas* or branch gatherings and found them to be very invigorating and character building. However, I am not a regular member."

My grandfather's mind is now churning out all kinds of scenarios, and his face shows the anxiety, as he is thinking what to say.

Daulat Ram continues, "I also have a very good relationship with Muslim organizations such as the Muslim League, as I have similar commercial relations with them also. If fact, my best friends are Muslims. Whenever there are any communal tensions, they call on me to straighten things out. They call me the Bridge, as in bridging the gap."

"Thank you, Suri Sahib, for offering the clarification. You did not have to do that. I have no problem with the *Sangh* or the Muslim League. Some of my wife's best friends are Muslim ladies of the neighborhood."

"Driver, take us to Lalaji's house in Prem Nagar. We will drop him off and then go home." As the car enters the street, kids are playing *Kanchas* or marbles in the street. The driver blows the car horn several times before the boys move out of the way and then start running after the car, as it slowly comes to a stop in front of the house.

My grandfather is thinking: *I was supposed to talk to Daulat Ram about the dowry, but when I should bring it up?*

As he is getting out of the car, the door of the house opens and Surinder is standing in the doorway. As soon as he sees Daulat Ram and his car, he steps out of the house to greet him. Daulat Ram also comes out of the car and gives an affectionate embrace to Surinder.

"Please come and have a glass of *Lassi*. My mother is just making it for me," "Surinder tells Daulat Ram.

"Not at this time; I am already getting late. I promised my wife to take her to Anarkali for some shopping," and he gets back in his car. As he is about to shut the car door, he says, "Surinder, some time next month, you will have to spare some time for us. We would like to take you for some marriage related shopping." And the car drives away, leaving Surinder thinking; *I wonder if Kamla will also accompany us for shopping?*

Surinder and my grandfather step into the house, and Surinder inquires of his father, "So, Pitaji, did you talk to Daulat Ram about dowry?"

"No, I did not get a suitable opportunity. I will talk to him, one day, during our morning walk. There is still a lot of time."

3
WAR

It has been a particularly hot and dry summer. Surinder has the afternoon off; a light drizzle is adding coolness in the air; the fragrance of slightly wet earth is arousing romantic emotions in him. He is in his room at home trying to mark the test papers, but Kamla is occupying his thoughts. It has been almost two months since he last saw her—the day they got engaged. He gets up, picks up his bicycle and rides away to the school where Kamla teaches. He has done this before a few times; he hides behind the large trunk of the Peeple tree about fifty feet south of the main gate of the school. The closing bell rings; he looks at his watch; it is 3:30 P.M. He waits; there is no sign of Kamla. He keeps waiting; it is 4 P.M.; still there is no sign of Kamla. He is getting edgy and then she appears and walks past him carrying a bunch of papers in her right hand. He springs forward, as if he is going to catch-up with her to talk to her, but, then, he stops; the superstition holds him back; it is not considered auspicious to talk to your fiancé, he knows.

As luck would have it, my grandfather and Daulat Ram see each other during one of the morning walks. Daulat Ram says, "Lalaji, with your permission, I would like Surinder to accompany me to make a selection of suits and shirts as gifts for the occasion."

"I have been meaning to talk to you about this." My grandfather replies. "You see, Suri Sahib, we would like to keep the marriage very simple and try and break from the shackles of tradition. My request to you is to do away with the tradition of gift giving. We feel that you were very generous at the time of the engagement. Bride's families are burdened with unnecessary expenses that can be easily done away with."

"Lalaji, we are not doing anything under duress or pressure from you. We appreciate your desire for simplicity, but we want to fulfill certain traditional ceremonies as a matter of pleasure and satisfaction rather than compulsion. We do not want you to feel under any obligation to match our actions," Daulat Ram replies.

"Suri Sahib, in my mind, this is not just a matter of this marriage, but *lakhs* of others that will take place in the future. I want to make this marriage an example of how we can celebrate marriages without breaking the bank. I hope you will join me in this noble cause. You are a prominent member of the Hindu community and equally respected by the Muslim community. The example you set may become a new tradition. Also, I think, with the War threatening to engulf the whole world, it would be in good taste to keep things simple."

Daulat Ram adds with a smile and a wink, "Lalaji, I respect your sentiments, and I will whole heartedly support them. However, I think you and I will have to stand united in front of our womenfolk; who, as you know, are the torch bearers of tradition in our society. With your permission, I want to take Surinder shopping for, at least, a token gift of one suit and shirt. What if we take him out on his birthday?" My grandfather smiles and nods his head in agreement.

Later in the evening, when Surinder comes home from the College after teaching, my grandfather tells him about his conversation with Daulat Ram. Surinder is delighted, and is looking forward to the shopping trip. He loves elegant English suits, ties and felt hats and possesses an impressive collection and is looking forward to adding to it.

Surinder gets up early on his birthday on November 15, 1940. He is 25 years old. *I am getting married at just the right age according to modern Hindu tradition,* he is thinking. He walks over to his parents to receive their blessings. As usual, he gets ready, takes his bicycle out and sets course to his college for his 8 A.M. class. He usually picks up the newspaper at a shop along the way. As he reaches the shop, he sees a group of people standing around the shop and listening to the news on the radio. The headline is: GERMANS BOMB COVENTRY TO DESTRUCTION. A similar headline appears on the front page of the newspapers. He listens to the details on the radio and to the comments of people standing around. For them, this is more news about the War that they hear everyday. Nevertheless, he feels very disturbed about the destruction and loss of life. Due to his long association with English literature and interest in the British Institutions, he feels very close to English people. He picks up a copy of the newspaper and rides away to his College.

In the evening, he walks over to the Suri residence; he is greeted by Daulat Ram. They both get into Daulat Ram's car and ride towards Anarkali, a shopping district in the heart of Lahore. As Daulat Ram is aware of Surinder's taste in elegant clothes, he tells the driver to take them to Richard & Sons, where he himself gets his clothes tailored. On the way, Surinder cannot help but bring up the topic of War and bombing of Coventry, in particular.

"*Bhai sahib*," he says, "You must have heard of the Germans bombing Coventry."

Daulat Ram replies, "It is a sad day. A number of my clients have their factories in Coventry and also live there. It seems that the whole world is going to be drawn into this War."

Surinder adds, "India also has been drawn in. Last year the British government of India declared War on Germany without consulting the Indian National Congress. In fact, Nehru was against India joining the War. Gandhi even wrote an open letter to Hitler denouncing Nazism for promoting violence. But, I think, finally the Indian politicians agreed to support Britain in the war effort by asking young Indians to volunteer to join the Army units being deployed around the world."

As the car stops in front of Richard & Sons, the owner's son, Vijay Richard, comes over to greet them. The Richards have been living in Lahore for several generations and have given their son a Hindu first name, Vijay. They belong to a community of English people who have come to be known as Anglo-Indians. The shop is about twenty feet wide and about forty feet long, with shelves of flat roles of cloth for suits and shirts. On one of the walls between the shelves there is a large brass plate with the name of the company engraved on it, and above the name is the royal coat of arms and below the name are engraved the following words:

By Appointment to His Majesty the King

Vijay asks Daulat Ram, "Sir, what may I serve you? Would you like to have a cup of tea?" Daulat Ram politely declines and looks towards Surinder, who smiles and says, "No, thank you."

Daulat Ram explains to Vijay, "We are looking for a suit, matching shirt and a couple of ties for the young man," pointing towards Surinder. Vijay pulls out several rolls of suit cloth and spreads them on the sales counter. Surinder selects dark grey pin striped cloth for the suit and a matching light blue cotton cloth for the shirt. As Vijay proceeds to take the measurements, Surinder is concerned about the cost, but, as it is a gift from Daulat Ram, he does not know how to say it.

Daulat Ram senses the hesitation and says, "Vijay, I will talk to your father about the cost later. Let us proceed with the measurement if Surinder is happy with the cloth."

Before he starts to take the measurements, he asks, "Sir, will this be Bespoke stitching or made-to-measure?" Although Daulat Ram knows the difference, he wants Vijay to explain it for the benefit of Surinder, and he replies, "Please explain to us the difference between the two forms of stitching."

"Bespoke is custom made and fitted with several trial fittings, while made-to-measure is fitted by adjusting an existing block pattern." Vijay explains.

"We will prefer Bespoke."

"Sir, do you have any special requirements for the shirts?" Vijay asks.

Surinder replies, "Yes. I prefer detachable collars."

"When can we come for the first trial?" Daulat Ram asks.

Vijay looks up the calendar and gives them a date. As Daulat Ram and Surinder start to make their way out, Surinder looks at the brass sign and inquires, "Vijay, I have seen the 'By Appointment' sign at many shops. Just for my information, what does it signify?"

Vijay replies, "For the supplier of goods to the royal household, a royal warrant is issued, and that gives them the privilege of adding this statement with the name of their business. A fee has to be paid for this warrant, and this fee is used by the Royal household for charitable purposes."

Surinder makes a mental note of this; something to be discussed in the next English class.

• • •

Surinder is not the only one getting new clothes. Surinder's mother is visiting jewelry shops and women's clothing stores to buy gifts for her future daughter-in-law. She has taken out some of her own old ornaments and is trading them for the ones of latest designs. The gifts that the bride brings to their husband's home are known as *Dahej* or dowry, and the gifts that the groom's family gives to the bride are known as *Wari*. Surinder's mother is collecting a respectable amount of *Wari*, as it is going to be displayed at the time the bride comes to her in-law's home after the marriage ceremony, and at that time all the relatives ask to see what the mother-in-law is giving her new daughter-in-law. She has two sets of 22 Kt gold ornaments already prepared; a set comprising a necklace, two earrings, two bangles and a ring. Two sets of new formal clothes have been given to the tailor for stitching, with pieces of Kamla's old clothing given as samples to copy from.

Kamla's family has plans to give a substantial dowry, despite the request from my grandfather to the contrary. *Dahej* is displayed at the time of the marriage at the bride's house and then at the groom's house after the marriage ceremony is over, and the bride comes to her in-law's house. In most cases, social pressure almost forces bride's family to give beyond their means. But not in this case, Daulat Ram is as affluent as he is influential.

4
MARRIAGE

December 15, 1940, the day of the marriage of Kamla and Surinder has arrived. There is lot of activity at Daulat Ram's house starting early in the morning. A tent is being pitched in front of the house. Middle of December gets pretty cold in Lahore; therefore, arrangements are being made to have coal burning *Ungithies* or fire boxes placed around in the tent to keep the guests warm. Lahore's top *Halwaii,* Maddhi Bhai, is setting up shop in the rear yard to cook food for the party in the evening. He has brought big cooking pots and several clay Tandoors, among other cooking materials. Daulat Ram, Pawan Lal and Lakhi Lal, Kamla's brothers, are supervising all the arrangements. Daulat Ram walks over to Maddhi Bhai and says, "Look, Maddhi Bhai," adding a few expletives for emphasis, "I want you to make sure that the food is sumptuous and served hot; otherwise, I will cut your ----ts off!"

Maddhi, after hearing the expletives, knows that Daulat Ram means what he says and assures him, "Oh, Suri Sahib, sir ji... not to worry. I will be here all evening making sure everything is first class. Your sister is like my sister. I will not let anything happen that will bring us dishonor.

About a hundred people are expected to attend the party. About thirty are Surinder's family and friends, and the rest are from the Suri family and Daulat Ram's friends and business associates.

At about 1 P.M., a car stops in front of Daulat Ram's house. An Englishman gets out and walks in. Daulat Ram's younger brother, Pawan Lal, is outside at that time. The Englishman hands over a letter to Pawan asking, "Are you Mr. Suri?"

"Yes," he says. However, he immediately realizes that it is his brother, Daulat Ram, who the Englishman is looking for.

"Let me call my brother," he adds, and he goes into the house.

Daulat Ram comes out to talk to the Englishman, and, as he is walking towards him, he sees a car standing outside the gate and realizes that it is David Rankin's car; he is the Commissioner of Police of Lahore and is one of the invitees to the evening gathering.

"I am Suri. I understand you want to see me," he says to the Englishman.

"Commissioner Rankin sends his regards, and, sir, this envelope is for you." Daulat Ram takes the envelope and asks him, "Won't you have a cup of tea?"

"Thank you, sir. I will be moving now."

Daulat Ram thinks that the Commissioner must have sent his regrets for the evening. He opens the envelope and reads:

Dear Mr. Suri,

Some senior members of Scotland Yard are visiting Lahore in connection with an investigation into some irregular activities in the import of machinery. They would like to talk to you today in the evening.

What the hell! Daulat Ram is thinking, as he is reads the letter; his face becomes red with anger.

Just joking old chap!
Oh Yes, we have a couple visiting from England, and they have never seen an Indian marriage ceremony. We are taking the liberty of bringing them along in the evening, with your permission of course.

Thank you.
David Rankin

Normal color and smile returns to Daulat Ram's face.

Surinder gets up early in the morning to oversee the preparations for the big day. The arrangements are relatively simple at his house, as all the ceremonies are going to take place at Daulat Ram's house. A small colorful tent has been pitched in front of the house to accommodate a small number of guests that are expected to make up the marriage party, the *Baraat*. A few chairs have been placed for the guests. Surinder and my grandfather inspect the arrangements, and everything seems in order and in keeping with the simplicity with which they want to celebrate the marriage.

By about 5 P.M., all the family members are dressed up. The women of the house—Surinder's mother, sisters and sister-in-law—start to sing some folk songs that add gaiety and joy to the occasion. They all hold him by his hands and walk him to the tent as they are singing. The colour of their clothing and the joyous and rhythmic sounds of the folk songs bring both smiles and tears of happiness. He is made to sit at the centre of the tent on a silk cloth spread on the carpet for the *Sehrabandi* ceremony. As the priest is reciting mantras in Sanskrit, his father begins to tie a saffron colored turban on his head. After the turban is in place, *Sehra*—an open mesh of flowers braided into a string—is tied to the turban and adjustments are made to ensure that he can see through the strings of flowers hanging in front of his face. His father, brothers and brothers-in-law also have pink turbans tied on their heads. His elder brother Shyam Nath's son, Sudesh, is acting as the *Sarbaala*—a young boy, who, as a matter of tradition, accompanies the groom. He is also wearing a suit, a turban and a *Sehra*.

After the *Sehrabandi* ceremony, Surinder's brothers walk him over to the ceremonial decorated horse standing just outside the tent. As this is taking place, all the relatives and friends gather around the horse. This is the first marriage being celebrated in the street, so my grandfather has invited some neighbors also. In addition, all the neighborhood urchins and some adults, who are not invited, also gather around and offer good wishes to my grandfather and grandmother. Men in the marriage party are dressed in English suits and ties and some in *Sherwanies*, the traditional formal attire of Punjab. The women are dressed in different types of formal traditional Indian dresses, such as *Sari, Salvaar Kameez and Lehanga,* in dazzling array of colors; only one lady is wearing an English dress. Out of the members forming the marriage party, there is only one English couple named John and Lynda Hughes. John was Surinder's professor at Forman Christian College, and he is the one who had agreed to arrange a scholarship for him when Surinder had met him at the home of the Wilsons. Surinder has maintained contact with him after graduation, and they have become good friends.

Surinder mounts the horse by stepping up on a wooden stool set up beside the horse. The *Sarbaala* is picked up by his father, Shyam Nath, and is made to sit on the horse in front of Surinder. Two *Dhollwallas* are starting to play on the drums hanging around their neck. The marriage party, the *Baraat,* is starting to move forward led by the drum boys and the horse carrying the groom and the *Sarabaala*. The rhythmic beat of the drums is adding a sense of celebration to the occasion. Some of the younger members of the marriage party have had some drinks to perk them up. In about ten minutes, the *Baraat* has reached the front gate of the Suri residence.

The bride's family is waiting outside to receive the *Baraat*. The drums stop playing. There is momentary silence. One of my grandfather's friends moves to the front of the *Baraat* and announces that he has been given the honor to sing the *Sehra*—a poem written in praise of the groom and his family. After he finishes the poem, it is time for the *Milnee* ceremony, a tradition in which the significant male relatives of the bride are formally introduced to corresponding male relatives of the groom. *Milnee* literally means "getting introduced". First to do *Milnee* are the two fathers. They are invited by the master of ceremonies to move to the centre of the crowd. They both embrace each other, and the bride's father gives a cash gift to the groom's father, but the groom's father is not required to give any return gift; another one of those traditions that are part of the dowry system. Next on the list are the three brothers and two brothers-in-law.

Why do they have to indulge in this giving to the groom's family every time? Damn this! Christians have a good system of getting married—clean and quick. Surinder is thinking, while he is getting impatient and is in physical discomfort sitting on the horse.

To his relief, the formalities are over for the time being. Surinder and the *Sarbaala* are helped by his brothers to dismount from the horse, and they all move onto the front lawn of the house. While most of the people stay outdoors, he is lead up the steps of the verandah. A little while later, Kamla dressed in a royal red Sari with golden embroidery walks slowly and elegantly out of the house and into the verandah area. The two of them stand facing each other, surrounded by their respective family members. They perform the *Jaimaala* ceremony as they exchange garlands, signifying that the bride and groom accept each other. Afterwards, the bride and the groom are taken inside the house where they are served dinner. After dinner, the groom is separated from the bride until the start of the main marriage ceremony.

Surinder moves out to the front lawn to be with the guests. He is seated on a chair near one of the *Ungithies*—the hot boxes—to keep warm. Friends and relatives are moving around and mixing with each other and coming around to meet Surinder and congratulate him. Commissioner Rankin, his wife Joan and his friends, who are visiting from London, also come over to meet Surinder. Daulat Ram proudly introduces Surinder to Commissioner Rankin and his guests from London, "Meet Surinder my brother-in-law to be. He is a professor of English literature."

"Pleased to meet you, Surinder; meet my friends Arthur and Julie Smyth. You will be pleased to know that Arthur also teaches English literature at King's College, London. He is in Lahore to teach at Forman Christian College for a few months."

Surinder is intrigued by this coincidence. He looks around and finds John and Linda Hughes and waves them to come over and introduces them to the Commissioner and his guests.

"John is also a professor of English literature at Forman Christian College," he tells them.

"I hope we are not going to enact a Shakespeare's play here tonight with three professors of English literature floating around," jokes Commissioner Rankin.

The dinner is served at about 9 P.M. It is a *Thaali* dinner. Vegetarian and non-vegetarian *Thaalies*—large brass plates with small bowls filled with vegetarian or non-vegetarian dishes—are brought around by the bearers. They ask each person for their preference, "Sir, veg or non-veg?" After dinner, the desserts are: *Firni*, a kind of Indian custard, and English Custard. The bearers bring around the two desserts in trays and ask the guests for their preference. The dinner is over by around 10 P.M. and the guests start to depart. Some guests have come in their own horse drawn carriages and others are waiting outside for a *Tonga*, a hired horse drawn carriage, to take them home. There are a few who have come in their own cars. Those who have their own transportation are waiting until their coachmen and drivers finish their dinner. Commissioner Rankin also gets up and calls his wife and friends, "Joan, dear, should we call it a night?" Expecting to get a reply in the affirmative, he starts to move towards the front gate. His friend, Arthur, intervenes, "David, we were wondering, if it would be appropriate for us to stay on and attend the marriage ceremony."

"Maybe we should ask our hosts," Commissioner Rankin says.

In the meantime, Daulat Ram sees them standing around preparing to leave, and he walks over to them with a questioning look, "Are you leaving already, Commissioner?"

"Well, we were wondering if it would be proper for us to attend the marriage ceremony."

"If you want to wait for a few hours, it is all right with us."

"Oh, wait a few hours?"

"Yes, the priests have determined that the auspicious time for the ceremony is between 3 A.M. and 5 A.M., December, 16."

"What do you want to do, Arthur?" Commissioner Rankin asks.

"It is a once in a lifetime opportunity for us. How about if we leave now and come back at 3 A.M.?"

"We won't have the driver at that time, but I will drive. We are not too far from here," Commissioner Rankin says, and they depart.

Surinder and some members of his family have been provided with a room in Daulat Ram's house, while some others have walked home, and some are snoozing on the sofas under the tent in the front lawn.

At about 2:30 A.M., the priests arrive. They start setting up the *Havan Smigri*—the materials such as the auspicious incense, and the *Havan Kund*—the pot for burning the incense. A little later, Surinder and Kamla's families congregate around the *Vedi*. It is an enclosure with open sides, with a canopy of silk cloth and decorated with garlands of fresh flowers. The floor of the *Vedi* is covered with a silk carpet for the bride and the groom to sit on. Kamla is brought into the *Vedi* by her mother and father who help her to sit down on the carpet. Surinder is also brought into the *Vedi* by his mother and father. Both sets of parents take their seats on the carpet under the *Vedi* and beside the bride and the groom.

The interplay of colors of the bride's clothes and the flowers, the fragrance of the flowers mixed with the intoxicating aroma of incense, and the heavenly vibrations of the Sanskrit Hymns, makes for a celestial setting.

Daulat Ram is wondering why the Commissioner and his friends have not come to see the ceremony. His thoughts go back to the ceremony as Surinder and Kamla get up to start to walk around the sacred fire, a ritual known as Saat Phere or Seven Rounds.

The priest ties the end of Kamla's sari to the end of a long saffron colored scarf hanging around Surinder's neck, into a proverbial knot. He is reciting mantras in Sanskrit, a language that neither Surinder nor Kamla understand. Although they do not understand exactly what the priest is saying in Sanskrit, they both know what each *Phera* or walk around the fire signifies.

In the first walk around the fire or *Phera*, the couple prays to God for plenty of nourishing food.

In the second walk around the fire or *Phera*, the couple prays to God for a healthy and prosperous life.

In the third walk around the fire or *Phera*, the couple prays to God for strength so that they can share good times and bad times together.

In the fourth walk around the fire or *Phera*, the couple prays to God for love and respect for each other.

In the fifth walk around the fire or *Phera*, the couple prays to God for beautiful and noble children.

In the sixth walk around the fire or *Phera*, the couple prays to God for a peaceful long life with each other.

In the seventh walk around the fire or *Phere*, the couple prays to God for loyalty and understanding with each other.

At the completion of the *Saat Phere*—the seven rounds—the priest declares them husband and wife. The couple approach each set of parents, by turn, and bow down to touch their feet and receive their blessings. All the relatives and friends approach the newlyweds to shower rose petals on them, to signify a shower of holy blessings from the Heavens.

After the conclusion of the formal marriage ceremony, some refreshments are served. As soon as all the formalities are complete, the time for *Doli*, the departure of the bride, is drawing near. Surinder's mother walks over to his father and whispers to him, "The auspicious time for the *Doli* is approaching; we should get ready." At about 7 A.M., preparations are being made for a ritual known as *Biddaii*. The bride is separating from her family for ever and making her home in her husband's home. Kamla's mother, father, brothers and sisters, one by one, embrace her, saying good bye with tears in their eyes.

Not too long ago she was a little girl, and now she is leaving us! Kamla's father and mother are thinking and are weeping like little children. Surinder is also getting emotional and wiping tears.

Her father, mother, brothers and sisters embrace her for the last time, and then her father takes her toward the waiting car and gently guides her to sit inside. Surinder goes around the other side of the car and sits beside her in the rear seat. Her brother, Pawan Lal, is supervising the servants who are loading some luggage into the dickey of the car. Her brother, Daulat Ram, is in the driver's seat, and her brother, Lakhi Lal, is sitting beside him in the front seat. It is a tradition that the brothers accompany their sister to her husband's home at the time of the *Doli* to make their sister feel that she will always have their protection as she enters her new life.

As the car slowly pulls away from the house, Surinder's father is walking behind the car and throwing coins in the air, a gesture of charity. As the rays of the rising sun strike the shinning metal of the coins, they look like a thousand *Golden Sparrows* flying in to bless the newlyweds. The coins fall in the form of a shower on the pavement, and a crowd of street urchins struggle against each other to get hold of a coin. As they hurriedly gather the coins, they blurt out an equally hurried blessing for the newlyweds.

It is in this shower of blessings that Surinder and Kamla enter their new life, and what a life they are about to have!

5
INTRIGUE

Now that all the formalities of the marriage of his sister are over, Daulat Ram's thoughts go to the incident related to Commissioner Rankin.
Why did he not come back to attend the marriage ceremony?
He has an ominous feeling that something is not right. It seems strange to him that the Commissioner's friend, Arthur Smyth, who is introduced as a professor of English and is in Lahore to teach for a few months, travels during the war all the way from London for the mundane purpose of teaching English. He comes to the conclusion that the two matters that need looking into are: Why did Commissioner Rankin not come back? And, is his friend, Arthur Smyth, really teaching at Forman Christian College or doing something else?

It is Sunday; a day he goes to the club to play tennis in the morning. He gets his gear together and tells his driver to take him to the Gymkhana Club. It is a cool sunny morning, ideal for a few sets of tennis. As his driver parks the car, Daulat Ram sees Commissioner Rankin and his friend, Arthur, getting into their car and are about to leave. Daulat Ram quickly gets out of his car and waves at the other car. And as soon as the Commissioner notices him, he directs his driver to stop. Both the Commissioner and Arthur step out of the car.

The Commissioner says, "Good morning Mr. Suri, I must apologize for not turning up to watch the marriage ceremony. Uh... we have been debating whether to tell you this or not. Nevertheless, I think, I owe you an explanation. The early morning of December 16, Arthur, Julie and I were on our way to your house to attend the marriage ceremony. As we were passing through the Gawaal Mundi area, a truck full of miscreants tried to run down my car. It appears to us that it was a planned act, and by that I mean that they knew ahead of time that we would be travelling that route to come to your house that early in the morning. It is fortunate that we escaped. My driver had the presence of mind to out-run them and drive the car to a nearby police station. The question now arises: How did the miscreants know that we would be coming to your house at the unearthly hour of 3 o'clock in the morning? My dear chap, it looks like an inside job; I am sorry to say. We have not told about this incident to any one except a few close associates in the police department, and I am requesting, or rather telling you, not to mention this to anybody."

Daulat Ram is flabbergasted to hear this. He is speechless, but blurts out, "I am so sorry to hear this. How can I help?"

"I will talk to you after we finish the investigation," the Commissioner replies and gets into his car and drives away.

After hearing this, Daulat Ram is in no mood to play tennis. He gets into his car and tells the driver to take him home. As he is sitting in the back seat of the car, he decides that he must get to the bottom of this matter. "Take me to Krishna Nagar," he tells the driver. Once they are in the area of Krishna Nagar, he begins to guide the driver through the various by-lanes till he reaches his friend Yogi Bindra's house, who works in the administration department of Forman Christian College. He gets out and knocks at the door. Yogi opens the door. After exchanging pleasantries, he asks "Yogi, *yaar*, I need a favor from you."

"What can I do for you, my friend?" Yogi replies putting his arms on Daulat Ram's shoulders.

"Can you please find out if there is a professor named Arthur Smyth, who is supposed to have come from London to teach at your college for a few months?"

Yogi looks up at the sky trying to think hard and says, "As far as I know, I have not heard anything like that, but I will make further inquiries. Why don't you come in and have a cup of tea, and we will talk?"

"Not at this time, I am in a bit of a rush right now."

He gets into his car and tells the driver to take him home.

After a few days, Daulat Ram drives over to the College, where Yogi works, to ask him if he has been able to find anything about Arthur Smyth. Yogi tells him that no professor from London has come to teach at the college.

Daulat Ram is now totally confused. He is not able to figure out why the Commissioner is playing this game with him.

He is thinking sitting in the rear seat of the car on his way home. He is mad like hell and blurts out: Oh, Bhen C… a strong expletive for the Commissioner.

The driver hears it and asks, "Sahib, did you say something?"

"No, no, nothing. Let us go home." He decides to say nothing to anybody about this matter.

A week later, one day, when he comes home from work, his wife gives him a letter. The letter is from Commissioner Rankin.

Dear Mr. Suri,

I will be thankful if you could meet me on Monday in my office at 10 A.M.

Thanking You,
Yours truly,

David Rankin

Daulat Ram knows that the Commissioner is playing some dreadful game with him, but he has no idea what it is. He recounts all the events of the last several months. The way he got introduced to Commissioner Rankin looked like a coincidence at the time, but now he realizes that it may have been a set-up. Over the last several months, the Commissioner has been over-friendly. Now thinking back, he does not see any reason why a Commissioner of police should have been trying to befriend him.

He reaches the Police Headquarters about fifteen minutes before the appointed time. He is greeted by the personal assistant of the Commissioner.

"Mr. Suri, the Commissioner will see you in a few minutes. Please be seated," he says pointing to a chair.

Daulat Ram's heart is pumping hard. He shifts back and forth in the chair due to nervousness, a feeling he has seldom experienced before. Normally, he is the one who makes people nervous.

After a few minutes, he is ushered into the Commissioner's office. As he enters the office, he sees the Commissioner and Arthur Smyth sitting at the desk—who he now knows is not a professor, but something else. He is eager to find out. The Commissioner gets up and shakes hands with Daulat Ram and says, "I am sorry to call you here like this. You have met Arthur before, but with a different identity. And I think an explanation is in order." He rings the call bell on his table and his assistant comes in, "Will you have some tea, Mr. Suri, Arthur?" Both nod in the affirmative. "Bring three cups of tea, Aamir."

"Oh, where were we now? Oh yes, as I was saying, Mr. Suri, an explanation is in order as to who is Arthur Smyth. He is not a professor of English–far from it. He is with the Security Service—you know, the spy stuff," he says with a sheepish grin and carries on, " I am sure you remember that incident I told you about; when my car was about to be rammed by a bunch of hoodlums. Our investigation has concluded that it was staged by somebody who attended the marriage of your sister and had the inside information. We are not going to pursue the matter any further because it may embarrass you, and we don't want to do that—being friends and all that. You know what I mean, Mr. Suri."

The Commissioner carries on, "Intelligence reports have been received that some Indian operatives sympathetic to the Axis Powers, mainly Germany and Japan, have infiltrated the Hindu and Muslim communities in the Punjab, the United Provinces and, maybe, other parts of India also with substantial Muslim population. Their purpose, we believe, is to spark communal violence in order to cause disorder and confusion in the country and to destabilize and weaken the Administration. And then the Japanese will attack India from the Burma front."

Daulat Ram is dumb founded as he finds himself in the middle of World War II. His hands are sweating. Perspiration appears on his forehead. He takes out a handkerchief to wipe his forehead.

He is thinking: *Why is he telling me all this?*

Finally, the commissioner drops the bombshell, "Mr. Suri, we would like you to help us avoid India coming under Japanese occupation. We want you to work for us as an informant. If you help us, we will not pursue the investigation into somebody from your household conspiring to kill me."

Daulat Ram's hands are shaking as he picks up the cup of tea to moisten his dry mouth so that words can come out. And then he says, "How can I help? I am just a businessman."

"Mr. Suri, you are sweating as if we are asking you to fight Hitler himself. You just have to keep your eyes and ears open and tell us if you see any new people enter the community, or if you hear any strange happenings. That is all you have to do for the time being. I can assure you that there will be a suitable reward for you."

"I am not sure if I can do this. I will have to think about it."

"Mr. Suri, do you realize the consequences of Japanese occupation? You must have heard what they have done in the Far East. I can assure you that everybody in India will be speaking Japanese within a year of the occupation of India by the Japanese."

Daulat Ram realizes that he has no choice but to say yes at this time and see what happens later. There is silence for a minute or so; and then, Daulat Ram says, "OK. I will do what I can." And he gets up and asks, "What do I tell others when they find out that I am visiting the police headquarters so often?"

"For the time being, you should say that there has been a robbery in your house, and you have been visiting here in that connection."

Daulat Ram goes out to his car. The driver opens the door, and he gets in and goes home to ponder on what has happened.

After Daulat Ram departs, the Commissioner and Arthur Smyth carry on their meeting.

"So what do you think, John?"

"John? I don't see any John here. I am Arthur, remember? You gave me the name, and now you have forgotten"

"OK John, you can take your mask off now. Seriously, what do you think of Suri. Do you think he can be a long term prospect?" the Commissioner asks.

"Well, I really can't say. I will try and send some new business his way through our connections with some companies in Britain. Money is a great motivator, you know old chap. And after that, we may have to get him a title of Rai Sahib for service to the Crown." They both laugh and John continues, "This is how we have built Loyalism in the past, and it is going to work in the future. Just see how many titles of Rai Sahib and Knighthoods we have distributed to buy loyalty in the colonies. Oh, these simple minded natives. Some times, I really feel bad about how we have treated them. Well, jokes aside, Mr. Suri's brother-in-law—the chap whose marriage we attended—could be an excellent long term prospect for helping our side. He speaks good English and is very presentable. I think we should keep him in mind."

The Commissioner replies, "Oh, what a splendid idea. I never thought about that. Why don't we arrange to get him a teaching fellowship at some college in London?"

"Well, I will see what I can do," John replies.

Daulat Ram is very pleased with how his business has picked up since his last meeting with the Commissioner. He has been contacted by two British companies to represent them in India and act as their Liaison with the Government. He remembers the words of Commissioner Rankin; *you will be suitably rewarded.* He has always wanted the title of Rai Sahib and he realizes that it may, one day, become a reality. And who knows the next step may be the Knighthood.

He is thinking: *Rai Sahib Daulat Ram Suri would sound very powerful and elegant. I will be able to stand up to my uncle Rai Sahib Parmatma Ram Suri, who always throws his weight around in the family because of his title.*

Daulat Ram is already well connected and is well regarded by both the Hindus and the Muslims. He begins to use his position in the community to collect information and pass it along to the Commissioner. The British have hooked another Toad.

6
THE HOUSEHOLDER

After only about a week of the marriage, Christmas—known as the *Barra Din or the Big Day*—has arrived. Christmas Eve, the evening of December 24, is celebrated by Christians and many Hindus with pomp and show. All the top restaurants organize special Christmas Eve parties with dinner and cabaret. Surinder is very fond of attending these and can't wait to attend one of these with his new wife.

He makes a reservation at Faletti's Hotel and comes home and goes to his room and finds Kamla and says, "I have made reservations at Faletti's for Christmas Eve. They have good food and also have a very nice cabaret."

She is a bit hesitant, "Listen ji, I still have my *Churra* on my arm. See these twenty ceremonial bangles. I am supposed to keep them on for another month. I will feel odd watching a cabaret with these on my arms. Why don't you take one of your brothers with you instead? Moreover, I do not think your parents will approve."

Surinder thinks of a brilliant idea. He says, "Your brother, Daulat Ram, likes to attend parties. I have seen him at Faletti's a few times. I will invite him to join us. I think, if we go with him, my parents will not object." Kamla does not say anything further.

The next day, on his way to work, Surinder stops by Daulat Ram's house. He sees him sitting in the front lawn reading a newspaper.

As soon as he sees Surinder, he gets up to greet him and offers him a seat, "Welcome, *Jeejaji*. Will you like a cup of tea or a cold drink?" Sister's husband is *Jeeja*; *ji* is added for respect.

"No, thank you. Kamla just cooked me a nice breakfast. I have come to invite you to join us for Christmas Eve dinner at Falaetti's."

Daulat Ram is thinking: *It will not be a good idea for me to go to Faletti's to see dancing girls in the company of my newly married younger sister and brother-in-law.*

"I would have loved to, but I have another engagement. We will make it another time."

Surinder is disappointed and gets up to leave and finds that the front tire of his bicycle is flat.

While he is looking at it, Daulat Ram strolls over and suggests, "Listen Surinder, I will drive you over to your college, and, later, I will have my driver get the bicycle repaired and bring it over to you. How is that for service, *Jeeja Sahib?*"

Surinder accepts the offer, and, after he is in the car, asks jokingly, "Dear brother-in-law, what will I have to do to return this favor? You have heard of the saying, *Saari Khudai Ek Taraf; Jodu Ka Bhai Ek Traf.*" Meaning: ones wife's brother carries the same weight as the rest of the Universe.

Daulat Ram replies with a smile, "Just make sure my sister is happy."

"That is my pleasure and the aim of my life, sir. You will not have any complaints in that regard."

Daulat Ram drops him off at the front gate of the college and drives back.

When Surinder returns home from work in the evening, he goes to his room and tells Kamla in a disappointed tone, "You know, your brother will not be able to join us for the Christmas Eve Party. I think we should drop the idea of going to Faletti's. We will plan it next year."

• • •

Surinder comes home late after finishing his last class. He always has some interesting stories to tell about his students. "How was your day," Kamla asks him, one day, when he comes home late.

"You know Kamla, something very interesting happened today. Rai Bhadur Seva Singh came to our college today to see the principal about his daughter. She is getting married later this year, and he wants to make sure that she completes her B.A. before that. This is her final year. He has made arrangements with three professors to give her private tutoring at her home once a week. I will be going to her home every Tuesday from 6 P.M. to 7 P.M. to tutor her."

"Are you going to get extra pay for this?"

"Of course, and a handsome amount too."

"How long will this arrangement last?"

"Till the end of March, and exams start after that. Rai Bahadur wants each professor to tutor his daughter the evening prior to the day of each of the exams. I told him that it would not be possible for me because I give a general lecture for all students the evening prior to the exam."

"What is a general lecture?"

"General lecture is a course I give to anybody who buys the ticket at the door, or an advance ticket at our college premises. We advertise by means of distributing pamphlets to all the colleges about my lecture. The advertisement gives the time, date and place of the lecture. In the lecture, we also distribute a "Guess Paper". A "Guess Paper" is a set of questions that, we have guessed, will appear in the question paper for the particular examination. In addition, we also provide written answers to the questions."

"Where is the lecture held?"

"At the YMCA hall."

"Do you charge extra for the "Guess Paper"?" she asks jokingly.

"Yes, of course. Not only do we charge extra for the Guess Paper, but there is a separate charge for the answers to the questions in the Guess Paper. This is a business, my dear."

He continues, "Kamla, do you know what Rai Bahadur said when I told him why I can't tutor his daughter the evening prior to the day of the exam? This is the interesting part I started to tell you. He says: I will pay you double of what you are going to make from the lecture."

"So, what did you say?"

"I told him; I will let him know later after consulting with my wife."

"What? Are you serious?"

"So, what do you think I should do?"

"I think you should do both." She replies.

"How would I do that?"

"Give her tutoring after the lecture."

"Do you know how long the lecture is? It is a three hour lecture. It starts at 7 P.M. It is too late to give her tutoring after that."

"But, why don't you give up the lecture and just give her tutoring for double the amount you are going to make from your lecture."

"I did the lecture last year, and it was very successful. I want it to become a yearly affair. If I miss it one year, some of my competitors will take all my students. I will tell Rai Bahadur's daughter, Sangeeta, that I will not be tutoring her, and that she should attend the lecture like other students."

"Do whatever is appropriate for your business," She replies.

The end of the college year has arrived. The students are preparing for the examinations, and the Lecture Season is in full swing. The date for Surinder's lecture is set the evening before the examination. That evening, the students start lining up outside the Lahore Y.M.C.A. at 5:30 P.M. The line goes along the street and then around the corner. There are about five hundred students lining up. Surinder arrives at the Y.M.C.A at about 6:30 P.M. He is accompanied by the college clerk and a peon, who is carrying all the stacks of papers. A table is set at the entrance to the hall. As the students enter, they either show the entrance ticket that they have already purchased or pay for tickets at the door and collect the Guess Question Paper and answers to those questions. The lecture is supposed to start at 7 P.M., but is delayed and starts at 7:30 P.M. instead, in order to accommodate the late arrivals. There is an unusually high attendance this year because of high degree of the correlation of the Guess Paper given by Surinder with the actual question paper set by the university last year. The lecture lasts till about 10:30 P.M. The students go home and cram up the answers to the questions in the Guess Paper till early hours of the morning and present themselves at the examination centre at 10 A.M.

The day of the exam, after all the students are seated, the invigilator distributes the question paper and blank answer books to the students. Three hours have been allotted to write detailed answers to any five of the seven questions in the question paper. As the students read the question paper, a ripple of *oohs and aahs* goes through the examination hall. Students look at each other with smiles—meaning the questions are easy. A number of students complete their answers in two or two and a half hours, handover their completed answer book to the invigilator and go out. As the time goes by, a mob of students collects outside the examination hall, talking to each other about how well they have done.

As it turns out, the Question Paper set by the university contains the same questions as the Guess Paper given by Surinder in the lecture the previous night. Not only are the questions the same, even the order in which the questions appear is the same. There are a lot of complaints, mainly by the Surinder's competitors. Some of them lodge a complaint with the University. The University sets up a Board of Inquiry. After a number of months, the Board of Inquiry declares that there is no evidence of foul play, and that the correlation is described as a mere coincidence. However, there are others who start rumors that Prof. Surinder Mehra has supernatural powers and is able to read the minds of other people at long distances. In a society that thrives on superstition and rituals, this rumour spreads like wild fire and takes a life of its own. In the field of private education in Lahore, Prof. Surinder Mehra has acquired a Star status. All the rich businessmen and politicians want Surinder—also known as *Shakespearewala*—to give private tutoring to their children; money is no object.

• • •

Kamla is thinking whether to bring it up with him or not, and then she finally decides to tell him.

"Listen ji, your mother keeps asking me now and then: Kamla, when are you going to make me a grandmother? I feel really embarrassed. I don't know what to say."

"Just tell her; it will be soon. Indian mothers-in-law want their daughters-in-law to be productive. This is the secret of India's growth. We want to grow so much so that there will be no room left for the British, and they will quit India!" And they both laugh.

"And she keeps telling me that she wants a grandson."

"Do you want me to talk to her?"

"No, no, don't do that. She will think that I am complaining to you against her. That won't look good."

"Then, just smile when she brings up the topic again. One day, her wish may come true." He says with a twinkle in his eye.

Three months later.

Kamla gets up from the bed in the morning, and she suddenly sits down. She is feeling dizzy and nauseated. Surinder gets up and makes her lie down and goes out of the room to call his mother.

"Beyji, can you please come here, Kamla is not feeling well. She is feeling dizzy and nauseated." Beyji goes to their room and finds that Kamla is standing and wants to get ready and go to school.

"Beyji asks, "Kamla, how long have you been feeling like this?"

"For the last few days." she replies.

Beyji is thinking: *This is it. I think my wish is coming true. I have been going to the temple every Tuesday to wish for this. God has granted my wish after all. I am going to have a grandson.*

Beyji immediately suggests, "Kamla, I think you should come with me to the lady doctor for a check up. The office is nearby."

"I am fine now, Beyji. I will see the nurse at school." And she gets ready and is about to leave for school, when she again sits down on a chair. She is not feeling well.

Surinder tells her, "Kamla, don't go to school today. I will go and deliver a letter for your principal, Mrs. Thakur."

Later in the day, Beyji again asks Kamla to come to the doctor with her. This time she agrees. They both walk to Dr. (Mrs.) Sandhu's office. It is located in her house. The doctor's office is facing the verandah. There are a few chairs for the waiting patients placed in the verandah. There is a nurse who takes down the name of the patient and collects the fee in advance; and then calls the name of the patient when her turn comes. All the patients are women. A movable screen separates the doctor's office from the examination room. There is a small enclosed area with a serving window where another nurse fills the prescriptions. Patients are addressing her as compounder *Sahiba*. Compounder is an in-house pharmacist who compounds the medicines prescribed by the doctor. As soon as Kamla and Beyji walk in, the nurse greets them. Both the nurse and the doctor are known to Beyji. She asks, "Nazira, I hope the doctor is not too busy today."

"No, there are only three patients ahead of you."

The nurse is curious and looks at Beyji and then at Kamla and asks, "Is she the new daughter-in-law?"

"Yes." Beyji replies.

"Good news?" she asks with a questioning smile.

Beyji does not say anything but smiles and gestures with her hands towards the heavens. In about an hour, the nurse asks Kamla and Beyji to go into the doctor's office.

Dr. Sandhu is a tall lady in her forties. She has a very stern look and is known for her no–nonsense style. When they enter the office, she is looking down and writing something at her desk. She gestures to them to sit down on the chairs across from her.

After she finishes writing, she looks up and, after a few pleasantries, asks, "What can I do for you today?"

Beyji starts to explain, but is interrupted by the doctor, "I want Kamla to tell me her problems."

After listening to what she has to say, the doctor asks Kamla to come with her to examination room. When they are inside, Beyji is waiting with anticipation.

When the doctor comes out she is telling Kamla, "Just eat rice and curd for a day or two and take care of yourself."

Beyji looks at the doctor with a questioning look on her face and asks, "What is the problem?"

"There is no problem. I am prescribing this medicine. She will feel fine in a day or two."

Kamla knows what the problem is, but is thinking how to tell it to Beyji.

Beyji and Kamla start to move towards the door.

The doctor calls back, "Oh, Beyji, I forgot to tell. You are going to be a grandmother. Congratulations!"

Beyji is beside herself and embraces and kisses Kamla and tells the doctor, "I want a boy."

"Everybody wants a boy, but it is not in my hands." Dr. Sandhu says, "Even if it were, I would be fair to both sexes. I will make one boy followed by one girl and followed by one boy and so on. God has meant to create equal number of boys and girls to have balance. If everybody gets their wish of a boy, there will be no girls born and eventually no boys also. I don't understand why people are so against having girl babies."

Surinder can't believe the good news, when he comes home from work. He was worried about Kamla all day at work. That night they both talk about whether they would like to have a boy or a girl. "Boy of course," he says. She tells him about what Dr. Sandhu said, and he agrees that they want a healthy baby boy or a girl. While he is still talking, he finds that she has gone to sleep.

He is a devout Hindu and believes in re-incarnation and the transmigration of the soul. He begins to wonder about the miracle of life. He looks at her and begins to wonder about the awe inspiring thought that a new life has just started to sprout. Has the soul entered the body yet? At what stage does the soul enter the body? He makes a mental note to ask his father, who is a student of Bhagavad Gita, the Hindu holy book. These metaphysical thoughts are running through his mind.

I wonder what would have been the previous life of this soul, he is thinking.

He suddenly feels rush of cool air blowing through the open window. He gets up to close the window, but stands by the window and looks out. It seems that it may rain, but there are no clouds. The rays of moonlight are shinning through the window on Kamla, as if the heavens are blessing the new life.

The next day, Surinder writes a letter to Kamla's parents about the good news. He tells Kamla to write a few words also, but she says she feels shy. After licking the envelope sealed, he walks over to the neighborhood letterbox to mail the letter. On his way back, he drops in at Daulat Ram's house and also tells them the good news.

Kamla takes a few days off and then resumes her duties at the school. By the time she comes home from school, she is very tired. One day, Surinder sees her in the kitchen trying to light the coal burning stove, the *Angithi*. The coal is not catching fire and she is blowing at it with a long steel pipe with the smoke all around her. He walks into the kitchen and angrily calls his mother, "Beyji, where is the servant? Why is Kamla doing this? Don't you know that in her condition, she should not be doing this?"

"The servant has gone out to fetch some vegetables from the market. It is OK. I will be fine," Kamla tells him trying to calm him down. She is afraid that her mother-in-law might think that she has complained to Surinder about her working in the kitchen.

Beyji comes running to find out what has happened.

Surinder is concerned that her having to walk to school everyday, the cooking and other household chores that she is still carrying on, will harm her and the baby. He suggests to her that she should resign her job and stay at home. He tells her that they don't need the money, so why should she work. She argues that she has spent five years to complete her B.A.B.T, the Teacher Training course, and that she would rather carry on working. She tries to convince him that no harm will come to the baby if she carries on working. He accompanies her to the next appointment with Dr. Sandhu.

"I am concerned that with all the exertion of walking to school, standing all day in the class teaching the children and, then, coming home and cooking for the whole family, will affect her health and health of the baby." He tells the doctor.

"Moderate amount of exertion is good for her. However, when she comes home, she should take it easy. I suggest that somebody else should help her in some of the household chores," the doctor explains.

As soon as they reach home, Surinder goes to talk to his mother, "Beyji, we were at the doctor's office for Kamla's checkup. She has forbidden Kamla from doing any of the household chores."

"Don't worry, don't worry," she replies trying to allay his fears, "I will find a *mai*, to help Kamla in everything." A *mai* is a woman servant.

As days go by, he is still not happy about Kamla walking to school, and then he gets a bright idea!

He is thinking: *Why did I not I think of that before? Her brother, Daulat Ram, has a car and a driver. I will ask him to have his driver drive her to school and back every day.*

He picks up his bicycle and rides over to Daulat Ram' house and tells him of his concerns about Kamla's health.

"I think, Surinder, you are over reacting because you are becoming a father for the first time. When you are on your third child like me, you won't be as concerned. Women are a very tough species. God has made them stronger than men."

Daulat Ram carries on his sermon, pointing to a pregnant sweeper woman sweeping his front yard, "Look at her. She has been working here for five years and this is going to be her third child. She cleans our house and carries all the garbage away. She has not had any problem."

Surinder suggests, rather forcefully, that Daulat Ram have his driver take Kamla back and forth to school.

Daulat Ram is not the kind of man who likes to be told what to do, but, in the matter of his sister and on the insistence of his brother-in-law, he agrees.

And henceforth, to her great embarrassment, Kamla is driven to and from school everyday. Her colleagues in school talk about it; and when she comes home, the neighbors look out of their windows and later ask her embarrassing questions.

As the due date draws near, they receive a letter from Kamla's parents. They remind them of the tradition that the birth of the first-born child takes place in the home of the maternal grandparents of the child. In the letter, they have requested Surinder to bring Kamla to Gurdaspur in the next week or so.

"What should we do now?" Kamla asks.

Surinder is very abrupt in his reply, "My son is going to be born in my house." He is convinced that he is going to have a son.

Kamla knows that Surinder is a very strong willed man. He knows what he wants and somehow gets it. "All right, we will do what you want. Please write a nice letter to my parents telling them that the doctor has forbidden me to travel in this condition. This way my parents will not feel bad."

Surinder does the needful and asks her, "Kamla, you should also write a few lines and request them to come to Lahore a week before the due date, so they can be with us when our baby is born."

7
I AM BORN

It is 12 A.M. Kamla wakes up Surinder, "Are you listening; I think it is time." Surinder has not been able to sleep, anticipating that this may be the night. He gets up with a start and goes out of the room to wake up his mother, Beyji. She comes out of her room and knows why he is calling her. Dr. Sandhu had already given her instructions about what to do. She goes in the kitchen and lights a coal fire in the *Angithi*, places a large pot of water on top and goes into the room where Kamla is resting. In the meantime, Surinder's father and brothers also wake up. Surinder and his brother, Karan, dress up, pick up a torch, umbrellas, and a long bamboo stick for security and set out to the doctor's house on foot, which is about a ten minute walk. It is dark and light rain is falling. They walk through the narrow streets followed by stray barking dogs.

"We should have brought a gun along to take care of the dogs," Surinder tells his brother, Karan, showing his impatience with being followed by dogs.

"Brother ji, barking dogs seldom bite," Karan tells him trying to calm him down and add some humour to the tense situation.

"Remember, it says 'seldom'; and in reality, it is the barking dog that bites," Surinder replies with irritation in his voice.

The dogs are persistent and keep following them.

"Moti, Moti, Jimmy, Jimmy!" Karan talks to the two dogs that are following them.

"How do you know the names of the dogs?"

Karan replies, "In Lahore, most dogs are either named Moti or Jimmy. The Anglicized rich Indians name their dogs, Jimmy, and poor people, Moti. Brother ji, it is the start of a happy occasion, let us talk of something pleasant." In the meantime, one of the dogs finds a large pothole that is filled with rainwater and starts slurping. The other dog finds a bicycle lying against a wall, lifts its leg, and starts to make water.

When they reach the doctor's house, they knock at the door a few times. A dog begins to bark. *There seem to be more dogs than people,* Surinder is thinking. They stand around waiting, and, after about five minutes, a male voice asks, "Who is it?"

"I am Surinder, Kamla's husband. I have come to take Dr. Sandhu to our house. My wife is in labour."

Dr. Sandhu opens the door, asks some questions and tells him, "From what you have told me, it will be a few hours before I will be needed. I will come to your house in about an hour. I will send for my assistant, and, as soon as she arrives, we will come." He just stands there and is thinking: *What if the doctor is needed early.* The doctor senses the anxiety on his face and reassures him, "Everything will be all right. I have already explained some emergency procedures to your mother. Now please go home and make your wife comfortable."

Surinder looks helplessly at his brother, Karan, and slowly turns around and both brothers start to go home. Surinder is known for his perseverance and power of persuasion. He does not give up easily. He is a past master at name dropping to get what he wants.

Suddenly, he turns around, and before Dr. Sandhu can close the door of her house, he tells her, "Dr. Sandhu, I know Rai Bahadur Seva Singh. Your sister-in-law, Sangeeta, is my student. I have tutored her at her home for some time. I am glad she passed her B.A. and is happily married."

As soon as she hears this, she steps out of the house and says, "Oh, I did not realize, you know my father-in-law."

"Well, I have met him several times at his home."

"Oh yes, of course, now I remember. He has talked about you. I just did not put two and two together." Dr. Sandhu replies.

Surinder senses a golden opportunity and says, "I will be thankful if you can walk with us to our house now, and your assistant can follow later."

She smiles, "Oh well, OK, why not? After all you are a family friend. Let me give some instructions to my servant and pick up some things. It will take me five minutes."

Dr. Sandhu comes out with two boxes of medical supplies and an umbrella. Karan and Surinder take the boxes off her hands, and the three of them walk to their home.

As soon as they reach home, she goes directly to the room where Kamla is in labour. Karan and Surinder place the medical supplies outside the room. After about an hour, there is a knock on the front door. Dr. Sandhu's assistant and her servant have arrived. Her assistant, Nazira, comes into the house, and the servant leaves. She knocks at the door of the room where Kamla is in labour and goes in to help out.

At about 3 A.M., Surinder's mother comes out of the room and tells other family members that the baby should be arriving soon. Soon thereafter, there is the sound of baby crying, followed by the sighs of relief and joy.

I am born.

Beyji runs towards the room with excitement and opens the door to get in. Nazira tells her, "Beyji, please wait, we have our hands full. We still have lots to do before you can come in."

"Is it a boy?"

Nazira closes the door without replying to her. Surinder is pacing up and down. He asks Beyji, "Why is the baby crying?"

"Babies cry when they are born."

Karan tries to lighten the mood and says, "I think the baby knows the kind of world he is going to be facing. He is just scared."

Surinder's father tells Karan to talk something pleasant and starts reciting Sanskrit mantras to bless the newborn. Finally, after about half an hour, the doctor comes out and announces, "Surinder, your Prince of Wales has arrived." This is a reference to the heir apparent to the reigning monarch of the United Kingdom. At first, nobody understands what she has said. It takes a few seconds for Surinder to realize what she has said. He turns around and tells Beyji, "You have a grandson."

"Can we go in?" he asks the doctor.

"Yes, Surinder, only you can go in first." He walks towards the room, slowly opens the door and finds Kamla sitting up with the baby in her hands.

"Here is your son. You wanted a son, didn't you?" She says with a weak smile, handing over the baby, wrapped in a white towel, to Surinder. He hesitates, not knowing how to hold the baby. Nazira, the doctor's assistant, shows him how. He finally holds him in his hands for the first time, and the baby gives out a loud shriek.

"This is his way of saying, hello Daddy," Kamla says feebly. She looks tired and run down with her skin yellow and circles under her eyes. Her hair is crumpled.

Surinder asks the doctor, "Can I take the baby outside the room to show him to my parents? She nods, and he takes the baby out to show to his parents and brothers. "The baby looks like you, Surinder," his father says.

"I think his chin takes after the Suri family." Beyji adds.

After a few minutes, Dr. Sandhu asks Surinder to bring the baby back to the room. A cradle has already been placed in the room. Kamla wants to hold the baby. She does not want the baby placed in the cradle. Dr. Sandhu and her assistant go out of the room. Surinder sits down beside Kamla and looks lovingly at his small family. He gently touches, one by one, the baby's feet, hands, chin and the forehead. "Cuckoo, cuckoo," he is playing with the baby as if he can understand him.

"What are we going to name him?" she asks.

"I don't know. We should also ask my parents."

"Do you want to have a formal *Namkaran Sanskar*, the naming ceremony?" she asks

"Whatever you want is fine with me." They decide to have a formal ceremony. Kamla lies down, with the baby close to her on the side. After a while, the mother and the baby both go to sleep. Surinder sits there quietly watching them.

Beyji, beaming with joy, says, "Dr. Sandhu and Nazira, please come in the sitting room. I have some ceremonial sweets to offer you to celebrate the birth of my grandson." All three of them sit around chatting for a while. After they finish their tea, both Dr. Sandhu and Nazira go to check on Kamla. When they go into the room, Surinder is dozing off sitting on the chair beside the bed, and Kamla and the baby are also asleep. They both stand there and watch. And then they wave at Beyji to come over to look at what Tranquility looks like!

Dr. Sandhu decides to wait a while before waking Kamla up for a check-up. In about fifteen minutes, Cuckoo starts to cry. The doctor and her assistant go to the room to have a look. After checking up on Kamla and Cuckoo, they decide to go home. It is 7 A.M. The sun is rising. Surinder opens the window. The rays of the sun fill the room with a golden hue. Birds are flying outside, chirping, and crisscrossing through the golden rays of the early morning sun, as if *Golden Sparrows* are welcoming the new born.

Surinder decides to go to the post office to send a telegram to Kamla's parents. On his way back, he drops by Daulat Ram's house to give him the good news.

"Congratulations, my brother. Delightful news! What have you named him?"

"We are planning to have a *Namkaran* ceremony to name him. We have given him a nick name, Cuckoo."

Surinder takes his leave and walks back home.

The *Namkaran*, the naming ceremony to select a name, is, usually, held at least ten days after birth. Kamla's parents come immediately to Lahore after they receive the telegram. Only the immediate relatives attend the ceremony. The ceremony is organized fifteen days after the birth. The sitting room is set up to perform the ceremony. A small carpet is spread on the floor with a round brass plate in the centre. Candles and incense are burning. The Pundit recites Sanskrit hymns. After consulting the holy books, and based on the date and time of birth, the Pundit selects the alphabet *V* as the auspicious sound that should be the starting sound of the name of the newborn.

Vikram, Vikram, Vikram, Vikram, my father whispers four times in my ear and my mother gives me an affectionate embrace and a kiss on my forehead and whispers, "My son, Vikram Jeet."—the word Vikram means 'Courageous', and 'Jeet' means 'Conquest'. I have finally arrived with my own identity.

In India, the birth of a boy is like finding gold. All parts of society want to partake in the find. It is a custom to distribute *Mithai*—the Indian sweets—to friends, relatives, neighbors, passersby and servants. A segment of society known as *Khusaras*—a name given to Indian Eunuchs—make it their profession to visit households where there is a newborn. It is believed that they find out this information, through the grapevine, and end up at the house uninvited.

As soon as the naming ceremony is complete, there are sounds of Eunuchs out in the street, singing and dancing to the beat of drums. It is almost expected. Everybody moves out to watch the spectacle, except my parents and I remain indoors because my mother believes that Eunuchs snatch young babies and run away. They are dressed as women, but the voices of some of them are like that of men. They sing and dance to the tunes of popular folk songs. This goes on for about an hour. At the conclusion of this spectacle, they demand to see me so that they may remove my diaper and check the sex and make sure that it is male and not one of their own. My grandfather gives them some money and asks them to leave.

They are not satisfied with what they get and shout at my grandfather, "Hey, you tight-fisted old man, show some generosity. If you are generous with us poor Eunuchs, we will pray for your grandson, and he will become a great man. Come on, open your fist a little and come out with more cash." After a little while, my father comes out with some more money. As soon as they see him, they ask, "Are you newborn boy's father? Why are you hiding the new soul? Bring him out and we will bless him, and he will grow up to be a police officer and make lots of money on the side!"

"But I want him to become an engineer in the Public Works Department." My father teases them."

"Whatever you say *Sahib*; we bless him to become an overseer in the Public Works Department when he grows up, so that he can make lots of money on the side from the government contractors."

The whole crowd breaks out in laughter.

My father offers them a few more coins and requests them to leave. After a while, they slowly move away singing and dancing to the beat of the drums.

Thus, I begin my journey on earth with the beat of drums and blessings from a group of dancing *Khusaras*!

• • •

After my birth, my mother has taken a six month leave of absence from school in order to recuperate and to take care of me. About two weeks before her leave is to finish, her parents send Roshni, an *ayah*—a nanny trained to look after infants. She is about 20 years old and well trained in all aspects of household duties, in addition to baby care. The reason for sending the *ayah* is to help my mother in my day-to-day care, household chores and eventually take care of me when my mother goes back to school. My grandmother, Beyji, likes the idea of having the *ayah* around and considers the *ayah* as another addition to the complement of household help, of which there is plenty. There is one full-time male servant, part-time female help to wash clothes—and now the *ayah*. As soon as the *ayah* arrives, Beyji puts her to work in the kitchen and gives her other chores. These include: massaging her head with mustard oil once a week before she takes a bath, pressing her legs in the afternoon before her afternoon siesta and ironing the clothes of the whole family.

This does not go down well with my mother because the *ayah* has no time left to assist her. She brings the matter to the attention of my father, and he agrees to talk to his mother. My father gives this matter a great deal of thought, as this a sensitive matter between the mother-in-law and the daughter-in-law—the proverbial war front in the Indian household. Up until now, the relations between my mother and grandmother have been reasonably cordial. I say "reasonably cordial" because there have been a few standoffs between the two about the matter of my upbringing. My grandfather and grandmother want my mother to give up her teaching career in order to give me full-time attention, rather than leave me in the hands of the *ayah*. My father feels that he is caught between the two grind stones—his wife and his mother! One day, when he finds his mother in good humor, he broaches the subject of *ayah,* or rather her using the *ayah* as her personal servant.

"Beyji, I want to talk to you about..." He does not even get to complete the sentence, when Beyji launches into a tirade, "Surinder, an infant must be brought up by the mother and not by hired help. I have seen the world. No child in our family has ever been left all day with an *ayah,* while the mother is working."

"But, Beyji, our baby is not going to be alone. He will be with you all day, under your care."

"No, no, I am not willing to take a mother's responsibility. At this tender age, the baby needs constant care and attention, and I am too old to do that. It is too much responsibility for me."

My father is left speechless. He slowly turns around and goes towards his room and stands outside, not having the courage to face my mother. He knows that she must have heard everything.

He imagines two grind stones going round and round against each other and grinding him in the middle.

His stomach is in a knot, and he is beginning to have a headache. Instead of going in to talk to my mother, he decides to go for a walk. While he is walking, he decides to go to see Daulat Ram. When my father enters the house, Daulat Ram is sitting in the front verandah sipping beer, deep in thought. He looks up and, half heartedly, invites my father to join him. After seeing my father, he senses that there is something wrong. My father, on the other hand, also realizes that Daulat Ram is not himself. Daulat Ram, of course, has been worried about the incident with the Commissioner of police.

"You seem disturbed, young man. What is the problem?" Daulat Ram asks.

My father is not sure whether he should talk about the problem between Kamla and his mother to his brother-in-law because he will not get an objective advice and, moreover, Daulat Ram will get concerned for nothing. He pulls up a chair and sits down. Daulat Ram asks the servant to get another glass. He pours some beer into the glass and hands it over to my father. He looks at it with a great deal of anxiety on his face.

"I don't know if I should drink at this time or not."

"Come on, Surinder *yaar,* have a few sips. It will relax you."

"You know Pitaji," referring to his father, "If he finds out, I will get a lecture on evils of drinking."

"You mean your father has never had a drink?" Daulat Ram asks.

My father replies, "So he claims. He also tells us that he has never seen a cinema and does not like to listen to any *filmi* music." My father decides to have a glass of water instead of beer and opens his heart to Daulat Ram. He tells Daulat Ram all that happens between his mother and his wife.

Daulat Ram, after listening to him patiently, presents him with an alternative that he has never even contemplated,

"Look here, Surinder. You are a family man now, and your responsibility should be first towards your child and wife. Moreover, tension and friction between mother-in-law and daughter-in-law is a traditional family drama. Sooner or later, it is bound to happen. When a man gets married, he should make a separate home for his family. This is the only way to maintain peace in the family. The more you meet, the more you have complaints against each other. And, eventually, family members begin to hate each other. You know better than me, the commonly known Shakespeare's saying, --------and what is it?"

"Familiarity breeds contempt." my father fills in the blanks.

"Yes, yes the same one. You are a disciple of Mr. Shakespeare. Why not follow his advice?" he says laughing.

My father is impressed.

He is thinking: *Here is a relatively uneducated man who has barely completed Matric, and he seems to be more worldly wise than I am.*

When my father is home, he tells my mother about his conversation with Daulat Ram. She has never thought of setting up a separate home, but now that it has been presented as an alternative; the idea appeals to her. She realizes that sooner or later, they will have to have their own home as a matter of necessity due to lack of enough space in the house. My father thinks of bringing up the subject with his father. It is becoming obvious that, with my birth and the arrival of the *ayah,* everybody is coming in each other's way.

My father decides that early Sunday morning is the best time to approach his father to talk about this subject, after his father has just completed his morning prayers and study of the holy book, Bhagavad Gita. He believes that with the lessons of Gita fresh in his mind, his father will look at the situation, he is about to present to him, rationally rather than emotionally.

Next Sunday morning, as soon as he hears his father singing a hymn that signals the conclusion of his prayer time, he quietly goes towards his room and peeps in to see if he has concluded the prayer and walks in. The first thing he does is that he touches his father's feet, a mark of highest respect given to elders. His father places his hand on his forehead, and gives him a blessing, "May you live a healthy, long and prosperous life" My father sits down on the bed, and his father sits down on a chair.

"Pitaji," addressing his father with utmost respect and humility, he says, "ever since Vikram is born, I have been having some metaphysical thoughts about reincarnation and transmigration of soul. I have never had such strange thoughts before."

His father replies, "Son, there is nothing unnatural about these thoughts. The birth of a child is the most wondrous happening. Thoughts, such as you are having, are natural. I will give you some books to read. After you have finished reading them, we will talk some more if you want."

As his father gets up to select the books from the bookshelf, my father says, "Pitaji, I want to ask your permission..."

My father has not yet finished his sentence, when his father interrupts him, "Yes, you have my permission."

"But you don't even know what I am going to ask."

"Son, parents have a natural bond with their children. You will learn that as Vikram is growing up. God gives a sixth sense to parents, which gives them the power to feel what their children feel. Go my son. You have your parents' blessings and permission to set up your own home. This is a natural cycle. Parents should let go of their children when they are grown up and can stand on their own feet. We are pleased to see that you have reached that stage. This house will always be there for you."

My father is again about to bend down to touch his father's feet, when his father holds him by his shoulders and embraces and says, " Son, your place is in my heart and not at my feet."

My father is feeling very relieved to receive his father's permission to move to his own place. He goes to his room, excitedly, to tell my mother, and, as soon as he enters, he finds his mother, Beyji, and my mother are sitting and talking. At first, he is not sure what they are talking about, but, after a while, he realizes that they are talking about our new home.

"Now, both of you make sure you rent a flat within walking distance to the school and our house." Beyji tells them.

"Beyji, don't worry. We will rent a flat nearby." My father replies.

After learning that we are going to move to our own home, my mother applies, in writing, to the school for an extension to her leave of absence by three months. Principal Thakur, who is in her mid-forties, is known for her strictness in enforcing the rules of the school. She sends a letter asking my mother to appear before her to explain the reasons. When my father learns about this, he suggests to my mother that he would like to accompany her, if she thinks it is appropriate. My mother agrees to it, and they go to see Mrs. Thakur. When they go to the principal's office, they are told by the principal's personal assistant, "Kamla, Mrs. Thakur is very busy today. It will be better if you come tomorrow. I can give you an appointment." My father is a very persistent man. He does not take 'no' for an answer easily. He has come to realize that he has a Star status in the field of private education, and he has begun to use this Star status.

"We will wait for Mrs.Thakur for a while. Maybe we can see her today." He tells the principal's personal assistant.

After about fifteen minutes, my father sees Mrs. Thakur walking around in the school for inspection. He gets up and walks over to where Mrs. Thakur is standing and explaining something to the gardener. He hands over his visiting card to her and says, "Good morning, Mrs. Thakur."

She looks at his visiting card and her face lights up with a smile—which, they say, happens only once in a blue moon, "You mean you are 'the Professor Surinder Mehra', the Wizard of English Literature, and whom the students call Shakespearewala?"

My father starts to blush and says, "Well, you are being very kind. I am the culprit who out guesses the university with the Guess Papers."

"To what do we owe the honour of your presence?"

"My wife, Kamla, is a teacher in your school. She has applied..."

My father does not even finish the sentence.

"I know. I know. No problem. I will grant her leave. Let us go sit in my office and have a cup of tea."

While this drama is being played, my mother is sitting outside the Principal's office, waiting and looking at my father and wondering what is going on between him and Mrs. Thakur. As she sees my father and Mrs. Thakur walk towards the office, she gets up and starts to walk towards them. As they come face to face, Mrs. Thakur says, "Kamla, you didn't tell me you are married to a Star."

My mother looks down and smiles shyly.

• • •

My father is not sure how to go about finding a flat. He talks to some of his fellow professors at the college. One of them suggests a *Dalaal*—a property broker—named Zaidi & Dayal. The office of the broker is located near my father's college. In between his classes, one day, my father decides to go to see the property broker. The broker's office is located in the area known as Lohari Gate. To get there, he has to maneuver his bicycle through narrow lanes, by-lanes and sub-lanes; where only two men can barely pass each other. So he has to walk his bicycle the rest of the way and, at the same time, make enquiries of the passersby about the location of the property broker's office. As he reaches there, he sees an old faded signboard barely hanging on the wall with the writing: "Busiest and Oldest Dalaal in Lahore". The office is about six feet wide and six feet long with a small desk and two chairs. To reach the office, one has to jump over an open drainage ditch. A man with a white beard, who looks to be sixty or seventy, is occupying the desk. He is chewing a *paan* and periodically sprays the red saliva into the drainage ditch about five feet away. My father just stands around for a while taking in the surroundings and trying to decide whether to go in or not. *Oldest maybe, but not the busiest, my father is thinking.* Finally, he decides to go in and talk to the old man sitting on the chair, who by now has noticed the young man on the bicycle inspecting his office.

It just so happens that both of them decide to say something to each other at the same time. "Khan Sahib..." as my father is about to say something, "Can I help you...?" the man on the chair starts to say and both start to laugh.

The man on the chair gets up and extends his arm and offers his hand, "I am Sayed Zaidi, the Flat King of Lahore."

My father is very amused to hear this introduction and extends his hand, "I am Surinder, a professor at J.N. Chatterji College."

"You know, young man, my son is a student at your college."

"What a coincidence? What is he studying?"

"He tells me that he is studying towards completing his B.A, but I am not sure. He has been trying it for six years. He has appeared in the examination twice, but failed both times." Realizing that he is wasting his customer's time, he says, "Professor Sahib, I beg your forgiveness for bothering you with my problems. What brings you to my office?"

"I am looking for a flat close to Prem Nagar."

"What are your requirements... number of rooms, etc.?"

"I need a three room flat with its own kitchen and bath and in a nice area."

"I know a Christian family on Sanda Road. They have three rooms vacant on the upper floor of their house. If you want, I can take you for a showing in the evening."

My father, mother, and with me in the pram, visit the flat on Sanda Road. It is a few minutes walk from my grandfather's house. The flat is owned by Joseph John, an Indian Christian. His wife, Samantha, and twin daughters, Iris and Mary, also come out to meet my parents. To everyone's surprise, the daughters turn out to be my father's students. They tell him that they have attended his lectures. They take a special liking to me. My parents are very pleased to see the flat. It is on the roof level of a single storey house and covers only part of the roof, with the rest of the roof used as a terrace. My parents decide to rent the flat. It is empty; we can move in anytime.

"See Kamla, so many people know me. You know, I have taught hundreds of students and wherever I go, there is always somebody who recognizes me." My father boasts as they are walking home, while my mother is pushing the pram with me in it.

My mother is very superstitious. She tells him, "Be humble, and do not let success get the better of you. Those who brag can be struck with Evil Eye."

8
HEALTH IS WEALTH

My mother begins to make preparations for moving into the new house. Most of the household articles are being taken from my grandfather's house such as beds, linen, utensils and some furniture. There is also a lot of stuff that my mother brought with her as dowry that is also going to Sanda Road—as our new house begins to be called. One day, two hand drawn carts, pulled by one man each and loaded with household goods, make several trips to Sanda Road. That very night, we sleep in our new home. Roshni, the *ayah,* also moves with us. After a few weeks, a male servant is engaged to do the major household chores. His name is Roshan. 'Roshan' means the Enlightened one, and 'Roshni' means Light. My parents take some time to recognize this dawn of light in our new home! Especially my father, being a student of literature, is fascinated with this inter-play of names of the two people who are going to take care of me when my parents are away at work.

When my grandparents come to visit us, my father tells them about it and wants to know from my grandfather if there is any significance to this. "Roshan and Roshni are two variations of the same universal phenomenon: Light," my grandfather says.

One day, our landlord, Joseph John, comes to see us. My father tells him also about Roshan and Roshni. Joseph John says, "You know professor, as is said in the Bible: *And God said, let there be light; and there was light.* Light is always associated with Good. I think both Roshan and Roshni are good people sent to look after Vikram."

Three months pass, and my mother goes back to work. I am about nine months old at the time. My parents are happy with the way Roshni and Roshan are taking care of me. My father is very busy with his work. In addition to teaching classes at the college and giving lectures at examination time, he also gives private tutoring to the sons and daughters of rich people at their homes. In some cases, he tells them to come to our home in the evenings and Sundays. He leaves home at 7:30 A.M. and comes back home at about 9 P.M. My mother tells him to slow down.

"My dear, there is tide in the affairs of men, which, taken at flood leads on to fortune." He quotes Shakespeare in reply and continues with further interpretation of the quote, "You know, Kamla, if I keep on making this income for another five years, we will be set for life. I want to build my own house and have a car like your brother, Daulat Ram. I know I can do it."

She keeps quiet.

One day, he comes home at night and complains of a severe headache. My mother gives him two tablets of Aspro, which he swallows with water and goes to sleep. He feels fine in the morning and again sets upon his grueling schedule. Another three months pass. In the middle of his lecture in the class, one day, he feels faint and sits down. His students notice that something is wrong and, immediately, give him some water and call the principal. He asks the peon to make a cup of tea. After taking tea, he feels better and continues with his lecture. After finishing his lecture at the college, he has to tutor two more students at their respective houses before going home. Instead, he decides to go home early. He writes a brief note to the students and asks the college peon to deliver the notes to the students' respective homes.

My mother is very pleased to see him at home early, but becomes concerned when he tells her about his near fainting spell.

"Listen ji," as she addresses him affectionately, "I think you should slow down. We have plenty. What are we going to do with more if your health is gone?" She is concerned.

"Don't worry Kamla, I am fine. From tomorrow onwards, I am going to take some refreshments with me to the college. Can you please ask Roshan to pack two mangoes and a thermos full of milk to take with me? In addition, I will also carry some almonds in my pocket that I can eat whenever I need."

This is to become his every day nutritional routine to fuel his grueling work load.

• • •

In early 1943, my father's health starts to deteriorate. He starts to lose weight and appetite. My mother and grandparents are very concerned. My mother finally convinces him to reduce his workload. He gives up individual tutoring, but continues his teaching at the college; it has no immediate effect. He hardly eats anything and continues to lose weight. After a few weeks, he also develops a mild fever and cough. My father, who is thin and lean to start with, has lost 20 pounds. He now weighs only 120 pounds.

One day, Daulat Ram comes over and suggests that he must consult an eminent doctor—his Doctor—Dr. Shiv Lal. My father, accompanied by Daulat Ram, goes to see the doctor. The office is in doctor's own house. There is a sign outside the house—Dr. Shiv Lal, D.M.L.R. My father is very interested to know the meaning of the four word qualification title. Usually, the doctors have M.B.B.S. after their name. He makes a mental note to ask the doctor. After about fifteen minutes wait, my father is called in to see the doctor. Daulat Ram also accompanies him, being an old patient of the doctor. The doctor listens to my father's condition and asks him to move into the examination area—a portion of the office separated by a foldable screen. He completes the usual examination, but with special emphasis on assessment of his pulse beat. My father finds out, during the examination, that Dr. Shiv Lal is an expert in the diagnosis of illness by studying the rhythm of a patient's pulse.

After the examination, the doctor says, "I will have to do some tests. I will write down the names of the tests. You will have to go the Government Hospital for the tests. Some blood tests, sputum test and an X-Ray of the chest are required."

"What do you think is the problem?" my father asks the doctor.

"I can't say anything definite, but it could be just fatigue from overwork. Professor Sahib, you are a young man and you want to drive yourself hard, but you must work within limits and take time to relax. You should take a month of holiday and go out of station."

"I have to work to make a living. I can't just take a month off."

"I will give you a medical certificate that should get you medical leave. Are you teaching in a Government College?"

"No. I work for a private College—J.N. Chatterji College. In a private college you can't just take a month off. If I don't work; I will not get paid. They will engage somebody else to replace me."

The doctor shrugs his shoulders and hands over the requisition for the tests to my father.

"The fee is ten rupees," the doctor says.

My father pays the fee and they leave.

One day, Daulat Ram takes my father for tests. There is a line up of some fifty people ahead of him. After waiting for two hours, they take his blood but an appointment is required for the X-Ray. The next available date is one month away. My father takes the appointment, and they come home. After a month, they go to the hospital to get the X-Ray done and also pick up the results of the blood tests at the same time. The X-Ray technician tells them that the photo will be available for pick up in two weeks.

They go back to the hospital to pick up the X-Ray pictures and take the results of the tests to the doctor's office. They are shocked to find out that the doctor is on holidays for two weeks. As they are coming out of the doctor's office, my father is in a depressed mood. He notices the sign board with the doctor's name followed by D.M.L.R. and asks Daulat Ram, " *Bhai Sahib*, do you know what does this stands for?" pointing to the sign board.

"I think it is **D**octor of **M**edicine **L**ondon **R**eturned."

"You mean Dr. Lal is educated in London?"

"Yes, I think so."

My father finds *London Returned* a very strange qualification.

Two weeks pass, and they come to see the doctor along with the test results. The doctor takes a look at the results and says, "Surinder, based on assessment of your pulse, weight loss, and the test results, I think you have TB."

The room is swirling around him as if the earth has shifted from under his feet. He steadies himself by holding the doctor's desk. All of a sudden all these thoughts come to him: What will happen to Kamla? How will she bring up Vikram on her own? Within a few seconds he visualizes a scenario without him. He believes that TB is like a death sentence.

"What is the treatment?" Daulat Ram asks the doctor.

"There is no medicine available in India. There have been some experimental medicines available in Europe."

"I will send a wire to my contacts in England." Daulat Ram says.

My father has composed himself by now, and asks the doctor, "What is the best course of action now?"

"My advice is that you should go to a hill station for two or three months, take care of your nutrition, have a positive attitude and hope for the best. The fresh air of the hills has been known to do wonders for TB patients."

Daulat Ram and my father thank the doctor and leave. Daulat Ram drops my father off at our Sanda Road home. It is lunch time. Roshan is getting the lunch ready. His usual routine is that he packs the lunch in a metal tiffin carrier and takes it to my mother's school, waits there till she finishes her lunch, and brings the tiffin carrier back. Today he finds my father home at lunch time; and therefore, he has to adjust the routine slightly. He gets all the food ready and tells Roshni to serve lunch to my father. As my father begins to have his lunch, I start crying. Roshni comes in the room to pick me up. At the same time, my father also comes in and takes me away from Roshni. He holds me for a while and looks at me wondering, if he will ever see me grow up as a young man. And then, suddenly, he gives me to back to Roshni, as he is concerned that he may pass along his infection to me.

While he is eating, he is thinking of the life insurance policy for twenty five thousand rupees that he has with the Lakshmi Assurance Co. Will that be enough? He is doing some mental calculations.

After finishing his lunch, he lies down and goes to sleep for a while. He hears me crying again and wakes up and finds my mother trying to placate me. He realizes it is already 4 P.M. He has taken the morning off from work, but he has to take his 6 P.M. class. He is not sure how he should break the news of the diagnosis of TB to my mother. She knows he was going to see the doctor.

My mother walks into the room and asks. "Listen ji, what does the doctor say?"

"He has suggested that we should take a holiday at a hill station for a month or two." He leaves it at that and decides not to tell her anything more for the time being. He gets ready to go to the college, but instead of taking his bicycle he tells Roshan to get a Tonga for him.

My father tells the principal everything about his health problems, including that the doctor has recommended a long leave. Principal S.L. Soni is very distressed to hear of the situation that my father finds himself in and is very sympathetic, "No problem Surinder, take as much time off as you need in order to get well. I will engage a substitute professor till you are back." My father is very relieved and gets up to go to teach his class.

At night, when he is back home and ready to sleep, he lies in bed, but is not able to fall asleep. He is tossing and turning, and my mother asks, "Listen ji, is anything bothering you?"

He is thinking whether or not to tell my mother that he has TB. He does not answer the question, but pretends that he has fallen asleep. After a while, he gets up to go to the bathroom and breaks out in a fit of cough that would not stop. My mother hears this and gets up to check on him. "Roshan, bring a glass of water," she shouts at the top of her voice. Roshan is sleeping on the kitchen floor. As soon he hears the commotion, he gets up, fills a glass of water and rushes to the bathroom. By that time my father's cough has subsided. He takes a few sips of water, and he and my mother move back to the bedroom.

My father takes a few minutes to compose and decides to tell everything to my mother, "Kamla, Dr. Lal thinks that I may have TB." He says the word TB so softly that my mother has to ask, "What did you say, TB?"

"Yes." my father replies.

She is stunned and is in a state of shock. For about a minute or so, she just sits there with her hands on her forehead, with a look of disbelief. "How can you have TB?" she says, "TB is found in people who live in dirty unhygienic conditions. I teach hygiene in school. You cannot have TB."

"Kamla, Daulat Ram was with me. You can ask him. The doctor says all tests are positive for TB."

Both of them sit quietly on the bed, looking at each other and holding hands. With tears flowing down my mother's cheeks, she says, "Somebody has cast an Evil Eye on you."

My mother looks up and finds Roshni standing in the doorway holding me, "*Sahibji*," she says in her rustic Punjabi, "Roshni will pray to Guru Nanak Devji for your good health. You will be all right." And she continues, "*Bibiji*" addressing my mother, "You should recite *Japji Sahib*, the essence of Sikh Religious Philosophy, every morning. You will see the power of prayer."

My father and mother are both touched by this gesture.

Later in the day, my mother and father go to see my grandparents. They walk across the open field, with Roshni pushing the pram with me lying in it fast asleep and oblivious to everything going on around me. My father knocks at the door. His brother, Dilip, opens the door.

He says, "*Namaste, Bhabiji* and *Bhai Sahib,* and how is little Cuckoo?"

My grandmother, Beyji, is busy with her embroidery work, "I am making a frock for Cuckoo," she says.

My grandfather is in the sitting room reading an Urdu newspaper. He gets up and comes out in the courtyard to greet us. "Surinder *beta* you seem to have lost a lot of weight. Are you missing your mother's cooking?"

"This is what happens when you eat food cooked by servants," my grandmother makes this sarcastic remark.

They all move back into the sitting room, and my grandfather asks, "So, Surinder, what did the doctor say?"

"He suspects TB."

"What? Don't believe that quack. I have heard a few stories about him."

"He is a very qualified doctor. He completed his training in London."

"I hope you are not impressed by the long list of alphabets after his name. You know, nowadays many professionals, including doctors, add alphabets after their names to indicate that they are foreign trained."

My father replies, "Daulat Ram has been his patient for ten years. I think he is a good doctor."

My grandfather adds, "Let me take you to Hakim Salim Rai. He is the best Ayurvedic doctor in Lahore. You know, our own Ayurvedic system is true and tried and works the best. I am also trying Homeopathic medicines—the German system. You should look into that also."

"Pitaji, please leave me alone." My father says irritably, "I don't want to be made a guinea pig. Especially, I don't want anything German. See what they are doing in Europe. We came to tell you that we are going to take two months leave from work and go to Kashmir to get well."

After hearing the bad news that my father has been diagnosed with TB, my grandfather and grandmother present a very brave face to my parents. However, after they leave, my grandmother, Beyji, has tears in her eyes. My grandfather consoles her, "He is a young man; he will be all right. The oxygen filled air of the hills will do him a lot of good."

"Why does it have to happen to our Surinder? You pray to God. You recite Gita, the Word of God. What good does it do?"

My grandfather replies, "God is testing our will to believe in Him. If we keep our faith in Him, every thing will come out fine. Just close your eyes and imagine: Surinder has recovered. He is hail and hearty. Keep this thought with you, always."

The clouds part and a shaft of sun light shines through into the courtyard illuminating both of them. A classical holy tune played on a *Bansuri* floats in from a neighbour's house. My grandfather looks at Beyji and, with a mystic smile on his face, says, "See. *Krishna Bhagwan*, our Lord, is smiling on us."

9
PARADISE ON EARTH

When my parents are walking back home after visiting my grandparents, they are planning their holiday in Kashmir. The capital of the state, Srinagar, is about 280 miles north of Lahore by train and bus. There are a number of logistics to be taken care of. "What do we do with Roshan and Roshni? My mother asks.

"I think we should take Roshni with us and leave Roshan behind to look after the house." My father replies.

"We should go and see my school principal, Mrs. Thakur, one day to ask for leave for two months." My mother says.

"I think I will go to the railway station tomorrow to buy the train tickets to Jammu. The train only goes up to Jammu. Onwards to Srinagar, it is a journey by bus. It is a long trip. We will stay in Jammu City for a few days. Then take the bus to Srinagar, stay a few days along the way, and enjoy the trip. We will take four to five days to get to Srinagar."

As they reach Sanda Road, they find Joseph John, our Landlord, standing outside preparing to go somewhere. My parents tell him all about my father's health problems and their forthcoming trip to Kashmir.

He expresses concern and asks, "Are you going to vacate the flat?"

"We will be keeping the flat. Roshan will stay here, but Roshni will go with us."

Joseph John puts his arm around my father's shoulder, "Surinder, don't worry too much about your illness; it will make your health even worse. We will send a prayer to our Lord, Jesus Christ. He will make you well."

My mother is touched by the gesture and wipes a tear with the end of her sari. As Joseph John and my parents are about to go into the house, Sayed Zaidi, the estate agent is walking by having just shown a flat in the neighborhood to another customer. He stops as soon as he sees Joseph John and my parents.

"What brings you here, Sayed?" Joseph John asks.

"I was just showing a flat to a foreign couple. From their accent, they sound like Americans. I asked where they were from, but they were very tight lipped. And they were accompanied by an Englishman. Anyway, we just fit people in flats. What they do in there is none of our business. A lot of foreign military personnel have been moving in this area because of the War on our eastern front in Burma... Professor Sahib, are you enjoying living in your flat? We guarantee satisfaction, you know!"

"Surinder has been feeling under the weather for the past little while." Joseph John adds.

"We will change the weather for our friend so that he feels on the top of, rather than under, the weather... what is the problem young man?" Zaidi asks.

"The doctor suspects I may have TB." My father replies." We have been advised to spend a few months at a hill station."

With his hands pointing towards the sky, Zaidi says *"Bismillah al rahman al rahim*, by the Guidance of the Divine, I will pray for your complete recovery and long life."

On April 1, 1943, under the protective umbrella of the good wishes of friends belonging to the three different faiths, my parents and I, accompanied by Roshni, set out on the fateful journey to Kashmir.

The luggage consists of three steel trunks, three holdalls and a number of small bags. Some of it is loaded on to Daulat Ram's car. In addition, three Tongas are engaged to carry the rest of the luggage and the people. The see-off party includes my grandparents, my Uncle Karan, Daulat Ram and his wife Nirmala, and Roshan. Daulat Ram's car is carrying my parents and me, in addition to Daulat Ram and his wife, Nirmala. The departure time for the train is 8:30 P.M. We leave home at 5:30 P.M. and run onto a torrent of traffic in the form of bicycles, Tongas and a few cars; and lots of people walking back to their homes after work. As soon as we start from home, the two Tongas are left behind and the car snakes through blowing its horn after each minute.

The car reaches the station at about 6:15 P.M. My father gets out of the car and shouts, waving his hands, "coolie... coolie." Three coolies, wearing red uniforms, walk towards us. My father asks the three of them to wait until the Tongas also arrive. In the meantime, he goes over to the ticket office to purchase platform tickets. These are required for the people who have come to see us off.

We wait and wait, but the Tongas do not arrive. My parents are getting worried. *Damn it, can nothing go right for us?* My father is thinking. They cannot leave till the Tongas arrive because most of the luggage is on the Tongas. The Tongas finally arrive at about 7 P.M. My grandfather gets down from the Tonga and starts directing the coolies about how to pick up the luggage and where to take it. He asks them to give him their brass registration plate that is tied around their arms. Each coolie is registered with the railway police. It is believed that if you take their registration plate away from them, they can't take off with your luggage because they will not be able to work as coolies without it. After unloading the luggage from the Tongas, the coolies load themselves up with steel trunks on their heads, along with one holdall each slung on one shoulder, and carrying bags in their hands. My grandfather walks along with them to ensure the safety of the luggage. My Uncle, Karan, is standing by watching this spectacle and, as usual, comes up with a gem of wisdom, "Pitaji, you need not worry about the coolies running away with your luggage; the poor men can hardly walk with the load they are carrying."

Uncle Karan is thinking: *Mahatma Gandhi fought for better treatment of the coolies in South Africa and see how they are being treated in their own country. It is always dark under the lamp!*

• • •

As the train catches speed, the whistling of the steam engine and the sounds of mating of the steel wheels with the steel rails has an intoxicating effect on the passengers. After a while, our fellow passengers begin to doze off. My father and mother are talking to each other. He tells my mother that he has a confession to make. She is very intrigued by this statement of his. "A confession?" she asks.

"Well, I saved it for this day. You know what day it is today?... It is April Fool's Day."

She has a smile on her face after a long time. Ever since she has heard of my father's illness, she does not smile. She just thinks and thinks and thinks... probably about her future. Lines of worry are etched on her forehead. My father is happy to see a smile.

He thinks of something that his father told him a few days back, when he had informed him of his of his illness.

"Son," he had said, "Believe that you are healthy, act that you are healthy and the Powers of the Universe will conspire to make your beliefs come true." He decides to play an elaborate hoax on himself, the Nature and my mother and play out his father's hypothesis. He decides that from today onwards, he is going to believe that he does not have TB.

"Kamla, my dear, I don't know how to tell you this but it is good news, … my confession is… that I lied about my having TB. It is true that I have not been feeling well, but I do not have TB. I made it all up to get away from it all. My college principal would not have given me the leave, and neither would have Mrs. Thakur given you the leave. I was feeling so tired that I had to get away."

My mother is somewhat confused and angry, and she says "Do you realize how much anguish this has caused me and all our relatives?"

"Yes, I realize my mistake. I should not have done this, or at least, I should have taken you into confidence."

My mother never argues too much and accepts the explanation. The sound of the steel wheels running on the permanent way of steel rails puts us all to sleep.

• • •

Several days have passed. We reach Srinagar, the capital of the state of Jammu and Kashmir, the early morning of April 7, 1943. As soon as we get off the bus, there is a crush of agents of various hotels and houseboats. My father selects an agent, who is standing quietly behind the crowd. He waves at the agent to move over to one side. The agent shyly moves over to one side. He is dressed in a white shirt, white pants and a red tie. Maybe it is his well groomed look that attracts my father. The agent walks over to where we are standing and introduces himself, "Sir, they call me Ramu Guide. I will be honored to be your guide during your stay here."

My father is very impressed that he can speak English so well, and he says, "Well, we want to stay in a houseboat to start with, and then we will see what to do next."

"I can suggest a few good houseboats, sir, where my previous clients have received good service. I suggest that you should rent a Houseboat on Dal Lake."

"OK, let us go and have a look," my father replies.

Ramu arranges two porters, known as *Hattoes,* to carry the luggage and a rickshaw to carry my mother and me. My father and Roshni walk along with

Ramu. As they are walking, my father engages Ramu in small talk to assess his abilities as a guide. "What made you take up the job of a guide?"

"It is not a job sir; this is my own business. I have completed my B.A. in history, and I decided to become a guide. I think with my knowledge of history, I can be a genuine guide."

Now my father is really impressed. He is thinking: *A guide with a bachelor's degree should be interesting. After this, maybe, I can take him back to Lahore. After all we do need a history professor.*

"Ramu, what is your full name?"

"Ram Avatar Kachru is my full name, sir, and I am a Kashmiri Pundit."

My father looks at him with a smile and satisfaction. He is pleased with himself that he has managed to get a Kashmiri Pundit as a guide. He will certainly add this to his brag bag to tell back in Lahore.

"What are your charges for acting as our guide, Ramu?"

"Sir, please do not be concerned with my fee. I have just started my business. Whatever you think appropriate will be fine by me."

My father is very pleased. He walks over to my mother and tells her about his conversation with Ramu. As my father is walking beside the rickshaw, in which my mother and I are travelling, Ramu also comes over and starts to walk alongside the rickshaw.

As my father is walking and talking, he is also looking around at the mountains with their outline in the distance rolling up and down. At a height of about 5600 feet above the sea level, the air is cool and fresh. After a long walk from the bus station, we reach the shores of the Dal Lake. My parents stand there and look around in amazement at the scenery. There are mountains on three sides of the lake—green mountains closer by and snow covered peaks farther away—with clouds flirting with their tops. With the sun shining on the snow covered peaks, the whole scene looks like a necklace of Pearls set in Emeralds. My parents just stand there spell bound.

Ramu breaks the silence, "Sir, let me show you a few houseboats."

Although, the houseboats are close by, the scene far off is so mesmerizing that my parents forget that they have to find a place to live. "Yes of course. How are we going there?"

"All the travel between the shore and the houseboats is done via *Shikaras*. See those small colorfully decorated boats?" Ramu says pointing not too far from where we are standing. "Sir, it is said that these are very similar to the gondolas of Venice, a city in Italy."

My father is intrigued by this concept of living on water, where the only way to reach you is also by water. He is even more fascinated by the comparison of *Shikaras* to gondolas of Venice. He immediately thinks of his favorite Shakespeare's play, the Merchant of Venice. He just has to tell Ramu about this, "Ramu, you should know that I am a professor of English Literature. What a coincidence that you mention Venice. I want you to know that one of my favorite plays is Merchant of Venice."

My mother laughs and says, "You know ji, somehow, you connect every event to Shakespeare. No wonder your students call you *Shakespearewala*!"

Ramu hails a *shikara*. My father and Ramu get in and sail away to inspect a few houseboats. They stop at one Houseboat and then to the next. And after a little bit of haggling on the rent, my father selects one. They come back, and my mother, Roshni and I also get in the shikara and set sail for our holiday Houseboat, while Ramu brings the luggage in another shikara. We all get aboard the Houseboat and look around. There is a drawing room and kitchen on the main floor and two bedrooms upstairs. The cooking is all done by the attendants of the Houseboat. After lunch, my father tells Ramu, "We would like to rest for the afternoon. Why don't you come back at about 4 P.M.?" Ramu gets up and, while he is walking out, my father thanks him for his help and slips some cash in his hands.

"No, no, please sir, you don't have to give me anything at this time. I have not really done anything as yet." He gradually slips the cash in his pocket, while he is still talking and goes downstairs.

My father strolls over to the balcony overlooking the water. After a while, he looks down and sees Ramu and the owner of the Houseboat in an animated conversation. The Houseboat owner gives some money to Ramu, which he appears to accept reluctantly.

My father is standing at the balcony and thinking: *Oh, well, commission! So, Ramu receives commission for bringing customers to the houseboats. The age old custom has found its way to Paradise on Earth, Srinagar, also. But Ramu is our guide. Is it ethical for him to accept commission from the owner of the Houseboat for which he helped me negotiate the rent? Smells like a bribe, he thinks.*

He goes inside and finds my mother and me asleep. He also lies down and falls asleep.

Ramu is back at the appointed time, and it is his knock at the door that wakes up my parents. "Come in Punditji." My father addresses him with sarcasm, by his high caste, having seen him accept commission from the Houseboat owner.

My father believes that, as he is going to be dependent on Ramu for the next few months, he wants to be sure about Ramu's character. He decides to ask Ramu.

"Ramu, tell me. Is it right for a guide to accept commission from the owner of a Houseboat?"

Ramu's face goes red with embarrassment, and he mumbles, "Sir, I know you were standing at the balcony. He forced the money on me. I never ask or expect commission; but sometimes the business owners give *Baksheesh* to the guides who bring them business. I will return the money. My integrity is more valuable to me than a few *paisas*. Please forgive me; it will not happen again."

My father is satisfied with what he hears and decides to let it go. "It is OK Ramu. Come have High Tea with us."

The wife of the owner of the Houseboat, accompanied by a female servant, brings a tray with a teapot covered with a tea cozy–to keep the tea hot–along with some cups and saucers; and another tray with a silver milk pot, a sugar pot with sugar cubes in it, and yet another tray decorated with assorted biscuits and pastries.

"This is very British!" my father remarks. It is all placed on the high table with chairs around. My parents and Ramu take seats around the table and Roshni sits down on the carpet. "Come on Roshni. Sit with us on the chair." My mother says.

"No *Bibiji*, I am fine here." She replies shyly. She addresses my mother as *Bibiji*, a respectful word in common use for the lady of the house. Roshni is respecting one of the "*great traditions*" of India: The domestic servants are not supposed to sit on the chairs in the presence of their masters!

Ramu pours tea from his cup into the saucer and slurps it. And while doing that, he asks, "Sir, why do they call this ritual, High Tea?"

"Late afternoon tea, as we are having, is known as High Tea." My father replies.

"Why not call it Late Tea, sir, why High Tea?"

"Another story is that the upper class English people in England used to have tea on low tables in their drawing rooms. And as the custom of late afternoon tea caught on, the middle classes also started having tea late in the afternoon. As they did not have low tables, they started having tea on high tables, like we are having; and therefore, they started calling it High Tea." And my father laughs.

Ramu politely nods, but does not appear convinced with the explanation and says, "Well, sir, English *Sahibs* and *Memsahibs* have their own customs. Here in Kashmir, we have tea all the time, High, Low and sometimes sitting on the floor."

My parents are amused with Ramu's take on High Tea.

My father asks, "Ramu, I have been eager to find out something for a long time. Tell me, how did the tradition of houseboats in Srinagar start? I have not heard about houseboats on any other lakes in India."

"It is a very unique story, sir. As you probably know, that Kashmir is not a part of India. It is independently ruled by Maharaja Sir Hari Singh. Although laws and regulations are the same as in India, there is one difference. No person from out-of-state can own land here. Because of the beauty and climate of Kashmir, the English people started visiting in large numbers and wanted to purchase land to build houses. Maharaja Sir Pratap Singh—the uncle of the present ruler—refused to entertain the proposal of foreigners buying land in Kashmir. And that actually led to the construction of houseboats. They could not buy land, but they could build and own houseboats on water to get around the law."

"This is very interesting, Ramu. You really know your history, don't you?"

My mother reminds my father, "Listen ji. We should send a telegram to Lahore informing them of our safe arrival and our address. I promised your mother that we will inform them as soon as we reach Srinagar."

"Ramu, how far is the telegraph office?" My father asks.

"Not too far, sir. We can all go for a stroll and stop on the way."

As we are going downstairs, my mother says to Roshni, "You know, we should have brought the pram along."

Ramu hears this, turns around and says, "*Bhenji,*" addressing my mother as sister, "I will ask Mustafa sahib, the Houseboat owner; they usually keep things such as prams, umbrellas and other household items."

As luck would have it, a pram is available. Everybody boards a Shikara and we are ashore in a few minutes. Roshni is pushing the pram with me sitting in it. My parents and Ramu are walking alongside. After walking for about ten minutes, my father begins to experience breathlessness, and he sits down on a bench nearby. He does not tell anybody of his discomfort and pretends that he is just sitting down and enjoying the scene. Meanwhile, my mother notices some shops that are selling Pashmina shawls. "Come on Roshni, let us go look at some shawls, while Professor Sahib is enjoying the scene." And they walk across the road to go to the shopping area.

It seems that my father is determined to bear the bout of breathlessness on his own without telling anybody. He thinks that this is his chance to practice what his father preached. He sits quietly and takes a few deep breaths, while concentrating on his breathing. After a few minutes, he feels fine, or maybe pretends to be fine and gets up and walks over to the shop where my mother and Roshni are shopping. My mother likes some shawls and wants to buy one for herself and one for, Beyji, my grandmother. She asks Ramu, who is just standing outside the shop, to come in and advise if the price is right. Apparently, he seems to know the shop owner and decides not to get involved. The shop owner is asking fifty rupees for one shawl. My father knows that everything is marked up during the tourist season, which is just starting. My father is all energized after taking some deep breaths of the fresh Kashmiri air and is ready to haggle. He introduces himself and hands over his business card to the shop owner. The shop owner looks at it, but does not say anything. From his looks my father realizes that the shop owner probably cannot read English. "We are from Lahore, and we have come to stay here for a month or so. I teach English in a college in Lahore," my father says.

"We have an agent in Lahore, named Verma & Company. He stocks our shawls. They have a shop in Anarkali area," the shop owner replies.

"What a coincidence! Sat Verma was my class fellow in college. I buy most of my clothes from him." My father is using his penchant for name dropping.

"What is your good name, sir?" my father asks him, addressing him with respect and with due regard to his age.

"My name is Rattan Dogra."

"Have you been is this business for a long time?"

"My grandfather started this business twenty five years ago. Over the years, we have started supplying shawls all over India."

"Do you go to Lahore sometime?"

"Yes, very often. My daughter, Lakshmi, studies at the Hansraj Mahila Maha Vidyalaya. It is known as HMMV. She is in ninth class and stays in the hostel. You must have heard of the women's college and school."

"Well, well, it is a small world. You know, my wife is a teacher at HMMV."

My father, usually, succeeds in finding a connection; sometimes by name dropping and sometimes due to the fact that both my parents being teachers, they come in contact with hundreds of students every year. The fact that Rattan Dogra's daughter studies at the same school my mother teaches in, is enough to melt his heart.

"Professor sahib, you people are teachers—one of the noblest of professions. Your wife is my daughter's Guru. I cannot accept any money from you for the shawls you want to buy. Consider it as *Guru Dikhshana* —a gift from my daughter to her Guru."

"Oh, please Dogra sahib, we will be embarrassed to accept such an expensive gift. Let us pay a fair price."

But Rattan Dogra does not budge. He asks his sales clerk to pack the two shawls, and he hands them over to my mother.

"We have to send the telegram," my mother reminds my father again.

Rattan Dogra hears this and says, "I will send one of my men to the telegraph office, if you can just write down the message and the address."

My father writes down the message and the address on a piece of paper, and as he opens his wallet to give some money to the salesman who is to go to the telegraph office, Rattan Dogra interrupts, "Please don't bother, Professor sahib, he will take care of it, and you can pay him when he comes back."

My father puts the money back in his wallet. The salesman leaves for the telegraph office and comes back in about ten minutes and says, "The telegraph machine is not working, sir. They told me to come back in an hour. The telegraph wires have come down in the hills."

"It is fine. Go back in an hour. In the meantime, we will talk and have some tea." Rattan Dogra says.

My parents sit down and wait, while Rattan Dogra is attending to other customers. After he is free of the other customers, he asks, "Where are you staying?

"We are staying at the Lotus Houseboat," my father replies.

After sitting at the shop for an hour or so and listening to all the talk about Pashmina, my father is eager to know more about it and asks, "Dogra Sahib, how is Pashmina made?"

"Well, if you agree to have lunch with us at our house, day after tomorrow, I will be happy to show you the making of Pashmina shawls."

"Where do you live?"

"Please don't worry about that. I will pick you up and take you there in my Jeep."

In the meantime, the salesman again goes to the telegraph office and comes back with the news that the telegraph wires will remain down for a number of days.

Rattan Dogra says, "Professor Sahib, I will advise you to write a letter to your family in Lahore. One of our salesmen is travelling to Lahore tomorrow; he will deliver the letter to your parents' house. Now, how do you like your personal post and telegraph service? You know, due to inclement weather, we are used to interruption in roads, and post and telegraph service– sometimes for days and weeks at a time."

My parents are really feeling weighed down by the burden of obligations that Rattan Dogra is placing on them. They don't know whether to accept the lunch invitation or not. In the meantime, Rattan Dogra gets busy with some other customers, and my parents look at each other and move out of the shop to get a breath of fresh air.

"What do you think we should do?" my father asks my mother.

"Well, he is making us feel welcome from the goodness of his heart; but don't forget, why he is doing this. He wants something back from us. It is basic human nature. He knows that if he looks after us, we will look after his daughter in Lahore. So let us not feel guilty. We should accept his hospitality gracefully, and we will return the favors when we go back to Lahore."

My father feels more comfortable with the situation after listening to my mother, and they move back into the shop. He writes a brief note to his father, puts it in an envelope, seals it and gives it to Rattan Dogra.

"So, Professor Sahib, what have you decided? Should I pick you up day after tomorrow?"

"Yes, Dogra Sahib, it will be our pleasure, and it is so good of you." My father shakes hands with Rattan Dogra, my mother picks up the package of shawls, and we all move out of the shop to go back to the Houseboat. My parents are walking in front, followed by Roshni pushing the pram with me sleeping in it, and Ramu walking beside her.

My father starts to brag, "See, Kamla I have such a sophisticated way of dealing with people." Before he can finish his statement, my mother interrupts, "Oh. Oh. Remember what I keep telling you. Bragging brings Evil Eye upon you." My father immediately places a finger on his lips, "OK.... OK. Mum is the word. No more bragging."

As they are walking, my mother says, starting a little bragging of her own, "Oh, just to set the record straight. Rattan Dogra is being nice to us because of my being a teacher in HMMV, where his daughter is studying, and not because you said something to him."

"OK, Madame, you are right. One thing we have to admit that Rattan Dogra is a gem of a man. After all, his name is *Rattan*, meaning Gem in Hindi. I think his parents gave him an appropriate name." They both break out in laughter. As they reach the shores of the Dal Lake and their home away from home, the Lotus Houseboat, they let Ramu go home for the day, and we all get in a *Shikara* and go to the Houseboat.

∴

Rattan Dogra is waiting for us to take us to his home for lunch. As soon as we reach the shore by Shikara, he comes out and helps us all to get in his Jeep. After about half an hour of winding drive through the hills, we reach his residence. It is set on top of a hill overlooking the Dal Lake, the Shalimar Gardens, and the Nishat gardens. It is a two-storey building with a sloping roof with clay tiles. Near the house, a little uphill, there is a small shed where Pashmina Shawls are made. My parents are awe struck by the scenery. They have seen the Dal Lake and the surrounding areas, and they were impressed by that, but now there is a higher level of admiration showing on their faces. My father comes out with his Shakespearean English, "Thou art living in Paradise, Dogra Sahib. Mughal Emperor Jahangir was right when he said: if there is Paradise on Earth, it is here, it is here, it is here."

Rattan Dogra's wife, Indirani, comes out to greet us, and Rattan Dogra introduces my parents to her. Roshni is standing nearby holding me, and Indirani says, "Oh, what a lovely child."

"Let me show you the making of Pashmina shawls." Rattan Dogra leads my parents to the factory shed and starts to explain.

"See, wool is known as *Pasham* in Persian. For making Pashmina, special wool is used from a goat known as *Changthangi* found at high altitudes above 14,000 feet in the Ladakh region of Jammu and Kashmir. The wool is first spun into yarn using *Charkha*—a manually operated spinning wheel—and then, a manually operated loom is used to make cloth. After that, other processes are used to dye the cloth and make borders. All in all, it is a very labor intensive process."

My parents move around the factory shed and watch the workers going about their work.

As they move back into the house, my parents find that some more guests have arrived. The new couple, Satinder and Sita, is introduced to my parents. Satinder is with the police department, and as soon as he hears that we are from Lahore, he says, "Our department has received a telegraph message from Lahore police asking us to trace some missing persons with names similar to yours. The message states that they left Lahore for Srinagar a week back and have not been heard from. In fact, the message was sent on behalf of the Commissioner of Police of Lahore."

"Oh, well, then it must be us they are looking for. The Commissioner is a friend of my brother-in-law, my wife's brother. We have been late in sending a telegram of our safe arrival. The day before, we found out that the wires are down, so we sent a letter, instead, through one of Dogra sahib's salesman."

"Well, you know, the news has come that there was a landslide yesterday, and the road is blocked. I am not sure if Dogra sahib's salesman made it through, or he is also stuck. Those of us who live in hill stations have to get used to interruptions in service—sometimes it is the telegraph service and sometimes it is roads."

My father shrugs his shoulders and says, "Well, there is nothing much we can do, except wait."

After lunch, Rattan Dogra drives us back to the Dal Lake and our Lotus Houseboat.

...

The next day, the day after, the day after that, and every day for two weeks, Ramu takes us to show us the sights of Srinagar and the surroundings. We visit the Shalimar Gardens, the Nishat Gardens, the Chashmashahi, the Moghul Gardens, Pehelgam and Gulmarg. On all our visits we are accompanied by Ramu, our Guide. We carry our lunch with us and spend the day strolling through the gardens. We usually have our lunch sitting on a bed sheet spread under a Chinar tree. Whenever my father asks him about the history of a particular garden, Ramu's eyes light up, and he starts an animated rendition of the Garden Symphony, as my father starts to call it. In every garden he recites the same story with a little variation for each, "Mughal Emperor Akbar visited Kashmir in 1579 and after that all his descendants, including Jahangir, Shah Jahan of the Taj Mahal fame, and even Aurangzeb the last Mughal Emperor, visited Kashmir several times during their respective reigns. They were so impressed with such abundant natural beauty of Kashmir that they contributed many beautiful gardens to the city of Srinagar."

And he says it with such fluency, rhythm and tone, with his hands moving around pointing to different areas of the gardens, that my father starts to call his rendition, the Garden Symphony.

River Jhelum meanders through Srinagar for miles; and whenever we travel through the City, and we see Jhelum River, my father says to my mother, "You know Kamla, I was born on the banks of the Jhelum River, and here I am 28 years later near the source of the River of my birth."

My destiny has brought me to the Origin of my life, when I may be nearing the end. There must be some meaning in it. He is thinking—lost in thoughts lying on a bed sheet under a Chinar tree in the Nishat Garden.

"Listen ji, what are you lost in?" my mother interrupts his thoughts.

And then, suddenly, my father says, "Ramu, I would like to visit the origin of the River Jhelum."

"Well, that can be arranged, sir. It is at Verinag Spring, in Verinag town, about 50 miles south-east of here. It will take about four hours, but the good thing is that the bus stops a few times along the way to let the passengers get down to enjoy the scenic lookouts."

10

THE DREAM

A few days later, we are on our way to Verinag. There are only a few passengers in the bus. Besides us, there is an *Engrez*—a white—couple and a young Indian couple on their honeymoon. We stop along the way to pick up passengers from small villages. The road winds around from one hillock to another. After a while, my father strikes a conversation with the *Engrez* couple. During the course of the conversation he finds their accent rather strange, and he asks them, "May I ask, which part of England do you come from?"

"Oh dear, you mistook us for the English. We are from Canada."

"Canada?" My father is surprised to see people from such a far off land visiting such a far flung place.

"What brings you to Srinagar?"

The lady replies, "We work with the government. We are in India on His Majesty's Government Service."

My father realizes that "His Majesty's Government Service" means that he should not ask any more questions. After a few minutes, the Canadian man says to my father, "Charming area, Eh?

"Yes. I really love sitting under the Chinar trees," my father replies.

"To tell you frankly, we, too, feel right at home amongst the Chinars. We call it the Maple tree in Canada. It is almost our national Tree."

"Is Canada also a hilly area like Kashmir?"

"Well, in fact, the maple trees are found in the plains in Canada. Because of Canada being in the North, the climate is similar to here."

"Do you also have a king in Canada?" my father asks.

"The same King my friend, the same King you have!"

"You mean you are also under the British rule?"

"Well, yes sort of... I think they treat us somewhat better because we are like cousins."

"I guess, it is then correct, when they say... the Sun never sets on the British Empire. When there is sunset in India, there is sunrise in Canada."

The Canadian couple breaks out into laughter and the Canadian man says, "Do you know that the British ruled over America also at one time?"

"You don't say old chap." My father says, trying to put on English accent... Oh, Ramu, you have studied history. Do you know all this?"

"Not really sir, I mainly concentrated on Indian history. I learned something new today."

My father introduces himself and my mother to the Canadian couple, "I am Surinder... my wife Kamla and... Oh, Ramu is our Guide."

"I am Adolf and... meet my wife Jane. Oh, and please forgive us if we mispronounce your names."

Adolf? Immediately, the word, Hitler comes to his mind. Is this his real name, or he is putting me on? My father is thinking.

"Is Canada involved in the War?" My father asks.

"Oh yes, in a big way. We have soldiers in Europe and even in India, on the Burma front."

"May I ask the obvious question? Are you here in connection with the War?"

"Well, we would rather not talk about it," Adolf replies.

After we reach Verinag village, we walk a short distance to the Verinag spring. It is an octagon shape, peaceful and sparklingly clear body of water surrounded by tall pine trees. My father, mother and Ramu walk around the spring. Roshni spreads a bed sheet on the ground nearby and makes me sit down on it. After eating lunch my father and mother stroll around the area. My father sits down on a rock outcrop and looks up towards the top of the pine trees and sees the beams of sunlight trying to penetrate the shaded area below.

He imagines the water in the Jhelum River starting from where he is sitting and flowing like a snake downhill, and reaching Jhelum City, his birth place. I wonder how long it takes for the water to travel that far, he is thinking. It took me 28 years to reach from Jhelum, my birth place, to the origin of the river.

After spending some time at Verinag, my father feels energized. A pleasant sense of wellbeing descends on him. He gets up and looks around. He notices a group of people congregating around a man in saffron clothes, a *Swami* or a holy man, sitting under a tree. He says to my mother, "Let us see what is going on there." And they walk towards the tree. The holy man is in meditation, while a few people stand around and watch for a while and then move on. After a while, the holy man opens his eyes and looks at my parents with a smile on his face. My father bends down to touch his feet—a mark of respect. The holy man holds his hands and asks my parents to sit down beside him.

"What brings you to Kashmir?" the holy man asks.

"We are here for a holiday. Swamiji... do you live around here?"

"Yes, I live in this area in an Ashram nearby."

"How do you spend your time, Swamiji?"

"Talking to visitors and people in the village and meditating. I have also learned palm reading. During the day I sit here and talk to people and tell them about the future; whatever I can see. In the evening, I go back to the Ashram."

My father looks at my mother, and she nods, and he, gradually, moves his right hand forward, "Swamiji, will you please?"

He looks at both my father's palms, closes his eyes and starts to speak, "You are passing through a difficult time... You have been feeling weak and exhausted... You will have two sons... and I also see a *Kanya*—a female baby—you will look after as your own... Long life, yes, I see long life for you. I am seeing you flying over oceans. Near the end of your life, you will live in a far off land... You will not come back after that." There is silence. And after a while, the holy man opens his eyes.

"How do you tell the future, Swamiji?"

"Just look up and see through the trees and you see the blue *Aakaash*—the sky. Behind the *Aakash* is *Kaal,* the Time. *Kaal* is like a sheet of cloth where the Past and the Future are written. The Future is constantly becoming the Past; what we call the Present does not really exist. It is just an illusion. *Aakaash* is also like a sheet of cloth. The stars that you see at night are subtle perforations in *Aaakash* like small peep holes. God has given some of us powers to see through the peep holes. We can sometimes get a small glimpse of the Past and the Future, and that is what we reveal to you."

"Swamiji, you said the present does not exist. How is that possible? We are in the Present."

"Yes, we are in the Present, but it is a combination of the immediate past and the immediate future, and our consciousness perceives it as present. I call it the Real Present. The actual present moment is infinitely small. It is beyond perception. This is why I say it is an illusion. If you want to be happy, live in the Real Present. Pay attention to what you are engaged in. Do not think of the Past or the Future while you are engaged in the Real Present."

"Swamiji, you say the Future is written on the *Kaal*. Does this mean that everything is already decided for us?"

"Yes, for most of us, but there are some strong minded souls, who by their shear belief and willpower, change their Future."

"Swamiji, how can you be sure that the future is cast in stone?" my father asks.

"Well, look at it this way. All the stars, the Sun and the Moon move about in predetermined orbits in accordance with the laws of nature. Is it not logical to think that we, humans, are also governed by the same laws of nature as the stars and move about in predetermined ways? This is why I say that the future is predetermined."

My parents just sit there for a few minutes to contemplate and digest what they have just heard. After a while, they touch his feet, place a small gift at his feet, and as they are about to get up and leave, my father asks, "Swamiji, can I please have your address? With your kind permission, may I write to you sometime?" Swamiji gives a sign with his hands asking for a paper and pen. Daddyji takes out his diary and pen and hands it over to him. He writes his name and address and hands back the pen and dairy.

As they are getting up, Roshni shouts from a distance, "*Bibiji, Bibiji,* Vikram is walking. Look, look." My parents run towards Roshni to watch me take my first steps. After a while, Ramu also walks towards where my parents are standing watching me stumble and get up and walk. As I see Ramu approach us, I also utter my first words pointing to Ramu, "*Punditji aah gaye*," Meaning: Punditji is coming.

My parents are fascinated to hear me talk, and especially that I address Ramu, as Punditji, by his caste.

"How does a baby know that Ramu is a Pundit?" my mother asks.

In the meantime, Swamiji gets up and walks over to where we are all standing and says, "An infant hears and absorbs everything and understands more than you think."

"Bus to Srinagar is leaving in ten minutes. Get aboard, get aboard," the bus conductor announces.

On the way to Srinagar, everybody in the bus is tired and sleepy, and there is virtually no conversation.

My father is thinking: *I am going to have two sons? Going to live in a far off land? If I believe what Swamiji said, I am not going to die of TB. He decides to believe Swamiji. Somewhere between Verinag and Srinagar, he decides to believe in the Future and live in the Real Present.*

My father wakes my mother up, who is dozing after a long day, "Kamla, are you sleeping? Do you remember what Swamiji said?... two sons and a daughter. I think we should get busy... thinking of the names." And he laughs, somewhat loudly.

Adolf, sitting on the seat just in front, looks back and asks, "Any thing funny we should be sharing in?"

"No, no... just doing some loud thinking."

The bus is winding around the hills. Cool air blowing in, and my father dozes off.

A man who looks like Adolf Hitler appears in his dream.
"Adolf Hitler, what are you doing here in Srinagar?"

"I am looking for the Brahmastra, the flaming weapon that can destroy continents. We Germans have studied all the original Hindu Scriptures written in Sanskrit. We have unearthed the secret, and it is buried in the valley in Srinagar."

"What do you want to achieve by destroying the world?"

"I want to rule the world like the British. I want to have an empire where the Sun never sets."

"Have you read Ramayana the great Hindu scripture? You sound like Ravana, the evil king of Lanka, who harbored illusions of ruling over the whole universe. Lord Rama, the embodiment of good and virtue, destroyed him. You will meet the same fate."

"Well, the British have been ruling the world for centuries and nobody has destroyed them yet. Nevertheless, I will destroy the British and take over the world. In order to accomplish that, I must have the Brahmastra. If you help me find the secret, I will make you the President of India. I like Indians. Do you know that we are all Aryans? I have even adopted the Hindu religious symbol, Swastika, as the sign of my Nazi Party, oh, well, with a little modification."

"Mr. Hitler, you are a cruel man. You are killing millions of innocent people. You should follow the principles of non-violence promoted by Mahatma Gandhi."

"Gandhi wrote me a letter, and I wrote back to him in which I told him that he will not get anywhere with non-violence."

"Mr. Hitler, we live in a different world now. The world is becoming more enlightened and liberal. There is no place for people like you in this world. The powers of good and virtue will destroy you."

The bus comes to a stop, and my father wakes up with a start. The bus conductor announces loudly, "Srinagar... Srinagar... we have arrived at Srinagar. Make sure you pick up all your belongings before you get down. Anything that is left, I get to keep."

Everybody is scrambling to get down. The sun has just gone behind the mountains, and it is suddenly dark. The Canadian couple and my father exchange addresses and names. Adolf writes down his Canadian address on a piece of paper and hands it over to my father, and my father does likewise. My father reads the address, "You live in Ottawa. What a coincidence! We also have a city in India with a similar sounding name. It is called Etawah."

"Is that right? That is interesting. Well folks, good-bye. Let us hope our paths cross again sometime." Adolf and my father shake hands and depart.

For the next month and a half, we make side trips to a number of small picturesque towns and villages. My father is feeling better with every passing day.

On May 29, 1943, we start our journey back to Lahore. As he is about to board the bus to Jammu City, he takes four or five deep breaths and says, "Let me breathe in the miraculous air of Kashmir that has restored my health." With that he bends down to touch the ground with his forehead, and then steps into the bus.

11
THIRD LIFE

Upon our return from holiday in Kashmir, my father's elder brother, Shyam Nath, suggests to him, "Surinder, you should get yourself checked by a competent doctor. You may be feeling fine now, but you never know what is going on inside you. And when I say 'competent doctor', I don't mean that quack, whatishisname, you went to last time. Dr. Bawa Harnam Singh Bhalla is a specialist in the diseases of the chest. He is a client of mine. His office is at his house at Lake Road. I am seeing him tomorrow about a property case. I will talk to him and make an appointment for you."

My father, accompanied by his brother, goes to see the doctor with all the results of his previous tests. Dr. Bhalla examines him and reviews all the test results and declares him fit. Not only that, he tells him, "Surinder, I have looked at the test results and the X-rays, and, in my medical opinion, you never had TB, and the diagnosis made by the other doctor was incorrect."

My father feels foolish having believed one doctor and not having sought a second opinion. He tries to justify or defend his action and says, "But Dr. Shiv Lal is a qualified doctor. He is educated in London. There is L.R. or London Returned after his name."

Dr. Bhalla explains, "Many professionals add L.R. after their names. Some also add other letters implying association with some non-existent, prestigious sounding, British Professional Society. It is a big racket. As far as medical profession is concerned, you should look for M.B.B.S. after the doctor's name. Anyway, Surinder, the important thing is that you are fit and fine now."

My father and his brother ride back home in his brother's horse drawn Victorian carriage. My father is enjoying the breeze blowing over his face; his hair is flying, and he is feeling free; he has just been given a second life. He says, "Maybe it was a blessing in disguise. I got much needed rest, and I feel rejuvenated. I met some interesting people and made some lifelong friendships. Above all, a wise man at Verinag told me that I am going to have two sons and a daughter."

His brother pats him on his back, and says, "Well done, Surinder."

My father replies, "*Bhai sahib*, wait a minute, it is just a forecast not a certainty." They both burst out laughing.

"And above all, I have learned a valuable lesson."

"What is that?" his brother asks.

"Never again believe in 'London Returned'." And they have another laugh.

"And, you know, brother, if we keep laughing like this, we will never fall sick." And they laugh again.

"Seriously, *Bhai sahib*, I have learned that one should live a life of moderation. I was running after money, and, in the process, I burned myself out."

As they reach Shyam Nath's home in the Gawaal Mandi area, the coachman pulls the horse to a stop with the characteristic ringing of the bells.

"Come in Surinder, your sister-in-law is eager to see you."

My father goes in for a few minutes, meets her and heads home on his bicycle. As he is peddling through the throng of humanity, bicycles, Tongas, rickshaws, and a car every now and then, his thoughts go back to what he and his brother were talking about in jest. They had laughed a lot and talked lightly about leading a life of moderation. But, as he is huffing and puffing riding up a small incline leading up to his home, he decides to put in practice the lessons he had learned as a result of his illness.

• • •

My father has taken up kite-flying as a sport for relaxation. Kite flying is a favorite pastime of the young and the old in Lahore, and, at the time of the festival of *Basant Panchami*—celebrated during the month of *Magh* of the Hindu calendar by Hindus, Muslims and Christians—it takes on a life of its own. The Muslims call this festival, *Jashan-e-Baharan*. People wear nice yellow colored clothes to signify the yellow colored mustard crop that is in full bloom at the time. Apart from religious ceremonies, kite flying is a big part of the celebrations.

On this *Basant Panchami* day in 1944, my father and Roshan are flying kites on the roof terrace right outside our flat; my mother and I are looking on. The sky is full of kites of different colors and shapes. There is unusual gaiety in the atmosphere, as if they are celebrating the gift of second life of my father. There is news that the Allies are gaining the upper hand, and the War will be over shortly. Millions of Indians are engaged in the War in various theatres around the Globe, and their families are anticipating that they will be home soon. Yellow is the color of the day. We are all wearing yellow, and there are lots of yellow kites floating high in the blue sky like *Golden Sparrows* flying around. My father has the kite string in his hand and is trying to pick a fight with the kite of one of our neighbors. The glass coated string is cutting into his index finger. He rubs his finger, shifts the string into his other hand and puts his injured finger into his mouth to soothe the burning sensation. As he is looking up at the kite trying to entangle our kite with that of the neighbors, he is also moving backwards towards the edge of the roof and, at one stage, is about to topple overboard. My mother runs towards him and shouts "Watch it, watch it. You will fall!" And runs, grabs him and pulls him towards her and starts weeping with her hands on her face. My father hands over the kite string to Roshan and goes over and tries to console her. I am watching them. I sit down on the floor and also start weeping. Due to the shock of all the loud shouting, and after watching what was about to happen, I wet my yellow knickers. Roshni, who is standing at a distance, also comes over and tries to calm down my parents.

My mother is still in a state of shock and is talking loudly to my father, "Listen ji, we have a small child to bring up. You must be careful in whatever you do. I am always in fear of something happening to you… What if you had fallen off the roof?"

"Well, I did not do this deliberately… OK, OK… I will be more careful in the future. I promise," my father says trying to placate her.

My mother is weeping and talking at the same time, "Do you know how many people get injured and die due to falls from the roofs while flying kites? …From now on, I am not going to let any of you fly kites."

My kite flying career comes to an end before it starts. My mother is always worried about something happening to my father. Whenever he is late arriving back from work, she assumes the worst. There is an aura of fear in our home. My father has become aware of it.

He wonders about the fact that he, almost, lost his life twice in one year, and got a third life. But this reinforces his desire to live fully, believing that God has bigger things in store for him. And he remembers what a wise man had told him sitting under a Pine tree in Verinag, at the origin of Jhelum River: You will have long life… I see you flying over oceans.

"Kamla, we have bigger things in store. The fact that God saved my life twice in one year is proof of that. Let us get out of the shadow of the fear of death, for it is nothing but just fear; it is not a reality. We have one wonderful son; we are destined to have another son and a daughter." He says playfully.

• • •

As my mother is walking out of our flat to go to her school, she runs back in and goes directly to the bathroom. There are loud gurgling sounds. My father has already left for his college; Roshan has gone out to buy vegetables. Roshni has just finished changing my diaper. Loud gagging and gurgling sounds continue. After about the fourth time, Roshni picks me up and goes to the bathroom to find out the cause of the uncouth sounds. "*Bibiji,* I thought you have already gone to school," Roshni says as we enter the bathroom. My mother is bent down with her face down on the commode and is vomiting. Seeing her in this condition, Roshni puts me on the floor, rushes out to the kitchen and brings a glass of water. In the meantime, my mother stands up with her face red and tears flowing down her cheeks. After a sip of water, she goes and lies down on the bed.

The next day, as soon as my father and mother walk into Dr. Sandhu's office, Nazira, her nurse, looks up with a smile and says, "Kamla ji, it looks like it is good news."

My mother looks at her with a shy smile and stops to talk to her, while my father goes and sits down on the bench in the waiting area. Nazira is well known to my mother, having assisted Dr. Sandhu during my birth. My mother asks, "Nazira, how can you be so sure?"

"Kamla ji, I see hundreds of cases every month, I can tell from the hue on your cheeks and the colour of your eyes."

My mother just gives her a mysterious smile as if she already knows and says, "Let us hope you are right." And she too goes and takes her seat beside my father in the waiting area.

"Mr. and Mrs. Mehra, you can go in now," the nurse announces after about half an hour.

When they walk into the doctor's office, the doctor is busy writing and signals them to sit down; but as soon as she sees my father, she gets up and says, "Professor Mehra, so nice to see both of you again. My sister-in-law, Sangeeta, and my father-in-law always talk very highly of you. What can we do for you today?"

My father replies, "Dr. Sandhu, Kamla is here to see you; I just tagged along."

The doctor gets up and leads my mother to the screened area in one part of her office that is used as the examination room.

After a few minutes, the doctor walks out of the examination room with a serious look and is followed by my mother a few minutes later. There is silence as the doctor again starts to write some notes. My mother and father look at each other with a worried look. The doctor finally speaks, "The good news is that Kamla is expecting, but the pregnancy is going to be a difficult one. I am saying this based on my knowledge of her previous pregnancy. She is going to have to be very careful and take complete bed-rest for the next one month."

My father says, "Dr. Sandhu, can you please give us a medical certificate. Kamla is a teacher; she will need it to apply for medical leave."

My parents walk out of the doctor's office with mixed emotions. My father says, "Kamla, you should apply for leave right away. I will go and see your principal tomorrow."

One day, three of us are sitting on the bed. My parents are reminiscing about their trip to Kashmir, and my mother says, "I am beginning to have faith in Swamiji of Verinag. He told us we will have two sons and a daughter; we already have a son; we are going to have a daughter now."

And she takes hold of my hand and makes me touch her stomach and says, "Vikram, can you feel your sister kicking. And sure enough, I can feel the movement."

"Kamla, how can you be sure we are going to have a daughter?" My father asks.

"I just know it; a mother just knows. I want to have a little girl; girls are incarnation of Goddess Lakshmi."

A few months later.

There is sound of a baby crying, and I wake up. My *ayah,* Roshni, comes and picks me up. The door to my parent's bedroom opens and the doctor comes out. She says, "Congratulations, Surinder, the mother and the child are fine. But, as I had told you earlier, it was a very difficult delivery."

My father says, "Thank you, Dr. Sandhu. Was it a boy or a girl?"

Dr. Sandhu appears nonplussed after hearing the question, and she says with a straight face, "I forgot to look. Let me go in and check."

Now my father has a blank look, and then Dr. Sandhu says with a mild laugh, "Surinder, I am just joking. You have a second son."

"But it was supposed to be a daughter; she was very sure. Kamla wanted to have a little girl," my father says.

Dr. Sandhu says, "In my practice, I have never seen parents who want to have a girl child; they all want boys. You are the first one."

My father says with a laugh, "Well, maybe, next time."

Dr. Sandhu is quiet for a few moments, deep in thought: She is thinking: *Should I tell him now or later?* She decides to tell him then and there.

"Let us take a breath of fresh air," and she steps out to the roof terrace. My father follows her; he has an ominous feeling that she wants to tell him something bad. She is still quiet and looking at a distance; it is a clear starry night; the Moon is rising just above the horizon. Strangely enough, two of the neighbours are flying kites.

Dr. Sandhu says, "I did not know that people fly kites at 2 A.M. See what a supernatural sight; the kites are dancing in front of the Moon… Surinder, you will have to be very careful in telling Kamla what I am going to tell you."

My father misses a heartbeat.

Dr. Sandhu continues, "Every day I bring little babies to this world. Some people get babies they want badly, and, then, sometimes, there are people who get babies that they do not want. There are also women who cannot have babies. God does not give everything to everybody. You have two healthy boys; you will never be able to have a girl of your own. Kamla will never be able to conceive again." And she walks back to the flat.

Although he knew that something bad was coming, he feels as if a bomb has exploded in his head. He holds the parapet, looks at the moon, takes a deep breath and remembers what his father had once told him when he was diagnosed with TB: Son, believe that you are healthy; act that you are healthy and the powers of the Universe will conspire to make your belief come true. He walks into the flat with the belief that everything will work out.

∴

"Well done, Surinder," Daulat Ram says, "Two boys! That is the way to go, just like me." He is the first one to visit us when he hears the news.

My father says, "*Bhai sahib*, your sister is very disappointed; she wanted a girl. And she is also talking as if she gave birth to a girl. She is even calling the baby, Suneeta; she has even made the baby wear pink clothes?"

"Don't worry, she will get over it. Maybe next time she will have a girl."

My father is not sure whether or not he should tell Daulat Ram that his sister is not going to have any more children. He decides to keep quiet.

My grandparents and my uncles are the next to visit. My grandmother is beside herself with the birth of another grandson. She says, "Kamla *Beti,* I am really proud of you." And she takes out a red box from her bag and places it my mother's lap. She opens it and is delighted to find a set of 22 kt. gold ornaments. My grandmother picks up the baby and notices that he is dressed like a girl, and she asks with surprise, "Kamla, why have you dressed my grandson like a girl?"

My mother replies, "Beyji, I wanted a girl so badly; and I was so sure of having one that I did not make any clothes for a baby boy."

"Times have changed, Kamla. Nobody wants girls anymore; just too many problems bringing them up; things have become so expensive. You know, one *Tola* of gold is now 50 rupees. Just imagine the cost of marrying off a girl," my grandmother says.

My mother replies, "Beyji, please forgive me; girls are the incarnation of Goddess Lakshmi. They bring balance and prosperity to life. If there were no girls, there would be no life."

My grandfather sensing the start of a daughter-in-law and mother-in-law argument changes the topic and asks, "Oh, let us see who the *Chotta Cuckoo* looks like?"

As soon as I hear the word Cuckoo, I move in, for I am the one with the nickname of *Cuckoo*. My father says, "Pitaji, I like your suggestion of giving the same nickname to both our sons: One Big Cuckoo and the other Little Cuckoo."

My grandfather says, "No, no, you *Shakespearewala,* you always want to add English language every where. We will give them Punjabi names: *Vadha Cuckoo* and *Chotta Cuckoo.*"

The day of *Namkaran* ceremony has arrived. The Pundit, after consulting the holy books, selects the alphabet K as the auspicious sound that should be the starting sound of the name of the newborn. My mother says, "I want to name him Krishan, after our Lord Krishan, our creator and protector, and the deliverer of our, holy book, Bhagavad Gita."

With the arrival of my younger brother, I have started feeling grown-up, a little jealous and neglected.

I am beginning to talk a little and start to call my mother as Mummy, and father as Daddy- same as Mary and Iris do. One day, Mummy places me on her lap and says, "Vikram, always add the word 'ji' to the name of your elders. You should call your Daddy, Daddyji, and me, Mummyji". As my brother is growing up and starting to crawl, I start calling him Kishi.

∴

On the day of the festival of *Jashne Baharan or Basant Panchami*, in February, 1945, Daddyji has bought a large collection of kites and glass powder coated string. Early in the morning, he is out on the terrace and gives wind to a new type of kite known as the *Tukkal*. Mummyji has just finished feeding Kishi; she hands him over to Roshni and walks out on to the terrace. As soon as she sees Daddyji and Roshan flying a kite, she shouts, "Listen ji, I told you last year: No kites. I do not want anybody falling off the roof and dying."

Daddyji hands over the kite string to Roshan and walks over to Mummyji and says, "Kamla, let us throw caution to the winds and sail into the wild blue yonder. Listen to what Shakespeare said in the play, Julius Caesar."

> *"Cowards die many times before their deaths;*
> *The valiant never taste of death but once.*
> *Of all the wonders that I yet have heard,*
> *It seems to me most strange that men should fear;*
> *Seeing that death, a necessary end,*
> *Will come when it will come.*

As soon as Daddyji finishes saying Shakespeare's quote, he says, "Kamla, just come and hold the kite string and feel the tug of nature, the sky, the sunshine, and see how the kite flies around moving with the winds without fear."

Mummyji walks towards Daddyji and says, "Let me hold the kite and fly."

12
1945: THE BOMB

Daddyji is a regular listener of radio news and keeps himself updated about the news of the War. On August 6 1945, when he turns on the radio, the headline is:

U.S. DROPS ATOMIC BOMB ON HIROSHIMA

He has no idea what an Atomic Bomb is. He listens to the rest of the news with his ear close to the radio, as the transmission is very erratic. He picks up some salient points of the broadcast:

The first Atomic Bomb has been dropped by a United States aircraft on the Japanese city of Hiroshima. President Harry S. Truman , announcing the news from the cruiser, USS Augusta, in the mid-Atlantic, said the device was more than 20,000 times more powerful than the largest bomb used to date............ The President said the Atomic Bomb heralded the harnessing of basic power of the universe............ By God's mercy, British and American science outpaced all German efforts...

Daddyji shouts and calls Mummyji, "Kamla... Kamla... Come here. Listen to the news. They have destroyed Japan. It is finished. I told you there was something to the dream I had. The Americans have produced something like the *Brahmastra*, the ultimate weapon mentioned in Hindu scriptures."

Mummyji is getting ready to go to school and comes running. "What can I do? I am getting late," she says and walks out to go to school. Daddyji also turns off the radio and gets up to go to work. As he is bicycling, he is thinking of the turn the War has taken. He stops along the way to his college, at his usual newspaper stand, to pickup the morning copy of a newspaper. He sees the same headline as he has heard on the radio. He looks around and nothing has changed. A whole city has been destroyed on the other side of the Earth and life goes on as usual. As he reaches his college, he goes straight to the principal's office but does not find him there. He just wants to talk to somebody. He then goes to the classroom and finds a few students standing around.

"Did you people hear what happened yesterday? The Americans dropped an Atomic Bomb on Japan. It is supposed to be 20,000 times more powerful than the biggest bomb ever made." Daddyji tells the students.

"No sir, we have not heard the news yet. What will happen now?" one of the students asks.

"Well, it depends on what Japan does in response. If Japan also has Atomic Bombs, they may retaliate and it can turn into the destruction of the world; Doomsday or *Pralaya*, as we have read in Hindu scriptures, may be around the corner." Daddyji replies. The students look disinterested. Meanwhile, the bell rings and it is time for the class to start.

Three days later on August 9, 1945, the United States drops another Atomic bomb on a second Japanese city, Nagasaki. On August 14, 1945 Japan surrenders to the Allies.

The World War II is over, but Daddyji's preoccupation with the relationship of the Atomic bomb to his dream about *Brahmastra* still carries on. Over the next several months, he reads articles about the Atom Bomb in any newspapers and magazines he can find. He discovers that the United States, Britain and Canada had carried out research that led to the making of the Bomb. When he finds out that Canada was also involved, he thinks of Adolf and Jane, the Canadian couple he met in Kashmir. Now his resolve to learn more about the Atomic Bomb and its relationship to his dream becomes even more intense.

He discovers some information that fascinates him. Robert Oppenheimer, who is famously referred to as the Father of the Atomic Bomb, has some interest in Hindu scriptures, as is indicated by the following quotes that are attributed to him.

While witnessing the first test explosion, he thought of the following verse from the Hindu holy book, the Bhagavad Gita:

"If radiance from a thousand suns were to burst at once into the sky that would be like the splendor of the Mighty One."

After detonation of the first Atom Bomb he is quoted as saying:

"Now I have become death, destroyers of the worlds."–another verse from the Hindu holy book, the Bhagavad Gita.

Another quote attributed to him:

"Access to Vedas is the greatest privilege this century may claim over all previous centuries."

Daddyji is also surprised to learn that Oppenheimer, too, was struck by a mild case of TB, like him. He finds all this very uncanny.

He has rudimentary knowledge of the Bhagavad Gita, having read the Urdu version that his father used to read.

He is thinking: *The information I have collected is very unique, but what does it really mean? Does it mean that Hindu scriptures played a part in the making of the Atomic Bomb? Was Robert Oppenheimer somehow inspired by what he read in the Bhagavad Gita or the Vedas? Are there scientific secrets in the Vedas that somehow contributed to the making of the Atomic Bomb? His mind is exploding with questions, but there are no definite answers. He is eager to talk to somebody knowledgeable in the Bhagavad Gita.*

Should I go Daulat Ram or my brother, Shyam Nath, or a priest from a temple? He forgets that his own father is a scholar of Bhagavad Gita. He decides to go to him to talk over his discoveries.

One Sunday afternoon, he walks over to his parent's house alone without his family. He is in the mood for some serious discussion, and he does not want any distractions. When he reaches there, he finds his brother's horse-drawn carriage standing outside. *Well, I will have two learned people to talk to today,* he is thinking. As soon as he knocks at the door, his father opens the door, as if he was just waiting to open it. "Pitaji, how did you know...? He asks his father.

"Well, look who is here... Surinder, we have not seen you for almost two weeks. You have become *Eid ka Chand*," his father says, referring to the Muslim festival of *Eid,* when Moon announcing the *Eid* appears after a long time.

"Well, *Pitaji*, I have been busy with work and the children. You know how it is... Have you been following the news about the War? You know, two cities in Japan have been destroyed. After hearing about it, I have read all about the Atom Bomb in the newspapers and magazines. It seems that it is similar to the *Brahmastra*, which is mentioned in the Hindu epic, the *Mahabharata*."

"Yes, there are references to all kinds of weapons in the Mahabharata." his father replies.

Daddyji says, "You know, I have read that a scientist named Robert Oppenheimer, who is referred to as the father of the Atomic Bomb, quoted *shlokas* from the Bhagavad Gita when the bomb exploded. I am surprised how an American will know Gita so well that he remembers it by heart. You know, Pitaji, I have copied down the *Shlokas,* he is reported to have spoken, from newspapers and magazines at the library."

His father says, "Don't be surprised that Gita is known in America. You may already know that Swami Vivekananda is well respected there. He attended the Parliament of Religions in Chicago in 1893. He represented Hindu religion at this conference and made a mark with the American public due to his knowledge of both Eastern and Western religions and cultures. He was a magnetic speaker and spoke fluent English, Sanskrit and Hindi. Also, Gandhi's work in South Africa and India, and his belief in non-violence, have come to the attention of thinkers all over the World and, due to that, so has the Hindu religion."

Daddyji continues, "*Pitaji,* please tell me what would an American scientist find in the Bhagavad Gita?"

His father replies, "I will tell you the two central lessons that are repeated in the Bhagavad Gita in different ways and are applicable in every day life, whether you are a scientist or a washerman:"

"You have the right to your actions,
But never to the fruits of your actions."

"The meaning is obvious. It means that do your action and Let Go. Don't worry about its result. Renunciation of the fruits of actions, Gandhi wrote, is the centre around which the Gita is woven."

"The second related theme is:"

"Act for the action's sake.
And do not be attached to inaction."

"This means do your duty, whatever it may be. You must act. You see, the American scientists were just doing their duty when they made the Atom Bomb and exploded it on the Japanese cities. It was their duty to protect their own country. While making the bomb, they may have had doubts; the lessons of Gita may have helped them to overcome their doubts. They acted as their duty required. Now you see what the American scientist, Robert Oppenheimer, may have learned from the Gita?"

Daddyji sits quietly for a while, absorbing what his father has just said. He wonders if the western scientists found the secret of the Atom Bomb in Hindu scriptures. He is thinking whether to tell his father about his dream about Hitler or not. In the end he raises the subject somewhat indirectly.

"What about Germany? I wonder if Gita is known there?" he asks.

"Hindu scriptures have been studied in Germany for over a hundred years. Max Muller, a German scholar, was responsible for the publication of a 50 volume set of English translations—The Sacred Books of the East. It has been established that Sanskrit is the origin of many European Languages. I am sure you know that Swastika, the symbol of Hitler's Nazi Party, is similar to *Savastik Sri Ganesh* sign we make in Hindu homes at the time of religious functions. It is drawn a little differently, but the basic shape is similar. However, it is believed in some circles that the fact that Hitler's Swastika is drawn differently was very inauspicious; hence his perverse thinking, and the War and destruction that followed."

"Yes, I have read about it. And you know, I had a dream about Hitler and Swastika, when I was in Kashmir" He is gradually bringing up the subject of the dream. He is afraid that his brother is going to ridicule him if he tells the whole story.

And true enough, his brother mocks him, "You had a dream about what?" and breaks into laughter. "Surinder, I think you have been tutoring too many students again; running around on your bicycle from home to home. It is about time you found yourself a job in a government college."

Daddyji looks down and mumbles a bit, and is apprehensive to say anything more for the fear of ridicule.

His father senses the typical sibling rivalry problem. He knows that Shyam Nath is a bit envious of Daddyji's success, and he intervenes. "There is nothing wrong in having dreams. Everybody dreams. In waking life, one is full of trials and joys. When our hearts are full of anxiety and taxing our mind to the utmost, the dream aims at relieving us of these. The dream either gives us something entirely alien, or it selects a few elements of reality and combines it with alien elements, and presents the combination in the form of a dream."

Daddyji sits down quietly for a while thinking, and inserts the little finger of his right hand in his ear, shakes it to clear the itch in his ear canal and takes out a bit of wax; his habit that his brother, Shyam Nath, loathes," Come on Surinder, for God's sake, stop putting your finger in your ears. It is a bad social etiquette, and you can damage your ear drum."

Daddyji quickly takes out his finger and cleans it with a white handkerchief, which he always keeps in the pocket of his trousers. He is not quite finished with his questions about dreams. He thinks, now that he has suffered so much ridicule at the hands of his dear brother, he might as well go all the way and ask the ultimate question.

"Please tell me Pitaji, do dreams tell the future. Do dreams come true?"

Pitaji replies, "Sometime dreams have been known to come true, but I think it is just a coincidence. On the other hand, in the Vedas, it is stated that waking state and dream state are both different states of consciousness and, in fact, both are unreal—*Maya,* an Illusion. Also, people with a sixth sense are known to see the future in their dreams. Who knows...?"

Pitaji is thinking: *Surinder, since his childhood, is known for his Sixth Sense.*

Shyam Nath interrupts, "Come on, Surinder, I think you should be more concerned with the Congress Party and the Muslim League; and how they are going to decide our future. In the Bar Association meeting yesterday, everybody was worried about the demand for a separate country for Muslims. Hitler is gone. Forget your dream and live in the real world. I came here to let you all know of my decision to move to Simla. Being in the hills, the summers are cool and you can all come and visit us during summers. Moreover, if India is divided, we will not have to move."

Daddyji is sitting quietly, listening. He takes off his spectacles, cleans them with his handkerchief and says, "Well, I think I will be going now. Kamla must be waiting."

• • •

As he is walking home, a brilliant idea comes to his mind. He smiles, as he is thinking about it, and decides not to do anything about it for a while.

...Several weeks pass.

He decides to write a letter to Swamiji of Verinag. He looks through his almirah where he keeps his books and old diaries. Buried under a pile of papers, he finds the diary in which Swamiji of Verinag had written down his address. In the same diary, stuck in the middle, he finds the piece of paper that Adolf had given him with his address on it. However, when he opens the diary, where Swamiji is supposed to have written his address, he finds it written in Hindi along with some numbers. He does not know how to read Hindi; he asks Mummyji to read it out to him.

"Well, it is not very clearly written. It is either *BrahmAshram* or *BrahmastrAshram;* Verinag, Kashmir. He has written his name as Ravi Anand."

Daddyji is intrigued because the two words have different meanings. The second word refers to the flaming weapon that was in his dream about Hitler, the *Brahmastra*.

They have no idea why the numbers are written below the address, but they decide to ask him in the letter.

He asks Mummyji to write, in Hindi, a letter to Swamiji of Verinag.

English translation:

Respected Swamiji Ravi Anand,

You may be surprised to hear from us after such a long time. It has been about two years since we met in Verinag in 1943. In fact, we are not sure if you even remember our meeting. We have some questions that we should have probably asked you earlier, but it was not to be; so here we are.

1. Just to make sure that we have the correct name of your Ashram: is it *BrahamAshram or BrahamastrAshram*?
2. Under the address you wrote in my diary on April 25, 1943, there are some numbers written and these are: 34 and 75. We will appreciate if you can let us know what they are so that we may benefit by the knowledge.
3. This is the most intriguing part of my letter. As we were travelling by bus from Verinag to Srinagar, I had a dream. A man who looked like Adolf Hitler appeared in my dream and started telling me that he is looking for *Brahmastra,* and he said the secret lies hidden in the Kashmir valley. There was a Canadian couple travelling with us; the man's name was Adolf. Your Ashram's name sounds like *Brahmastra*, the word Hitler uttered.
4. And what we find uncanny is that, a little over two years after I had the dream, the Atom Bomb was dropped on Hiroshima; a weapon very similar to the *Brahmastra* described in Hindu scriptures.
5. We will be thankful, if you can take the time to enlighten us with your thoughts about the above happenings.

Yours Respectfully,
Surinder and Kamla

.... A few weeks later, he receives a reply in English, rather than in Hindi. The choice of the language is surprising.

Dear Surinder and Kamla,

I send Blessings to you from all of us at the *Brahamashram*. I hope this clarifies the name of our Ashram. The numbers that you refer to are the Latitude and Longitude, respectively, of the Ashram; may not be exact, but almost exact for all practical purposes. Why the numbers at the bottom of my name? Well, it is a long story, but suffice it to say that I am a physicist, mathematician and an astronomer—hence my love for numbers. Just so that you know; zero is my favorite number.

Now about your dream: I should tell you that, at the Ashram, we do studies and research in Hindu scriptures and their effect on modern scientific knowledge. Over the last several years, we have played host to many scholars from foreign lands. They have stayed at the Ashram for extended periods of time to study Sanskrit and gain some knowledge of our scriptures, *Vedas, Puranas, Ramayana, Mahabharata and Gita.*

Since the mid thirties, there has been special interest expressed by foreign scholars in the various armaments mentioned in the above noted scriptures.

Another interesting fact I should tell you is that the Canadian couple, who was with you on the bus, had been in Verinag before and had stayed at the Ashram on their earlier trips. He is connected to some research institute in Canada.

As far as your dream is concerned, it was very relevant. At the time you visited Verinag in 1943, there was intense research going on in the Western world, including the U.S.A., the U.K., France, Canada and Germany, about the power of the Atom. They were all looking for the Key to the Atom. From the visits to our Ashram by researchers from those countries, we conclude that they thought that the Key to atomic power lay buried somewhere here. So, maybe, your dream was due to the intense concentration of brain waves about atomic research in this area, or may be it was your *Sixth Sense*. And for your information, we, at the Ashram, are also doing research in Long Range Brain Wave Transmission but more on that later. Do keep in touch.

Serve All, Bless All.

Ravi Anand.

010101

P.S. My last name is Anand. I am a Punjabi from Gurdaspur.

After reading this letter, both Daddyji and Mummyji go to sleep; it puts their mind at rest... *Gurdaspur? Mummyji is thinking: That is also my birthplace.*

The next day, Daddyji writes a letter to Adolf Hoffer of Canada.

Mr. Adolf Hoffer,

I trust you are keeping well. I am not sure if you remember me. We met at Verinag, in the State of Jammu and Kashmir, in April 1943. You must be wondering why I am writing to you after more than two years. The end of the War has been a great relief for everyone involved. I am surprised to read in the newspaper reports that Canadians played an important role in the War on the Burma front and the defense of India and Burma. However, the explosion of the Atom Bomb certainly adds a new dimension to international relations. I was surprised to read the newspaper accounts that Canada was an active participant in the research and development activities related to the Atom Bomb. We certainly owe a debt of gratitude to Canada for help in the defense of India on the Burma front.

As you must have heard, pressure is increasing on Britain to quit India. I am wondering if there is any such movement in Canada. I am not sure what form of government you have in Canada, but as I understand, King George VI is your head of state and also ours, and hopefully, not for too long.

It will be nice to hear from you. May be we can become Pen Friends.

Surinder

P.S. I am still curious to know more about your visits to India. I am writing to you at the Canadian address you gave me, but I am not sure if you have gone back, or if you are still in India.

• • •

As Daddyji is walking in after posting the letter to Max Hoffer, he seeks out Mummyji, "Kamla, where are you?"

"Listen ji, I am in the kitchen. What is the matter?"

He goes into the kitchen and says, "Kamla, when I was walking back from the post office, I was thinking: The English speaking countries won the World War II. As America has the Atom Bomb, you will see they will rule the world. This will mean that the English language will become the predominant language of the world. And that means that demand for those of us who teach English will also go up. God bless Mrs. Wilson for encouraging me to become a professor of English. If I had listened to my father, I would have been working as a mechanic in the railways repairing steam engines."

Mummyji is just nodding her head as she is stirring the pot on the *Angithi*, and Roshan is standing nearby helping to cut some vegetables. Roshan is listening to what Daddyji is saying and says "Sahib, can I also learn English?"

"Yes, you can. I think you should start learning along with Vikram when he starts to go to school. We have admitted him in the International Public School in Kindergarten; it is an English medium school and is run like the British Public Schools."

13
1946–47: COMMUNAL CONFLAGRATION

I am standing outside the school waiting for Roshan to pick me up to take me home after school. A large *Jaloos* of people is passing by. They are all shouting in unison, *Toady Bachcha Hai Hai, Toady Bachaa Hai Hai, Firangi Hai Hai*. There must have been hundreds of people. I get swept away by the rush of people. After the procession has passed by, I have no idea where I am. I am just standing and looking around with tears running down my cheeks. As luck would have it, I see Joseph John, our landlord, walking by on the other side of the street. I am not sure how to get to him. I am four years old and have never been out of the house alone. I decide to run across the street. As soon as I reach him, I grab his trousers and pull at them. He suddenly looks back and says, "Oh, hello Vikram *beta*, what a surprise!" He looks around expecting to see my father or mother. "Where are your parents?" he asks.

"Roshan is supposed to bring me home, but he has not turned up." I explain to him in voice full of fear and tears flowing down my face. We wait there for a while, and then I walk with him to his office at the YMCA. After a while, he takes me home on his bicycle, with me sitting on the rear carrier and holding him tightly from behind.

As we reach home, he takes me inside their flat and calls his daughters, "Iris and Mary come and see who is here. We have a guest." Iris comes into the sitting room. Mary is not home.

"Oh, Vikram, I hear you have started going to school," she says. Joseph John tells her what has happened.

"Come on Iris; bring him some biscuits and *burfi*. He must be hungry."

Iris brings some sweets, puts the plate on the centre table, picks me up and makes me sit on her lap. She is very fond of me, and I like it.

While I am sitting eating sweets, Iris sees Roshan walk by the window. She runs outside and calls him in. Roshan walks into the room and stops and then rushes to me and lifts me up.

Joseph John asks, "Roshan what happened? You were supposed to pick up Vikram."

Roshan says, "Sahib, I was also stuck in another *Jaloos* on my way to the school. Upon reaching the school and not finding Vikram, I rushed home. Thank God, he is here; if he was lost somewhere, I would have killed myself."

"Well, Roshan, you would not have had a chance to kill yourself; Surinder would have killed you before that."

In the evening, when Mummyji and Daddyji come home from work and find out what has happened, they are furious at Roshan. But after he presents the explanation, they realize that it was due to extraordinary circumstances.

The next day, they both accompany me to the school in a Tonga to talk to the Principal. He is known to my father, both being educationists. For the future, it is decided that all children shall wait inside the school compound to be picked up.

On our ride back home in the Tonga, I ask, "Daddyji, what does *Toady Bacha Hai Hai* and *Firangi Hai Hai* mean?

He explains, "*Toady Bacha* refers to the lackeys or flatterers of the Government of British India. The general public believes that it is they who are helping the British to rule over us. *Hai Hai* means down with them. *Firangi* refers to the foreigners—in this case the British or English people. Indian people want the British to leave India."

"Why do they want the British people to leave? My teacher, Miss Smith, is British. She is a very nice lady. Do the Indians want us to leave also? We also speak English."

"No, no, we are Indians. Your teacher, Miss Smith, comes from England; so she is English or British. She looks different from us," Mummyji replies.

"So, they want all people who look like Miss Smith to leave."

"Yes."

"Is it because they don't like the way she looks?" I ask.

"No. It is because they do not want to be under the King of England," Daddyji replies.

"Oh, I see. Is he a bad king? Is he like Hitler or Ravan, the bad king of Lanka?"

"Hey, how do you know about Hitler?"

I reply with a laugh and a twinkle in my eye, "When you listen to the radio, I also listen. And when you discuss the news with Mummyji, I listen then too."

"So, now we will have to be careful in what we say when you are around."

"Oh yes, Daddyji, I am becoming a big boy now."

"He may not be a bad King, but we Indians do not want to be under the King of England because of the way he treats us. We want to have our own King," Mummyji replies.

"We have so many Kings in India. Do people like them? We can have one of those as the King of India, can't we? Daddyji, how does one become the King?" I ask.

"If one's father is King, then the son becomes King," Daddyji replies.

"What if the son is not a good person, does he still become King?"

'He should not. This is why, in India, people want to decide who the King would be," Mummyji replies.

The Tonga comes to a stop in front of our home and so does my first lesson in political science.

When we get off from the Tonga and are walking into the house, we find Joseph John sitting in the verandah reading a newspaper. He looks up and says, "Good morning, I trust you people found out what happened yesterday."

Daddyji replies, "Mr. John, we thank you for bringing Vikram home yesterday. We were at Vikram's school today to talk to the principal about this matter. We are satisfied that it will not happen again."

Joseph John says, "Surinder, the incidence of processions and riots is going to increase as the time goes by. If you read the British Cabinet Mission Plan of June 16, 1946, the partition of our country is now inevitable. Moreover, the Muslim League is asking all Muslims to observe 'Direct Action Day' on August 16, in support of the demand for a separate Muslim country, Pakistan. All this is going to result in a lot of disturbance of normal life."

"So what do you suggest?" Daddyji asks.

"I think you should not send Vikram to school in the month of August and then see how things shape up."

• • •

In early 1947, as the plan of partition of India and the formation of a separate Muslim country, Pakistan, is being finalized by the British, large scale riots—between Hindus and Sikhs on one side and Muslims on the other side—break out in Lahore.

This is a terrifying night.

Distant Wails of *Allahu Akbar*—God is great—by the Muslims, *Jai Bjarang Bali*—hail to God Hanuman—by the Hindus, and *Jo Bole So Nihal*—whoever utters shall be filled with bliss—by the Sikhs pierce through the darkness waking us all up. It is a hot summer night. We are all sleeping on the roof terrace. Daddyji gets up and goes out to parapet of the roof terrace to see what is happening. He comes back in and says, "It is four or five streets away. In a way we are safe where we live because our landlord lives on the ground floor. They are Christians and are considered neutral by both the Hindus and the Muslims; and therefore, chances of the house being attacked are very slim." And we go back to sleep.

The sound of ringing of the bells of the fire brigade wakes us up again. We are standing at the roof terrace watching the fire at a distance, and I ask, "Mummyji, why are people burning each other's houses?"
"*Beta*, Hindus and Muslims, are fighting with each other."
"Oh. What are Muslims and Hindus?" I ask.
"Different people have different Gods. Depending on which God they believe in, people call themselves, Hindu, Sikh, Christian, or Muslim."
"What are we?"
"We are Hindus. Our Gods are Bhagwan Krishna, Rama and Hanuman and many others."
"What is Iris?
She and her parents are Christians. We also call them *Isahi* in India."
"How did we become Hindus?"
"As our forefathers were Hindu, we also are Hindus."
"What is my friend, Ashraf?"
"He is a Muslim."
"But, Mummyji, how do you know?"
"By his name."
"What is Roshni?"

"She is a Sikh. Her full name is Roshni Kaur. The names of Sikh women are followed by Kaur and the names of Sikh men by Singh. But remember, all Sikhs are Singh, but not all Singhs are Sikh."

Still trying to figure out the meaning of her last sentence, I ask "OK.... what is my friend Iqbal?"

"Umm... what is his full name?"

"I don't know."

"Well, there are some names that are common to Hindus, Muslims and Sikhs. Iqbal is one of those names."

"You mean some people have same names and they still fight. Does their God tell them to fight?"

"No, no... God always tells people to live in peace."

"So why are they fighting?"

"You know, we live in India. Peoples of all religions live here. You know that the King of England is our King also. Well, English people have decided to leave India and go back to England, and let people of India decide who their new King would be. Hindus and Muslims are not able to agree on who the King should be. Should it be a Hindu, or a Muslim? So, the Muslims want their own country and name it Pakistan. That is what the fighting is all about."

"I think they are fighting about something else," I say.

"Oh, what is that?"

"Kite-fights are the cause of the fighting, my friend Iqbal says. He says one man stabbed another man near Rajgargh because one man's kite was cut by the other."

Mummyji becomes quiet.

I have some more questions, but there is the sound of gunfire nearby and we move indoors.

I am thinking: *Why don't Muslims and Hindus have a Kite-fight competition, and whoever wins gets to choose the new King.*

• • •

Mummyji opens the letter and starts to read it; it is from her parents. The worry lines on her forehead are increasing as she is reading. Daddyji is looking and says, "Come on Kamla, please read it aloud."

She starts to read it aloud, "Dear Surinderji and Kamla. As you already know, conditions in Punjab are becoming from bad to worse. There are all kinds of stories circulating. Some people are saying that Gurdaspur will become part of Pakistan, and we are very worried. We have already started making plans for moving to Delhi. Also, Roshni's parents came to see us. They want her back right away. Please send her by bus as soon as possible. Love to Vikram and Kishi."

Mummyji and Daddyji are quiet for a while trying to absorb what they have read in the letter. Mummyji shouts, "Roshni, can you come here?"

Roshni comes into the room where they are sitting, with Kishi and me in tow. Mummyji says to her, "Roshni, there is a letter from Gurdaspur. Your parents want you back as soon as possible. Today is Wednesday. Is it fine with you if you leave by the Sunday morning bus?"

She replies, "*Bibiji*, Why do they want me to go back? Who will look after Vikram and Kishi? I am not leaving them like this. You can write to them that I am not coming back yet."

Mummyji explains to her, "Listen Roshni, your parents love you as much as we and you love Vikram and Kishi. It is natural on their part to be worried about you. So you should go back now to make them feel better and come back when rioting subsides. Is it fine with you?"

Mummyji gets up and embraces Roshni, and both of them breakout into tears.

On Sunday morning, Roshni completes her packing. I am old enough to understand what is going on. Roshni has looked after me, and my brother Kishi, ever since we were babies. She is like a second mother to us. I am very sad because I have a premonition that I will, probably, never see her again. Mummyji has got the doors of a small cupboard open, and she is trying to pry some cash loose from a secret hiding place. As Roshni is standing near her baggage, I run to her and embrace her, and she picks me up and gives me kisses on my cheeks and says, "Listen, *Vadhaa Cuckoo*, look after Mummyji, Daddyji and Kishi till I come back."

I nod my head and cling to her with tears rolling down my cheeks. She puts me down on the floor, picks up Kishi and gives him hugs and kisses. He is only about two and a half years old at the time and does not really understand what is going on. He just starts to play with Roshni's earrings. Roshan has gone to get a Tonga. Mummyji comes out from her room with some cash and a few pieces of jewelry wrapped in a piece of cloth. She hands it over to Roshni and tells her, "Come Roshni, let us hide these things on your person so that you will not lose them."

She takes Roshni inside her room, and after five minutes they are back. As soon as the Tonga arrives, the luggage is loaded, and both Mummyji and Daddyji go with Roshni to the bus station to see her off.

When they are back, everybody sits down quietly wondering what life would be like without Roshni. Mummyji says, "I think it is time for me to resign my job. Ever since the partition of the country is being talked about, there is talk of closing down the school and moving it to Jullundur."

Daddyji says, "I think it would be advisable for us to move back with my parents and brothers. There is strength in numbers. And we should seriously think about getting out of Lahore. It is something to think about anyway."

Daddyji goes downstairs to see, Joseph John, our landlord to tell him of the planned move back to his parent's house. As he steps in the verandah, he can see through the window of the drawing room; some neighbors are sitting along with Joseph John. They are all residents of Sanda Road—two are Hindus, one Sikh and two Muslims—sitting down sipping tea and discussing the security situation in the City and Sanda Road area in particular.

Daddyji peeps in and says, "I came down to see you, Mr. John. I see you have company; I will come back later."

Joseph John says, "No, no, don't leave. It is fine; just come right in. We were talking about what is happening to our fair city. Lahore used to be the pride of India, as far as communal harmony was concerned. Now people are at each other's throat. Something does not seem right."

One of the neighbours adds, "It seems there are some interested parties who are fanning the flames. I have many Hindu and Sikh friends who are saying the same thing. Nobody knows where the rioters appear from at night."

Another neighbour, says, "I think we should create a watch party of able-bodied young men. A group of three or four should give watch duty, a few hours, every night and look out for any hoodlums who may be thinking of targeting Sanda Road. We have some firearms, and we can get some more, if required."

"We should name our watch party *Lashkar-e-Aaman*, the Army of Peace," another neighbour adds.

"What do you think Surinder?" Joseph John asks.

Daddyji replies, "I came down to tell you that we have decided to move back to my parents' house in Prem Nagar. It is not that far; it is just a few hundred yards from here. I am sure we can participate in the watch party. "

Joseph John says with anger and frustration, "Who are these mysterious rioters, which appear at night? We see Hindus helping their Muslim neighbours and vice versa. So who is lighting the fires? Are they members of the Congress, the Sangh, the Muslim League, the British Agents, the Japanese Agents, or are they common illiterate people just settling old scores?"

With this outburst from Joseph John, they all get up and decide to meet again.

• • •

This evening, we are all sitting down listening to the radio for any news of the riots. A postman comes upstairs. "A Telegram for you, Surinder Mehra," he announces. Daddyji gets up, goes to the door, signs for the telegram and gives a small *bakshish* to the postman and walks back to the room, while opening up the envelope at the same time.

"Oh, my God... oh my God... It says the bus that Roshni was travelling in met with some kind of accident. Kamla, the telegram is from your father."

Mummyji gets up, takes the telegram from his hands and reads it again. I understand what has happened and start weeping; and Kishi, who is too young to understand, also starts weeping, as he sees me weeping. Roshan comes in from the kitchen and stands at the doorway and asks, "*Bibiji,* what has happened?" Mummyji explains to him what has happened, and he sits down on the floor with his head in his hand and says, "She is like my younger sister. Let us pray that she is fine."

There is nothing they can do now at this time but wait. Mummyji says, "Let us listen to the 9 P.M. news. There may be something about the accident."

There is nothing in the news, except news about the politics of the day and the plans for the partition of India.

The next day, Daddyji is up early in the morning, waiting to go out to pick up the newspaper. At about 7 A.M., he goes out to buy a newspaper and brings it home. There is a news item about the accident. It says: The bus driver was attacked by one of the passengers with a knife. The accident took place near Amritsar. The driver of the bus succumbed to the injuries. Several passengers died in the accident. The attacker also got injured in the accident and was taken into custody by the local police. The authorities have decided not to disclose the religion of the driver or the attacker. This is being done to avoid an already tense communal situation from becoming worse.

Daddyji comments, "This means that it was a communal attack. We just don't know who attacked who."

"Let us hope that Roshni is fine," Mummyji says.

She prays for Roshni all day long by reciting *Japji sahib*, the essence of the Sikh religion, Roshni's faith. We are all waiting for some word about Roshni. Our landlord, Joseph John, and his family and many neighbors come to know of what has happened. They all come to visit us to offer their good wishes and prayers. Monday passes just waiting for some further news. On Tuesday evening, Mummyji goes to the Hanuman Temple to offer prayer for the safety and well being of Roshni. She is a regular at the Temple on Tuesdays and makes a special offering to God this Tuesday. After she is back from the Temple, she breaks her fast by partaking in the evening meal. As soon as we finish our meal, the postman comes upstairs and says loudly, "Telegram, telegram, sahib…"

Mummyji gets up and rushes to receive the envelope and opens it in a hurry. And there is smile on her face and tears of joy, and she says, "Thank you *Sachea Padshah*—the Lord of Truth… it is all because of your kindness."

Daddyji says, "Kamla, please tell us what is written."

She reads it aloud, "Roshni is with us safe and sound."

• • •

By May, 1947, we move back to my grandparent's house. Roshan, our domestic servant, is still with us.

Daddyji tells him one day," Roshan, I think you should go back to Kangra, your home town. It is in the hills in a predominantly Hindu area. You will be safer there with your family."

He replies, "*Sahib*, you, *Bibiji*, Vikram and Kishi are also my family. How can I leave you behind during this troubled time? If we leave Lahore, we will all leave together—dead or alive."

Daddyji is touched by his loyalty and tells him, "Roshan you are an amazing person."

"The school has been closed indefinitely and may be moving to Jullundur," Mummyji tells all the family members as she comes back from school. Daddyji is still continuing his teaching work.

Upon hearing the news of the school closing, Daddyji tells his father and brothers, "We should be seriously thinking about moving out of Lahore, at least temporarily, to Simla. In addition to Shyam Nath, Kamla's younger sister, Sumitra, and her husband, Raghu, also live in Simla. He is an official with the Central Water and Power Commission."

My grandfather is very adamant. He says, "All of you are cowards. There is a little bit of disturbance, and you all want to leave your home and run away. We should stand steadfast and defend our home. I have spent my lifesavings to build this house. I am not going to just leave it and run away. I will defend it to the last drop of my blood. You can all leave, but my wife and I are not leaving."

Daddyji tries to convince him, "Pitaji, we are so close to Rajgarh. It is a Muslim stronghold. We can be attacked any time."

My grandfather says, "The government has created a new force, known as the Punjab Boundary Force, comprising half Muslim and half Hindu soldiers from the Indian Army under the command of a British officer to control civil unrest and maintain communal harmony. A contingent is going to be stationed just behind our house. We are safe."

...

Lashkar-e-Aaman, a watch party of Muslim and Hindu young men of the area, has been formed to give watch duty at night and day.

Daddyji, his brothers, Roshan and some hired help are working sixteen hours a day to fortify the house against attacks by Muslims. The amazing thing is that the masons and painters are provided by one of the Muslim neighbours, who is a building contractor. In mere one week, all the wooden doors on the exterior of the house have been painted with fire retardant paint. The windows have been bricked up. A hand-operated pump is ready and tested to make sure it can pump water to the roof top in case fire lit torches are thrown there. Bricks have been stacked on the perimeter parapet wall of the roof, to be used as weapons to thwart any attack. Fire arms and ammunition has been procured. In spite of the government's assurance that the Army is going to keep watch on the area, Pitaji is not taking any chances. Our house has been converted into a fortress.

Nights are becoming more and more terrifying. The glow of distant fires mixed with the wails of religious slogans, the sporadic sounds of gunfire, and the war like atmosphere at the house keeps me awake.

The young men of *Lashkar-e-Aaman* stand on their respective roof tops at night to keep watch on the activity in the neighborhood. They signal each other either by voice signals by taking out sounds of animals, or by code using battery operated torches. The news of *Lashkar-e-Aaman* spreads, and other neighborhoods also start such watch groups.

My Uncle Karan, who is also a member of the *Lashkar-e-Aaman*, receives a letter. When he opens it, a chill runs down his spine. The letter is in Urdu language with alphabets cut out from a newspaper and glued on to a piece of paper. It is signed—*Lashkar-e-Shaitaan*, the Army of Devil. It says: Fools and Cowards of *Lashkar-e-Aaman* group, if you continue your activities, you will all be struck down one by one. The members of the group have a meeting to consider the threat, and they decide to continue their watch duty. The effect is that there are no untoward incidents in the neighborhood.

• • •

This day in July 1947, Daddyji goes to work in the morning and does not come back. He is usually back by about 8 P.M. It is 10 P.M., and he is not back. Mummyji is in our room, sitting on the bed with me and Kishi in her lap, with her face full of anxiety. Beyji, my grandmother, comes in every few minutes to console her that he will return soon. He is supposed to have gone to tutor Vishnu, who is the son of a rich and influential industrialist, Din Dayal, with the title of Rai Bahadur; a title given by the British to Indians for their services to the Crown. My Uncle Karan offers to go look for him at the Rai Bahadur's house. He takes out his bicycle and leaves, but he is back after about fifteen minutes. He says, "Police have closed all roads, and they are going to impose a curfew at night."

Mummyji is in a state of panic. Assuming the worst, she starts weeping.

Panic!... thinking what will happen ...if he does not return. Two young children... without him... How will I survive? Her mind is churning out a thousand different scenarios... all terrifying. I am helpless, she is thinking. And then, she remembers Roshni who gave her strength the last time when my father was ill. She had told her to recite, Naam, the name of God.

And then, she slowly starts to recite the *Hanuman Chalisa*, a poem in praise of God *Hanuman*, with her voice choked with tears. As she keeps reciting, she feels determination, courage and faith flowing to her. As soon as she finishes one full recitation of *Hanuman Chalisa*, there is sound of three beeps of a car horn—very similar to the ringing of the bell of Daddyji's bicycle. After a while, there is knocking on the front door; it sends a chill through us all. My grandfather takes out his gun and loads it. There is another round of knocking on the front door. He asks loudly, "Who is it?"

A voice sounding similar to Daddyji's voice replies, "Pitaji, it is I, Surinder, open the door." My grandfather moves to the door and asks again, keeping his ear close to the door, "Surinder, is that you? Where were you born?"

The reply comes, "Germany." The code is correct, and the voice sounds right. My grandfather opens the door, but there is somebody else standing outside beside a car. My grandfather raises his gun at the man. The man raises his hands up and says, "Sir, sir, please don't shoot, I am Vishnu, professor sahib's student."

Daddyji has got the dickey of the car open and is in the process of taking out his bicycle.

My grandfather sees him and says, "Oh, Surinder, where were you? We have been worried to death."

"Pitaji, what could I do? The authorities imposed a curfew, but I am lucky that Vishnu's father was able to get us a pass to drive through the curfew," Daddyji replies.

Vishnu also comes in and starts chatting with other family members. He says, "Professor sahib, I think you should move out of Lahore to Delhi or Simla. It is not safe in Lahore anymore. We have been moving lot of our belongings to Delhi for the last few months. Let me know, if I can help in any way."

When Mummyji is standing in the courtyard in the middle of the house with Vishnu and all the family members, she makes an impassioned plea.

"You know, I am just exhausted with anxiety… I am worried to death… Look at these helpless children," pointing at Kishi and I. "They are clinging to me all day… They keep asking me all day, Daddyji? Daddyji? I don't know whether you will be back or not… I can't take this any longer. Please let us all get out of here." And she breaks into tears again.

Pitaji appears to be moved by what she has said and says, "Surinder, I think you should take your family to Simla as soon as possible. The Indian Independence Bill has received Royal assent on July 18. The partition is now certain and conditions are going to become worse. Your mother, Karan, Dilip and I will stay back and see what happens. If Roshan can also stay back, it will be a great help."

Daddyji replies, "It is up to Roshan. I think we should let him decide."

"I will stay behind," Roshan adds.

Vishnu is standing in a corner watching the family drama, and after the decisions are made, he adds, "Professor sahib, I can make all arrangements for your travel. Please sir, just let me know when and where you would like to go?"

"Thank you, Vishnu, for your offer. We have already decided that we want to go to Simla. Let us pick a date… hmm, Kamla, what do you think? I think we can wrap up things within a week… Let us say in one week… Vishnu, please let me know when you have made the travel arrangements."

• • •

This evening, a few days before our departure for Simla, Daddyji and Mummyji go to see Daulat Ram, Mummyji's brother, to inform him of their decision to leave Lahore and move to Simla. As usual, he is sitting in the front lawn, enjoying the evening with a few friends and a bottle of Scotch. Mummyji goes into the house to meet her sister-in-law and Daddyji joins the group.

As soon as he learns that we are leaving Lahore, Daulat Ram says, "Oh, Surinder *yaar*, you are a coward, running away at the first sign of trouble. I am not leaving my property here so easily. Nobody dare come near my house to cause any trouble. Come on *yaar*, have a seat and have a peg." And he laughs and carries on talking, "Surinder, let me introduce you to my friends; meet Afzal Baig, we have known each other since school; and this is Sukhvinder Singh Walia, he has an insurance business; he lives in the house next door."

Daddyji takes a glass of water and tells Daulat Ram, "*Bhai sahib*, as I told you earlier, we will be leaving in a few days. And, in Simla, we will be staying with your younger sister, Sumitra, for sometime, till we can make our own arrangements. We came to say good bye. God knows when we will meet again."

"Afzal Baig, a Muslim, says, "Surinder ji, I think you are over-reacting to the situation. There are a few ruffians who are causing the riots. You will see that it will all simmer down after the partition of India and Pakistan."

Daddyji finishes off the glass of water, gets up and replies, "Let us hope so. Well, gentlemen, I will be making a move now."

Daulat Ram also gets up. In the meantime, his wife and Mummyji also come outside. There are emotional goodbyes and tears.

Daulat Ram embraces both Daddyji and Mummyji and wiping a tear says, "*Shabba Khair*," God will take care. A phrase generally in use by the Muslim community; such is the extent to which the two communities, their languages and cultures have inter-mixed together that Daulat Ram, a Hindu, uses a Muslim phrase to give blessing to his sister and her husband.

As they are walking out of the house, Daulat Ram says, "Are you going home now?"

Mummyji replies, "No, *Bhai sahib*, we have some arrangements to make at the bank before our departure."

"Why don't you take my car?" he says, and asks his driver to drive them.

As they reach the Punjab National Bank, they go in to see the manager. As soon as he notices Daddyji standing outside his office he gets up and comes to receive them. His daughter is Daddyji's student. "Please come in. What can I do for you, Professor Mehra?"

"We are shifting to Simla for some time till the conditions improve. My father is still going to be here. I would like to give him authority to operate our bank accounts and safety deposit box."

The manager opens his desk drawer and takes out a stack of forms. They fill and sign the forms in the presence of the manager.

Daddyji asks, "Is it safe to leave our valuables in the safety deposit box? What I mean is that, in view of the political situation, is the bank safe?"

"As far as I know, it is safe." the manager replies.

Mummyji says to Daddyji, "Listen ji, why don't we take everything with us to Simla?"

The bank manager says, "My advice is that you should withdraw half the money and jewelry and leave the other half here. In case some untoward incidents take place on the way to Simla, you will still have something to fall back on."

They accept his advice.

When they reach home, Vishnu had already dropped off their tickets for the Train to Simla.

14
LAHORE: JULY 1947
TRAIN TO SIMLA

"Come, Vikram and Kishi, you have to take a bath right now and get ready tonight; we are going to Simla early tomorrow morning," Mummyji shouts.

Kishi is too young to understand what it is going on, but I know. After Kishi and I are dressed up in our shorts and shirts, Mummyji shows me the secret pockets she has sown inside of our shirts. She takes out some money and two pieces of paper and tells me, "Vikram, this paper has our address in Lahore and the address of Sumitra *Massi* in Simla. And here is some money also. Let me place it in this secret pocket. Do you understand why we are doing this?"

"Mummyji, I know."

"Just tell me what you know," she says.

"If Kishi or I get lost, then somebody can bring us to one of the addresses."

"I am proud of you. You are a big boy now," Mummyji says pulling me towards her and embracing me with tears in her eyes.

Kishi is standing nearby chewing his shirt collar. My legs are shaking, and, if the fear level goes up a bit more, I could wet my knickers.

By 10 P.M., everybody is in bed. Kishi is asleep after a few minutes, but I am tossing and turning. Daddyji and Mummyji are talking.

He says, "Kamla, we should have left Lahore a few months back. There are reports of trains being attacked by the rioters. In the last four years, God has brought us face-to-face with our destiny for the third time. I wonder what he has in store for us."

Mummyji says, "Listen ji, Swamiji told us that you have a long life, so you have nothing to worry about. And he also told us that we will have two sons and a daughter. We have two sons, and, as we cannot have a daughter without me, therefore, I still have a life to live. So let us have a good sleep tonight; we have a long journey ahead."

There is silence, but I am still awake. I can hear Mummyji's rhythmic breathing. Daddyji is still stirring in bed. As I am just about to fall asleep, Daddyji shakes Mummyji by her shoulder and says, "Kamla... Kamla, are you asleep?"

She gets up with a start, "What is happening? Are they attacking?"

"No, no, Kamla, nobody is attacking... I want to tell you something."

"Can it not wait until morning?"

"I will not be able to sleep without getting it off my chest; it has been almost three years."

Mummyji sits up in bed, rubbing her eyes. And Daddyji finally gets it out, "Kamla, you said Swamiji told us that we will have two sons and a daughter, but Dr. Sandhu said something else."

Now, he gets Mummyji's full attention. She turns the table lamp on and says, "What did she say?"

Daddyji stammers a bit, trying to compose his words in a way that will have the desired effect with a minimum of hurt. His mind is searching all the works of English literature that he has read, hoping to come across a situation that he can draw upon—Pericles, Comedy of Errors, the Tempest—and then he remembers that baby Marina was given up for upbringing by another family in Shakespeare's play, Pericles. He decides to present the adoption of a baby girl as an alternative.

He says, "Kamla, God does not give everything to everybody. Dr. Sandhu told me, just after Kishi was born, that you will not be able to bear a child again. But, as Swamiji told us that we will look after a baby girl as our own, so maybe, one day, we will adopt a baby girl... Kamla, we are at cross roads of our destiny. Who knows where we will be tomorrow at this time; I did not want to keep this information from you any more."

Mummyji is shocked to hear this and says, "Let us see what He has in store for us."

• • •

It is July 27, a Sunday. Vishnu arrives early at about nine in the morning. He says, "Sir, let us try and depart for the railway station as soon as possible because there are some demonstrations planned later, and the authorities may impose a curfew."

"Roshan, come and load the stuff in the car." Daddyji shouts. My uncles, Karan and Dilip, also join in to help put some of the luggage in the dicky of the car and some on top of the car on the luggage carrier. They tie a rope around the luggage on the top of the car and make sure that nothing can fall. There are two tiffin carriers full of food that are placed on the rear seat along with two Thermos flasks full of water. Everybody moves out of the house to say final good byes. Daddyji bows down to touch his father's and mother's feet, who in turn hold him up by his shoulders and embrace him and kiss him on his forehead and shower him with blessings. There are tears in their eyes, but they do their best to present a stoical image. Daddyji has tears flowing down from his eyes. He is afraid for them being left behind. Mummyji also touches Pitaji's and Beyji's feet and receives blessing from them. Both Pitaji and Beyji bend down to kiss Kishi and me on our heads and give us blessings, and both of us wipe tears and cling affectionately to their legs. Roshan, after he is finished giving finishing touches to loading the car, comes round to hold Kishi and me and give us hugs. Beyji, my grandmother, is standing by the front door of the house, with a silver plate with a *Diya*—a small clay lamp filled with oil and lighted cotton wick—and a silver cup full of sweet curd. As we pass by her, standing at the door threshold, she puts a little of the sweet curd in our mouth with a spoon and blesses, "May Lord Krishna protect you all."

Mummyji, Kishi and I sit at the rear seat of the car, and Daddyji and Vishnu sit at the front. Vishnu gets hold of the self-starter between his fingers and pulls it for a while, but the engine does not engage. He tries again; there is the noise of the engine turning, but still the car does not start. He tries for a third time and still nothing.

"I don't know what has happened. It was running fine when I came here," he mumbles to himself.

"Why don't you try with the crank handle?" Uncle Karan says.

Vishnu gets the crank out from under his seat and goes out. "Vishnu, give me the crank, and you go in the car and press the accelerator, and I will turn the engine with the crank," Uncle Karan says.

He goes in the front of the car, inserts the Z-shaped crank handle into the opening at the front of the car and gives it a few circular jerks, and the engine spurts into action.

We are on our way. As we are pulling away, Pitaji, my grandfather, says, "Surinder, if you have any problem at the railway station, go and see Kabir Malik; he is the Station Master. He knows me. He was the Assistant Station Master at Mian Wali, when I was the PWI."

The car slowly moves away. I turn around and look back and see my grandfather, grandmother, uncles and Roshan standing outside the house waving at us and becoming smaller and smaller, and then the car turns the corner and they are gone. I turn around and start looking into the rear view mirror and see everything behind us moving backward, as we are leaving everything behind. And suddenly, the things are not moving backward so fast anymore. I turn around and see a sea of people surrounding the car and looking in.

The car comes to a stop. We have run into a mob of people some of whom are shouting, Pakistan zindabad—long live Pakistan. Then there is another group shouting Hindustan zindabad—long live India. And some of them have surrounded the car and are hitting the windows of the car with their fists.

Daddyji says with panic in his voice. "Keep calm. Don't open the door or the windows."

"Oh... no. I think we have rotten luck; out of the frying pan into the fire," Mummyji adds.

"Oh, look Kamla, we are just outside Daulat Ram's house." Daddyji says. Mummyji starts to recite verses from Hanuman Chalisa and puts her arms around my younger brother, Kishi, and me and pulls us in a protective embrace towards her.

Again... there is panic. Sounds... of... death. That is what we wanted to escape, and we find ourselves facing it. I am thinking: As a five year old, I have seen and felt panic and seen fear of death so many times and found that nothing happens; in the end everything turns out fine. I am sure that this will also pass, as others did before.

And as if by divine intervention, Mummyji's brother, Daulat Ram, accompanied by two friends, is moving out of his house with his double barrel shot gun in his hand and shouting what appears to be a healthy dose of expletives.

"Oh, see there is *Bhaji* Daulat Ram, carrying his Remington," Mummyji says. Daulat Ram has raised his gun barrel up towards the sky, and we hear two shots fired. One man standing just outside my side of the window looks around and sees Daulat Ram, and says, "Oh, come boys let us run. Daulat Ram is coming."

Daulat Ram is a strongman of the area and has, what is locally called, *Dhubb Dhubba*—a personality that instills fear in the local hoodlums.

Somebody else looks into the car and says, "You stupid idiots, that is Daulat Ram's sister and her family inside the car. Let them go; otherwise, he will make minced meat of us all."

Slowly the mob melts away, and Daulat Ram comes close to the car. Some men in the mob are obviously known to Daulat Ram, and they seem to be apologizing. Daulat Ram is now close to the car and tells us to open the windows and says jokingly, "And you people thought you will leave without meeting me? This is just my way of saying good bye to you."

He peers into the car, still laughing in his characteristic manner, gets hold of my right cheek between his two fingers and says calling me by my nick name, "Oh *yaar*, my friend *Vadhe Cuckoo*, you are leaving us alone and going away... God bless you... take care."

He slowly moves towards his house. Our car slowly moves away on way to the train station.

As we reach the railway station, it appears that everybody is leaving Lahore. Rickshaws, Tongas, cars and buses are all competing with each other for space at the entrance to the railway station to disembark their passengers. Vishnu is furiously sounding the horn of the car; the louder you sound the more attention you get. After a few minutes of jostling, he gets a space near the front steps of the station. The ground in front of the entrance is muddy due to a light drizzle and excreta from the horses of the Tongas. Mummyji opens the door, gets out and helps Kishi and me to step out. As I get out of the car, I step into a freshly deposited mound of horse dung. I scream and Mummyji, who is standing nearby and is trying to collect the thermos bottles and tiffin carriers from the rear seat of the car, looks around and says with irritation and concern in her voice, "Vikram, be careful *beta*... Oh my God, what have you done? Come here. Let me clean you."

On the other side of the car, there is Daddyji shouting, "Coolie... coolie come here." There are so many passengers that there is shortage of coolies. We are standing and waiting for good ten minutes before we find a coolie to take our luggage to the train. My foot is still dirty and smelling. As the coolies are carrying the luggage inside the station, Mummyji tells Daddyji, "Listen ji, I want to take the children to the bathroom. Just wait till I come back." As we approach the bathrooms, we find that there is a long lineup. Mummyji is in a fix as to what to do. We go back to the place where Daddyji is waiting with the coolies; they are grumbling that they are losing customers by idly waiting, and are demanding extra payment.

As we reach there, Vishnu also comes in the station after parking his car, and Daddyji tells the coolies, "All right fellows, you will get extra money."

Mummyji asks one of the coolies, "Where can we find some water to wash?" pointing to my foot.

The coolie replies, "*Bibiji,* there is a hand pump at the train platform; you can wash there."

As we reach the platform, where the train to Amritsar is waiting, there is more chaos than we saw earlier outside the station. Daddyji looks at the tickets to find out the train compartment where our seats are reserved and points it to the coolies. As the coolies are trying to enter the compartment with the luggage on their heads and shoulders, people who are already in the train compartment are trying to get out at the same time. Mummyji finds a hand pump, and the situation there is no different than the bathrooms. There is a lineup but with a difference. There are some people filling water in brass pots for sale. She buys a pot of water and washes my shoe, and we move towards our train compartment. As we reach there, we see Daddyji and Vishnu in argument with some people inside. We look through the window of the train compartment. It appears that some other people have occupied the seats that are reserved for us. Daddyji is showing his tickets to them, and they are showing some papers to him and are refusing to vacate the seats. At last, Daddyji comes out and says with frustration on his face and beads of perspiration on his forehead, "I think I am going to call the TT." TT is Train Ticket Examiner.

He looks around for some uniformed official. He finds one some distance away. Vishnu goes over and persuades him to come over to settle the dispute. When the TT reaches where we are standing, Daddyji says to him with tact and charm, "TT sahib, I am Surinder. My father is a retired PWI. He knows Station Master Kabir Malik. We have reserved seats, and some other people have occupied them. I will appreciate if you can help us."

The TT seems impressed with the fact that Daddyji knows his boss. He raises his cap a bit, but is somewhat non-committal and says, "Let me see what I can do. May I see your tickets?"

Daddyji hands over the tickets to him. The TT looks them over and says, "Every thing seems in order here. Let us go in and see what the problem is."

Daddyji and the TT go inside the train and confront the people who are sitting on the seats that belong to us.

The TT asks them, "Can I see your tickets?" One of the men takes out a piece of paper and shows him."

The TT looks at the piece of paper and says in a terse voice, "This is not a ticket. Are you trying to pull wool over my eyes? Take your luggage and get out."

The man says, "We have paid a lot of money for this paper. We paid cash. The man at the ticket counter told us that nobody will bother us."

The TT replies angrily, "First move out, and let these people take their seats, and then we will see what to do with you."

They move out. The coolies, who were waiting outside, bring in our luggage, and we take our seats. Vishnu says goodbye and embraces Daddyji and touches his feet, as a student usually would to his Guru, and says, "Professor sahib, God willing, we will meet again. We are moving to Delhi. Do look us up." And he departs.

We are seated in a First Class Compartment, where no more passengers than the number of seats available are allowed. Nevertheless, there is so much chaos, and there is such a throng of people coming into the platform that the authorities do not appear to have any control. People are trying to enter our compartment. The passengers inside are preventing them from entering. The door to our compartment has been bolted from inside. People who are outside are pleading to be let in. As people are not able to enter the compartments, they are climbing on the roof of the train by holding on to and stepping on the steel security bars at the windows. Some are planning to hang on to the exterior handles of the doors. The steel bumpers between the railway cars are another place where people are hoping to find a seat.

While seated inside the train, all we see are legs outside the windows standing at the window ledges and screaming people. It is a pathetic scene. Many women and children are waiting and looking dejected, because they are unable to perform the trick of climbing on the window ledges. People are standing outside, begging to be let in.

One *Nihang* Sikh, wearing saffron colored clothing with a sword hanging on his side and a blue turban with a shinning steel ring , suddenly gets up and opens the doors of the compartment and says, "Only women and children can come in."

A throng of people rush the door. He selectively lets in some women, children, along with some men who claim to be part of the family of the women and children. The people who just entered have occupied whatever space they can get on the floor. The train is supposed to depart at 12 Noon, but the time has come and gone and there is no movement.

After a while, a number of military personnel begin to appear on the railway platform. As the passengers are waiting and speculating about the reasons for delay in the departure of the train, another train on the adjacent track arrives from somewhere and slows down as if coming to a stop. I am watching the movement of the other train. After a while, it appears to me that our train has started to move. Not only I, but a few other passengers mutter something to the effect that thank God we are moving. And as the other train comes to a stop, we realize that the movement of our train was just an optical illusion. As the other train slows down to a stop, the passengers in our compartment are in shock at what they see, and there are gasps. The passengers in the other train are wailing and crying. After a while, the military personnel move into the other train and start evacuating injured passengers. Nobody knows what has caused the injuries. As everybody in our compartment is watching the other train, there is a lot of commotion outside our train on the platform. A mob with sticks, swords and knives has stormed the railway platform. The military is trying to fight them off. As this is all happening, the steam engine gives three long whistles that sound as if the humanity is screaming—enough is enough. The train starts to move with people running along side hoping to find a little space somewhere to grab and hang on to the train. Nevertheless, the train rumbles along, gathering speed a little bit at a time. We are slowly moving towards Amritsar that is about 35 miles east of Lahore.

Our train comes to a stop just at the outskirts of Amritsar railway station. The passengers, who are dozing peacefully, suddenly wake up in panic. Those who are travelling on the roof top, or are hanging on the exterior of the train coaches, gradually start to disembark and walk around. Rumors start about the cause of the sudden stoppage. Reports of communal attacks on trains are becoming common. Passengers are fearful of being attacked or set on fire. After sometime, a few military personnel appear on the side of the train. All the passengers in the train are Hindus leaving Lahore to avoid communal violence. Some of the soldiers are Sikhs. Passengers feel relieved. The train starts to move again. At last, the train slowly glides on to platform Number 3; with the hiss of the steam being let off by the engine, as if all the pressure has dissipated in the boiler of the engine. However, there is no relief on the faces of the passengers on the platform. The hawkers are shouting selling tea and sundry eatables. The coolies are running by the slowing train to find passengers whose luggage they can carry. The train stops. For us, we have come out of the inferno, but there are others who are running around to get out. The Muslims of Amritsar are as scared, as we were in Lahore; the mirror image of the fear that we felt is being felt by them.

We get out of the train and move to the waiting room. Our train to Kalka is not until 9 P.M. There is hardly any place in the waiting room but we make do. It is full of people like us. Mummyji spreads a small piece of cloth on the floor, where Kishi and I lie down. Another family is camped beside us in the waiting room.
"I am Shafik," he extends his hand to Daddyji.
"I am Surinder. Where are you going, Shafik sahib?"
"We are going to Lahore. We live in Delhi, but the communal violence there is becoming worse by the day. We live in a Hindu dominated area. As you can tell from our name, we are Muslims. You know what I mean. We thought we will go to Lahore for a while, until the political situation settles down."
"Well, we are going to Simla for the same reason. We are Hindus, as you can tell from my name. We left Lahore for fear of attacks by the Muslims." Daddyji adds.
"Do you own property in Lahore?" asks Shafik.
"No, not me personally, but my father has a house in Lahore."
"We have a house in Delhi, in Daryagunj area."Shafik replies.
"Oh, well, we have relatives who live in that area."
"As you have probably heard, there is talk of exchange of property between refugee migrants in the event of partition of the country," Shafik says.
Daddyji replies, "Yes, I have read about it, but it is a very premature concept as yet. Until the partition of the country is legalized and new laws come into effect, it is difficult to say how it will play out. It is better to wait and see."
Mummyji and Shafik's wife also talk to each other off and on. They have two children; a boy and a girl, but they keep to themselves, and Kishi and I keep busy on our own. This is how we spend a few hours at the waiting room. At about 8 P.M. we board the train to Kalka.

The overnight journey to Kalka is uneventful. We reach Kalka early in the morning after travelling for about 150 miles. Kalka is at the base of the hills. From Kalka to go to Simla by train, one has to take a narrow gauge train. It is an uphill journey. We board the train to Simla at 10 A.M. It is a much narrower train than the ones we had travelled in the previous legs of our journey.

As the train is straining to gain traction due to the steep slope of the rails, Daddyji starts to explain to me, "Do you hear the sound of grinding? This is the sound of steel of the wheels of the engine rubbing and slipping against the rails because of the slope. Engines have to work harder on the slope… and in winter, the rails become slippery due to ice. The workers have to pour sand on the rails to make them rough and help with traction."

"Daddyji, how do you know this?"

"You know that your grandfather was in the railways, and I have grown up around rail lines. Rails are in my blood."

"What else do you know, Daddyji?"

"OK, let me tell you a few more things. You know, in front of the engine there is a "cow catcher". This is a machine that catches a cow and throws it away if it comes in the way of the engine. And you see this chain with a handle near the ceiling, if anybody is in trouble and wants to stop the train, all he has to do is to pull hard at it, and the train will stop."

"See… see… Daddyji we are going into the hill." I have just finished saying this when it becomes dark. "See Daddyji, I told you we are going through the hills."

"This is a tunnel. When they built the railway line, they dug a hole through the hill for the railway line to go through. You know, there are 103 tunnels on this line. It was completed in 1903."

After a few hours, the train reaches Solan. Daddyji, excitedly, starts to tell Mummyji about the town, "You know Kamla, the beer people drink in Lahore comes from Solan. You see that building with a chimney; it is the Dyer-Meaken brewery. You see that sign, it says 4,432 feet, that is the height of this place above sea level."

The air is cool and fresh, but it has started to rain. The engine whistles and the train moves again. After a while, the sound of the engine pulling the train has become very rhythmic. It sounds something like… *pull-push-pull-push-pull-push*… and with that sound I doze off for a while. As I am waking up, the train is gliding to a stop at a place called Kandaghat. The characteristic sounds of the hawkers selling tea, biscuits, cupcakes and newspapers fill the air. Daddyji buys a newspaper.

After leaving Kandaghat, the rain becomes very heavy. The passengers have drawn down the glass shutters over the windows to stop the rain from coming in. There is a little chill in the air that is infiltrating through the little openings. Mummyji takes out a Pashmina shawl and covers Kishi and me to keep us warm.

"God bless Rattan Dogra who gave us these shawls," she says. Daddyji smiles, but does not say anything as he is busy reading the newspaper. After a while, he starts talking to a passenger sitting near him about what he has read in the newspaper.

Then he turns around and tells Mummyji, "You know Kamla, the train that stopped beside our train in Lahore yesterday was full of Muslims and was attacked by a mob near Amritsar. The rumor is that hundreds of people were injured." Many other passengers turn their attention to what Daddyji is saying, and he continues, "Kamla, after reading this, I am very concerned about the safety of our family in Lahore. Now, in hindsight, we should have insisted that they come with us." And he is just staring at the newspaper, pretending to read, but in fact, he is lost in his thoughts about his family in Lahore.

Passengers look cozy and secure; especially Mummyji is dozing with a sense of peace on her face. *Pull-push-pull-push-pull-push...* the rhythmic sound is back again. I begin to associate this sound with normalcy; meaning that the engine is working fine. However, in my short life of 5 years, I have begun to feel uneasy when things are going too smoothly. And things have been going too well for the last few hours. I am awake and looking around and up at the ceiling. The Pull-Chain that stops the train fascinates me. I am wondering how the driver of the engine knows when somebody pulls the chain. And for fun, I imagine that I am getting up and pulling the chain. I put my right hand up as if trying to pull the Chain. I pretend to pull it down. And suddenly, there is bang, bang, and bang—the sounds of screeching as the rail cars are coming to a stop, the rubbing of the wheels of the rail cars with the rails, the articles of luggage falling down from the overhead storage racks, and the passengers falling over each other. I am petrified and say, "Daddyji, Daddyji... I did not mean to pull the chain... I was just imagining." I am thinking that, some how, the train stopped because of my imaginary pulling of the chain.

All of a sudden, the peaceful atmosphere turns into chaos. A little while back some of the passengers were talking about what happened to the train in Lahore, and now, suddenly their train has stopped. "I hope it is not an attack." One of the passengers says loudly. Everybody is collecting their belongings and placing them in order. After a while, some people can be seen walking outside.

One of the passengers pulls up the glass screen of the window and puts his head outside, and asks loudly, "Do you know what has happened?"

The man outside the train shouts back "It is a landslide."

The passengers seem relieved. Especially, I am relieved that I had nothing to do with it. Daddyji and Mummyji look at each other, and Mummyji says to him, "Do you think Vikram had a premonition of the landslide? Just like you, *does he also have the Sixth Sense?*"

"Do you mean he saw the landslide *before* it happened, and that is why he tried pulling the chain to stop the train?" Daddyji asks.

It takes about four hours to clear the landslide, and the train starts its climb towards Simla. We arrive in Simla at about 8 P.M. July 28, 1947.

We are received at the railway station by Daddyji's elder brother, Shyam Nath and his wife, Sona Devi; and Mummyji's sister, Sumitra and her husband, Raghu. As had already been agreed, we are taken to my aunt Sumitra's home. We travel in rickshaws pulled by two men in the front, two in the rear and one walking beside us. We are travelling up and down the hills, and finally down and way down to a place called, Lower Kaithu.

15
LAHORE: AUGUST 1947
BEQUEATH

As Daulat Ram's car turns into the driveway of his house, he notices a police car with a policeman carrying a Sten Gun standing beside it. The driver of the police car gets out and walks towards the gate and, as Daulat Ram gets out of his car, the police driver hands over an envelope to him.

Daulat Ram opens the envelope, and, before he can read it, the police driver says, "Sir, Commissioner Rankin has requested your presence in his office. It is urgent, and he would like you to come with us in the police car. It will be safer for you in view of the riots."

Daulat Ram enters the rear seat of the car as the driver holds the door open for him.

When he enters his office, Commissioner Rankin gets up to greet Daulat Ram and says, "Please have a seat, Mr. Suri. Well, the time has come for us to move over to let the new Government of Pakistan take the reins of the new country. I have been given orders to move to New Delhi. I would like to thank you for all the help. It appears that, in the future, we are going to continue our relations. We are concerned with Russian Intelligence moving into India and, eventually, India becoming a Communist nation. We would like to maintain good relations with friends like you to counter this threat."

Daulat Ram is thinking: *What the hell is the Commissioner talking about—five years ago it was the Japanese threat, and now it is the Russians?*

"When are you moving to New Delhi?" Daulat Ram asks.

"Oh, within the next month or so… Mr. Suri, have you decided about your future?"

"Well, I have my house here, and my Muslim friends have given me assurances that I can stay here in Lahore without any fear as they consider me one of their own."

"Mr. Suri, my advice to you is that you should move to a safer place, for the time being, and watch and see what happens. We will offer you police escort and safe passage if you leave with us. A special train, with a military escort, is being arranged to transport senior British and Indian officials to Delhi. As a friend of the Crown, you are welcome to join us. My family will also be leaving by this train."

Daulat Ram rubs his chin with his right hand, deep in thought and says, "Well, let me talk it over with my family."

The Commissioner writes something on the writing pad on his desk, removes the sheet of paper, folds it, puts it into an envelope and hands it over to Daulat Ram, "Mr. Suri, this is my contact address in Delhi. If you send me a letter by mail at this address, it will eventually get to me. This is the address of the British Liaison office in Delhi. It will eventually be known as the British High Commission. We will be maintaining a large contingent of officials in India in order to maintain Political and Commercial Contacts. As you know, there are big plans for the future development of India, and British companies will be eager to participate in supplying expertise. There will be ample opportunity for you; we will see to it."

Daulat Ram says with his characteristic laughter, "Mr. Rankin, you will have to promise one thing: No East India Company this time." He is referring to the British East India Company that came to India for trade and eventually came to rule large parts of India with its private army.

Commissioner Rankin also breaks out in laughter and gets up to shake hands, but Daulat Ram stands up and embraces him and says, "You know, Mr. Rankin, I was hoping that, one day, I would beat you in Tennis, but it was not to be."

...

Daulat Ram is taking a brief stroll in the front lawn of his house. He stands there and reminisces how he had built the house ten years ago. His black Morris is standing in the driveway. Ashraf, his driver, is washing the car. He always keeps it sparkling clean; as soon as the car reaches home, he cleans it for the next trip.

Daulat Ram is thinking: *Everything I worked for will be left behind. Probably this house will be occupied by people I do not even know.*

"Nirmala, Nirmala, where are you?" He is looking for his wife.

She comes out of the house to the front lawn. "Nirmala, Rankin has advised that we should leave Lahore. He thinks it is too dangerous for us to stay here, and he has offered to take us with him in a special train"

"I have been telling you the same thing, but you never listen to me."

"OK, OK *baba*, you were right. Now let us prepare to leave."

The fact that unknown people will occupy his house is bothering him. He walks over to Advocate Azam Sharif's house–three houses down from his. He is a Muslim; and therefore, Daulat Ram decides to go to him because he is sure that *he* will be around after the riots settle down.

"Azam *bhai, Salaam-e-Lekam*," Daulat Ram greets him in Urdu.

"*Namaste*, Suri sahib," he returns the greeting in Hindi. "How may I be of service to you?"

"Azam *bhai*, I want you to prepare an affidavit bequeathing my house and car to my driver, Ashraf Mohammed, and domestic servant, Mushtaq Ali, in equal proportions, in the event that we do not come back to Lahore. They have given us ten years of their lives. Rather than let my possessions be forcibly occupied by unknown people, I much prefer to give them to these two. Do you think this is possible?"

"Yes, this is possible, but you should think it over. If you decide to come back, it may cause complications. But I will see what I can do. I will draft the affidavit today, and you can have a look at it in the evening."

Daulat Ram looks at the affidavit in the evening and signs three copies; appointing Azam Sharif as the executor.

Next few days, he spends organizing his financial affairs. One day, he goes over to see my grandfather and his family and tells them about the fact that he will be leaving Lahore for Delhi in the next few days.

16
SIMLA: AUGUST, SEPTEMBER, 1947
DAWN OF INDEPENDENCE

This is our first morning in Simla. When we wake up in the morning, it is cold in the room, and I can see the high mountains around with clouds touching their tops. Daddyji and Mummyji are also up, but Kishi is still asleep. "Why is it so cold here?" I ask Daddyji.

"*Beta,* Simla is at a height of about 7,000 feet above Lahore. We are in the clouds here. That is why it is cold." I do not really understand it. All I know is that it is cold, but it feels nicer than the heat of Lahore.

"Daddyji, when are we going back to Lahore?" I ask.

He laughs and replies, "*Beta*, we have just arrived."

"Will we go back when Hindus and Muslims stop fighting?"

"Yes, we hope so."

"Are there any Muslims in Simla?"

"Yes, there are Muslims in Simla also."

"Are they fighting here also?"

"No, there is no fighting here," he replies.

In the meantime, Aunty Sumitra enters the room with cups of tea and says, "Oh, *Vadha Cuckoo*, you are very thin and lean. I am going to feed you well, while you are with me and make you fat and healthy."

"OK Auntyji," I say shyly.

"Oye, don't call me Auntyji, I am your *Massi*, your mother's sister. So from now on call me, *Massiji*. OK?"

"OK. Aunty... oh no... no. *Massiji*" I say, blushing.

"So what should he call your husband? Mummyji asks.

"Oh, he should call him *Masserji*."

"Oh, come on, Sumitra, it is too old fashioned. Let Vikram call him *Uncleji*." Mummyji replies.

Sumitra Massi pulls my cheeks, making them blood red, and says "*Nee*, Kamla, your son is very shy."

The first day in Simla just passes by, lazing around and getting used to the cold weather.

• • •

At about 10 P.M., and as we are all getting ready to go to sleep, there is a lot of noise outside. People are shouting at each other. There we go again, I say to myself; it reminds me of the scary nights in Lahore. Daddyji and Uncleji go out to check what is happening. I also get up and walk out with them to the verandah. The street, in front of the house, is on a steep slope. A slight rain is falling. A number of people are dragging furniture up the slope. I see a dressing table being pulled up the sloping street, along with a dining table and some chairs.

One man is shouting to the other, "*Oye*, the Sheikh family have left Simla and gone to Lahore. They told me to take whatever I wanted."

"But they said they may come back," the other man says.

"Oh, *yaar*, if they come back then we will see."

And they keep dragging the furniture uphill.

All the neighbors get out of their homes and join in the looting of the home of the Sheikh family, a family of Muslims.

An elderly Englishman, who lives next door, is standing outside his house and is looking on, shaking his head in disgust. Daddyji and Uncleji go out to the street and tell the looters to cease what they are doing. The Englishman, who is being addressed as Mr. Hunt by Uncleji, also joins them in persuading the looters to stop. The looters stop after Mr. Hunt intervenes.

The next day, we are all invited to the home of Uncle Shyam Nath, Daddyji's elder brother, for lunch. We all decide to walk. When we get out of our house, we see Mr. Hunt standing outside.

As we are walking by, he says, "Sixteen days to Freedom on August 15."

We all stop to say hello to him, and he carries on speaking, "You know my friends, freedom does not mean license to loot, fight and kill each other. My young friends, with freedom comes responsibility; not only to oneself but to the whole community. I am seventy five years old and have lived in India for fifty years. I may be born in England, but I have grown up here. I consider India my home. Have you seen today's newspaper? You Hindus and Muslims have gone mad. Maybe, you are not ready for freedom. One thing I will tell you that if you people do not develop a feeling for your community and country, one day, the whole Indian society will decompose."

All my elders just stand there speechless—not for long, though. Daddyji is looking at Mr. Hunt very intently and eager to say something. Although, he appears to be trying to control himself, he suddenly blurts out, "Mr. Hunt, with due respect, the British had something to do with what is happening nowadays. Don't get me wrong. I am not anti-British; on the contrary, I am a professor of English Literature and may even be considered pro-British. However, the remarkable ability of the British to project an aura of intellectual, moral and racial superiority, combined with standard colonial practice of divide and rule was relentlessly utilized to create conditions of communal disharmony. Cohesiveness with exclusiveness has been the essence of the Raj."

And Mr. Hunt stands there looking at Daddyji with a little smile on his face and says, "Young man, I do not entirely disagree with you, but the people of India, both Hindus and Muslims, also have to take responsibility for being ruled for centuries by a relatively small number of Britishers. Do you know that there are only approximately 100,000 British soldiers and officials governing 300 million people in India? If the people of India had the sense of community and pride, they should have driven out the British long ago. On the contrary, they fell for the policies that divided and subjugated them. You should not lay all the blame at the feet of the British. They have also done some good things. Look at the infrastructure, the institutions of higher learning, the Civil Service, the Police, the Army; and most of all, a lingua franca— the English Language that people of India have got because of the British."

Mummyji is getting uneasy, "Listen ji, we are getting late. You can carry on after we come back." Daddyji excuses himself and we move on.

Being from the Plains, for us, the walk uphill is tiring and slow. After about 10 minutes of walk, we find a rickshaw. Mummyji and Kishi get on it, and the trek starts again. The next casualties are Daddyji and me. After another ten minutes, Daddyji asks for a rest break. Uncleji laughs and says, "You people from the plains are lazy." We find another rickshaw. Daddyji and I get in. The rickshaw is being pulled by two men in the front and two in the rear, and one walking beside us acting as a relief puller. The rickshaw pullers are walking barefoot. It takes us about 20 minutes to reach Sunnyhill, the residence of Uncle

Shyam Nath. It is located at the edge of a steep slope. It is a large accommodation. He has a large family consisting of three sons and four daughters.

He is standing outside with his family to receive us. "Welcome to Simla, the summer Capital of India and soon to be of divided India… Well but… I am not sure if the new government will continue with the tradition to move to Simla in the summers. Surinder, I think you made a wise move to come here before August 14, the day of the partition. You will see that there will be widespread bloodshed after that."

The families meet after a gap of several months. Mummyji covers her head with the end of her Sari and bows down to touch the feet of both Uncle Shyam Nath and Aunt Sona Devi. There is lot of chatter amongst all the family members. My Aunt is a strict disciplinarian; she has to be if she has to run a family of nine. Mummyji goes to the kitchen to help her set the lunch. It appears that Mummyji is in awe of her and follows her directions to the letter. The lunch is served at precisely 1:30 P.M.

At about 4:00 P.M., we all prepare to walk back to Sumitra *Massi's* home in Lower Kiathu. Uncle Shyam Nath calls his servant to go and get some rickshaws. Daddyji says looking at his brother, "I will not be riding a rickshaw; I just feel guilty being pulled and pushed around by five men with bare feet. Why don't they wear something on their feet?"

Uncle Shyam Nath replies smiling, "You know, Surinder, we have heard that before when Mahatma Gandhi came to the Simla Conference in 1945, even he had no choice but to ride a rickshaw, in spite of the fact that he had previously expressed disapproval of this mode of travel for the same reasons you are giving. Anyway… I think Kamla is going to need one; she has young Kishi to carry along."

Finally, one rickshaw arrives and Mummyji, Kishi and I get into it, and the rest of them start walking home.

As we reach near Sumitra *Massi's* home, we see Mr. Hunt pruning the plants outside his house. Uncleji says, "One thing you have to admire about the British men: They are very active and are always doing some physical activity around their house and keep the area clean and well tended. We Indians just sit around reading newspapers, slurping tea, eating Samosas and getting fat."

Daddyji laughs and says, "Hello Mr. Hunt, you have very nice flowers."

"Well, it needs a lot of work to keep a garden looking good and same applies to your country, my friend."

Daddyji is thinking: *here we go again.*

Mr. Hunt walks over and puts his right hand over Daddyji's shoulder and says, "You know old chap, I really enjoyed having a chat with you this morning. You said something this morning which was a very thoughtful observation on your part: cohesiveness through exclusiveness is the essence of the British Raj. The key word is cohesiveness. This is what people of New India should practice. Forgive me for saying so, but in the past Indians have been practicing some thing very contrary. *Divided we stand united we fall.* Look at the history of India; the people always *stood divided*... What is your name, my young friend?"

"Surinder."

"When you were speaking this morning, you reminded me of somebody I used to know long time ago; your gestures, way of talking, and your voice are very much like his. He used to work with me."

"When was that?"

"Oh... Let me think now. It must have been 1922. I used to be an overseer in the North Western Indian Railway. We were doing a lot of construction in the Mianwali–Jhelum Sector."

As soon as Daddyji hears the word 'railway', his eyes lit up. "My father was in the Railways."

Mr. Hunt does not pay attention to what Daddyji has said, and carries on, "He was a Quantity Surveyor. You know... he used to measure quantity of materials that were supplied by the contractor. All other quantity surveyors used to cook the Measurement Book known as MB, but not him. And for cooking the MB, they all used to receive a percentage from the contractors, but he refused to accept even a *Paisa*. We used to call him Yodh Raj, the Lion."

Daddyji jumps up with excitement, "He is my father, Mr. Hunt."

At first, Mr. Hunt does not hear what Daddyji has said. And then suddenly he says, "What did you say? Are you serious? My God! What a coincidence... Where is he nowadays?"

"He retired in 1939. He is living in Lahore."

"In Lahore? My dear chap, things are going from bad to worse over there. How could you leave him alone?

"We did our best to persuade him to come with us to Simla, but he did not want to give up his house. He thinks we are cowards in deserting our home and fleeing to the safety of Simla."

"My son is a Colonel in the Army and is the Area Commander in Lahore. He wrote in his last letter that they are expecting a lot of bloodshed."

"Oh God... Mr. Hunt, I am really very worried about my family now, after what you told me. I am not sure what to do."

Everyday we go out, partly on foot and partly on rickshaws, to do some sight seeing. Like Mahatma Gandhi, Daddyji also gets over his altruistic streak and begins to ride the rickshaw. The justification given is that, after all, the rickshaws create employment; and if it is good enough for Gandhiji, it is good enough for Daddyji.

Annandale is what I find most fascinating—the only plateau in Simla that is about one thousand feet in elevation lower than the main town. It is very near, Kiathu, the area we live in. About quarter of a mile in diameter, the ground is used by the British for Polo, a Race-Course, a Gymkhana Club, Dog Shows, Flower Shows and other public functions. One day, we pack up lunch and set on a descending journey to Annandale. As we reach there, a game of Polo is in progress. We all stand there and look all around us at the towering hills. In the middle of it all a bunch of people in uniforms are riding horses, with long sticks in their hands, chasing a small white ball. What a sight it is, and this prompts Daddyji to say, "No wonder the British want to hang on to India as long as they can! Look at the life they are leading."

After lunch, we start our uphill trek home. Daddyji and Mummyji start walking. Kishi and I sit in a rickshaw, with one rickshaw as a spare, just in case one of my parents needs it. We stop at many places along the way to see the sights and hear the sounds of wind whistling through the needle-like leaves of fir trees, clouds playing hide and seek with the mountain tops, and monkeys swinging on the tree branches.

As we are nearing Kaithu, we see an elderly man, in a military uniform, standing on the roadside.

"See, he is selling flags," Mummyji says.

As we come closer, we are surprised to see that the man is selling the *Teeranga,* as it has come to be known—the Tri-color flag of New India. None of us has seen it before, having been only recently adopted by the Constituent Assembly on July 22, 1947. Daddyji is very excited to see it, and so is Mummyji. I am not really sure what it means to have a flag. The only flag, I remember having seen flying in Lahore, is a flag they call the Union Jack—the flag of Great Britain. Our caravan, consisting of two rickshaws, comes to a stop in front of this makeshift roadside shop.

"Let me tell a little bit about our beloved new flag," the man says.

And he begins to sing in Hindi, the description of the flag.

English translation:

The Saffron at the top depicts the courage, the sacrifice and spirit of renunciation of our Freedom Fighters.
Lest we forget,
The white in the middle is for purity and Truth
Lest we forget.
The deep green at the bottom is for Faith and Fertility,
Lest we forget,
The Wheel in navy blue with 24 spokes, is the wheel of Life
The *Dharma Chakra*,
Lest we forget.

The song is performed in such patriotic vain that my parents have to wipe a few tears from their eyes.

Mummyji asks him, "Sir, May I ask what prompted you to make these flags and sell them?"

"Young lady, I have fought in two wars; The World War II and the War of Freedom; the first War was for the freedom of other lands, and the second, for the freedom of my own land, India. The first I fought alongside the British and the second, against the British. I am giving away these flags, the symbol of our hard fought freedom. I want all Indians, be they Hindus, Muslims, Jews, Christians or Parsis, to keep one flag at home; lest they forget."

Mummyji picks up six flags and places some money in the donation jar standing on the side of the table on which the flags are stacked.

Daddyji goes over and shakes hands with him and asks, "May I know your name, sir?"

"My name is Major Hari Singh Nautiyal, Retd; Indian Army." And he gives a military salute.

Daddyji is somewhat taken aback and also impressed at the same time, and he salutes back. A small wooden signboard, with "LESTWEFORGET" written on it, is sitting on the table. Mummyji and Daddyji both stand there and look at it with curiosity.

Mummyji says, "Oh… it says Lest We Forget."

Major Hari Singh Nautiyal says, "LESTWEFORGET is an organization we have started to help India, our motherland—which used to be known as *Golden Sparrow* at one time— to get up and fly again."

"But most Indians don't know English. So why give it an English name?"

"We have a Hindi name also. It is "YAADRAHE", meaning REMEMBER. Both names are opposite of each other, but complementary—opposites like Yin and Yang of Chinese philosophy."

Until now, Daddyji is thinking of the Major as some frustrated elderly man smitten with patriotism, but after listening to him he changes his opinion. He realizes that he is not talking to an ordinary man, and that there is something more to him than meets the eye.

"What is your raison d'etre?" he asks Daddyji.

Daddyji looks at Major Hari Singh Nautiyal—a bit confused with this question from him.

There is silence for some time, as Daddyji is thinking how to reply.

To gain time he asks, "I beg your pardon?"

Hari Nautiyal repeats, "What is your raison d'etre?"

Still there is no reply. Mummyji senses that probably Daddyji does not know the meaning of the phrase, 'Raison d'etre'—a French phrase. She says, "Reason for being…" She has studied elementary French in college.

"I know Kamla; I know what it means."

This really hurts his ego; Mummyji is telling him what the French phrase means. Daddyji takes his cue and carries on, "We are refugees from Lahore. I am a professor of English Literature. My wife teaches in a Girl's school. Major sahib, how do you plan to make the *Golden Sparrow* get up and fly again?"

"My plan is simple; 3E's. Yes, not 3R's but 3E's; 3E's stand for **E**ducation, **E**thics and **E**nglish. Give education to all our people. Teach people to be ethical and honest. Teach English to as many people as possible because English is the language of the world and, to get ahead, you have to be able to do business with the rest of the world. You know, literacy rate in India today is only 12%. We are essentially a nation of illiterates; imagine if 60% of the people become educated. I think India would become the knowledge market of the world. Give them education, and the rest will take care of itself."

Daddyji replies "Yes, in principle, I agree with you, but educating 300 million people is a Herculean task."

"Yes, of course, but we have to start somewhere. And there is another leg of our plan; it is *Brahmastra*, the flaming weapon that is now called the Atom Bomb. Do you know how the War ended in 1945? It is because of the Atom Bomb. I call it the Peace Bomb. It is unfortunate that thousands of people lost their lives, but many times more would have died if the War had continued." As soon as Daddyji hears this word, he is transported back to the dream he had in 1943 in Kashmir about Hitler.

"What about *Brahmastra*, the Atom Bomb? How is that relevant?" he asks.

"I believe that India must develop a *Brahmastra*, the Atom Bomb, of its own if we want to grow as an independent nation. We must have the Peace Bomb if we want to deter future traders, and future East India Companies to become raiders of our freedom. In order to preserve Independence, we must be capable of independently defending our homeland... You know, I forgot to tell you, we are having 'Dawn of Independence' celebration at the Ridge starting at 9 P.M. on August 14. Please make it a point to attend."

"Is it being organized by the government?"

"Yes, but our LESTWEFORGET is an active participant".

We say good bye and move on.

After we are some distance away, Daddyji asks, "Kamla, what do you think of Major sahib? To me he seems to be behaving strangely. Did you see him saluting us? But something about him also tells me that he is not an ordinary eccentric patriot."

They have a hearty laugh, and we keep walking towards our home.

• • •

As we reach home, there is a note from Uncle Shyam Nath: "Family from Lahore arriving tomorrow, August 10, by train at 4 P.M."

Daddyji just lets out a loud, hurray, "They are all arriving tomorrow. Oh, thank God they are all safe."

The next day, we all walk to the railway station. We are getting used to walking. The train is late. And as the time passes, we are getting edgy. It is 6 P.M and there is no sign of the train. The news from the Station Master is that the train is definitely arriving by 7 P.M. Well, arrive it does... but our family is not on it. Uncle Shyam Nath and Daddyji are just standing there feeling helpless. After talking things over, they go to see the Station Master. There are some other people standing in his office with the same dilemma. It just so happens that the people who did not arrive are all from Lahore. So the obvious conclusion is that something happened to the train from Lahore to Amritsar or from Amritsar to Kalka.

One man says, "I have heard that trains from Lahore are being stopped at Wagha, a town near the proposed border between India and Pakistan, and there have been killings on the trains." There is only one train a day from Kalka to Simla. The Station Master promises to send messages to Kalka, Amritsar and Lahore to find out what has happened. As there is nothing more that can be done, we all go to our respective homes.

The next day, all of us are sitting, worrying and sifting through the newspaper and listening to the news. The news is all bad. Reports of massacres and bloodshed are being broadcast on the radio and the newspapers. We are imagining the worst.

"We should have forced them to come along with us to Simla," Daddyji says with a tone full of guilt. He decides to go to the railway station again, hoping that his parents and brothers may arrive. As he gets out to go to the the train station, he sees Mr. Hunt standing outside his house.

"How goes life young man?"

Daddyji relates the story of his family from Lahore not arriving. Mr. Hunt offers to walk with him to the train station. Along the way, Daddyji tells him about his meeting and conversations with Major Hari Singh Nautiyal.

"Surely, old chap, you have heard of the Nautiyal Industrial Empire. Major Nauti—as he is known to his friends—is Adarsh Rai Nautiyal's son. They made a ton of money during the War supplying material to the Army."

As they reach the railway station, the train from Kalka is just steaming in. Uncle Shyam Nath is also waiting there. As the coolies rush to the train to pick up clients and their baggage, Daddyji gets a glimpse of a man in a turban sitting in the train. "I think I see my father." And both brothers rush to the compartment where they spotted their family. They push through the crowd to get to the compartment where they had spotted their father. They look through the windows; the man sitting inside is not their father but somebody else. Both the brothers look at each other and decide to go and look into other compartments, but they do not find their family. As this struggle is going on, Mr. Hunt comes close to them to find out what is happening, and he sees both the brothers standing looking dejected.

He holds both the brothers by their shoulders and says, "Surinder, as I told you earlier, my son is the Army Commander in Lahore. I will send him a telegram and ask him to find out what is happening."

"Thank you Mr. Hunt. We really appreciate your help."

There is nothing more to do at the station. They all go to their respective homes. Along the way, Mr. Hunt tells Daddyji, "We should go to the Telegraph office and send a telegram to my son." They send a telegram to Mr. Hunt's son along with the address of my grandfather's house in Lahore.

As they are walking back home, Daddyji is thinking: *The red ball of fire behind the western mountain—the slowly setting Sun—reminds him of his childhood days in Jhelum…*

he is four. "Come, come, Surinder...take this.... take this" *Beyji offering him a ball of freshly made butter from the earthen churn pot, with the white strings still in her one hand and rolling the butter ball in the other. He would grab it and run away... "I will still tell Pitaji, he would say and run away"... the Hookah, she used to smoke, was a secret she wanted him to keep—the ball of butter a small bribe!*

He sits at the edge of the cliff on a stone parapet, looking over the gorge to the ever sinking red ball, still rolling over random thoughts: *a rainbow on the left... just like the Tiranga, the Tricolor Flag of New India... What a dance of Nature? The red blood colored Sun and the seven colored rainbow and out of it is born the Tricolor Flag of free India... I wonder if you mix red blood with the colors of the Rainbow, what colors will you get... red blood Malta, an orange like fruit... common in the Jhelum—Mian Wali area...a favorite of his father... You actually have to fertilize the tree with the blood of Sheep to get the red color ...but there is plenty of blood now being spilled... Hindus and Muslims bathing each other... in blood. Wonder where are they now?.... my family.*

A light drizzle starts. "Come on my friend everything will be all right. Just a little delay, that is all," Mr. Hunt wakes him up from his reverie.

They both walk home.

• • •

The same night, as they are having dinner, Uncle Shyam Nath's servant comes to deliver a note addressed to Daddyji. As he unfolds the piece of paper, he raises his hands up in delight and shouts, "Oh, they have arrived from Lahore. They are here... they are all alive and well." He holds the piece of paper between his hands and raises them towards the heavens; closing his eyes, he says a prayer, "Oh Lord, you are very kind. Protector of your disciples, Thou art great. Thank you for giving us our family back." And suddenly, he moves out of the house running to go to Uncle Shyam Nath's house. And, as suddenly, he comes back in and says, "Come on Kamla. Get Vikram and Kishi ready; we are going to Sunnyhill."

As we reach Uncle Shyam Nath's house, there are scenes of tears and joy. Everybody is telling everybody else what happened, and what they did, and how they got out of Lahore and landed in Simla. Roshan, our domestic servant, has also come with them. I find him in the crowd. As soon as he sees me, he embraces me and lifts me up and says, "Oh *yaar*, Vikram, we will fly kites here one day."

Later, as we are sitting around, Daddyji asks, "Pitaji, we were at the train station, and you were not in the train, so how did you come?"

"We came by the Rail Car," my grandfather replies.

"By Rail car?... But that is only for the British."

"Son, the British Raj is now about to become history. I knew the Station Master, and he let us ride the Rail Car."

Rail car is like a bus that travels on the same rails as the train. The British used it exclusively for themselves and some upper class Indians.

After dinner, my grandfather and Uncles, Karan and Dilip, start to tell the stories of horror and mayhem that is going on in Lahore.

Uncle Karan relates excitedly, "You know, Pitaji did not want to leave Lahore at any cost if I had not insisted. The straw that broke the camel's back was: One day there was a knock on the door. As I opened the door, Suttoo, our washerman, was standing outside and he, suddenly, fell in my arms. There was a long dagger stuck in his back with blood oozing out. There were two men outside with daggers in their hands, and, as they were about to jump at me, Dilip, who was standing behind me, fired one round at them. One of them got hit on the shoulder, and they both ran away, vowing to come back at night. After hearing the sound of gunfire, some of our neighbors came to our rescue. One of our Muslim neighbors, a good friend of Pitaji's, suggested that we should move into his house for protection, but we did not agree to that. He suggested that we should remove the name plate on the house, because the attacking Muslims can identify the house as a Hindu house, based on the name. The next day, he brought a name plate with a Muslim sounding name. That same night our house and houses of many Muslims got attacked by a Hindu Mob. What an irony we thought. It did not matter, whether you were a Hindu or a Muslim, the mobs were just after revenge. After the last incident, Pitaji was convinced that the time has come to leave Lahore."

Mummyji has not heard anything about her brother, Daulat Ram, who is presumably still in Lahore. She asks, "Pitaji, have you heard of any news about my brother, Daulat Ram?"

"Oh yes, of course. He came to see us, one day, to say goodbye. He said that the Police Commissioner had advised him to leave Lahore as soon as possible. So he must have moved to Delhi."

My grandfather carries on with his narration.

"Let me tell you about a tragedy. Curfew was strictly imposed at night with shoot-to-kill orders. One night, a group of houses were set on fire. The occupants ran outside to escape the flames, only to be shot at by the Police, who had strict orders to shoot-to-kill in order to enforce the curfew."

Uncle Shyam Nath gets up and says, "I think we are all tired now. Surinder, how about if we all retire for the night. Come for dinner tomorrow. At the stroke of Midnight, India will be free. Jawaharlal Nehru is giving a speech. We will listen on the radio together and celebrate. I will have a new bottle of Solan Whisky ready."

After a little while, we get up and ride home on rickshaws.

• • •

Next evening, we all again descend at Uncle Shyam Nath's house to celebrate the dawn of the Independence Day. As Pitaji frowns on alcohol consumption, the bottle of Solan whiskey is kept in another room. Daddyji and his brothers go there, by turn, to have a sip and come back to the drawing room where we are all sitting. I am sitting on the floor, leaning against a chair in one corner of the drawing room, half asleep, just watching the goings on. Kishi is already asleep in another room. The women folk are busy in the kitchen and are sending, through Roshan, fried fish and chicken pakoras as accompaniments to the Solan Whiskey.

Pitaji is sitting on the chair beside where I am sitting. He comes to me and lifts me up and puts me on his lap. "*Oye yaar*, Vikram, I missed you. Son, how do you like it here?"

"I miss my friend Iqbal... Did you see him?"

"I saw him from a distance, but his father came to see us before we left."

"Pitaji... I want to go back to Lahore. When will they stop fighting?"

"I don't know son... I think we will probably never go back."

"You know Pitaji... Iqbal told me that all the fighting is because of kites."

At this time, Uncle Karan comes into the room after taking his sip of Solan and says, "Oye Vikram, you have become a politician talking about why the fighting is taking place." And he laughs at what I had said.

"Oh, Karan, don't laugh, there is a hypothesis going around that the first fight between Hindus and Muslims may have been triggered by a kite fight," my grandfather says.

Uncle Karan does not say anything more. He goes outside to light a cigarette.

Roshan comes into the room and announces, "*Bibiji* says, the dinner will be set on the dining table at 9:30 P.M. sharp."

After dinner I fall asleep.

Like father, like son. I too have a dream!

The sky is full of kites of all colors; green, white, saffron and red. When a Green kite cuts the string of a saffron kite, the Saffron kite turns red and slowly glides down to the ground. And when a saffron kite cuts a green kite, it also turns red and glides down to the ground. Slowly and slowly, all the kites are cut and the sky is full of red kites all falling to the ground. Lots of people are running after the kites to catch them... strange... sight. People are all colored red. ..... No, no wait a minute ...it is red blood flowing down their bodies that makes them look red... They have all become Independent... the kites!

• • •

"Red Blood Maltas... Red Blood Maltas" ...a street hawker is selling a fruit that looks like an orange. Suddenly, I am awake. I am at Sumitra Massi's house. How did I get here? I went to sleep in Uncle Shyam Nath's house.

The hawker is persistent. "Buy *Azaadi ka Phul*, Red Blood Maltas... *Azaadi Mubaarak. Azaadi Mubaarak.*"

As I hear the word *Azaadi,* meaning Independence, I realize that it is August 15, 1947 today, the first day of free India. The hawker is distributing good wishes for the Independence Day.

Red Blood Malta being his favorite fruit, Daddyji goes out and calls out for the hawker to stop. The hawker puts his, *Chabri*—a large basket made of straw—on the ground. Daddyji picks up one Malta at a time, presses it with his fingers, takes in the fragrance and asks, "How much for each?"

"*Sahibji*, it is 15th of August today, our first day of Independence, give me whatever you wish. Malta is the Fruit of Independence... see." He picks a knife and cuts one open into two pieces; each piece has red blood colored pulp inside.

"Oh, this is really a good piece. But why do you call it the Fruit of Independence?"

"*Sahibji,* look at the blood that has been, and is being spilled to gain Independence. Red blood Malta is a reminder."

Daddyji is left speechless and says, "OK. Give me eleven Maltas." And he hands him a one rupee note.

The hawker replies, "*Sahibji*, You can have a dozen for one rupee. It is my *Boni* time, I don't have change."

"Keep the change. I want only eleven Maltas."

"Sahibji, may I ask why eleven?"

"Because it is an auspicious number—you know, 11, 21 and 51. Oh, on second thought, make it fifteen. It is 15 August today, so I will buy 15." And he hands him one more rupee.

"*Sahibji,* I don't have change. Will you accept 21 Maltas? You know, 21 is also an auspicious number."

"OK." He replies.

The hawker fills in two large paper bags made from old newspapers and hands them over to him. Daddyji, as a gesture of goodwill, helps the hawker lift his heavy *chabri* on to his head and the hawker is on his way to his next customer.

I am standing there watching, and so is Mr. Hunt.

"Surinder, old chap, you fell for the old hawker trick: I don't have change. He sold you twice the quantity you wanted."

Daddyji smiles at Mr. Hunt and hands over a few Maltas to him and says, "Happy Independence Day, Mr. Hunt. Tell me honestly, how do you feel? Do you feel independent or dependent?"

Mr. Hunt has a hearty laugh.

"Oh, look Mr. Hunt, my family is walking down the hill. See the man on the left, with the turban. He is my father and your old friend, Yodh Raj."

And we all start walking uphill to receive them.

Mr. Hunt and Pitaji embrace each other and start talking about the good old days.

· · ·

On August 16, the day after the Independence Day, nothing has changed. As usual, as soon as Daddyji gets up in the morning, he walks out to the front verandah looking for the newspaper, but Uncle Raghu is already siting there with the newspaper in hand. He looks up and says, "Professor sahib, how goes life?"

Daddyji replies, "Let me first breath in the fresh air of independence," And he pulls a chair and sits down close to where Uncle Raghu is sitting."

Uncle Raghu separates the front and the back pages of the newspaper and hands them over to Daddyji and goes back to reading what he was reading before.

The complete text of the speech of Prime Minister Nehru, delivered the mid-night of August 14, is in the newspaper. Daddyji reads out a few words in an oratorical style.

Long years ago, we made a tryst with destiny, and now the time comes when we shall redeem our pledge, not wholly or in full measure, but very substantially. At the stroke of the midnight hour, when the world sleeps, India will awake to life and freedom. A moment comes, which comes but rarely in history, when we step out from the old to the new, when an age ends, and when the soul of a nation, long suppressed, finds utterance. It is fitting that at this solemn moment we take the pledge of dedication to the service of India and her people and to the still larger cause of humanity.

When he is finished Uncle Raghu says, "Professor sahib, you sound almost as good as the Prime Minister."

Daddyji says, "Raghu, are you making fun of me?" And they laugh, and Daddyji keeps talking as he is looking at the newspaper, "We should keep today's newspaper as a souvenir. See the newspaper is full of stories about the Independence Day. I like this picture of Nehru and Lord Mountbatten, hoisting the Tricolor flag. Raghu, did you see this. Just below this headline on the front page, BIRTH OF INDIA'S FREEDOM, there is also a smaller headline: 'Lord Mountbatten Greets Pakistan; Pakistan having attained independence a day earlier on August 14.' So this means that Mountbatten was in Pakistan on August 14, morning and came back to Delhi in the evening in time for Nehru's speech at midnight."

And then Daddyji's attention goes to the advertisements on the front page of the newspaper and he says, "Raghu, did you notice the ads?"

Uncle Raghu moves closer to his chair and says, "Oh, let me see. Look at this ad about a carpet showroom and the other one about an optician."

Daddyji points to another bigger advertisement at the bottom right corner and says, "Look Raghu. The British have not left yet, and the Americans have already moved in with their cultural artillery in the guise of Hollywood. See this big ad about the American movie: It Happened in Brooklyn; starring Frank Sinatra, Peter Lawford and Jimmy Durante."

Uncle Raghu shows him his part of the newspaper and says, "Look at the large crowds, at Kingsway and India Gate following the open carriages carrying the Mountbattens and the Nehru family, with people shouting: Pundit Mountbatten *ki Jai Ho*, Jawaharlal Nehru *ki Jai Ho*." Meaning: Glory to Mountbatten, Glory to Nehru.

Nehru becomes the Prime Minister and Lord Mountbatten the first Governor General of India. Mahatma Gandhi declines to join the festivities in Delhi. He goes on a 24 hour fast in Calcutta and holds prayers for communal harmony and to usher in the new Era.

Daddyji deposits the newspaper of August 16, 1947 in safekeeping as souvenir.

Apart from the change in government, nothing has changed. After a few days of euphoria, the reality of millions of refugees dawns on the leaders of India. The effects of Bengal famine have not gone away, just because the British are leaving.

Bombay film industry is producing movies to depict all aspects of life. About 175 movies will be produced in 1947—among them are some fascinating titles: Atom Bomb, Tiger Queen and Song of Baghdad. Life still has to go on.

Roti, Kapra and Makaan—bread, clothing and roof over their heads—are the three needs that the common man has, along with some movies, of course, as dessert for the mind!

And that is what my parents, grandparents and uncles are thinking about. How will they survive? Most of what they owned has been left behind in Pakistan. To start with they need a roof over their head. They know that they cannot live with their relatives for too long. My grandparents and uncles rent a small place near Uncle Shyam Nath's home. It is a small storage room behind a large house owned by an English family. There is no latrine, so they use the facilities at Uncle Shyam Nath's house. There is a water tap outside that they can use. They buy some necessities and set up a household. It certainly is a *hold,* but hardly a house. Five adults are living in a 10 feet by 15 feet storage area with a roof that leaks even when dew falls. It remains to be seen what will happen when it rains. And rain it does one day—cats and dogs. And yes, there is a dog house nearby, where Jimmy lives. Uncle Karan likes to play with Jimmy. He is amused when he finds out that the dog is named Jimmy. "I knew it. Jimmy again; half the dogs in India are named Jimmy," he tells himself. "One day, I will have to find out why every other dog in India is named Jimmy." For the time being the problem is: How to keep the roof from falling over their heads. The choice is between water falling over their head or the whole roof falling over their head. My grandfather knows, being experienced in construction, that if he stops the water from leaking, it will buildup on the sagging roof and it will sag even more with the increased weight of water, and ultimately come down. And down it comes one day. Fortunately, nobody is home when it happens. They have all gone to see a movie, the Tiger Queen, in order to divert their minds off the *Khich Khich*—the pull and push—of daily life of *Khana Badosh*—the Nomads.

Well now, they have no choice but to move back to Uncle Shyam Nath's house. It turns out that it is not a good move—14 people living under the same roof. What if the roof does not leak water, but there are plenty of opportunities for leaky egos to collide. And collide they do, the egos of my grandmother and Aunt Sona Devi, Uncle Shyam Nath's wife. They are just keeping up the traditional drama of mother-in-law and daughter-in-law getting one up on each other; no one is to blame but the circumstances. Forced by conditions beyond their control, fourteen human beings adjust their habits and idiosyncrasies and start living, or shall we say existing together. Uncle Dilip is lucky that his profession of Tailoring is in demand in Simla at that time. Most tailors were Muslims, and a large majority of them have migrated to Pakistan, resulting in an acute shortage. Who says misery does not have benefit? As soon as he starts his job, he finds his own living quarters. Same thing happens in the case of Uncle Shyam Nath. He cannot keep up with the demand for legal services; a number of Muslim lawyers have moved to Pakistan. Uncle Karan's previous employer, Dewan & Company, has also moved to Simla, and he gets his old job back, but the business does not take off—not enough speculators in commodities, and the company decides to relocate to Delhi. We are still living with Sumitra Massi and Uncle Raghu Nath.

Daddyji makes inquiries about starting a private college. His principal, S.L. Soni, has also moved to Simla. They both put their heads together and form a plan to start a coaching college in Simla, but the weather is not cooperating. It is a particularly rainy summer and the weather is also cooler than usual. And along with the ups and downs of the pathways, the enthusiasm for starting a new business is also up one day and down the other. After staying in Simla for a few weeks, Daddyji realizes that Simla is too small a city for the business of coaching to take off. Moreover, a few months in a year, because of cold weather and snow, the population of Simla, which is usually only about twenty thousand, goes down even more. As the rest of the family is in Simla, Daddyji and Mummyji decide to consult with them. One day, we all walk over to Uncle Shyam Nath's residence in the evening.

As we are all sitting down before dinner, Pitaji asks, "So Surinder, have you found any prospects for coaching business here?"

"Well Pitaji, the problem is that Simla is too small a city. The prospects are going to be very limited. We have to have a large number of students to be able to make money."

Uncle Shyam Nath says, "Surinder, you have a family to feed, so you should try and find a job rather than this coaching business, where one day business is up and down the other. I know Major Hari Singh Nautiyal. He is the chairman of the Board of Trustees of a new college they are going to set up. It will be recognized by the Punjab University. He is a client of mine. I can talk to him about you."

"We met him a few days back, when we were coming back from Annandale. He seems to have started a nationalist Organization, LESTWEFORGET."

Uncle Shyam Nath says, "They are a very influential family. I am going with him to Delhi to negotiate a big land deal for a new housing colony. You know, Surinder, I have spent a lot of time with him. He is a visionary. Their family has played an important, behind the scenes, role in the freedom of India. You will see that their ideas will play an important part in shaping the future of India."

As they are finished talking, Pitaji brings in a letter and says, "Surinder, when we were in Lahore, a letter arrived for you. Here it is."

Daddyji takes the letter, looks it over, but does not open it. He knows who the sender of the letter is. He cannot wait to open it and read.

After dinner, two rickshaws are called, and we set out for Lower Kaithu, our temporary home.

As soon as we reach home and settle down in our room, Daddyji opens the letter and is smiling while reading, and then his smile turns to amazement, and then to concern about something he has read.

Still looking at the letter, he says with excitement, "Kamla, you should hear this. My God, this is amazing. I can't believe this." And he is still reading the letter. After he finishes, he turns it over and over to make sure he is not missing something and says, "You know Kamla, it seems the letter is incomplete."

"Daddyji... Mummyji is not here. She is outside talking to Sumitra Massi," I say.

He bends down to look under the bed as if he has lost something.

"Have you lost something?" Mummyji just walks in, and sees Daddyji looking under the bed.

"It seems I have dropped a page of this letter. See the writing at the end of the page; the sentence is not complete."

"Who is it from?"

He laughs and says, "Can you guess? I will give you one hundred guesses and you will not be able to."

"Come on ji, tell me."

I decide to join in the guessing game. "Daddyji, what will you give me if I can guess it right."

"I will get you whatever you want."

There is a knock on the door. Daddyji signals with his finger on his lips. We are all quiet.

"Come in."

Uncle Ragu Nath walks in. "How goes life, Professor sahib?"

"Well, with the grace of God and, of course, your kindness, we are doing well. However, it seems that we will have to move to Delhi to set up our college."

"I guess we will go to Delhi together."

"What do you mean?"

"We are being transferred to Delhi. I have to join my new job the first of next month."

After some more small talk, Uncle Raghu leaves, and Daddyji is back reading the letter. Actually he is right. One of the pages of the letter had fallen off and gone under the bed. While he was busy reading, I had picked it up and put it in my pocket. I slide under the quilt to feel warm, as it is getting cold. Mummyji is sitting on a chair, and Daddyji is siting on the edge of the bed and starts to read the letter aloud to Mummyji.

They think I am asleep; a common mistake made by parents!

The letter reads:

Hello Surinder ji,

I am sure you will be surprised to receive this letter about two years after you wrote to me. The address you have is my parents' home in Ottawa, Canada. I was in India till the end of 1945. After the War officially ended, with the signing of the instruments of surrender by Japan, on August 15, 1945, a lot of work had to be done to wind down our operations in India. After that, we came back to Canada, and I joined my regular duties. Your letter was received, but for some reason, I did not respond to it. As soon as we came back to Canada, I changed my first name to Max from Adolf, short for Maximillian. Max Hoffer sounds very Canadian, eh?

Recently, I read that the British are about to leave India, and that India is about to become a Dominion like Canada. I understand the date is August 15, 1947, exactly two years to the day Japan surrendered. I was thinking that peace is finally upon us, till I read about the communal riots taking place in India. It is after I read about India's Independence, that I decided to write to a few people I know in India. Best wishes for a bright future!

You must be surprised to see me use "ji". Well, my friend, do not forget that I lived in India for about three years. During my stay, I gained a working knowledge of Hindi and even Sanskrit. For Sanskrit, I should like to thank an Indian colleague I was working with in India; his name is Major Hari Nautiyal; also known to his friends as Hari Nauti. Pun is intended, as he was a naughty man in all senses of the word. He introduced me to Swami Ravi Anand of Verinag. During my stay in India, I made three trips to Verinag; I think it changed my view about life. During each of my trips to Verinag, I had supernatural experiences, but the one I had when I was in the bus, with you, tops them all. It was a dream. Here is a brief description:

A man who looks like Adolf Hitler appears in my dream and says, "Herr, Adolf Hoffer."
 "Herr Hitler, what are you doing here? Who is minding the War?"
 "I am here looking for what America and Britain are looking for; the Ultimate Weapon, the Atomic weapon."
 "Why here in this remote place?"
 "We have studied the original Hindu scriptures written in Sanskrit, and we have unearthed the secret, and it is buried in the valley of Srinagar."
 "The secret lies in the laboratories of the Western World, Herr Hitler, and not in the Ashrams of India."
 "Herr Hoffer, you are wrong. Do not under estimate the power of the Vedas and the Puranas. When you want to unearth the secret of smashing the smallest particles of matter, the basic building blocks of the Universe, you have to get close to the Creator and understand His ways—mind over matter. That secret lies in the Hindu scriptures. You should help Germany, your fatherland. Your father was born in Stuttgart. If you help me find the secret, I will make you the King of Canada, when I conquer the world. I want to have an Empire, where the Sun never sets."
 "Herr Hitler, you are a cruel crazy man. You are killing millions of innocent people. We will destroy you. There is no place in this world for a person like you. The Sun will soon set upon you."

The letter from Max Hoffer continues:

The dream takes on a larger significance, in my case, because of my profession and my role during the War. I wrote to Swami Ravi Anand about it. He wrote back to say that you also had a dream similar to the one I had, and at the same location and time. According to him... (*The writing in the letter ends here and the next page is missing.*)

By the time I get up the next morning, I have forgotten about what happened last night. I find a paper in my pocket, and I decide to make a paper airplane. After Mummyji had banned kite flying, Roshan and I had taken to making paper airplanes. And this one goes flying right into the eye glasses of Daddyji. He picks it up and starts to read the writing on the paper. "Oh, Vikram, where did you find this? This is the paper I was looking for last night."

He unfolds the paper and starts to read. The balance of the letter:

Our birth dates may be the reason why both of us had the same dream at the same time. My birth date is November 15, 1915. It will be interesting to know yours.

Daddyji gets up from the chair and goes excitedly to Mummyji, "Kamla, look, we were born on the same date; my God, what a coincidence!" And he keeps reading the letter.

The letter continues:
The dream set me thinking. May be the dream was a divine intervention to set our endeavors on the right path. During the following months, I spent some time at Verinag Ashram with the help of Maj. Hari Nautiyal. During my stay at the Ashram, I was surprised to learn that the financial support for the Ashram was being provided entirely by the Nautiyal Family Trust. I was also surprised to learn that scientists from many Western countries had been visiting and staying at the Ashram for the last many years. Especially, after reading the Quotes attributed to Robert Oppenheimer, it appears to me that the techniques of *Sadhana*—a means of accomplishing a spiritual realization that I learned and others may have learned before me—may have contributed to furthering of the scientific knowledge that led to the development of nuclear physics.

As he is reading the letter, Mummyji is sitting nearby knitting and shaking her head. I can feel anger rising in her. After finishing the letter, Daddyji is in deep thought, as if planning his next move. Mummyji gets up angrily, snatches the letter from his hands, tears it up in pieces and throws it out the window into a gorge just outside the window. "Listen ji, what are you getting from dissecting this dream of yours after so many years. We should be concentrating on trying to find a way of earning a living."

I run towards the window and get up on the bed to see where the pieces of my paper airplane have gone. I see the pieces of paper gliding down into the deep gorge reminding me of kites of Lahore. As I am leaning outside the window, looking at the floating pieces of paper, Mummyji comes running to catch me and pulls me back shouting, "Do you want to fall over? You both father and son are going to kill me with worry." And she starts to weep, wiping tears with the end of her Sari. After this incident, Daddyji does not talk to Mummyji for the whole day. Mummyji tries to talk to him many times during the day but to no avail.

I did not know Mummyji could sing. But at night, after she thought both Kishi and I have gone to sleep, (a common mistake by parents) she tries to make amends by singing a couplet from one of his favorite films. No, no, not Tiger Queen… yes, yes, yes… Atom Bomb. It is running now-a-days, and its music has taken off. The couplet in English goes something like this; but an appropriate translation of a Hindi couplet is never possible:

Oh, my love,
You have blown me away,
With the blast of your love,
Let our love mushroom,
Like a mushroom cloud.

A few repetitions of this couplet lull me to sleep. When we get up in the morning, everything is normal. Both Mummyji and Daddyji are laughing and talking lovingly to each other as if nothing had happened.

A knock at the door disturbs the status quo… Uncle Raghu always enters at the wrong time. "Professor sahib, how goes life?" His favorite opening line and continues, "*Abb Dilli Dur Nahin*," meaning, Delhi is not far off now—being a reference to our forthcoming move to Delhi.

• • •

Roshan, our domestic servant and my kite flying partner and Guru, decides to move to his native village of Kangra, situated about 150 miles North of Simla. I have spent almost all my life of 6 years with Roshan. I am very upset after hearing that he is going away. First, Roshni left us and now Roshan. It seems that the Light left me earlier, and the Enlightened one is also leaving me. "Oh, *Yaar* Vikram, I am going away for a few months only. I will be back. After that I will come and live with you in Delhi."

And one day, as he walks off to the train station, he looks back, waves and keeps walking and walking and his image becomes smaller and smaller, till he walks over a hillock and disappears.

Will I ever see him again? I am thinking.

The storm of partition of India has caused so many separations that people who used to live together like petals in a flower have been blown around like the leaves of a tree in autumn. Nevertheless, seasons never remain the same. Autumn is followed by winter, by spring, and then new flowers bloom and new petals….new beginnings.

On September 25, 1947, we pack up and board the Train to Delhi in search of new beginnings; with hopes and aspirations of a new spring… Oh yes, with spring comes *Basant,* the festival of kites. Will Roshan be back by then to fly kites with me again? Let us see. He said he would.

17
DELHI: SEPTEMBER 1947
NEW BEGINNINGS

After travelling through 103 tunnels, over 568 bridges and descending 7,000 feet in elevation, we steam into the Railway Station of Delhi, the erstwhile Capital of the Mughal Empire, the British Raj and now of Free India. Coolies in red uniforms are running beside the slowing train jostling with each other for the privilege of carrying our luggage to the waiting Tongas.

"Oh, Kamla, look there, RK and your sister Devika waiting on the platform."

I am not sure who RK is, but I assume he must be the Uncle that goes with Devika Massi, my mother's sister.

As soon as the train comes to a stop, coolies come inside and stake their claim on the right to carry our baggage to the waiting Tongas. Two coolies drag the pieces of luggage out of the compartment; and then load the luggage on their heads, arms and shoulders; it looks like they are superhuman.

I am standing there watching and thinking: *Will I be this strong one day? With such strong men around, how could people of other countries rule over us? Why are they wearing red clothes? If they are free; then why are they not wearing the tricolor clothes of the colors of the flag of free India?*

"*Oh Vadha Cuckoo yaar*, how are you?" Uncle SK is standing in front of me holding me by the shoulder with one hand and pulling my cheeks with the other. I am shaken out of my thoughts, as I am reminded that I am still known by my nick name as *Vadha or elder Cuckoo*.

And then, I have to face the loving wrath of my Devika Massi, "*Nee* Kamla, your son is very thin. Is he OK? He looks somewhat ill." Devika Massi, having been herself endowed with physique somewhat on the heavier side, considers that all thin people are either inflicted with some disease or are deprived of food. With my cheeks already red from the fingers of Uncle SK, the comments by Devika Massi make me blush. We are finally outside the railway station looking for Tongas, and I am glad to be out of the centre of attention; I am still rubbing my cheeks, which are burning from the attention they received from Uncle SK. It seems the whole world is moving to Delhi. Throngs of people, rickshaws, Tongas and motor cars are everywhere. As we are standing around waiting, Daddyji points out the flag mast outside the station with the Tricolor Flag flying proudly on the top, and he says, "You know, till only a few days back, a Union Jack used to fly there."

In the meantime, the coolies get two Tongas and start to load them. I can see the poor horses, with their bones visibly protruding beyond their skin, being weighed down with their legs buckling under them. Some how, four adults, two children and eight pieces of luggage are made to fit with barely any room for the coachmen. They have to stand on the side boards.

"Why does it take so long to get a Tonga," Daddyji asks the coachman, just to make small talk.

"Sahib, many Muslims, who used to own Tongas, have moved to Pakistan, so a large number of Tongas are lying idle for lack of owners."

After living in Simla for a few months, we have been spoiled. Having got used to the cool and fresh air of Simla, the weather in Delhi feels sultry. In addition, I am standing on the front floorboard of the Tonga just facing the rear extremity of the horse. There are so much excreta being ejected by the horse that it appears, as if, I am being fired upon by a cannon. The horse seems to be straining under the load of the passengers and luggage. After a great deal of coaxing and untold strikes of the *Chaabuk*—the leather whip—the horse finally gets us to Uncle SK's home in Daryagunj, a locality in the north east part of Delhi on the western banks of the Yamuna River. We are told that one room has been rented for us on the third storey; the landlord having reluctantly agreed to give away the room for a few months to help out because we are a refugee family. We are looking to the Tonga coachmen to haul our luggage. They, of course, see an opportunity to make amends for the cheap fares that Uncle SK has negotiated at the railway station. "Come on *Tongawalas*, you have to carry all this baggage to the third storey." Uncle SK coaxes them.

"Oh sahib, we are not coolies. We don't transport luggage. You will have to make some other arrangement."

"Well, we will pay you something extra."

"OK. Sahib, it will be four *annas* extra." (An *anna* coin is 1/16 of a rupee.)

"Well, we'll see. Hurry up now. Get moving." Uncle SK is trying to push them to start moving the luggage.

The two *Tongawalas* start to carry the luggage upstairs. The canvas holdalls are not a problem, but when they start to move the heavy steel trunks, they have a hard time maneuvering them within the confines of the staircase. They blurt out between themselves, "Seems like the trunk is full of bricks."

Uncle SK overhears it. Annoyed at the comment, he gives a kick on the rear of one of the men and shouts at them saying, "You are talking nonsense, you bloody idiots." The man loses his grip on the handle of the steel trunk, and the trunk falls on his foot crushing his toenail, and it starts to bleed.

This upsets Uncle SK even more, "Don't you people know how to do things properly? You have spoiled our staircase floor."

The man tears up a piece of cloth from his head wrap and ties it around his toe to stem the flow of blood and says, "Do not be concerned sahib, we will clean up before we leave."

Daddyji is standing at the bottom of the staircase. He goes in the house and brings a bottle of Mercurochrome, an antiseptic lotion, and tells the injured man, "*Eh bhai*, apply this on the wound otherwise you may get septic."

"Eh, sahib, we poor people are used to cuts like these. The germs don't affect us; we affect them. They die when they touch our blood." And with this, he brushes aside Daddyji's offer.

Uncle SK comments softly to Daddyji, "Surinder, you should leave these labour class people alone. You should not sympathize with them; otherwise, they start taking advantage of you. Let them take care of themselves."

Daddyji does not like Uncle SK's comment, but does not say anything.

They finally manage to move the luggage to the third storey. After the *Tongawalas* finish their tasks, they wait outside the house to get paid. Uncle SK gives them the agreed amount for the trip from the railway station and hands them additional two *annas* for moving the luggage.

"Sahib, we told you it will cost you extra four *annas*."

"Go, get away now. This will do." And Uncle SK turns his back on them and goes into the house muttering under his breath, "Oh, these people, the more you give them the more they want."

And then he reluctantly takes out one more *anna* and says, "Take this and disappear."

The *Tongawalas* are not happy with the way they have been treated, and they move away with an air of disgust on their faces. One of them mumbles to the other, "The English sahibs are better than Indian sahibs. At least the English are fair and honest and do not go back on their word. For the last two hundred years the English sahibs kicked our rear end, and for the next foreseeable future the Indian sahibs will be kicking us around."

The other replies, "My friend, have faith in Mahatma Gandhi. He will take care of us."

It is now our turn to climb the three storeys to the roof top. Having negotiated the steep hills of Simla for a few months, climbing the three storeys of the building seems like nothing for us. Finally, we are inside the room that is going to be our home for the next few months. The room has windows on two sides, with a small kitchen area in one corner, and a small bathroom outside on the terrace with walls on four sides and no roof. Mummyji sits down on one of the steel trunks looking despondent and says, "Oh God, what have you done to this poor country of ours? We were happy the way we were. Nobody told us that freedom would mean getting uprooted from our homes and hearths and banished to distant lands as refugees."

Daddyji, trying to cheer her up says, "My dear, we may be refugees, but the future is bright, and I have seen it." He looks up at the sky and continues, "In fact, it is so bright that I have to wear sunglasses to watch it." With this, he wears his sunglasses and recites aloud a couplet from Shakespeare's "As You like It".

"Now we go in content,
To Liberty and not in Banishment."

And continues, "My dear, who said the price of freedom is cheap?"

Mummyji replies with irritation in her voice, "Oh, there you go again. Do you think Shakespeare has the answer to all the woes of the World? You try to trivialize every problem by quoting from the plays. We are not actors in some play. This is real life."

"OK, dear wife, do not take life too seriously. Life is a play. If you play with it, it will play with you. If you complain, it complains back." And out comes another quote from 'As you Like It' by Shakespeare:

"All the world's a stage,
And all the men and women merely players."

Watch out Delhiites, *Shakespearewala* has arrived. You can take him out of Shakespeare, but you cannot take Shakespeare out of him.

Uncle SK is shouting from the ground floor, his deep voice reverberating through the central open courtyard and floating to the top, "Oh Professor sahib, lunch is ready. Come on down."

And thus we discover the culinary delights that Uncle SK is capable of producing. As we are having lunch, we find out that Daulat Ram and family have also arrived in Delhi and have rented a flat nearby; his family had earlier lived in the same room that we are now occupying.

As the time goes by, Daddyji is beginning to think about the future of our family and some way of earning a living. Only after a few days of arriving in Delhi, he has purchased a bicycle made of black steel frame with white streaks on the mud guards. There is also a guard on the chain wheel, which the bicycle in Lahore did not have. This is to prevent trousers of the rider from getting stuck in the chain or, otherwise, getting soiled by the grease on the chain. There is a carrier over top of the rear mud guard, and a child's seat on the front rod behind the handles. Two adults and one child can easily ride on it. With the purchase of the bicycle, Daddyji has become mobile and is beginning to take trips to investigate opportunities.

He has his mind set on a business venture and says, "Kamla, I am going to look into buying a few Tongas for hire as a business. What do you think?"

"Listen ji, what are you saying? Such a famous Professor of English literature is going to be working as a coachman? What will people say? Instead of *Shakespearewala,* people will call you *Tongawala.*"

"Come on Kamla, we will be owners of a Tonga business. The population of Delhi is increasing everyday. You remember the *Tongawala,* who brought us here from the train station, said that there is shortage of Tongas in Delhi. We will start with four Tongas, and as the demand increases we will purchase more. I am already dreaming about owning a fleet of a hundred Tongas. If we make five rupees from each Tonga in a day, we could make five hundred rupees a day—fifteen thousand a month. Kamla, you know this is five times of what I was making in Lahore, and we used to think that it was a fortune."

Without further ado, he goes and negotiates the purchase of four Tongas. One day in the afternoon, four Tongas with four coachmen arrive in front of uncle SK's home. Fortunately, there is some land in front of the house, across the street, which has some trees. It is an Evacuee Property; the Muslim family that used to own it has since evacuated to Pakistan. Daddyji starts to use the land for a stable for horses. The horses are de-harnessed at night and tied to the trees. The tree leaves and grass also serve as a snack for the horses. One of the coachmen, named Sabua—a tall man with a bulging belly—is in-charge of managing the stable. He sleeps there at night with his ten year old son; the boy also helps him with feeding and washing the horses. Sabua has built a small shelter by stretching and tying a sheet of canvas, known as *Tarpaal,* to the tree branches around. To answer the calls of nature, they go behind the nearby thick historic stone wall; which, at one time, formed the boundary defense of the walled City of Delhi during the Moghul Empire. This wall, having borne the brunt of many an invasion over the centuries, now serves the fundamental needs of the refugees who have settled in the area without adequate facilities. The horse manure serves as a source of additional income. Nearby shanty dwellers buy it from Sabua to make fuel cakes for burning in their hearths for cooking.

Tongas go out in the morning to do the business of transporting people and return home at night. The fodder for the horses is bought by the coachmen during the day, as required. At the end of the day, the coachmen give all the money they have earned to Daddyji, and he gives them their daily wage of one rupee. The first problem is the smell of horse dung, and the second problem is also a smell, but of a different kind. He smells rat. Most days, after expenses, nothing much is left. The explanation that the coachmen give is that there are not enough customers, so they are idling most of the day. Finally, he takes matters in his own hands and decides to investigate. He sends three Tongas out to do business and rides himself in the fourth Tonga to survey the scene. After spending one day in the field, he realizes that he is being cheated by the coachmen. The coachmen are pocketing some of the cash they receive from the customers. He confronts them and things improve a bit. At least the coachmen start to bring in a little bit of net income. Complaints from neighbors are increasing. Many times the neighbors are compensated for bearing the smell of the horse dung by free rides on the Tongas.

Uncle SK is a freelance Insurance Adjuster. He works on contract for various insurance companies. Whenever there is fire or other accident, he is contracted by the insurance company to survey the scene at the site, make an assessment of the damage and submit a written report to the insurance company. He owns an old typewriter that is used for typing the reports. He is technically good in his profession, but his English language skills leave a lot to be desired. One day, Daddyji sees him struggling with writing a report and offers to help.

Uncle SK replies, "Oh *yaar,* Professor sahib, you are God sent. Why don't you help me in writing the reports on a regular basis? This way I can take on more business, and we can share the fee."

"Well, I will be pleased to do that, but I will have to accompany you to the sites of the accidents to see what happened so that I can describe it properly."

When the next opportunity comes along, they take a ride in one of Daddyji's Tongas to the site of the fire. After the visit, Daddyji is told by Uncle SK what to write. Daddyji writes it by hand, and Uncle SK types it. Daddyji then reads the draft to make sure that there are no mistakes.

As he is reading the report, he says, "SK sahib, there appears to be a mistake here. I saw only one building that burned down. You have changed it to read that two buildings burned down."

"Oh *yaar,* Professor sahib, this is how insurance business is conducted. It is a matter of give and take. You give some and you take some. Do you get it?

Daddyji gets it all right; he knows that Uncle SK is misrepresenting the facts, but he lets it go.

Between the income from the Tongas and the fee from Uncle SK, he begins to earn enough to sustain the family.

• • •

This day, Daddyji appears very uneasy; he is walking back and forth in the room. Mummyji looks at him and says, "Listen ji, is anything bothering you?"

Daddyji looks back at her, while he is still moving around the room, and replies, "Kamla, I am missing something in life–it is my old friend, Shakespeare."

"Why don't you buy some of his plays?" She says.

"I think I will do just that." And he walks out of the room, runs down the stairs and comes out on the street and finds our coachman, Sabua, getting a Tonga ready.

"Come on Sabua, we are going to Nai Sarak to buy some books," Daddyji says as he hops in the front seat and takes the reins of the horse. Sabua sits beside him, and they are off to Nai Sarak– or the New Road, a street where school and college students buy textbooks and stationery.

In about twenty minutes, they are in the Chandni Chowk area and at the entrance to Nai Sarak–this is as far as they can go as Nai Sarak is too narrow for the Tongas to go through. Daddyji goads the horse to enter the street, but Sabua stops him, "Sahib, the street is too narrow; it becomes even narrower as you go further. The horse will get claustrophobic and start to jump around and hurt somebody."

Daddyji reluctantly gets down from the Tonga and decides to walk the street. As he is getting down, he asks, "Sabua, this street is so old and narrow; why do they call it Nai Sarak, the New Road?"

Sabua replies jokingly, "Sahib, this was new in 1857 when the British built it after the Mutiny to let their cavalry ride through easily. After 90 years...."

Daddyji replies, "OK...OK" And he starts to walk towards the entrance to Nai Sarak with a spring in his step. He is looking forward to meeting his old friend, William Shakespeare, and his cast of characters: Antony and Cleopatra; Julius Caesar, Macbeth and the old King Lear. As he is walking and looking around for the appropriate book shop, he sees a very interesting sign: Kabaria Old Books and News Store. He stops to look.

The shop owner comes out and asks, "Sir, may I help you?"

"Yes. I am looking for Shakespeare." Daddyji replies.

The shop owner says, "Sir, for that, you will have to go back in time some 350 years and to Stratford-upon-Avon."

Daddyji is, at once, amused and amazed to find somebody knowledgeable about Shakespeare in the narrow crowded street. He laughs and says, "Well, I mean, Shakespeare's plays."

The shop owner takes him into the shop and shows him a shelf full of used books. Daddyji, after browsing for a while, picks up two books and hands them over to the shop owner and asks, "How much?"

"It will be two rupees, Sir."

As Daddyji is taking out his wallet, he notices a book shelf on the opposite wall. There is a red cloth draped over the bookshelf with a sign: Blood Bath. He looks at the shop owner and asks, "What do you have here?"

"These newspapers and magazines tell you all about the Muslim and Hindu blood that was spilled as a result of the riots before and after the partition of the country."

Daddyji moves closer to the shelf and picks a few newspapers and magazines and selects two newspapers and two magazines to buy. After making the payment, he walks back to the Tonga, takes a seat in the front alongside the coachman, Sabua, and they head home. As soon as the Tonga starts to move, he opens one of the newspapers and starts to read with the papers fluttering in the breeze. Sabua is talking about all kinds of things, but Daddyji's face is buried in the newspapers and the magazines that he is devouring one after the other. When they reach home, Sabua rings the bell of the Tonga to announce their arrival. Daddyji, without a word to Sabua, picks up his books, newspapers and magazines and gets down and walks up the stairs to our home on the third storey.

When he walks into our room, he goes quietly to his bed, spreads out the newspapers and starts to read. Mummyji finds him very quiet and asks, "Did you find the books you were looking for?"

He looks up and shakes his head with disgust and says, "This is a disgrace. I never knew this. Do you know this newspaper says that 500,000 to 1,000,000 Hindus and Muslims were massacred during the riots? And 10,000,000 to 15,000,000 people changed countries—the largest migration in the history of mankind. Do you know what we are being called by these foreign magazines? They are calling us a decomposed society. Do you know how the killings took place? The killers used whatever they could get their hands on—axes, knives, hockey sticks and bare hands." And he takes his glasses off and rubs his eyes to relieve himself of the emotional strain.

Meanwhile, Mummyji has moved close to him and says, "According to Vishnu Purana, the ancient Hindu Holy Book, we are now in Kali-Yug, the fourth and the last epoch of human existence; what you have described are some of the signs. 1,000,000 people were massacred; no wonder there is so much smoke in the skies—with so many cremations taking place."

18

DELHI: JANUARY 1948
ASSASSINATION

Life has acquired a rhythm. We are settled in a routine. I am of school going age. The school year is already started. As we are not sure where we are going to settle down, Mummyji has started a small school where she teaches the children of refugees. Three neighborhood boys attend; including me, we are four. The mothers bring their children at 10 A.M. They sit around as the class is going on, and go home at 12 P.M.

This eventful Evening:

During most evenings, all my classmates and I play in the street. It is a regular January evening. It is close to 6 P.M. It is getting a bit cool. Households are starting to cook the evening meal. Our coachman, Sabua, and his son, are lighting a fire in their hearth; using the dried horse dung cakes and some coal he borrows from Uncle SK's servant. Windows of nearby homes are open. The characteristic tune of All India Radio is floating out the windows, while the smoke from Sabua's hearth is floating in. Due to a mass of cold air that engulfs the city in January, the smoke is seen to be floating like clouds. Four of us are playing a game of *Pithoo*—two on each side. All four of us have nick names that we call each other by; A1, B1, C2 and D2 etc. Why this strange nomenclature? It follows from the class that Mummyji teaches. We learn the English alphabet and numerals in the class. Mummyji has decided that we will give each other nick-names using alphabets and numerals. The interesting part is that we change our nick names everyday. The challenge is to remember them. The addition of all four numbers must add up to the date of the month. Today is January 30, 1948. The nick names are A 13, B7, C7 and D3 (13+7+7+3=30). A13 and B7 are on one side, and C7 and D3 on the other. My name is D3, and C7 is my partner. A13 is older than the rest of us and is bigger and better built. He throws the rubber ball at *the Pithoo*—a pile of six or seven pieces of flat rocks. As soon as the ball hits the *Pithoo,* the pile breaks, and the ball bounces and hits the glass pane of the window of a nearby house. The signature tune of the All India Radio Delhi comes to an abrupt stop. As soon as the glass shatters in one house, there are screams from inside the house where the radio is playing. All four of us are stunned and scared. We look at each other. A13, who threw the ball, stands still, and we see water flowing down his knickers. After that, all hell breaks loose; not only on our street, but all over India. Not because of a pane of broken glass but something more.

As a pane of glass broke at a non-descript street in Daryaganj area of Delhi, not only India, but the whole world finds out that Mahatma Gandhi had been shot to death about an hour earlier. An apostle of peace and non-violence met his end with violence. People pour out of their homes and fill the streets. All our family also comes out on the street. Daddyji is not home, Mummyji is worried. As soon as she finds out that Mahatma Gandhi has been assassinated at Birla House, she goes into a panic. Daddyji has gone in that area to meet somebody, and had told Mummyji that he will attend the prayer meeting that takes place every evening.

Uncle SK tells some neighbours. "Let us hope the killer is not a Muslim; otherwise, Hindus will not leave a single Muslim alive."

And then, one of the neighbours comes running from his house shouting, "Two Hindu men, named Nathuram Godse and Narayan Apte, shot Mahatma Gandhi."

Everybody heaves a sigh of relief. Nevertheless, Mummyji is standing outside with other ladies of the neighbourhood, waiting for Daddyji to arrive. Her face is full of worry. In her mind she is assuming: What if there are riots along the way, and Daddyji is caught in the middle. Devika Massi consoles her, "Kamla everything will be all right. You believe in God, so have faith in Him. There is no report on the radio of any disturbance. The streets are full of mourners, but there are no riots."

All four of us friends are also standing around the adults not knowing how to react. We almost feel as if we caused the tragedy with our ball. My friend

A13, who threw the ball, says, "I think we should stop playing with the ball... You know I have heard that number 13 is inauspicious. We should not use the number 13 again."

C7 replies, "My house number is 13B. What are we supposed to do? Change the house number?"

As we are talking, Daddyji's Tonga rolls in. As soon as he gets down, he is surrounded by the neighbours and one of them asks, "Surinder, were you present at the prayer at Birla House?"

"Well, yes I was there... Let me have some water." Mummyji goes in the house and brings a glass of water. After having a sip, he continues, "I reached there before 5 P.M. Sita Ram, my coachman, dropped me off right in front of the gate of Birla House and then went and stationed the Tonga on the opposite side under a tree. I walked down the walkway to the grounds. People were arriving on foot, in Tongas and cars. I was just walking around waiting for Gandhiji to arrive. A newspaper photographer was walking around, also waiting. I started a conversation with him. He pointed out two men standing beside a wall talking to each other. He told me that one of them was an American reporter, and the other was the Delhi correspondent of the BBC. I was not surprised to hear this. Newsmen from around the world visited India to report on the partition. The photographer told me that he frequently covers the prayer meeting and Gandhiji is very punctual, but today he was late. At about 5:15 P.M., Gandhiji walked in, leaning on two girls and followed by other devotees. He was wrapped in homespun shawls of *Khadi*. He just walked by me. I felt my body becoming warm as he passed by. I just could not believe that I am standing so close to him. I started walking behind his entourage."

Daddyji stops talking for a few minutes. The neighbours, who are standing around him, stay motionless. There is silence. A few of them have tears rolling down their cheeks. After a while, Mummyji realizes that Daddyji is overcome with emotion and is just unable to talk.

"Listen ji, have some water," she says.

He takes a few sips and continues to describe the last few moments in the life of beloved *Bapu,* the father of our nation.

"Gandhiji climbed a few steps to the prayer ground. A small group of people milled around and in front of him, some standing and some kneeling to offer respects. I was barely ten feet away. And then, I saw two men move to the front, right close to him and facing him. One of them joined his hands together in the traditional Hindu greeting, Namaste, took out a pistol, extended his hand and fired a number of shots. A well built man in the front got hold of him and wrestled him to the ground. People started screaming and running. The photographer started to take pictures... Just at that moment, I felt a rush of warmth passing through my body... I heard the words Hey Ram... as if Gandhiji's soul passed by me... I felt dizzy and sat down. I don't remember anything until I found myself in the Tonga, and Sitaram was trying to shake me into consciousness. He was saying: Sahib, wake up it is me; Sitaram... Sitaram... these are the words of Gandhiji's favorite hymn... and then... I woke up"

Everybody is silent for a few minutes. A number of neighbours move close to him. They touch him and his hands, and then touch their own face with their hands to receive the blessings of the noble departed soul of Gandhiji. All India Radio is only playing hymns. And as the tune of one of Gandhiji's favorite hymns floats out of one of the houses, everybody joins in.

Eventually, everybody moves indoors to their respective homes. We go inside Uncle SK's home on the ground floor of the building. The radio is still playing religious hymns.

Daddyji takes off his glasses, closes his eyes and covers them with his cupped hands to relax and asks, "SK sahib, when do you think the cremation will take place?"

"Well, it will have to be tomorrow."

"Don't you think they will wait for foreign dignitaries to arrive?"

"Well, I don't know if any member of the Royal family will come to attend, or Mountbattens will stand in for the Royals. After all he is the Viceroy."

"I would like to go to the cremation to pay my respects."

Uncle SK does not seem interested and says, "Well it all depends on where it is going to take place. It will be difficult to move around the city tomorrow. There will be large crowds everywhere."

Suddenly, the radio stops playing hymns and an announcer comes on, "Ladies and gentlemen, the Prime Minister of India, Pundit Jawaharlal Nehru."

The speech is delivered in English:

Friends and Comrades, the light has gone out of our lives and there is darkness everywhere. I do not know what to tell you and how to say it. Our beloved leader, Bapu as we called him, the Father of the Nation, is no more. Perhaps I am wrong to say that. Nevertheless, we will never see him again as we have seen him for these many years. We will not run to him for advice and seek solace from him, and that is a terrible blow, not to me only, but to millions and millions in this country. And it is a little difficult to soften the blow by any other advice that I or anyone else can give you.........

All of us listen to the speech spell bound, but with tears and sobs punctuating the speech.

• • •

From about 9 A.M. onwards, crowds have begun to collect. We see people walking past our house to the river banks. By early afternoon, crowds have swelled to hundreds of thousands. Daddyji and Uncle SK decide to attend the cremation ceremony. They leave the house at about 12 P.M., and walk to the cremation ground that is within walking distance from our home. Mummyji and Devika Massi stay at home. We all go to the third storey to watch the procession that is supposed to pass by very close to our house. At about 3 P.M., we can see the procession moving ever so slowly towards the River Yamuna. We can see a long green colored military vehicle carrying the body of Gandhiji. It is being pulled by rows of army personnel, with hundreds of more army soldiers leading and following. Three planes of the Indian Air Force fly past the area and shower flowers on the procession. Slowly, the procession moves past our house and then outside of our visual range. After a while, we all go inside our room and turn the radio on to listen to the eye witness account of the cremation ceremony: It looks like about one million people have gathered to say good bye to Gandhiji. Lord Mountbatten, in full military uniform, and Lady Mountbatten are sitting on the ground next to Jawaharlal Nehru, Indira Gandhi and other Indian leaders. Gandhiji's body is laid on a pyre of sandalwood. As soon as the pyre is lit by Gandhiji's son, Ramdas, the vast crowd groans, the women wail, the men weep.

Daddyji and Uncle SK return home at about 7 P.M.; they are emotionally and physically exhausted. Everybody has an early dinner and we all go to bed.

• • •

Daddyji is thinking and is slowly falling asleep, but his mind is swirling: *Oh God, what a twist you have given to the events. You took away the Peacemaker. The word 'twist' sticks in his mind. For some strange reason he is reminded of Swami Ravi Anand of Verinag and his concept of Kaal or Time as a stretched sheet of fabric and past and present all etched on it. But who has done the etching? God? Did He etch the death of 1,000,000 people? No... no it is 1,000,001... million and one, including Gandhiji. No, no, Gandhiji is not just a statistic. His death is a tragedy. Somebody important has said that you can't add a tragedy to the statistics. It seems the fabric of Kaal —Time got twisted accidently and 1,000,000 souls just disappeared from earth... Just like somebody washing his face and wiping it with a handkerchief and 1,000,000... one million germs gone! Use a mouth wash and 1,000,000 germs killed. Human beings seem to be nothing but germs... and it makes perfect sense... When things become real dirty in the world, like in Kalyug, the epoch of darkness, God has to wash the Kaal-Time fabric to clean it... Twist Twister Twisted, and twist it hard to wring out all the dirt ...When the Kaal-Time fabric gets twisted, the past becomes the future and the future the past... oh and... then all the souls get reincarnated with new ration cards.*

19
HORSING AROUND

Daddyji gets up in the morning with a headache. Sabua, the coachman, comes upstairs, "Sahib, a terrible thing happened last night."
"Eh, Sabua what more can go wrong?"
"Sahib, Julius left us last night."
"What? Wasn't he tied?"
"No Sahib, he has not run away..... he has left us for his heavenly abode."
"Oh Sabua, you idiot, horses don't go to heaven."
"Sahib, why not? He did so much service to the human race. He was a nice horse. He deserves the best."

Daddyji appears flabbergasted by this turn of events. All kinds of questions rush through his mind. How to dispose of the body? Should he purchase another horse? Also, he suddenly realizes that Sabua has made a profound statement. Horses have been serving humanity for time immemorial; so much so that, in Physics, the units of Work are known as Horse Power. It has been the most useful animal for the human race. If any beings are entitled to a place in heaven, it has to be horses. With these thoughts in mind, he is calls for Mummyji:
"Kamla... Kamla, Julius has died. What should we do?"
She comes hurriedly out of the room, "Oh, Sabua, how did he die?"
"*Bibiji,* it looks like a snake bite."
"How can a small snake kill such a large animal as a horse?"
"*Bibiji,* how would I know? I am not a *Dunger* Doctor."
"I think, we will have to call in a veterinary doctor. I want to find out the cause of death of Julius because I don't want Romeo, Anthony and Shylock to meet the same fate."

Daddyji takes a quick bath, dresses up and goes downstairs to see the situation. He finds that the neighbours are all milling around looking at dead Julius. He walks around Julius, and Sabua points out the suspected snake bite.

"Sabua, if there is a snake around, that means that other horses are in danger also."

"Sahib, you are sixteen *annas* right—hundred percent correct."

"Sabua, what do you suggest we do now?"

"Sahib, I have been a coachman for 20 years. I have seen all types of problems with horses. The first thing we have to do is to dispose of the body. I know some *Chamaars*. As you know they deal in leather. We should let them take the body."

"All right Sabua, go ahead and do the needful."

Sabua gets one Tonga ready and goes away to bring the *Chamaars*.

In the meantime, other coachmen also arrive and are surprised to learn that Julius has died. They look around the dead body and give their individual opinions about the cause of death. By early afternoon, Sabua is back, and is followed, a little while later, by a number of men with a bullock cart and ropes. They tie ropes around Julius's body and drag it over to the bullock cart. The cart is pulled with two bulls. After about two hours of effort, Julius's body is taken way.

"Sabua, what should we do about the snake?"

"Sahib, we will have to find a snake charmer to catch the snake, but they are not easy to find. I will take one Tonga and go around some places and see if I can find one."

At about 3 P.M. Sabua arrives with a snake charmer sitting in the rear seat of the Tonga. The snake charmer gets off the Tonga and brings down two baskets, a pole and a *Been* or *Pungi*—a wind musical instrument. He starts to play the *Been* and takes the covers off the baskets. The tune floating out of the *Been* mesmerizes the two snakes in the baskets. The snakes come out of the baskets and start to crawl on the ground. The snake charmer gets up and moves around the area, while he is playing the *Been;* trying to charm the wild snakes out of their hiding places. After about fifteen minutes of effort, the snake charmer announces that, in his opinion, there is no snake in the immediate vicinity; otherwise, it would have come out. Daddyji is disappointed.

He asks the snake charmer, "What should we do now?"

"Sahib, I will give you an antidote that you should give to the remaining horses; it is supposed to protect against some snake bites."

Daddyji buys the medicine wrapped in a package made from an old newspaper. After the snake charmer leaves, Sabua tells him, "Sahib, I think we should not give this medicine to the horses. God knows what concoction is in this packet."

After some discussion, Daddyji decides to take Sabua's advice not to give the concoction to the horses. It is quite a large packet, and he decides to open it and look at the contents. The packet contains powder that appears to be turmeric powder, by look and smell.

"Come, Sabua. Have a look at this,"

"Sahib, this looks and smells like turmeric powder; it must be turmeric powder."

Daddyji is disgusted that he has been sold one *paisa* worth of turmeric powder for one rupee.

He picks up the discarded newspaper cover and looks at it, while he is thinking:... *Is nobody honest around here?*

There is a news item in the piece of newspaper in his hand that catches his attention. He is able to read only a part of it; the rest of it is covered with the turmeric powder. Only part he can read is... "Thousands of orphan children... looking for homes." He holds on to the newspaper and decides to look at it later.

"All right Sabua, keep an eye on things at night." And Daddyji goes up to our room at the third storey to think things over. He goes into the room, sits down on the bed and cleans the part of the newspaper that is of interest to him so that he can read it. The news item states: Thousands of children have become orphans because of the riots. A number of charitable organizations have set up camps and orphanages to look after the children and find suitable adoptive parents for the orphans. He is surprised and impressed to read that Lady Mountbatten, the wife of the Governor General, is the president and patron of numerous such organizations and takes active role in visiting and directing them.

"Kamla, come and read this. See how so many generous and kind people are looking after the destitute women and orphans, and we are so absorbed in our day to day problems. Here, we are distressed by the death of a horse, and out there thousands of people have lost their loved ones."

Mummyji is busy lighting a fire in the hearth and has not heard a thing Daddyji has said.

"Are you listening Kamla? We should also do something for our community."

• • •

Two weeks have passed.

Daddyji is just waking up in the morning, when he hears Sabua coughing outside the room clearing his throat as if getting ready to say something, "Sahib, it is me Sabua."

"What is it?" Daddyji gets up from the bed, opens the door and comes out on the roof terrace. He is bracing himself for some more bad news.

"Sahib, something unbelievable has happened. I know you will blame me, but I did not hear anything. We just slept through it all. They must have made me inhale something, while I and my son, Babua, were asleep, to make me unconscious; otherwise, I must have heard it."

"Oh, Sabua what the hell has happened? You are killing me with suspense," Daddyji says.

Sabua sits down and starts to weep loudly like a child. Daddyji thinks, may be his son, Babua, has died.

"Oh, Sabua at least tell me what has happened?"

"Sahib, I swear by my son, Babua; I had nothing to do with this. If I am lying, may God reincarnate me as a lizard."

Now Daddyji knows that it is not his son who has died; otherwise, he would not be swearing by him. Daddyji goes close to where Sabua is sitting and sobbing. Sabua suddenly gets hold of Daddyji's feet and begs forgiveness for what has happened. He, then, slowly gets up and leads Daddyji downstairs and out of the building in the area where the stable is located.

And then he starts to weep loudly, "Sahib, they are all gone; Romeo, Anthony and Shylock. Somebody stole them last night."

Daddyji says, "What are you saying, Sabua? How is this possible? I have never heard of anybody stealing horses."

"Sahib, I have been in this business for over twenty years, I have seen this happen before."

"You idiot, why did you not tell me before; we could have taken some precautions."

"Sahib, I used to tie them securely at night. I don't know what happened. Are you going to call the Police?"

"I don't know… I don't know what we are going to do."

Uncle SK, after hearing all the commotion outside his window, also comes out.

"Surinder, what has happened?"

"All our horses got stolen last night."

Uncle SK asks Daddyji to come inside with him and says, "You know Surinder, this bastard, Sabua is a crook. I think he has arranged all this in collusion with some thieves. Now they know that you have no horses left, they will try and buy the Tongas from you for nothing."

And sure enough, that is what happens. After a few days have passed, Sabua comes up to our room and says, "Sahib, two men have come to see you. They are interested in buying the Tongas."

Daddyji goes downstairs to meet the two men. As he is talking to them, Uncle SK also comes outside, and a deal is struck to sell the horseless Tongas.

Uncle SK says, "Surinder, I have an idea. I can get you some money from insurance."

Daddyji is puzzled, "How will you do that?"

"I will get you a commercial insurance policy for the Tongas. But, we will have to back date it. One of my friends is an insurance agent; it should not be a problem. After that, you will report that the horses have been stolen. I will process the claim for the insurance company, and you will get the insured amount."

Daddyji is not surprised that Uncle SK has made such an outrageous proposal, but he decides to keep quiet and ignore it. The Tongas provided him hope and some income; both have disappeared. Also he was genuinely attached to his horses, having named them after his favorite characters from the Shakespearean plays. They offered some connection to his passion. However, it is all gone now, and he remains depressed as he has nothing much to do and very little income; except from the report writing he does for Uncle SK.

"Listen ji, don't be despondent. I have seen the future; it is very bright. In fact, it is so bright that I have to wear my sunglasses to see it." Mummyji is using the same technique Daddyji uses on her to cheer him up.

20

PLANE TO LAHORE

Daddyji is busy writing a report in Uncle SK's office. While he is writing, he starts to think about all the cash and jewelry they have left in the bank locker in Lahore. There is a knock at the door and a man walks in. "Come on in, Imran. Have a seat." Uncle SK says.

"Meet Surinder, my brother-in-law and my adviser-in-English." And he laughs at his own oddity.

Daddyji and Imran shake hands, and Imran sits down on a *Moorah*—a round drum-like stool made from bamboo—the only seat in the room, which seems to have disappeared under Imran's large bottoms. Imran is a large man of small height with unusually large hands.

Imran Khan says, "SK sahib, I am going to Lahore within the next few days. General Insurance Company has asked me to survey some of the damages to the properties they have policies on."

"Is it safe to go there?"

"Yes, I am told that things have settled down. Due to the shock of Mahatma Gandhi's assassination, the riots between Hindus and Muslims have almost stopped. Isn't it an ironical twist of events that an apostle of non-violence meets his end by violent means, and that results in the cessation of violence?"

"How do you plan to travel?"

"Bharat Airways has direct flights to Lahore. I plan to leave some time next week, depending on availability of seats, of course."

"Imran, Surinder has left a small treasure in a bank locker in Lahore; why don't you take him along so that he can retrieve his fortune." Uncle SK says jokingly.

"My uncle is with the National Bank; may be he can help."

As soon as Daddyji hears the name of a bank, he suddenly jumps up and says, "Imran *bhai,* can you really help?"

"If you give me the necessary papers, I can certainly try."

"I will go and get the papers from our room upstairs."

He goes upstairs and tells the whole story to Mummyji.

"What if he takes off with everything? He is a Muslim, and we are Hindus. What if he decides to stay in Pakistan? You should talk it over with SK before you give him the papers."

"Kamla, there is no time. How will I ask SK? Imran is sitting there also. SK seems to know him well. We have lost the money anyway, why not take a chance? Kamla, Imran seems like a decent man."

"OK. OK. You take out the papers and the key, and I will go downstairs and ask sister Devika about Imran?"

Mummyji goes downstairs and finds her sister and tells her the story and asks, "Devika is Imran a reliable man?"

"Don't worry Kamla; we have known him for years. He is a gentleman."

Mummyji meets Daddyji in the courtyard. He is waiting there with the bank papers in hand. Mummyji says to him, "Devika is sure Imran is a reliable man."

Daddyji goes back to Uncle SK's office, "Imran *bhai,* here are the papers and the key to the locker. I have a copy of the Power of Attorney I had given to my father, and I will also write a letter giving you the authority to operate the account and the safety deposit box."

After some time, Imran Khan collects all the papers and gets up, "I will be taking your leave now. I hope to be back in about a week. *Insha Allah,* I will come back with the little treasure."

They all get up and embrace each other and say, "*Shabba Khair*"—God will take care."

• • •

Imran Khan leaves his home at 8 A.M. in order to board the flight to Lahore that departs at 11 A.M. He reaches the Willingdon Aerodrome by 9 A.M. He realizes that there will be delays at the airport. The two newly born countries, India and Pakistan, have just started operating as separate entities. The procedures for trans-border travel have not yet been fully established. Imran has a letter from his employer and his ration card to indicate Delhi as his place of domicile. It has been raining since early morning with strong winds. He has been told by the airline staff that the flight will not take off until the weather clears up. He deposits his suitcase with the airline, picks up his hand bag and walks over to a nearby tea stall outside the airport to have some samosas and tea. He looks up at the sky and sees some parting of the clouds, raising his hope that the flight may take off earlier. While having tea, he looks at the magnificent building of Safdarjung's Tomb nearby. He briefly thinks of the days of the grandeur of the Moghul Empire, finishes his tea and walks back to the aerodrome building.

The plane, a DC3 Dakota, finally takes off at about 3 P.M. As the plane ascends into the clouds, he is imagining an artificial line—the Radcliffe Line—in the clouds where the newly born India ends and Pakistan begins.

He is thinking: *The birds do not have to respect such boundaries. What a view from up here; the birds must enjoy. I wonder what the birds must think of us humans when they look down at the proverbial Bird's Eye View.*

Once in a while, he is known to dabble in poetry. He opens his hand bag, takes out paper and pencil, and begins to write in Urdu. The title of the poem in Urdu is: *Parindoun ka Nazaria.*

English Translation:

A Bird's Eye View

Birds flying in the brown smoky sky,
Looking down at us,
They must wonder
At the thunder down-under.

The noise, the dust, the smoke,
The fires and explosions,
Humans moving around in smoking boxes of steel,
Humans must love smoke,
The birds must wonder.

What a species these humans,
The birds must wonder.
Living in smoking cubes,
Flying around in smoking metal tubes,
Trying their best to kill each other,

With Nukes.
What on earth is going on?
They must wonder.

Birds must wonder,
What a species, these humans,
A God's blunder.

I wish we could look
At ourselves
With a bird's eye view.
Take a green leaf
Out of the birds' book.
And live our lives as they do.
The birds,
God's wonder.

The plane arrives at Lahore at about 5 P.M. Imran hires a private car to take him to his Uncle's house in the Krishan Nagar area of Lahore. As the car is winding its way through the crowded areas of the city, a few hoodlums stop the car, pull the driver and Imran out of the car and take them into a nearby house. They are looking for Hindus. As the leaders of the hoodlums are not sure who Imran is, both Imran and the driver are asked to take off their clothes to check if they are circumcised or not—a sure distinction between Hindus and Muslims at the time. They both are found to be Muslims and set free. Imran finally reaches his Uncle's home all shaken up.

"I thought the madness of Hindu-Muslim killing was over," He tells his uncle.

"Well, things are much better now, but there are still a few madmen who sometimes take things in their own hands."

"Uncle, a relative of an old friend of mine left his valuables in a locker in the Punjab National Bank when they migrated to Delhi. They have given me the key and written authorization. Do you think I will be allowed to take the contents of the locker back to Delhi?"

"Well, the registered office of the Bank was moved to Delhi in June 1947, but they are still operating in Lahore. I know the manager. I will be happy to accompany you and see what can be done."

One day, they go to see the Bank Manager. After looking at all the papers and with the surety provided by his uncle, the Bank Manager allows Imran to take out all the contents of the locker. The contents are removed in the presence of the Bank Manager, an itemized list is prepared, and Imran and his uncle have to sign the receipt of the contents. Five thousand rupees cash and considerable amount of gold jewelry is found in the bank locker.

Imran tells the Bank Manager, "I think it will be difficult for me to carry so much cash on my person. Do you think you can give me a bank draft or some other financial instrument that is negotiable in India?"

"Yes, we can prepare a bank draft payable to Surinder Mehra in Delhi."

"Oh, I think that would be marvelous."

Imran asks the Bank Manager, "What do you think is the best way to carry the jewelry? Would I be permitted by the government of Pakistan to take it out of the country?"

"There should not be any problem. I don't think anybody is going to question it. There are still quite a lot of people migrating back and forth between India and Pakistan, and they are allowed to take their belongings without restriction."

After finishing his insurance business, he takes the return flight to Delhi. The plane lands in Delhi at about 7 P.M. As he comes out of the aerodrome building, and as he is going to cross the road to hire a taxi, a black cat crosses his path. He just stops in his tracks. He is very superstitious. He goes back into the building and sits down on a chair for a while. He believes that if one lets fifteen minutes pass, without undertaking any task, the curse of black cat crossing one's path withers away. After a while he gets up, having, supposedly, shed himself of the 'black cat spell' and walks out of the building to find transportation to his home. He finds a private taxi with the driver standing beside it.

"I am looking for a taxi," Imran enquires.

"Where are you going, sir?"

"I am going towards Darayagunj side."

The driver opens the door for him, puts his luggage in the dickey of the car, and they are on their way.

It is getting dark. Imran is concerned about passing through some older areas of Delhi to get home. He makes sure that the car doors are locked. The driver informs him that some of the roads have been closed to allow passage of Prime Minister Jawaharlal Nehru's and the Governor General Lord Mountbatten's cars. The driver takes a detour through some older congested areas that Imran had wanted to avoid. These are predominantly Hindu areas and were the scene of trouble for Muslims living in these areas. As the car is snaking its way through narrow lanes, it is stopped by a group of miscreants. The driver tries to keep moving, but some of the men get on top of the bonnet of the car and the driver has no choice but to stop. The hoodlums signal the driver and Imran to get out of the car and open the dickey of the car. They both comply, reluctantly. One of the men, who appears to be the leader, asks Imran to empty out his handbag. Imran takes out everything, but leaves the package of gold jewelry in the bag. The man takes hold of the handbag, turns it over and tries to empty it out by shaking it; and out falls the bundle of jewelry. Imran's heart starts to pump rapidly, his mouth is dry, and his mind is racing trying to come up with some way of saving the jewelry.

He thinks of saying something. He thinks that if he tells the Hindu boys that he had gone to Lahore to retrieve the jewelry for a Hindu friend of his as a favour, they may appreciate it and may let him go. He tells them the whole story. The leader of the hoodlums says, "Sir, you are a gentleman and obviously rich. We will let you go as long as we keep this little treasure," pointing to the bundle of gold ornaments.

He is thinking: *What would SK and Surinder say? They will think that I have stolen the gold jewelry. But at least I have the bank draft.*

Imran pleads with the hoodlums to give the jewelry back, "Please, I beg of you to return the jewelry. My honour is at stake. My friends will think I am a crook."

"Eh, Muslim sahib, you are worried about your honour? You should be worried about your life that we can take in a minute if we want to. We are letting you go because you went on a mission to help one of our Hindu brothers."

Imran realizes the limitations of his choice. The leader of the hoodlums signals to Imran to enter the car and leave. Imran gets into the car and asks the driver to drives away.

• • •

Uncle SK and Daddyji are sitting down writing an incident report for the insurance company. Imran knocks at the door and walks in. Both Daddyji and Uncle SK get up to greet Imran.

Imran walks in and slumps into a chair without any greetings and fanfare.

"What is the matter Imran? Is everything all right?" Uncle SK asks.

"Well, no."

Imran narrates the whole story to both of them. Daddyji's immediate thought is: What would Mummyji say about losing her jewelry. Nevertheless, he is happy that, at least, Imran has brought five thousands rupees back from Lahore.

Uncle SK says, "Oh, professor sahib, you are a lucky man, and suddenly you have become a rich man also. I think we should have a *Jashan*. You get a few chickens and some bottles of Solan Lager, and I promise that I will cook *chicken Korma,* the like of which you have not eaten before."

The party is on for the evening. Daddyji goes upstairs to our room to tell Mummyji that Imran has lost her jewelry, but he immediately shows her the bank draft to soften the blow.

"Are you sure he is not making up a story about losing the jewelry?"

He replies, "If he had to steal, he would not have given us the bank draft."

"Well, he had no choice in the case of the draft because he can't cash it."

"Look Kamla, there is nothing we can do about the jewelry. We have received a lot of money that we had taken for lost. You know how much five thousand rupees is? It is two years worth of salary of a professor. Let us thank God for all the blessings. We have come through the most violent time in the history of our country relatively unscathed. All our family is intact. We have a roof over our head, and we have enough to eat. And look at our two handsome sons—our Golden Sparrows."

They all enjoy the party in the evening.

However, Mummyji does not forget the jewelry. She keeps talking about the bangles that she had received from such and such aunt; the necklace she had received from another of her aunts; and the earrings that her brother, Daulat Ram, had given her when she had completed her B.A.B.T; and then she starts to weep. And after reciting all that time and time again for the next many days, she would start to weep again and again.

I am thinking: *What a love for jewelry my mother has?*

One day, she is sitting down stitching buttons on to Daddyji's shirt. She suddenly gives out a shriek and puts her finger in her mouth to sooth the needle prick. Here we go again, I am thinking; she is starting to weep again and I say, "Mummyji, when I grow up and start making money, I will buy you all the jewelry you want. But for the time being, here is my piggy bank."

She looks at me lovingly, embraces me and starts to weep again.

"I told you Mummyji; I will buy lots of jewelry for you when I grow up."

"Silly boy, I am not weeping because I lost my jewelry. It is the emotions that are attached to the pieces of jewelry that are distressing me."

I am all of six years old. What do I know about emotions, attachments and all that and I say, "Mummyji, I will buy you all the emotions and attachments also."

She kisses me on my right cheek and starts to smile.

"Promise me Mummyji, you will not weep again."

"Promise!"

21
APRIL 1948
ACCOMMODATIONS

It is only April and the temperature is already soaring into the nineties and the anxiety level even higher. Daddyji comes into our one-room flat after climbing three storeys and says, "Kamla, I met the landlord downstairs. He says that his sister in coming in two weeks; we will have to vacate the flat."

"It is good that we are being forced to vacate. Now we will have to find some other accommodation. I am tired of climbing three storeys five times a day," Mummyji says.

Daddyji explains, "With the influx of millions of refugees, living accommodation is very hard to find. I have made enquiries about any flats to-let in the immediate vicinity but without success. You want to live in the Darayagunj area, close to your relatives, but there is nothing available here. I will talk to SK."

In the evening, Daddyji goes downstairs to see uncle SK. He is sitting on his old typewriter punching away. Daddyji sits down beside him. As Uncle SK looks up, Daddyji says in a dejected tone of voice, "SK sahib, we are in a quandary. The landlord wants us to vacate in two weeks. How are we…"

Daddyji has not even finished the sentence, and uncle SK say, "Oh, professor sahib," as he fondly likes to address Daddyji, "Not to worry; what are we for? You are always welcome to our humble abode. If you cannot find a flat, we will make do somehow."

"SK sahib, thank you very much, it is with your support that we have survived."

"Oh, please mention not," Uncle SK says in his characteristic English.

• • •

This day, Daddyji and Mummyji decide to visit, her brother, Daulat Ram and his family. They live within about fifteen minutes walk from where we live. We all get ready at about 11 A.M. and walk over to his house.

When we reach there, the front door of the house is open. There are two cars parked in the lane in front of the house with their respective drivers cleaning the cars. The black Austin is what Daulat Ram had bought a few months after moving to Delhi. The other car is a maroon coloured Morris. Daddyji stops beside the cars to admire their styling.

"Kamla, I think your brother has some visitors." And we enter the house as Daddyji is still saying this. We are met in the courtyard by Nirmala, Daulat Ram's wife.

Mummyji asks her, "Whose car is it outside?"

"Oh, your brother has invited David Rankin and his friend for lunch. They are sitting upstairs in the drawing room."

The ladies go to a room at the ground floor to continue their chat, and Kishi and I start playing in the courtyard with our cousins. In the meantime, as Daulat Ram hears the voices on the ground floor, he appears in the balcony that looks down into the courtyard and calls Daddyji to join them upstairs.

As Daddyji enters the drawing room, all three men stand up to greet him.

Daulat Ram does the introduction, "Meet David Rankin; Surinder, you remember he attended your marriage. And this is his friend, James Griffiths."

Daddyji shakes hands with them, and David Rankin blurts out with a smile, "Oh, hello *Shakespearewala!*" And they all have a hearty laugh, and he explains the context to James Griffiths.

"So, how is flat hunting going, Surinder?" Daulat Ram asks.

"It is not going well. There is no game to hunt. We have to move out in less than two weeks. But, SK has offered to accommodate us for as long as we are unable find any suitable accommodation."

"Surinder," Daulat Ram say, "You are invited to move in with us anytime. We have plenty of accommodation. You can live with us as long as you like. Don't forget that this is your in-law's house; you have the right," And he laughs and carries on, "After all, I have to make sure that my sister and her family are well looked after." And he laughs again. May be it is the beer, but he is always laughing when he has company. And then he turns his attention to David Rankin, "So Mr. Rankin, how do you spend your time nowadays?"

"Well, you know, there is a lot of paper work to clear up, and my wife and I are also involved in work at some refugee camps and orphanages. As you know, the carnage that preceded and followed the Independence left hundreds of thousands, if not millions, homeless and thousands of orphaned children."

Daddyji suddenly remembers that he had read in the newspaper about this, and he is very interested to find out more, "Mr. Rankin, I read about it a few weeks back. We would like to help in some way. I know that thousands of orphaned children and women are living in refugee camps."

"There is a camp, not too far from here; it is just across the road from where Mahatma Gandhi was cremated."

"Can we just go there to see the place?"

David Rankin replies, "Yes, you can do that, and you may use me as a reference."

Lunch is served at 1 P.M. The menfolk have lunch in the upper floor dining room, while the women and children eat downstairs in the kitchen. After lunch, the menfolk again move back into the drawing room for desserts and conversation.

Daulat Ram asks, "Mr. Rankin, what do you think is going to happen in Kashmir?

He replies, "As you know, fighting is going on between the armies of India and Pakistan. And, as we speak, debate is going on in the United Nations Security Council. You know, Mr. Suri, I think Kashmir is going to become a bone of contention between India and Pakistan for a long time to come."

Daddyji says, "We were hoping that, after the riots are over, things will settle down, and we will move on with our new lives."

David Rankin says, "The world has been in some form of conflict or the other since 1939. After the War was over in 1945, we were hoping for a protracted period of peace, but a new type of war started just after the VJ day."

Daddyji adds, "Are you talking about the riots between Hindus and Muslims in India?"

"No, no, I am talking about the Cold War, the war for public opinion, between Russia and the Allies."

Daulat Ram asks, "So how did the Cold War start? After all, they were all on the same side in the War."

"Well, it is a story that I think started in Canada. If I remember correctly, it was in September 1945. A cypher clerk, in the Russian Embassy in Ottawa, Canada, named Igor Gouzenko defected and brought with him documents that proved that Russia had an extensive network of spies in Canada, the United States and Britain. This was made public by the Canadian Government in February 1946. They say that this is the incident that sparked the Cold War."

As soon as he hears the words Ottawa, Canada, Daddyji cuts into the conversation even before David Rankin could finish the story and says, "Sorry for the interruption, I want to tell you something that you will find interesting. In April 1943, we were visiting Kashmir, and we met a Canadian couple from Ottawa, Canada. They were working for the Canadian Government."

James Griffiths and David Rankin look at each other hurriedly, as if to say: Let us pursue it further.

David Rankin says, "Surinder, this is interesting; tell us more about it."

Daddyji has noticed them looking at each other and decides not to tell anything further. To change the topic, he asks, "Mr. Rankin, what were the Soviets looking for through the network of spies in the western countries?"

David Rankin realizes that he has been outsmarted and replies, "Well, I think they were looking for nuclear secrets. You know, they are lagging behind. They have still not tested a nuclear device."

David Rankin takes the last few sips from his cup of tea and gets up and says, "We should make a move. Mrs. Rankin must be home by now. She was visiting some of the refugee camps."

All four of them get up, go outside the room and start walking down the staircase, while engaging in small talk at the same time—nothing in particular, just weather. My brother Kishi and I are playing in the courtyard; and as they are descending down the stairs, the sound of their voices becomes progressively louder. For the first time in my life, I notice that Englishmen speak differently than Indians. They speak the words, as if their mouth is full of air and in melodious tones; especially, when they are ending a sentence. Indians speak their English in a way that almost sounds as if they are speaking Hindi. I am fascinated by the way the Englishmen speak. After they have left the house, I try to speak like the Englishmen, just to see if I can. I also notice that when Daddyji and Daulat Ram are in the company of Englishmen, they speak English differently than when they are speaking to each other.

After the Englishmen have left, Daddyji asks Daulat Ram, "Is David Rankin with Delhi Police now?"

"No. He told me in Lahore before we left that he will be going back to Britain after spending some time in Delhi, but now he seems to have changed his mind. He says he has got a job with a British company; James Griffiths is his boss just visiting from Britain."

• • •

When they are driving back, James Griffiths says, "David, that brother-in-law of Daulat Ram, Surinder, seems to be fairly well informed. What do you think about him?"

"What do you mean?"

Before replying, James Griffiths points towards the Indian driver of the car asking silently, with a sign, if the driver is reliable.

David Rankin replies, "He is deaf, and he speaks very little. He has been with me for over ten years."

"I was talking about the brother-in-law. You know, he could be useful for us in the future. What does he do for a living?"

"He used to be a professor of English in a private college in Lahore; I am not sure what he is doing now."

"He speaks good English and is a presentable chap. Why don't you get him a job with Bond & Sons? You see, that way Daulat Ram will feel obliged, and we will have better control on him. And we will be able to put Surinder to good use."

• • •

As we are all walking to our home after lunch, Daddyji is thinking about his pen friend, Max Hoffer, of Ottawa, Canada; his interest having been stirred by the conversation at lunch time. As he is thinking about what he is going to write to him about, he realizes that Mummyji does not like him even talking about Max Hoffer; she will certainly not approve of him writing a letter to Max. Although she had torn up Max Hoffer's last letter, Daddyji still has the address in his diary. As these thoughts are swirling in his mind, Mummyji says, "Listen ji, When can we go to the refugee camp and the orphanage?"

"We will go one day. Let me first concentrate on finding a flat."

As we reach home, it is time for the afternoon, after lunch, nap. We draw the curtains to make the room dark, switch the ceiling fan on and lie down. Mummyji and my younger brother, Kishi, quickly fall asleep. But as usual, I am just pretending to be asleep; in fact, I am wide awake. When Daddyji thinks we are all fast asleep, he gets up and picks up a pen and paper and starts to write, and what a speed he is writing at; his hand is moving up and down, and his arm is shaking; and he is moving his lips with no sound coming out of his mouth.

Hello Max,

I received your letter some months back, but could not reply to it as we have been on the move and trying to settle down after migrating from Lahore. A lot has happened since your last letter: India has gained independence; we have become refugees; have seen Simla and Delhi; are about to be evicted from our one room flat, which is hot like the inside of the boiler of a railway engine; I should know because my father was in the railways and he is now in Simla enjoying the cool air of the hills, while we are being cooked in the *Barsati* of a three storey house in Daryagunj area of Delhi… and now let us see what else is in store for us. And in case you don't know what a *Barsati* is; it is a room on the roof terrace of a house, where people move in when it begins to rain, when they are sleeping on the roof terrace… I am almost breathless.

Sorry for throwing all the grammar to the winds, especially for a professor of English; I am sorry, but I must finish this letter before my wife wakes up; sorry to tell you that she does not like me rehashing the dream I had on the bus to Verinag. Talking about Verinag, yes, I had a dream very similar to yours and yes again, I have the same birth date as yours, November 15, 1915, but what does that really mean, I don't know; we will see what the future brings.

I must tell you that I am impressed with Canada; having been part of the dawning of the age of nuclear fission and then, soon thereafter, sparking the age of Cold War with the help of Igor Gouzenko; just imagine hot and cold at the same time! I can see Canada being the place to spark the Cold War; being itself a very, very cold country, I mean in temperature only, not in the temperament of the people.

I am also impressed that Canada is front and centre in the Kashmir conflict between India and Pakistan. I hear one of your esteemed Generals is coming to India for mediation and peace keeping. Oh, yes, I think his name is Gen. McNaughton. I have been reading a little bit about Canada, and as I understand, one of your provinces, is totally French speaking. It is not surprising; we also have provinces in India that totally speak other languages. What I was going to say is that if Canada ever got independence like India; as you know you have the same masters as we used to have; and I should tell you that they are very fond of creating partitions of countries; so if they granted you independence, they will want to partition Canada into at least two countries; if not three. How is that, you may ask? One: English speaking; two: French speaking and three: this might come as a surprise to you; Indian. No, not our type, but the native Indian and they could also make a case for the fourth part also; Eskimo country. The British specialize in creating partitions.

In conclusion, I can only give one advice: Do not ask the British for independence, if you want to stay whole!

My wife is waking up; I must go now.

Bye.

Surinder

After mailing the letter in the evening in the neighborhood mailbox, he goes for a walk on Fiaz Road to talk to a few shopkeepers to find out if any flats are available. He wants to rent his own flat because he knows that we can live with the relatives only for so long. At first, he wanted to live near the relatives, but now he has decided to widen his search. Gupta Provision Stores is owned by Prakash Gupta, an old resident of Delhi. We have been buying provisions from his shop for the last few months, and Daddyji has formed a friendly relationship with him. In addition to stocking provisions and stationary, he also stocks medicines for common ailments—both Allopathic and Ayurvedic. In the evenings, when customers come to buy goods, they sit around and chitchat. Sometimes, Prakash sends his servant to bring hot *Chai,* from the neighbouring *Halwaii.* Some customers walk over to the *Paan* and cigarette shop next door to order their favourite *Paan*—a Betel leaf wrapped over Areca nut and slaked lime. While chewing on the *Paan* and talking, they light their cigarette with the help of a smoldering rope hanging from the ceiling of the shop. One day, Daddyji also buys two *Paans* with sweet *Supaari.* They are wrapped in a piece of old newspaper. Daddyji has developed a habit that as soon as he sees an old newspaper being used as a wrapper, he starts to read the newsprint on it. So, as soon as he gets the packet in his hands, he starts to turn it around trying to read what is written on it.

"Is there any problem with the *Paan*?" The *Paanwala* asks him.

"No, no, just trying to see if there are any advertisements for flats to-let in the newspaper."

As some of the customers are sitting around and chatting, the topic comes around to shortage of accommodation in Delhi due to the influx of refugees.

Prakash Gupta points out to a man standing outside the shop and says, "Oh, you don't have to worry about accommodation, while Chaturvedi sahib is here with us. He works with the Home Ministry."

As Chaturvedi sahib hears this, he is all smiles as if he is the Home Minister, but he is just an upper division clerk in the ministry.

And as soon as people hear the words: Home Ministry, a number of the men shout at the same time, "There are no homes available. What on earth is the ministry doing? These people working in the Home Ministry are tying red tapes around the files and just giving out accommodations to their own kith and kin. You will not find a single employee of the Home Ministry or their relatives without a place to live."

Daddyji also joins in, "Chaturvedi sahib, if you walk around any place in Delhi today, you will see people living in make shift houses made of wood with tin sheets on the roof, or tents made of bed sheets pitched in the open. People are also building houses with mud, cow dung, and any old piece of wood they can find."

Prakash Gupta says, "Chaturvedi sahib, please say something." As Chaturvedi sahib starts to speak, his speech is drowned out by the shouts of the crowd.

Prakash Gupta intervenes, "You people are complaining to Chaturvedi sahib, as if he is the Rehabilitation Minister Mehar Chand Khanna. If you have complaints, you should take them to the Minister. Chaturvedi sahib wants to help you; just listen to him."

Chaturvedi is finally able to get in a few words, "Oh please, let me at least finish what I have to say. What I was going to say is that there are flats available in the west side of Delhi in the area bound by Rohtak Road, Camp Road and Original Road. There are hundreds of quarters in that area that were built for government employees during the War. The government has given permission to the residents, who are government employees, to rent out parts of them. This will create new accommodation for hundreds of people."

Daddyji asks, "Who should we contact? Is this area called Karol Bagh?"

"Yes, the area is known as Karol Bagh. If you go in that area and go to the Enquiry Office, you will find the staff there very helpful."

Daddyji immediately gets up and goes home. He has decided that he will go tonight to look at the area and see if he can find some place to rent. As soon as he reaches home, he runs up the stairs and finds Mummyji struggling with the *Ungithi*—the coal fired hearth; she has a long steel pipe in hand and is blowing into it to light the fire.

"Kamla, I think we may have a chance to find a flat, but we will have to move to Karol Bagh area on the west side of the city."

"I don't know where this Bagh is, but I am ready to move anywhere as long as we have a roof over our head. There is just one week left to vacate this place."

How to go to Karol Bagh? That is the question. It is already evening; and by the time he takes a Tonga to go there, it will be dark and the Enquiry office may be closed.

"Kamla, if your brother, Daulat Ram, lends us his car and his driver; we can go there and, possibly, find somebody to talk to? What do you think? Should we ask him?"

She lifts her face from the *Ungithi* just long enough to say, "I think you can ask him; there is no harm."

Daddyji runs down the stairs, saying at the same time, "Kamla, get ready and get Vikram and Kishi ready also; we are going on a family outing to Karol Bagh."

In about twenty minutes, we are driving to Karol Bagh in Daulat Ram's car, with him sitting beside the driver, and our family on the rear seats. He decides to come along to see if he can be of any help; he considers his duty to help his younger sister settle down. It takes about 45 minutes to reach the area. After asking for directions, a few times, from some children playing on the streets, we finally reach the Enquiry office. It closes at 8 P.M., and we have only a few minutes to meet the officials. As the car pulls in front of the office, we see a line up of people. They all start to look at us. They are wondering, what these rich people are doing in this lower middle class neighbourhood. Just the mere confidence, with which Daulat Ram and Daddyji get out of the car and walk in with complete disregard to the queue of people, is enough to convince the onlookers that we are some important people.

"Who is in-charge here? I am the Managing Director of Government Liaison Services," Daulat Ram says, using the high sounding name of his company and his self proclaimed title to impress the officials.

The peon, who is standing outside the office, opens the door and lets them in. The official, sitting on a desk in the office, is talking to two men. As soon as he sees Daddyji and Daulat Ram being shown in by the peon, he looks up and tells the men siting with him to leave. Daulat Ram hands over his business card to him.

Daddyji says to him, "We have been sent here by Mr. Chaturvedi of the Home Ministry. We want to rent a flat around here." He is again using his penchant for name dropping.

The official replies, "We have a long waiting list. It is on a first come first served basis. I will let you also add your name to the list." And he hands over a thick register to Daddyji and points out the place where he should add his name, his father's name, number of family members, and the current domicile and address. Daddyji starts to look through the register. After seeing hundreds of names, his face shows discouragement. He is not sure if there is any point in adding his name to the long list. And then he notices that after every fifteen or twenty names there is a blank line, with no name written on it. Daulat Ram is also looking down at the register. As Daddyji looks up, their eyes meet. Daddyji winks at him—meaning that they know the purpose of the blank lines.

Daddyji looks at the official and says, "What is your good name?"

"I am known as Jeetu."

"Jeetu sahib, why don't you look after us, and we will look after you—if you know what I mean. Moreover, you will also be doing social service; we are really in dire need of accommodation. You know, there is nothing wrong with that," Daddyji says.

Jeetu replies, "Fine sir, I have no problem with that."

Daddyji writes down his name in one of the blank lines closest to the top of the list, slips some cash within the pages of the register and hands over the register to Jeetu.

Jeetu accepts the register and puts it in the drawer of his desk. He then picks up the business card given to him by Daulat Ram and asks, "Sir, what business are you in?"

"We make the wheels of government machinery move smoothly. As you know, ours is an ancient civilization; therefore, with time, the rust has set in. You know what rust is? In Hindi, it is called *Zung*. We apply lubrication to the parts of the wheels of the government, and, after that, things start to move smoothly. Indian companies and foreign companies use our services to facilitate their dealings with the governments of all levels; be it central, state, or municipal government. If you ever need any help, just come and see me. You helped us; we will help you."

I am standing nearby and watching butter being applied to the slow moving wheels of bureaucracy. Another one of the "lessons": Whenever there is friction and things don't move, one should apply lubrication.

Daulat Ram is standing looking at Daddyji proudly and thinking that his brother-in-law has a bright future ahead of him! And his sister will be well looked after.

When we go out to the car, Mummyji says, "Is it possible to see one of the Quarters?"

Daddyji goes in to see Jeetu and asks him, "Jeetu ji, is it possible to see one of the Quarters?"

"Certainly," he says and comes out with Daddyji.

He then leads us to a nearby Quarter that is unoccupied and explains to us, "You see, the existing landlord will be occupying one half of the Quarter; you will occupy the other half. The rent is fixed by the government at thirty rupees per month. Your portion consists of the front verandah with the exterior covered with an open wooden lattice work known as *Jaaffery* in Punjabi, one main room, a small room in the rear with another verandah, a kitchen, a bathroom, and a separate toilet. The rear courtyard is common space and has an eight feet high wall around. The Quarters are laid out in a u-shaped plan called a Square. There are fifteen attached Quarters in one Square and open ground in the middle with grass. Laneways at the rear separate the Squares from one another. There are many such Squares in the neighbourhood. All in all, it is a small flat, but the whole locality is very well laid out. There are plenty of open spaces and very airy atmosphere full of natural light, as all buildings are one storey high."

We all walk through the Quarter; Mummyji is happy; no more climbing three storeys of stairs.

In about two weeks, we get an official letter of allotment of a rental flat in the E-Type Quarters in Karol Bagh.

22
DELHI: MAY 1948
RAY OF HOPE

Two Tongas and Daulat Ram's car are lined up, outside the building we live in, to transport our belongings to our new residence in Karol Bagh. Having lived at this place for almost six months, our possessions have multiplied. Daddyji has arranged some labourers to bring our belongings from the third floor to the ground; he remembers what happened when we moved in here from Simla, and the *Tongawalas* refused to carry the baggage upstairs. Mummyji is upstairs, and Daddyji is downstairs supervising the operations. Uncle SK and Devika Massi are also standing around looking things over. At last, the caravan of two Tongas, followed by the car, make their way to Karol Bagh.

When we arrive at our new residence, we are met at the entrance by our landlord, Karnail Singh, a tall, well built Sikh. He is married with no children. On May 1, 1948, we move into Quarter number E185. It seems that the move has brought a ray of hope to my parents. It has almost been one year since we left Lahore–this being our third move. However, it seems that our nomadic life may have come to an end.

A few days after we settle down a bit, Kishi and I are playing on the ground in front of our Quarter. Daddyji is sitting in the verandah shuffling the pages of the newspaper looking for job openings. Mummyji is sitting nearby peeling onions with tears flowing down her cheeks. She says while wiping her eyes, "Listen ji, we should be doing something about Vikram's schooling. I was talking to a neighbour, and she told me that the schools close on May 15 for the summer vacations and re-open on July 15. We must finalize his admission in Grade 2 before May 15."

"I was talking to Karnail Singh, and he told me the same thing. He says all the students in this area go to Ramjas School No: 2 located at Anand Parbat, a hill a little west of here. I think I will go there in the next few days and also take Vikram with me. I want to talk to the teachers before we make a final decision."

One morning, both Daddyji and I get ready to go to visit the school. The bicycle had been cleaned the previous night. On this fateful day, we set course towards Anand Parbat. I am riding on the rear carrier of the bicycle with my legs hanging on each side, and holding on to Daddyji by the waist from behind. This is my first ride sitting on the rear carrier with Daddyji riding the bicycle. As we ride away, Mummyji and Kishi are standing in the verandah waving at us. This reminds me of the first day of school in Lahore when I nearly got carried away by the procession and got lost.

The bicycle ride is very smooth and uneventful for the first few minutes. However, after a few minutes, I find that Daddyji is straining hard. I can hear his heavy breathing. The speed is getting slower and slower. I also find that it is very hot, although it is only about 9 A.M. I am holding on to his waist. I can feel that his shirt is all wet with perspiration. After about ten minutes, the bicycle stops. Daddyji gets down with me still sitting on the rear carrier.

"Daddyji, what happened?" I ask.

"See the hill in front of us. It will be very hard to ride the bicycle up the hill. Vikram, you just keep sitting; I will walk the bicycle up the hill."

"Oh, Daddyji, we have climbed bigger hills in Simla. Have you forgotten?"

"Yes, but it was not this hot in Simla."

After a few minutes, I notice that Daddyji is having a difficult time pushing the bicycle up the hill with me sitting on it.

"Daddyji, let me get down; I want to walk."

As we are walking up the hill, we notice that there are houses on one side and a rock face on the other. People who are riding their bicycles down the hill are coming down really fast right in the middle of the road. Daddyji moves over to the extreme left of the road in order to avoid any accident.

After a few minutes of walk, we reach the top of the hill. The road after that is almost flat with a very gentle slope. We again get on the bicycle and start riding towards the school.

"Daddyji, I am thirsty."

"There are no shops here, Vikram, but I am sure we will find some shops near the school."

After travelling for a little while he says, "Oh, look Vikram, there is a *Chabeel* there, let us drink some water." *Chabeel* is a shack erected by a charitable individual or organization to dispense free drinking water to the general public.

We stop and get off the bicycle. As luck would have it, the *chabeel* is under a large *Neem* tree providing ample shade. Both of us drink some water using both our hands to form, what we call in Punjabi, a *Bookk*—a channel formed by joining both hands to direct water to the mouth—as the man inside pours water from a pot into our hands. After drinking some water, Daddyji requests the man inside to pour some more water so that he can wash his face to cool down.

In a few minutes, we are at the school; a small sign in Hindi proclaims the name of the school: Ramjas School No: 2, Primary School, Anand Parbat. *Anand* means bliss and *Parbat* means Mountain— Mountain of Bliss.

Not a bad place to start my school life, I am thinking.

Daddyji places his bicycle on a stand adjacent to other bicycles. He looks around and finds the Headmaster's office. He knocks at the door and enters the office with me following him. The peon tells us that the Headmaster is taking a class and offers us a wooden bench to sit on. After about fifteen minutes, a short stocky man, in pants and a bushirt, walks in and says, "Hello!"

Before he can say anything more, Daddyji gets up from the bench and says, "My name is Surinder Mehra; I am also a teacher like you. This is my son, Vikram Mehra. I have come to find out if Vikram can get admission in your school in Grade 2."

The headmaster extends his hand, "My name is Atma Ram. I am the headmaster of the primary school. I am a *Hindustani*, a care taker of the *Golden Sparrows*."

Daddyji looks at him with a blank look; his expression is showing that he has not understood the point of what Atma Ram has just uttered.

Daddyji starts to say, "I have not…"

Before Daddyji can finish, Atma Ram starts to explain, "I know, I know, I am talking in riddles. I have this standard line that I speak when I come in first contact with expectant parents. Oh, by *expectant* I mean expectation about school admission. Oh, and by the way, the school admissions are becoming so difficult that in the next few years expectant parents will have to register their unborn child." And Atma Ram and Daddyji break out into laughter together, and he continues, "Anyway, jokes aside, you said that you are also a teacher. Where do you teach?"

"I used to teach English in a college in Lahore. I have not started working yet."

"Oh I see; now about the question of admission of Vikram. He is very lucky. We have only one seat left in Grade 2."

And the headmaster takes out a few forms and hands them over to Daddyji. He looks at the forms and turns them over to see if he can find English anywhere, but, to his embarrassment, the forms are all in Hindi language.

"Atma Ram ji, do you have the forms in English?"

Atma Ram has a strange smile on his face and asks, "Why?"

"I am sorry, but I don't know English." Daddyji is so embarrassed that instead of saying 'I don't know Hindi, he ends up saying, "I don't know English."

He quickly corrects himself, and says, "Oh... I mean I don't know Hindi."

"We do not have forms in English. And the rule is that the forms have to be filled in Hindi Language," Atma Ram says.

"Well, in that case, I will have to bring my wife, Kamla, along to have the forms filled. Or if you can give me the forms, I will have them filled and bring them back tomorrow."

"I will prefer if you bring your wife along tomorrow to fill the form. I want to see that somebody in your family can read and write Hindi. Because the medium of instruction in the primary school is Hindi, it is essential that somebody at home knows Hindi. That way the student will be able to get some help at home."

"Atma Ram ji, tell me one thing. What if some student's family is illiterate? Does that mean that the student cannot get admission in your school?"

"No, no... in that case, one of the teachers becomes his guardian and helps him in all matters concerning his schooling. I am sure a person of your qualifications will not want that kind of arrangement."

"I will bring my wife along tomorrow; and by the way, she is also a teacher."

"Oh, Mehra sahib, that is a wonderful coincidence. My wife is also a teacher in a girl's school. Well, as your wife is a teacher, you don't have to bring her along here tomorrow. I will give you the forms; you can get them filled and bring them back tomorrow."

Atma Ram takes us on a brief tour of the six room school. Each of the four grades is allotted one room. The students are sitting on the floor on coir matting. A verandah runs the entire length of the one storey rectangular school building with sloping roof made of tin sheets. The courtyard, in front of the classrooms, is enclosed on three sides by a brick wall, with the classrooms on the fourth side. As we are walking in the verandah, Atma Ram says, pointing to the students in the classrooms, "See, Mehra sahib, all these are my *Golden Sparrows*. As you probably know, India was, once upon a time, known as the *Sone Ki Chiriya—the Golden Sparrow*; these are all her children. We want to ensure that all our students receive grounding in Hindi—the mother tongue of the *Golden Sparrow*. This is why we have kept only Hindi as the language of instruction in the primary school."

In his mind, Daddyji does not agree with what Atma Ram is saying, but he keeps quiet. But, to change the topic, he says, "I have noticed that there are very few girls in the classes."

"Both the primary school and the higher secondary school are 'boys only' schools. Only girls permitted are the teachers' daughters."

"Oh, I see... Atma Ram ji, if you can kindly give us the admission forms; we will make a move now."

We pick up the admission forms and head home. The ride back home is downhill all the way. Daddyji gets up on the bicycle, and I climb on the rear carrier. As the pedal completes its first revolution, it becomes clear that the front tire has no air. We both get off the bicycle and start to walk. Daddyji is looking around for a bicycle repair shop to have the puncture fixed.

"Daddyji, I had seen a bicycle repair shop on our way just near the *Chabbeel* on the right hand side." I tell him.

After walking for a few minutes, we come across a shop on the roadside in a *Khokha*—a small shack of wood with a tin roof. In the front of the *Khokha*, the shop has some general household provisions for sale. A few bicycles are leaning against the wooden walls. A man is leaning on a small table writing something on a piece of paper, and a woman is standing nearby. We stand there watching. It seems that the man is writing a letter on behalf of the woman; she is dictating. After he is finished writing, he looks up and asks, "Yes sir. What can I do for you?"

"I have a puncture in the tire. Do you repair bicycles?" asks Daddyji.

He replies with his hands waving in the air and with a smile, "Sir, what to speak of punctured tires, I can also repair punctured hearts and souls".

Daddyji is impressed with his confidence and his friendly nature, and replies, "Oh *Shah ji*," using an informal term of endearment, "It seems that you are a refugee like us. Where do you hail from?"

"We are from Jhung, which is now in Pakistan. We used to have an agency for new bicycles, and now we repair bicycles. Just because of the bloated egos of our leaders, we had to leave our homes and become refugees. I wish I could puncture them; their egos I mean."

As he is speaking, he comes out of the shop, lays our bicycle down on the ground and opens up the tire exposing the rubber tube. I have never seen a rubber tube in a bicycle tire before. He pumps up the tube with a hand pump, dips the tube in a pan of water to look for the puncture; he locates the puncture as soon as he sees bubbles coming out of water. Within a few minutes, he has the bicycle ready to go, and he says, "Sir, see we should learn from the rubber tube. One should always keep oneself pumped up if we want to keep going. Never let yourself deflate; and, if that happens, pump yourself up again." And they both have a hearty laugh.

"Where do you live?" Daddyji asks.

"Right here, just behind the shop."

"How did you get this land?"

"All land belongs to God. It was empty, so we just built a small *Khokha*. After all, I have to feed my family. But I can tell you one thing; we will not be here for long. I have applied to Atlas Bicycles for an agency. Once it is approved, we will open a bicycle store."

Both Daddyji and I are all pumped up. We get up on the bicycle and ride it downhill, going faster and faster. Daddyji's shirt is getting pumped up and blowing outward with the wind blowing against us as if we are flying. As we reach the bottom of the slope, Daddyji applies the brakes and we slow down, and he says, "Vikram, we should be pumped up and fly like this all the time."

As we reach home, Mummyji is very eager to find out the result of our school visit. Before Daddyji can speak, and as he is putting the bicycle aside, I get off the bicycle and run to Mummyji to tell her the whole story.

"Mummyji, the *cyclewala* says we should always remain pumped up like the tube of a tire." I tell her. She is very amused to hear the story.

Daddyji gives her the forms, and she sits down to fill them right away. After she is finished completing the admission forms, Daddyji tells her, "Kamla, in this school the medium of instruction is only Hindi. This concerns me some what. I think learning the English language is going to be the key to landing good positions in private companies and the government. I wish I could get Vikram admission in an English medium school, but there is no such school around with the same reputation for academic excellence as Ramjas School."

Mummyji replies, "At this time we have no other choice. We can always change the school in the future as more schools open up. In the meantime, we will, ourselves, teach Vikram how to read, write and speak English."

In the evening, Daddyji meets our neighbour, Karnail Singh, in the rear court yard, while he is sitting there sipping a cup of tea. He starts a conversation with him about the school, "Karnail Singh, Vikram and I went to see Ramjas school on Anand Parbat today. We were lucky; there was only one seat left for Grade 2."

"It is the best school in Delhi and, moreover, it is located at a serene location. There is very little population and traffic in the area. Sometimes, I go for a walk up the hill and around the rear of the school. Very recently, the government has opened a refugee camp and an orphanage there. There are only women and children in that camp."

As soon as Daddyji hears about the refugee camp and orphanage, he calls, "Kamla, just listen to what Karnail Singh is saying."

Both Mummyji and Karnail Singh's wife, Gurinder Kaur, come out to join their husbands.

"Kamla, Karnail Singh says that there is a refugee camp and an orphanage near Ramjas School at Anand Parbat."

"Oh, I see. In that case, when you go to the school to drop off the admission forms, I will also accompany you. That way, I can see Vikram's school, and we can also visit the orphanage."

The word 'orphanage' rings bells in her mind. She has not forgotten what Daddyji had told her on their last night in Lahore about adopting a girl child as their own.

Next morning, Mummyji, Daddyji, Kishi and I get ready to go to my future school. After a few minutes' walk, we find a Tonga standing on the north side of Original Road. We all get on the Tonga.

"Where to, sir?" the Tongawala asks.

"Ramjas School, Anand Parbat."

"Eh sahib, it is very hard on the horse; the hill is very steep. Last time I tried, the horse stopped on the way up and refused to go any further. I had to turn back."

"So how do people go there if they cannot walk?"

"Sahib, how do I know?"

We all get down from the Tonga and start to walk with our enthusiasm deflated. I immediately think of the *cyclewala* and say, "Everybody, get inflated like the bicycle tube."

It is already getting hot. There is another Tonga standing on the other side of the road. As Daddyji looks towards that Tonga he says, "Kamla, it seems that our old coachman, Sabua, is manning that Tonga."

At the same time, Sabua looks towards us and waves his hand in recognition, turns around his Tonga, and brings it to our side of the road. He gets down from the Tonga and greets us warmly.

Daddyji looks at the horse and the Tonga and realizes that it is the same Tonga that we had sold earlier when we used to live at Daryagunj. He walks around the horse to see if he can see the branding mark that he had got affixed on his horses. And, sure enough, he notices the mark and points out the mark to Sabua and says, "Oh Sabua, Beh...d"—using plenty of expletives—he continues, "You were in collusion with the people who stole our horses, you bloody *Namak Harram*. I will hand you over to the police."

"Sahib, I swear by my son, I had nothing to do with it. After I left you, I was not able to find any employment. I came across this Tonga Company and got a job. It was very recently that I discovered that they had the stolen horses that you used to own. The owner told me that he had bought these from somebody else. As you can see, there is nothing I could do. Sahib, please believe me."

Mummyji intervenes: "Listen ji, let us drop the matter now. We are going for an auspicious task—the admission of Vikram to his school. Let us forgive and forget. Those who perpetrated this crime upon us will suffer the consequences of their deeds. God is watching."

"Sahib, where are you going? I can take you there."

"We want go to Ramjas School at Anand Parbat, but the other Tongawala says that the horses refuse to go up the hill."

"Eh, sahib, Leave it to me; I will get you there."

Mummyji sits on the rear seat with Kishi, and Daddyji and I climb on to the front seats. But I make sure that I am not sitting in line with the rear end of the horse this time; I still remember my ride from the railway station to Uncle SK's house with the horse blowing wind at me. As we reach the bottom of the hill, Sabua gets down from the Tonga and gently starts to walk the horse up the hill at a very slow pace. As the Tonga is moving, I am looking at the wheels of the Tonga. I am looking for the tires, but there are no tires. So if there are no tires, there are no tubes. How are the wheels supported?

I ask, "Sabua ji, where are the tires of your Tonga?

"Vikram *Baba*, Tongas don't have tires. The wheels of Tongas have the black rubber treading," Sabua points out.

In a few minutes, we are on top of the hill. Sabua gets back on to the Tonga, and we move speedily towards the school. We are at the school in no time. We all go in and are lucky to find Head Master, Atma Ram, in his office.

Daddyji introduces Mummyji to him, "Meet, my wife, Kamla; our family's specialist in Hindi." At the same time he hands over the admission forms to him.

The Headmaster looks over the forms and says, "Vikram, you are now one of the *Golden Sparrows.*

Daddyji decides to offer him some bait and asks, "Atma Ram ji, do you give private tutoring? If Vikram needs some help, can we call on you? Of course, we will compensate you for your effort. I also know some more people whose children need help."

It seems Daddyji is applying Daulat Ram's Principle that everything is for sale, and everybody has a price.

Atma Ram says, "Of course, I am always ready to help."

With this exchange between them, and by showing the greener pastures of extra income to Atma Ram, Daddyji has assured smooth sailing for me through school.

As we are preparing to leave the school, Daddyji asks, "Atma Ram ji, how do we get to the Refugee Camp?

"There is a walkway from the playground in the rear of the school. It goes downhill, and you will be there in ten minutes. If you want to go by road, then you go down the hill, turn right, and you will see some military barracks; the camp is right there."

We decide to go by Tonga. Daddyji explains to Sabua how to get there. Again Sabua walks the horse gently down the slope. As we reach the bottom of the slope, we turn right, and after about five minute, we reach the entrance to the compound of the refugee camp. A barbed wire fence surrounds the area. A Gorkha guard, wearing a green Army uniform, is standing at the entrance. The Tonga comes to a stop. We are not allowed to go in.

"We want to meet the manager of the Camp," Daddyji tells the guard.

"Sahib, do you have a letter from the government?"

"No, we do not. We have been given permission by Mr. David Rankin to come and see the manager."

Daddyji again uses his penchant for name dropping to see if it will work or not. After hearing the English name, the guard seems to take notice. He puts his hand up and says, "Sir, please wait here. I will go in and ask."

It is almost 11 A.M., the Sun is almost at the Zenith and heat is piercing. The canopy over the Tonga provides some relief. We wait and wait. Almost 10 minutes have passed, but there is no sign of the guard.

Daddyji tells Sabua, "Let us go in." The Tonga slowly rolls in, and we come to a stop in front of the office. We get off the Tonga, walk up the three steps and walk into the office.

There is nobody in the office. We stand there looking around. Daddyji sees the guard standing at the other end of the verandah. He is talking to a tall and well built matronly lady with glasses. Daddyji starts to walk towards the lady, and at the same time, the lady, accompanied by the guard, also starts walking towards us.

As soon as the guard notices our presence, he starts to run towards us shouting, "Get out, you cannot come in without permission."

Daddyji repeats what he had said before, "We have been told by Mr. Rankin that we could visit the camp."

As the lady comes closer she says, "Are you looking for somebody in the camp?"

Mummyji says, "No, we are not looking for somebody, but we are looking for something—a way to help our fellow human beings. We are also refugees from Lahore. We have been fortunate to come through this ordeal unscathed. We have come here to see if we can help in any way. We are both teachers."

"My name is Sita. I am the manager of the camp. Please have a seat." And she waves at the guard to leave the office.

Daddyji introduces us all, "I am Surinder Mehra …my wife Kamla and my sons… Vikram and Kishi."

Sita starts to tell us about the camp, "You see, this refugee camp is for women and children only. We have young girls from 8 years to 18 years old. And then there are infants about 2 years to 3 years of age. Each age group presents its own problems. Some of them are so traumatized that they hardly talk. Our aim is to wait and see if their families will come and claim them. It has been almost a year, but very few have been claimed by their families."

"Are they Hindus or Muslims?" Mummyji asks.

"We have both. You see, it is easy to find out in case of grown girls; we just ask them. However, in the case of infants, we just do not know."

"So, what does the government plan to do with them?

"In the case of infants, it is reasonable to assume that their parents have been killed, and the children were left behind. So the logical thing to do is to give them out for adoption, but this presents a number of problems. We have to be careful, who the adoptive parents are. There are reports of trafficking in children. There have been cases of children being adopted and used as child labor, and young girls as domestic servants and prostitutes."

"Have you had requests for adoption?"

"No, there have been no requests in this refugee camp."

After some pause, Sita continues, "Mrs. Mehra, in which way would you like to help? But I would like to tell you that we do not allow men inside the camp as workers, except for very special tasks."

Mummyji replies, "I am a trained teacher, and I can teach a variety of subjects."

Sita says, "If you want, I can give you a form to fill. But you will have to be approved by the Ministry of Rehabilitation."

Mummyji replies, "Yes please, I would like to fill the form."

Sita takes out a form from her desk and hands it over to Mummyji. She folds the form and puts it in her purse.

"Thank you for the form. Is it possible to see the camp?" Mummyji asks.

"Yes, please follow me." Sita gets up from her chair, and we all follow her through the six barracks that form the camp. Some classroom and playground facilities have also been provided. The most touching area of the camp is the barrack where infants are kept in small cots and cradles, the room Sita calls *Tarron ki Shaala—Galaxy of Stars*. Mummyji stops in that area and starts to play with each child. She picks each child up and plays with them.

As she picks up the baby girl, she looks at Sita and says, "Look at the eyes of this little one; how old is she?"

"We don't really know her exact age, but, I think, she is about 18 months old."

"What is her name?"

"Well, we have started calling her Suneeta. She just started standing up a few weeks ago."

Suneeta is dressed in a pink cotton frock with a pink hair clip on the left side of her head. Mummyji puts her down on the floor to see her take a few steps, but she just moves her hands towards Sita, holds her by her sari and looks down with shyness, still stealing a few glances up at Mummyji. Mummyji picks her up again, plays with her chubby cheeks and Suneeta smiles a bit. Mummyji then tickles her chin with her index finger, and she breaks into a wide grin.

"Mrs. Mehra, she seems to like you. This is the first time I have seen her smile; otherwise, she is always looking down and playing with her feet."

Kishi and I start playing with some wooden toys in the room. Mummyji carries Suneeta around while we walk through the *Taaroan Ki Shaala* looking at other children. We spend almost an hour in that room. As Mummyji starts to put Suneeta back in her cot, she looks at Mummyji with a pleading look and holds on to Mummyji's blouse. She just does not let go. Mummyji picks her up again and holds her tight to herself kissing her lovingly on her cheeks and forehead.

Sita takes Suneeta from Mummyji's hands. We all gradually start moving away. As we are about to go out of the room, Suneeta gives out a sweet little sound, "Mama, Mama... Mama," pointing her little finger towards us. We all turn around, and our hearts melt as we see Suneeta with her little hand stretched towards us.

My younger brother, Kishi, says "Mummyji, how about we take Suneeta home?" And we all stand there with smiles on our faces and moistened eyes.

"Come Kishi, we will come to see her again," says Daddyji. With these words, we quietly walk out of the room. Sita hands over Suneeta to one of the women helpers in the room and comes out with us.

"I will fill the form and bring it to you tomorrow."

"See you tomorrow, Mrs. Mehra."

"Oh, please call me Kamla."

"All right, Kamla, we will meet tomorrow."

Sabua takes us home in his Tonga and departs. We eat lunch and lie down for the afternoon nap.

Mummyji too has a dream:

Suneeta is sitting with her hands outstretched... mama... mama..., won't you be my mama? ...fog, there is fog... no, no, not fog... it is smoke... fire... the house is on fire... screams, there are screams... and then silence... mama... my mama is gone... won't you be my mama? Suneeta again... sobbing... mama I am left alone... won't you be my Mama... red kites are flying and then all falling into... the fog... no, no, fire. Mama... I am alone. Mama.

And Mummyji wakes up with a start, looking around, and Kishi also gets up, weeping... saying Mama... Mummyji... Suneeta is alone... He too had a dream.

The next day, Mummyji fills the forms and, along with her Ration Card to prove her identity, goes to the refugee camp to handover the forms. She is again stopped by the guard, but he lets her in after she reminds him that she had visited the previous day. As she hands over the form to Sita, the manager, Mummyji asks, "How long will it take to get approval?"

"I really cannot say. There are so many problems being managed by the Rehabilitation Ministry that it may take months before somebody even looks at it," Sita replies.

Mummyji sits down in the chair with a disappointed look.

Sita continues, "Kamla, don't be disappointed. I have some discretion in this matter. After I have had a chance to look at the form, I will be able to recommend your provisional acceptance as a volunteer until we receive formal approval from the Ministry." Sita looks at the forms and the Ration Card to compare the signatures, returns the Ration Card to Mummyji and says, "Kamla, can you start from next week? Will you be able to come every day?"

Mummyji replies, "No, Sita, I can come only three days a week from 10 A.M. to 12 P.M. starting July 22, a week after my elder son, Vikram, starts his school. Moreover, I will have to bring my younger son along because he has not started school as yet."

"That seems fine. I will see you then."

23
JUNE 1948
CLOSE QUARTERS

As usual, Daddyji is sitting in the verandah turning the pages of the newspaper looking for opportunities of making a living. And every now and then, he looks up from the top of the pages of the newspaper to watch the happenings in other Quarters in the Square. Since we have moved to the Quarter, he spends most of his free time sitting outside reading newspaper and watching the life of the neighbours unfold. The Quarters are so close to each other that he can hear people talk to one another. As many times during the day the mothers or the fathers call their children by name, he knows the names of many of the children.

"Kamla, I have found a new profession," He says

Mummyji is sitting nearby peeling *Karelas* for lunch. She looks up and asks, "Oh?"

"I am going to start writing plays like Shakespeare, my Guru. You now, Kamla, after sitting in the verandah for two weeks, I know the life story of all the residents of this Square. There is plenty of material for at least ten plays."

The *Daakia* is about to place the letters in the letter box, when Daddyji gets up from his chair in the verandah and extends his hand towards the Postman asking for his letters to be given to him. He is expecting a letter from his parents, who are in Simla. The Postman has not noticed his extended hand. He opens the lid on top of the letter box, drops the letters in and moves to the next Quarter. As he approaches the next Quarter, he notices a dog sleeping in the Verandah, as has been the case for the last few days. He hesitates, and then decides to quickly drop the letters in the letter box and move on. As soon as he opens the letter box, the dog jumps at the Postman; as if it had been pretending to be asleep and was waiting for him. In a matter of seconds, the Postman is on the ground and the dog is on top holding on to his khaki pants between his teeth. Chatterjida, the resident of the Quarter and the owner of the dog and, ironically, an official of the Post and Telegraph department, comes running out in his *paijamas* and undershirt and commands his dog, "Tiger, Tiger, sit, sit."

By this time, all the letters, money orders and parcels in the Postman's bag are sprayed all over the ground. Daddyji gets up from his chair to go to the Postman's rescue. Although, Chatterjida is commanding his dog to sit, the dog is still going at the Postman. Daddyji notices that the dog is not listening. After some quick thinking, he realizes that either the dog is deaf, or it is being given the wrong command.

Daddyji starts to say, "Come on Moti, Moti, good boy sit down." The dog immediately complies. The Postman gets up and tries to compose himself and dusts off his clothes, or whatever is left of them.

Chatterjida moves closer to the Postman, "I am sorry Postman ji. I just bought the dog a few days back; I did not know that he was so ferocious. Let me help clean you up." He makes the Postman sit down on a chair and brings a glass of water for him. But he seems puzzled and asks Daddyji, "Surinder ji, I am puzzled by the fact that the dog responded to your commands and not to mine."

"Well Chatterjida, I am also puzzled by the same. Why did you name your dog, Tiger?"

Chatterjida replies, "It is an intimidating name. I want him to be like a Tiger."

"In that case, he did just what you wanted him to do. He attacked the poor Postman like a Tiger would."

"But Tiger did not listen to me. That is what is bothering me."

"Let me tell you something. My younger brother, Karan, has done a lot of research about dogs. He tells me that the two most common names of dogs in India are, Moti, and Jimmy."

"I have never heard of that before. How is that relevant?" Chatterjida asks.

"Well, did you know the name of your dog before you bought it?"

"No. I just brought it home and started calling it, Tiger." Chatterjida replies.

"Then that explains it. I think your dog's previous name was Moti. That is why he responded to my commands."

"What does your brother do? Why is he interested in the names of dogs?"

Daddyji replies, "Karan is an economist and works for a stock broker. He got interested in dogs when we were in Lahore. There were a lot of stray dogs in Lahore. They used to loiter here and there. Karan decided that, as dogs are known to be a man's best friend, he should do something about their plight. He formed a group with common interest in the welfare of dogs. They used to encourage people to adopt a dog in the neighbourhood and give their leftover eatables to the stray dogs. In the evenings, after coming back from work, he used to play with the stray dogs, and this is how my brother acquired special knowledge about dogs; so much so that he started using dogs in his professional work."

"I have never heard of this before. I am also an economist with the Indian Post and Telegraph. How do dogs figure in his business?"

Daddyji replies, "As dogs are known as man's best friend, he utilizes the services of a trained dog to pick stocks."

In the meantime, the Postman has picked up his bag and has moved on to the next Quarter.

Chatterjida is scratching his head and is quiet for a while. As all the barking and screaming is taking place, our neighbour, Karnail Singh, has also come out to investigate the goings on.

"Chatterjida, your dog also ran after me yesterday, and if it had bitten me, I swear, I would have taken out my *Kirpan* and taken his head off. Make sure you keep him tied or otherwise…" Karnail Singh leaves the rest to Chatterjida's imagination.

Chatterjida is standing with folded arms and says, "Karnail Singh, my humble apologies,"

Babli, Chatterjida's wife, hears the entire ruckus and also comes out to investigate and, after hearing what happened, says, "I told you not to get such a big dog, but you never listen to me. I hope you people can put some sense into him and convince him to get rid of the dog."

Chatterjida's jaw drops after receiving a tongue lashing from his wife. He looks really deflated and quietly walks into his Quarter. Daddyji and Karnail Singh are still standing talking to each other. Karnail Singh says, "He is really dejected, isn't he?

Daddyji replies, "I think he is going to have a hard time getting inflated today."

They both have a hearty laugh and start walking towards the road for a stroll, "Karnail, which government ministry are you working in?" Daddyji asks.

"I am with the Defense Ministry." Karnail replies.

"What do you think is going to happen in Kashmir?"

"Fighting is going on, and India is moving large number of troops to Kashmir. Debate is going on in the United Nations Security Council. Let us hope peace prevails soon."

As soon as he finishes the sentence, Chatterjida's wife, Babli, is heard shouting in panic. The sound of a gun shot pierces the air. Both Karnail Singh and Daddyji run to Chatterjida's Quarter. As they enter, they find Babli running out of the rear door. Both of them follow her. And as they get into the rear street, they find Chatterjida standing with a shot gun in his hand and his dog, Tiger, lying in a pool of blood tied to a tree nearby.

"Why did you shoot him?" Daddyji asks him.

"You all told me to get rid of it; that is what I did. He is not going to bother anybody anymore. Karnail Singh, he will neither bother you nor the Postman. Tiger has made me feel so ashamed in front of everybody. Can you imagine? I am an employee of the Post and Telegraph department and my dog bites the Postman. I will be the laughing stock of the office tomorrow—Man's best friend, my foot!"

Karnail Singh asks, "Why did you bring Tiger in the first place? What are you afraid of?"

"You want to know? I will tell you something that will shock you. There are a number of older boys who get on the roof tops and penetrate our privacy during day and night. They look at people sleeping outside in the courtyards and peep through the glass panes of the ventilators. They have left objectionable letters in my mail box."

Karnail Singh and Daddyji are furious to hear this and say, "Tell us, Chatterjida, and we will go to see their parents. You are not alone in this; we are with you."

"I have seen their shadows only. I am not sure who they are?"

"Let us, all three, keep an eye on all the older boys."

Afterwards, Daddyji goes over to the letter box, which is shared between us and our neighbour Karnail Singh. He looks at the letters and finds the one addressed to him, but it is not from his parents. It is from an organization unknown to him. He carefully tears off a side of the envelope and blows into the envelope, blowing it up a bit. It reminds me of the blowing up of the tube of the bicycle. I have noticed, in the past also, that Daddyji has this characteristic method of opening a letter. Anyway, he takes the letter out of the envelope and starts to read it.

"Kamla, Kamla," he starts to call for Mummyji. She comes out. At first, he tells her about what happened to the Postman and then says, "I have received this letter, from a company named Bond & Sons, asking me to appear for an interview for a job next week. I have never applied to this company for a job.

They write that they are looking for a person who is well educated and fluent in English."

"Well, think it over. You certainly meet the qualifications they are looking for."

· · ·

On a moonlit night, Karnail Singh and Daddyji are out for a walk after dinner. As they are walking on the road in front of the Square, they clearly see two figures crouching on the roofs of the front verandahs. "Surinder look. Do you see what I see?"

"Oh my God, look at those rascals. I wonder how they got on to the roof."

"Let us just stand here and see what they do."

The boys look into each ventilator, one at a time, and then stop at one of the Quarters, and keep peeping in.

"Karnail let us quietly get a few other men, surround the area and then challenge them to come down."

They quietly go to Chatterjida's Quarter and Jains' Quarter and ask both of them to come out.

Daddyji suggests, "Let us each take one corner of the Square and then shout and challenge them."

As soon as they take positions, all four of them challenge the boys with a shout, "Hey, you boys. What are you doing on the rooftop? Get down right away." The boys on the roof top are startled; especially, when they see not only these four men, but a number of other men and women coming out of their Quarters.

The boys start running, but freeze when one of them is recognized by his own mother. She shouts at him with a mouthful of expletives, "Oh, Nindi, *Khasmaa Nooo Khaneya*, what are you doing on the roof? Come down right away. Are you not ashamed of peeping into peoples' homes?"

Nindi says to his mother, "Mama, we were just looking for the ball we had hit on to the roof, while playing cricket."

As soon as the boys come down, Nindi's mother swings her right hand landing a slap on his face, and Nindi goes tumbling to the ground. The other boy is from the Square opposite to our Square. Daddyji gets hold of him by his collar and asks him, "Where do you live? What is your name?"

"Sir, I live in 220. My name is Raju Kataria."

Daddyji, followed by some other men and women, drags him to his Quarter and tells his parents what their dear son has been up to.

Raju's father, instead of giving him the treatment that Nindi got, says, "Leave my son alone. What right do you have to treat him in this manner? I will report all you people to the Police for assaulting my son. Tell me Raju. Is what these people are saying true?"

Raju replies, "Babuji, we mistakenly hit the ball to the roof, and we were there just looking for the ball."

"See, I know my son. He is not a vagabond that he will get up on top of roofs and peep into other peoples' homes."

Karnail growls, "Raju make sure we don't see you on the roofs again, or you will have to deal with me."

And everybody goes home for the night.

24
INTERVIEW: THE NEW EAST INDIA COMPANY

On the day of the interview, Daddyji dresses up in a white shirt with collar studs and cuff links, white shark skin trousers and red tie. He gathers some papers, puts them in his brief case and moves out of the Quarter with a spring in his step. He appears confident and ready to take on the world. Rather than take his bicycle, he decides to hire a Tonga for the ride to Connaught Place, where the offices of Bond & Sons, Importers & Exporters, are located. The time for interview is 11 A.M. Daddyji reaches there about fifteen minutes early. An Anglo-Indian receptionist greets him.

He says to her, "Hello, I have been invited for an interview." And shows her the interview letter,

And she politely shows him the sofa, "Please, sir, have a seat."

He makes himself comfortable and picks up a copy of a newspaper lying on the side table. Every now and then, he looks around to take in the surroundings. He is impressed with the office decor. The receptionist is wearing a red, low-cut blouse, green skirt and a red flower in her bobbed cut hair; she seems to be exceptionally well dressed, or rather provocatively dressed for an office setting.

A voice, with an upper class English accent, comes from the front office, "Shelly dear, can you help me with shorthand?"

"Yes, sir, I will be right in."

She takes out a lipstick from her purse, refreshes the lipstick on her lips, arranges her hair, picks up her steno pad and goes into the front office without knocking at the door.

After reading through most of the newspaper, Daddyji looks at his watch and realizes that it has been almost an hour since he arrived. He is wondering if he should ask somebody, or wait a little longer. This is the first time he has come to a commercial establishment for a job interview. Every now and then, he looks over top of the open newspaper towards the front office, and then towards the office area further down, shifting nervously in the sofa, expecting some officer of the company to walk out of his office and ask him to come in for an interview. The only thing that keeps him interested is the sound of the receptionist's giggling coming from the front office.

He is thinking: *Once there was a time, when in Lahore, the students used to line up to attend my lectures, and here I am sitting waiting for one hour and nobody cares. Those were the days my friend!... True it is that we have seen better days; The time is out of joint; that ever I was born to set it right............................ Shakespeare is swirling through his mind.*

He finally decides that he has had enough. He gets up and begins to stroll up and down the reception area. As he looks out the window, he can see the Odeon cinema theatre right across the road. People are lining up for the matinee show. Bill boards indicate that The Film *Aag*, starring Raj Kapoor and Nargis, is playing. He slowly starts to walk towards the interior of the office and sees the back office with ten or fifteen people working on their desks. One of the office workers notices Daddyji standing there, and he comes over and asks, "Can I help you?"

"I have been waiting in the reception area for over an hour. The receptionist asked me to wait, but she has gone in this office." Daddyji says pointing to the front office. The man giggles and says, "The sahib is having *Jull Paan*; you know... refreshment. We call it shorthand refreshment; you know what I mean."

Daddyji does not know what to do. He takes out the interview letter and shows it to the man.

"Yes, Bond sahib does all the interviewing; he is the one inside. He is getting ready for the interview, but before that he is "Bonding" with Miss Shelly." And he giggles again.

As soon as he is finished talking to the office worker, the door of the front office opens, the receptionist walks out rearranging her hair and straightening out her skirt. After seeing her, the office worker recites a well known Urdu couplet under his breath, "*Terii Urri Urri si Rungut, Terre Khooleh Kholeh se Ghessoo, Bataa Rahi Haai, Terah and Bond sahib Kaa Afsaana.*

Translation: Your disheveled look is telling the story of your Bonding with Bond sahib.

At the same time, Mr. Bond comes out of his office and greets Daddyji. He is a tall, well dressed Englishman in a suit and tie, and half moon reading glasses perched on his nose; he looks about 45 years old.

"Hello. Sorry to keep you waiting. I had to attend to some urgent correspondence. You can come in now." Mr. Bond shows him into his office and offers him a chair across his desk.

Mr. Bond continues talking as he takes a file out from the drawer of his desk, "Yes, here we are. You come highly recommended by a very good friend. He said he knows your brother-in-law. Oh, let me first introduce myself. My name is Bond, Kevin Bond."

"My name is Surinder Mehra," Daddyji says, getting up from the chair to shake hands with him. "I received the interview letter last week, and, ever since, I have been wondering: Why did I get invited for an interview without applying for the job? But now I know."

"Let me tell you a little bit about our company and about the position we are trying to fill," Kevin Bond says.

Daddyji says, "Oh, I would like that."

Kevin Bond clears his throat and says "All right then, let me start from the beginning. My great grandfather started the company over 100 years ago. He used to be a servant of the East India Company. He started his career as a Writer, the entry level position, and worked his way up the ranks to Factor, Junior Merchant and then Merchant. The East India Company permitted its servants to do their own trading, in addition to looking after the business of the Company. They used to purchase pepper, textiles, tea and other commodities for sale in Britain. After he had been working with the Company for 20 years, the East India Company was disbanded, and he started his own business. So in a way, one could say that we are the descendants of the East India Company," Kevin Bond says with a kind of guilty smile and continues, "I hope you have no hard feelings against the Company!... We have offices in Delhi, Calcutta, Bombay and Madras. We also have one retail store in each of these cities. Our stores are named, The Imperial Stores; you must have seen one in the Inner Circle of Connaught Place. We are four brothers and each manages one region of the country. We are looking for a Manager for this office. I travel all across Northern India on business; therefore, I am looking for a right-hand man."

Daddyji says, "Well, I do not have any real business experience. I have been a professor of English literature in Lahore. After we moved here from Lahore, as refugees, I started a small business owning Tongas for hire, but it did not work. However, one thing I can tell you that I will try my best to make it a success, if given the opportunity."

They talk for about 45 minutes, and Kevin Bond is very impressed with Daddyji's command of the English language, his social skills and personality in general.

"Well, Mr. Mehra, I would like to offer you a job with our company as the Manager of the Delhi office. You do not have to make a decision right at this time. I will give you a letter of appointment while you wait. You can go home, think it over and indicate your decision to me, by post, within one week."

Kevin Bond goes out of his office to the reception area, where Shelly is sitting. He explains to her something and comes back in. Daddyji and Kevin converse for a while, until Shelly brings in the appointment letter. Kevin looks it over, writes down the salary by hand on the letter, puts the letter in an envelope and gives the original and one carbon copy to Daddyji.

"Thank you Mr. Bond, I will get back to you in a few days." And Daddyji deposits the envelope in his briefcase. He then gets up and shakes hands with Kevin Bond. And then walks through the reception area, nods at Shelly, walks out of the office and runs down the stairs and comes out on Radial Road No: 5. He stands there and takes a deep breath and feels like a winner. He finally seems to have found a job in keeping with his hopes and aspirations. It is almost 1:30 P.M. He is feeling hungry. He starts to walk towards the Outer Circle of Connaught Place, the Connaught Circus. He stands there looking for a place to eat. Across the road, he notices that a number of small wooden shacks have come up. A variety of shops have sprung up in them. One of them appears to be a restaurant. He carefully walks across the road, and, as he gets closer, he sees a sign *'Kake Da Hotel'*. He remembers a restaurant by the same name in Lahore. As he enters, he is warmly greeted by the owners.

"You used to have a restaurant in Lahore. Is it not?" He asks them.

"Yes sir, it is the same *Kake Da Hotel* and the same best Chicken Curry in the World."

He has a hearty lunch and a heartier laugh with the happy go lucky owners of the restaurant—the Chopras of Lahore.

• • •

When he reaches home, he tells Mummyji all about his experience at the offices of Bond & Sons. The special topic of conversation is Shelly's shenanigans with Kevin Bond, which Mummyji does not find amusing. She says, "If what you say is true, I think it is an immoral place to work."

"Kamla, I did not see anything. What I am telling you is what one of the office workers told me. Moreover, you know the world has become advanced; morality is not what it used to be. Western society is more open in their dealings amongst the members of the opposite sex. In India, relations between the sexes are kept under wraps... no pun intended! This is the reason why we have young men climbing over roof tops to get cheap thrills."

She decides to change the topic and says, "What have you decided? Are you going to accept the job?"

"I am leaning towards accepting the job. It is a great opportunity, and the salary is good; although, I must say, I will miss the thrill of teaching. What do you think?"

"I think you should take the job. It will have regular hours, and you will not have to run from house to house giving private tutoring to students."

As they are talking to each other, I come running in after playing with my friends. Daddyji gets hold of me by my arm and asks, "What do you think, Vikram?"

"Think about what Daddyji?"

"I have been offered the job of a Manager in an English firm."

"I don't know. It is up to you." And I go on to the subject of interest to me, eating, and I say, "Mummyji, I am hungry."

She gets up, and we go to the kitchen for an afternoon snack.

As I come back to the front room after eating, Daddyji is sitting on a chair with some papers spread on a table across him and is writing something.

"What are you writing, Daddyji?"

"I am signing my letter of appointment."

"Oh." I say. I have no idea what it is all about, and I run out to join my friends.

• • •

Daddyji—by a stroke of chance, luck or whatever one may characterize it—has decided to join the East India Company'; as it is known in the owner's own words.

"Kamla, I never thought that I would be working for a British company at a time when the British Raj has come to an end." He tells Mummyji, as she is sitting turning the pages of the newspaper.

She replies as she is reading from the newspaper, "It says here: Tomorrow June 21, 1948, is the day when the British Raj will really come to an end. Do you know why?"

Daddyji gives her a blank look. He does not want to admit that he does not know the answer. He is diving into the depths of his mind to recall but comes out blank. Mummyji, like a dutiful Indian wife, does not want her husband's ego diminished. So, rather than tell him the answer, she pretends that she also does not know the answer. She passes along the newspaper for him to read the answer himself.

"Oh, the Governor General Lord Mountbatten and his family are departing tomorrow, and the first Indian GG, Rajagopalachari, will take over. You are right. India will be truly free tomorrow. Kamla did you read the account of yesterday's farewell to the Mountbattens? It says here that the procession started at the Delhi Gate, and they drove up to the Red Fort in a Rolls Royce car—the Mountbattens and the Nehrus. Both sides of the road were lined up with crowds throwing flowers and garlands and shouting Mountbatten *Zindabad*—long live Mountbatten. You know Kamla, tomorrow is an historic occasion that we must witness."

She replies, "There will be large crowds. I don't want to go. Why don't you ask one of the neighbours to accompany you?"

Daddyji asks our landlord, Karnail Singh; he agrees, and they both decide to witness the winding up of the long chapter of the Indo-British history.

They are up early in the morning of June 21 and ride their bicycles to the Government House. As they reach there, they find thousands already present to witness history in the making. The Mountbattens climb into an open horse-drawn carriage and ride away to Palam aerodrome for their flight to London.

Daddyji is thinking as he is watching the farewell ceremony: *India is finally free after a thousand years. First the Moghuls and then the English people ruled over us. At last, we can shape our own destiny, or can we? Only if we have power... strength... at the end of the day it is the 'Jis Ki Laathi Oos Ki Bhense.' Meaning: 'The one who wields the Stick owns the Buffalo'; Old Indian saying... How did they do it? A mere few hundred thousand English people ruled over 300 million of us... Divide and rule, my friend, divide and rule... Don't you see, old chap, that they have divided us again into: India and Pakistan.*

• • •

As Daddyji and Karnail Singh are riding their respective bicycles home, Karnail Singh shouts over, "Surinder, how about stopping in Connaught Place for a cup of coffee?"

They stop at the Gaylord Restaurant, at the Regal Building, to have coffee and cup pastry. This is the first time Daddyji has visited an English style restaurant after leaving Lahore. It is nice and cool in the restaurant, and they use this opportunity to get to know each other.

Daddyji says, "I have accepted a job with an English firm, Bond & Company."

Karnail Singh replies, "Yes, I have heard of them. They have been supplying provisions to the military."

"Which department of the Defense Ministry do you work in?"

"I am with the Procurement Directorate. I am a Gazetted Officer."

"What is your background?"

"I have completed M.A. in Political Science from Punjab University. What is your background?"

"I have completed my M.A. in English from F.C. College, Lahore. I used to teach in a private college. Karnail, as a student of political science, what do you think was the contribution of the British to India."

Karnail smiles and says, "It is interesting that you ask this question. When I was in my final year, my professor was an Englishman named, Jason Martin. He asked us to write an essay: 'What would India be like today, if the British had not come to India.' It was an amazing mental exercise to imagine the various scenarios. One needed a good knowledge of the past history in order to reconstruct the new fictitious history, with the British taken out of the equation."

Daddyji asks, "So, what was the conclusion?"

"Well, we found it very hard to come to any substantial conclusions. None of the students could write much about it. During one class, Professor Martin decided to have a frank discussion about the matter. It became a very emotionally charged discussion. The Indian students were on one side, the English students on the other, and Professor Martin in the middle."

Daddyji says, "I would have liked to have been there."

Karnail says, "Determining the impact of the British Raj on India is not a small undertaking. We came to the conclusion that a large team of political scientists, historians and economists would be required to complete the study."

"Tell me Karnail. How were a few hundred thousand people from Britain able to rule over us for centuries?"

"Fault, dear Surinder, lies with us that we let them rule over us. There were hundreds of small and big rulers fighting with each other, while the British were taking over. The British conquered us by their Cohesiveness. We lost by our Divisiveness."

Daddyji says, "I hope we learn a lesson from this for the future."

"I hope so too. But from what we saw during the riots of 1947, I don't think any lessons have been learned."

Karnail Singh waves at the bearer for the bill. While they are waiting for the bill, Daddyji says jokingly, "If the British had not come to India, we would not be eating pastries in the Gaylord. Instead, we would be eating *Jalebies* at the *Ghantewala Halwai* in Chandni Chowk."

Karnail Singh retorts back, "What is wrong with that?

Daddyji says, "There would have been no Connaught Place, India Gate and Parliament Buildings; and no trains, no bridges, no electricity, no cars and no planes but only bullock carts. I am not sure if there would even be bicycles."

Karnail Singh replies, "Surinder, you are so pro-British."

"No, no, don't get me wrong. This is what Mr. Hunt, our neighbour in Simla, used to say. Not only that, he used to say: You Indians are not ready for self-rule judging by the way you are killing each other."

The waiter brings the bill. They pay the bill and move out into the June heat of Delhi. As they are peddling hard in the afternoon sun, Daddyji says, "Karnail, now that I think about it; what did we gain by going to see Mountbatten get on the carriage and leave for the aerodrome?

Karnail Singh replies, "I just wanted to see him off–the last vestige of the British Raj."

Daddyji wants to have the last word and says, "Karnail, don't forget; you got your name by courtesy of the British. As you know, the word, Karnail, is the Punjabi derivative of Colonel. Anyway, I think, we should come up with some good natured way to avenge all the atrocities the British perpetrated on Indians."

Karnail says jokingly, "We will have to do some serious thinking. Here is my suggestion. First: we should beat them in the game of cricket. Nothing would humiliate them more than getting beaten at their own game by the colonials. Second: We should impregnate the English language by adding Hindi language into it and call it *Hinglish*. Third: We should flood Britain with Hindus and Muslims and take them over by shear numbers; and build Temples, Mosques, Restaurants and Ghettoes for Indians. Four: Food Revenge. Make thousands of Indian Restaurants in Britain; so much so that instead of fish and chips, the

British start eating Butter Chicken. Instead of Guinness Beer, they start drinking *Lassi* in their Pubs."

Daddyji is laughing his head off and says, "I think that should be enough to teach them a lesson not to colonize again."

Karnail Singh says, "I think we should give our plan a name. What should we call it?"

Daddyji replies, "How about naming it: Operation *Vilayat*"

"I think it is very appropriate."

Vilayat, in Persian, means Foreign. As Persian was the language of the court of Emperor Jahangir when the British first came to India, they began to be called *Vilayti*. Over the years the word stuck, and the Britain began to be known as *Vilayat*."

They are both laughing at their ingenuity in coming up with an amusing Operation *Viayat*.

"Surinder, we should talk to some influential people about this."

"I know Hari Nautiyal, the famous industrialist, and his son Veer. I will talk to them about it."

And they both again have a hearty laugh.

After a pause, Karnail Singh suddenly says, "Surinder, *yaar,* I forgot to tell you something most people don't know."

Daddyji asks, "What is that?"

Karnail Singh replies, "Britain owes India a lot of money."

Daddyji replies, "Come on Karnail, you can't be serious."

Karnail Singh says, "No, I am serious. A friend, who works in the Finance Ministry, told me that Britain owes India a lot of money. As we speak, negotiations are going on about the Terms of Payment."

Daddyji asks, "How did that happen? I would have thought that India would be owing money to Britain."

Karnail says, "Britain used the services of the Indian Army during World War II. The cost was all paid by India as a loan to Britain."

"I think we will have to look into this matter when we launch Operation *Vilayat*." And they both laugh again!

25
JULY 1948
MY SCHOOL

It is almost a year since we left Lahore, but it seems like eternity. Having gone through what we went through... knives, swords, guns, bullets, fires, killings, landslides, dead horses, assassination... one would think that the first day at school would be child's play for me. Nothing could be further from the truth. We are all up at 5 A.M. I have been up all night, along with Mummyji. I have lost count of how many times I must have visited the bathroom. I am ready in my new shorts and shirt, along with a new *Busta* to carry my books in, a *tahkti* and a slate, an ink bottle, *Kullumn* and a *Saletti*. At 6:45 A.M., Arun and Satti, our neighbours who are in Grade 4, are at the door to take me with them. Daddyji wants to take me to school on the first day, but I refuse. I do not want to be known as a Daddyji's boy in the class; being a Grade 2 student, I want to be seen to be standing on my own feet. With *Busta* on one shoulder, *Takhti* in one hand, and the other hand held by Arun, I am given a ceremonial send off by Mummyji. She is standing in the verandah with a silver cup full of sweet curd placed in a flat silver plate. She fills a silver spoon with sweet curd and slides it into my mouth. I slurp it and move on. All three of us move forward like little soldiers in lockstep, ready to take on the world.

"Move quickly, Vikram. The school starts at 7:30. We have to be there by 7:15; otherwise, Head Master Atma Ram will make you stand like a *Murgha*."

I am thinking: *They are Grade 4 boys; they should know.*

Arun and Satti are taller than me; therefore, I have to, practically, run to keep up with them, but I ask in my breathless voice, "What is standing like a *Murgha*?"

"You will soon find out."

I know *Murgha* means chicken, but what has a chicken to do with school. We start to walk up the sloping road that leads to the school. I remember how even a horse had a hard time climbing the hill when we came earlier in a Tonga.

"Why do they have to make the school on top of a hill?" I ask my friends.

"Just keep walking; you will get used to it."

As we reach the top of the hill; I see the bicycle repair shop on the left. It reminds me of the inflated bicycle tube, and how the man had said that one should always keep oneself inflated like a bicycle tube. But I am breathing so hard that there seems to be more air going out than coming into my body. So, I am in danger of getting deflated rather than inflated.

We are finally there. The school bell has just started ringing. Arun shows me to my classroom and goes into his own classroom. The bell is still ringing. I enter the classroom. The teacher, wearing a white Gandhi cap, is sitting on the chair writing something. The boys are starting to take their seats on the coir matting on the floor. I am one of the new boys in the class. The others, having attended Grade 1 in the school, know each other and are talking to one another. I go and stand in front of the teacher with folded hands and say, "Namaste Masterji." My legs are shaking under me. I am not sure if the legs are shaking due to exhaustion of climbing the hill or plain fear. Masterji looks up over his glasses sitting at the edge of his nose.

"What is your name?" he asks.

"Vikram Mehra, Masterji."

He looks at me to size up my height and then assigns me a specific spot on the choir matting. There are three strips of coir matting on the floor laid down along the length of the class room. I am given a seat in the middle of the middle row. Later, I find out that the students are seated in order of their height; the shorter ones are allotted seats in the front, and the taller ones at the rear. As all the students get seated, Masterji gets out the attendance register and calls each student by name. The students stand up, one by one, in response to their name.

After the formalities are over, Masterji gets down to business. "Today, we are going to review what we learned in Grade 1." The first order of business is Hindi writing practice. Everybody takes out their Takhti—a ½ inch thick piece of wood coated with a paste of clay. The ink pots and *Kullumns* are out of the *Bustas*. The *Kullumn* is a piece of ½ inch diameter bamboo stick, about 6 inches long with one end shaped like a nib. I dip it into the ink pot and begin my first attempt at writing Hindi *Varnamala*—the alphabet that is written using the Devanagari script. After a few tries, I am successful in copying some letters from the blackboard, but there is more ink on my fingers and ink drops on the Takhti than letters in Hindi *Vernamala*. Most of the morning, before recess, is devoted to learning the basics; 40 consonants, 10 vowels and many *matras* that are used to modify the sounds of the vowels. After the first period is over, out come the slates and the *Saletti*—long and thin pencil made of soft rock that is used to write on the slate—hence the word *Saletti*. This is where the strong foundation in arithmetic is laid. I thought I knew my numerals, until Masterji starts writing the Hindi numerals on the blackboard. 1, 2, 3 are similar in shape—with a little modification—as English or Arabic numerals, but after that the similarity ends. With the *Saletti* in hand, every student is copying from the blackboard. Masterji has written the Hindi numerals up to only nine.

After a few minutes, Masterji gets up and draws a small circle on the blackboard, and as soon as he is finished, the school bell starts to ring.

He says, "Today, being the first day of school, it is *Adhichootisaari*—halfdayfulloff. But tomorrow, I will show you a Magic Numeral—the magic of *Shoonya*—Zero."

All the students pick up their *Bastas* and *Takhties* and run out of the classroom into the courtyard. I am looking for my friends Arun and Satti. I see Arun bent down and doing something on the floor. As I go nearer, I see him bent in a strange pose with his legs bent and his arms going through his legs and his hands holding his ears.

"Hey Arun, what are you up to?"

"You wanted to know what *Murgha* is. Well, I am doing the *Murgha*."

"Why?" I ask

In the meantime, he lets go of his ears and straightens out a bit. As soon as he relaxes a bit, the Headmaster comes and gives him a light kick on his rear and says, "Up, up, with your behind."

Arun raises his behind, and Satti and I move away and wait for him to live out his punishment.

As we are walking back home I ask, "Hey Arun, what were you being punished for?

"Oh, I was just talking to the boy behind me. Masterji just likes to punish his students for every little thing. If it is not *Murgha*, it is Moti Ram."

On hearing the word "Moti", I immediately think of Moti as a dog's name, as Daddyji had told Chatterjida that most dogs are either named Moti or Jimmy, and I ask, "Does he have a dog?"

"No, no, stupid, Moti Ram is the name of the cane he uses to punish the students. But he usually gives a choice; Murgha or Moti Ram."

As soon as we reach home, I run to Mummyji and tell her all about the first day at school.

"Vikram, are you already back from school?"

I start to talk at full speed, "Yes, Mummyji, being the first day, they gave us *Adhichootisaari*—halfdayfulloff, and you know something, Arun had to do *Murhga,* and Masterji is going to show us magic with numerals, and I saw the bicycle shop along the way, and Headmaster Atma Ram likes to punish his students for every little thing, and I dropped ink on my shorts and shirt, and there are no toilets in the school, and we have to go to the big school if we want to go, and Masterji is going to select a class Monitor tomorrow, and I want to be the one. And now I am hungry." And I finally pause and take a deep breath.

The next day, we are in school even before the bell starts to ring. As the students are waiting for the bell to ring, we are all queuing up in the courtyard for the prayer meeting—short ones in the front and tall ones in the rear of the queue, with one exception, Santosh. She is the tallest in the class, but still gets to sit in the front of her row and gets to stand in the front of the queue. It seems to me that the tall boys are being penalized for being tall; they are being left behind. I decide that I will have to rethink my strategy of becoming tall and big if it is considered a disqualification. We all follow the lead of the group of Grade 4 students, who are the lead singers of the prayer hymns sung in Hindi. After the prayer meeting is over, we all go to our respective class rooms walking in single lines. As soon as all the students settle down on their designated seats, Masterji starts the process of selecting a class Monitor.

"Who wants to be the class Monitor?" he asks.

Only two hands go up—mine and Santosh's. Masterji looks at her in amazement, but does not say anything.

He is thinking: *She is a girl, how can she be the class Monitor of a class in a boys' school. She is the daughter of a teacher who teaches in the big school, and that is the reason why she is in the boys' school in the first place.*

I am reading Masterji's thoughts, as he looks at me. As his and my eyes meet, I can see that he wants me to be the Monitor.

It is quick, but painful. Masterji asks both, Santosh and I, to come to the front of the class. Both of us go and stand on each side of Masterji's table. Santosh folds her hands with her eyes closed, in the prayer position, and starts to chant a Sanskrit mantra, popularly known as, the *Gayatri Mantra*. Everybody appears nonplused; as we have just finished prayers. After a while, we all reluctantly join in. We repeat it 9 times.

After the conclusion of chanting, I am standing still, not knowing what to do, but I maintain my composure.

Masterji says, "Students, those of you who want Santosh to be the class Monitor raise your hand." Every student, except me and Santosh, raises their hand. I don't know what comes upon me, I try to embrace Santosh. As I embrace her, I find out that I am only as tall as her shoulders. She moves away from me, and all the students burst out in laughter. This ends my first and the last attempt at becoming a leader.

After the election is over, Masterji goes and stands next to the blackboard and says, "Students, yesterday I promised to show you the magic of *Shoonya*—Zero; or *Sifr* as it is called in Urdu."

I suddenly perk up.

Masterji continues, "*Shoonya* means nothing, empty." He shows his hands and says, "See my hands are empty. There are *Shoonya*—Zero things in my hands. All of you close your eyes and think of *Shoonya*—Zero."

When I close my eyes, my mind is blank. Have I found *Shoonya*—Zero, I am thinking.

"Open your eyes now." Masterji announces after a minute or so.

When I open my eyes, I see the blackboard full of numerals and zeros.

"See, zero on its own is nothing, but zero added to the right of a numeral makes the numeral ten times larger."

The blackboard has 10, 100,1,000,10,000, and so on.

I raise my hand and ask, "Masterji, what does ten times larger mean?"

He shows one finger and then all the ten fingers, "This is one and this is ten times. You can write ten by writing the numeral one and then adding a zero. And if you keep on adding zeroes, the number becomes larger and larger."

I again raise my hand and ask, "Masterji, what if we add zeroes equal to all the stars in the sky; then what happens?"

He replies with a smile on his face, "Then it will be a number as big as the sky. In Hindi it is known as *Anant*—something that never ends, and, in English, it is known as infinity. "

Another boy sitting behind me asks, "Masterji, how many stars are in the sky?" Masterji seems to be having a wonderful time watching the sense of wonderment on the faces of his students, and replies, "More than we can count."

I raise my hand, "Masterji, who made the stars?"

"God made the stars."

"Then He must know how many stars He made."

"Yes, He must, but we do not. This is why we call it *Anant*–without bound or end–Infinity."

I raise my hand again, "Masterji, what was in the sky before God made the sky and the stars?

He replies, "*Shoonya*, nothing, zero."

There is absolute silence; *Shoonya*, zero noise.

The school bell rings, and we are all transported back to reality–the land of finite numbers and noise.

As Arun, Satti and I, are walking back home after school, the happenings of the day are swirling through my mind.

Arun asks, "Hey, Vikram, you are very quiet. What is the matter?"

I tell him all that happened in the class, and he tells me, "You know, they say that girl, Santosh, is possessed by a *Bhoot*–a Ghost. When she was in Grade 1, she used to, suddenly, start shouting, and then she would lie down on the floor and become unconscious. Everybody stays out of her way. We have heard that once she got angry at somebody at her home, and that person caught fire."

Arun keeps on talking, and I keep on walking while looking at the ground. I have no idea what he has said, and before we know it, we are near our Square. A lot of people are standing outside Quarter E189. As we get nearer, I see Mummyji also standing there. As she sees me coming, she walks towards me, gets hold of my hand and takes me inside our Quarter.

"What is happening in E189, Mummyji?"

"Jaggi is ill with high fever."

After eating my snack, when I go out to play with my friends, there are still people going in and out of E189. Standing just outside E189, we can see inside. They are placing big wet towels on Jaggi. A doctor is standing over him doing something. After a while, he turns around and says something to Jaggi's parents, and then there is silence; *Shoonya*–Zero noise. And then I hear loud wailing of a number of women. Mummyji comes running out of our Quarter, and so do all others who are at home.

We are shocked to learn that Jaggi is no more; he was a victim of Typhoid fever. Jaggi was eight.

In the evening, we all stand and watch as Jaggi's body, wrapped in saffron coloured cloth and placed on a wooden frame, is lifted on their shoulders by a number his relatives and taken away with the chants of holy hymns.

"*Ram Naam Satya Hai... Ram Naam Satya Hai... God is Truth... God is Truth...*"

All the residents of our Square are outside saying good bye to Jaggi, with a river of tears flowing. Many of the neighbours join the processional walk to the cremation ground.

I am thinking: *Has Jaggi become Shoonya—Zero or Anant—Infinity?*

26

A THREAD THAT BINDS

It is Thursday, August 19, 1948. The *Raksha Bandhan* day has arrived; a festival when a sister ties *Rakhi*—a holy thread—on the wrist of her brother, and in turn, the brother gives gift of money and a vow to protect her for the rest of her life. The school is closed. Daddyji has taken the day off. We are all ready by 10 A.M. and walk to Original Road to pick up a Tonga. There are a few Tongas standing waiting for passengers. Daddyji is looking around to see if, our old coachman, Sabua is around. And as luck would have it, he is manning one of the Tongas; and as soon as he sees us, he comes around to our side of the road.

"Namaste, sahib," and he looks at Mummyji and asks, "*Bibiji*, let me guess. You must be going to Daryagunj to tie *Rakhi* to your brother, Daulat Ram ji."

"Yes, Sabuaji you are right, but before that we have to go to the refugee camp. Vikram and Kishi want to have *Rakhi* tied by Suneeta, a little girl at the refugee camp."

In a few minutes, we are at the camp. Unlike our first visit, nobody stops us. They all know Kishi and Mummyji as they have been going there regularly. We all get down from the Tonga and go into the baby area: *The Galaxy of Stars*. Sita, the manager, is already there and says, "Kamla, you gave us a very good idea. We are having all the girls in the camp tie *Rakhies* to all the men here."

Daddyji laughs and says, "I think it is an excellent idea. Then you will have so many men vowing to protect the infant girls and young women."

As we walk closer to the cot where Baby Suneeta is playing, she gets excited after seeing Mummyji and Kishi and starts babbling, "mamma mamma."

Sita brings in two *Rakhies* and hands them over to baby Suneeta. She starts to play with the threads. Sita holds baby Suneeta's hands and wraps the *Rakhi* first on Kishi's wrist and then on my wrist. Baby Suneeta holds on to the *Rakhi* threads and does not let go. Sita gently opens her grip on the threads and takes the threads out of her hands. Sita then ties the *Rakhi* threads firmly around our wrists. We get some sweets to eat and give some new clothes, that Mummyji had stitched herself, to baby Suneeta.

We move from one *Rakhi* tying stop to the next. As soon as we are finished with the ceremony at the refugee camp, we all get into the Tonga and are off to Daryagunj to Daulat Ram's house. As usual, I am sitting in the front of the Tonga and bearing the brunt of the explosive excretions from the rear end of the horse. In about 45 minutes, we are at Delhi Gate, take right turn on to Ansari Road, and, after a few minutes of negotiating the by-lanes, we reach our destination. The rest of the family has already arrived. Mummyji's two sisters, Devika and Sumitra, are there and so are her brothers Daulat Ram, Pawan Lal and Lakhi Lal. So now, three sisters have to tie *Rakhi* threads to three brothers. All three brothers sit down on three chairs in a row and cover their heads with small pieces of ceremonial cloth. The three sisters, one by one, tie the threads on each of the brother's wrists and place a red *Tikka*—a red mark—on their foreheads. The brothers give gifts of cash to each of the sisters, and the sisters place a little bit of sweets in their mouths, and the ceremony is complete. The women move into a different room leaving the men alone to talk politics and whatever else.

"Surinder, how do you like your job," Daulat Ram asks.

"I like it. Thank you, *Bhai* sahib. I have not seen you since I started the job. I really appreciate you recommending me to them."

Daulat Ram says, "I have known your boss, Kevin Bond, for a long time. Bond brothers are very nice people."

Surinder replies with a sarcastic smile, "I like the job, the salary is good, but I sometimes feel that I am working for the East India Company."

Daulat Ram laughs after hearing this and says, "Surinder, I don't know what you mean."

"Well, I feel I am still under the British Rule. In fact, I never felt like that even before independence. Now that I am reporting to the English bosses, I feel that India never got Independence. Although they are very nice, there seems to be an underlying arrogance in them that bothers me. You know, it is the way they treat other employees, and the way they talk to other Indians that I don't like; they seem to feel that the Raj is still continuing."

"You will get used to it. I think it is the way the English people speak that gives us the impression that they are displaying a superiority complex, but I think it is all in your mind. You should act with confidence, and everything will be all right."

The other uncles don't seem to be interested in this conversation. They, one by one, move to the other room where the womenfolk are sitting and chatting about much more interesting topics.

Daulat Ram and Daddyji carry on their chat. Daulat Ram says, "There is a party at the Imperial Hotel next month. The party is being arranged by your employer, Bond & Sons. I am sure they will invite you also."

Daddyji replies, "Yes, I know about it. I have been asked to make some of the arrangements. We are inviting top officials of the Government of India, top Indian business people and some diplomats also."

A servant enters the room meekly and keeps standing with his hands joined, as if in prayer. Daulat Ram looks at him, and the servant says meekly, "Sahib, *Bibiji* has sent a message: Lunch is served."

Daulat Ram says, "Tell her that we will be there in five......"

Daulat Ram is not quite finished with what he is saying, when Uncle SK enters with a plate full of food and comes and sits near Daddyji and says, "Sorry Surinder, I forgot to tell you; I have a letter for you."

He looks for it in his pocket, but does not find it and realizes that he had given it to his wife, Devika, to keep it in her purse before they left home. He leaves his plate on a table nearby, goes and gets the letter from his wife and hands it over to Daddyji; he quietly deposits it in the pocket of his pants and gets up to fetch his lunch. It has not escaped Daulat Ram's attention–from the type of envelope–that the letter is from outside India. And due to his dominant and nosey nature, he can't help but ask, "Surinder, the letter looks to be from a foreign country... is it?"

"Yes, it is from a pen friend I have in Canada."

• • •

After lunch, we all head to our respective homes. As we are riding home in the Tonga, Daddyji is thinking whether to tell about the letter to Mummyji or not. He is not sure how she will react to it. In the end, he decides not to tell. As soon as we each home, he makes an excuse to go out for a stroll in the park. He sits down on a bench and gently starts to open the envelope in his characteristic style: he tears a slice of the envelope on the short side of the envelope, blows into the envelope inflating it a bit, takes out the letter and unfolds it and begins to read:

45.27 N, 75.42 W

Dear Surinderji,

I found your last letter most interesting for the following reasons. First being, of course, that we have the same birthday. This fact places our pen friendship in a different class. Second being the part about the possible partition of Canada, if we were to ask for Independence from Britain. In fact, I showed your letter to one of my friends—a Member of Parliament—and he found that there is a lot of truth in what you wrote. Most probably, I will be visiting India as part of the United Nations' Kashmir Peace Keeping Mission. I will keep you informed.

You may find it of interest that I have exchanged a few letters with Swamiji of Verinag Ashram. I am pleased to learn that considerable progress has been made in Long Range Brainwave Transmission or Communication by Thought. I am really excited to learn about this celestial technique. In my opinion, this is the next frontier after Nuclear Fission, and its secret lies in India and its scriptures. In fact, Verinag Ashram is the most advanced in this extra sensory science. Imagine if people could communicate with each other just by thinking about one another! Brain waves are crisscrossing the Universe all the time. It is just that we do not know how to sense them. Developing the technique of Communication by Thought would be what developing an antenna was to electronic telecommunications; I have given it a new name—Braincom. Instant communication would change the world like nothing else. With advanced Braincom, one could not only read thoughts, but also see the views at another location.

Regards

Max

The next day, as he is riding to his office on his bicycle, he is thinking of what Max Hoffer had written in his letter. He agrees with Max Hoffer's conclusion that instant communication would change the world like nothing else, but he believes it would be a change for the worse. As he is peddling hard up the incline near Jhandewalan, he is trying to imagine what it would be like as millions of people communicate with each other just with their thoughts. He thinks that human race would go mad, with the brain being bombarded by messages all the time. They will have to devise some way of shutting off the brain function at night so that people can sleep.

As he opens the front door of the office, Shelly is sitting at her desk in a bright red dress and says, "Good morning, sir. Did you have a happy *Rakhi* day?"

He smiles and replies, "Good morning Shelly, it was a nice day. But as my sisters live out of station, they send me the *Rakhi* by post, and I have to tie the Rakhi thread myself on my wrist."

And he moves through the reception area into the area where his office is located. Morning passes by quickly, and it is lunch time. He usually eats lunch at *Kake Da Hotel* nearby. But today, he is in a hurry to finish lunch so that he can spend part of his lunch break writing a letter to Max Hoffer. He goes downstairs and picks up some food from the hawkers standing in front of the Odeon cinema. After he is finished eating, he goes to the bathroom to wash his hands and clean his teeth; and comes back and starts writing the letter.

Delhi (He does not know the Latitude and Longitude of Delhi; otherwise, he would have, like Max, started his letter with Latitude, Longitude)

Dear Max,

I am delighted to receive your letter and learn that you may be visiting India. But I am somewhat skeptical about Communication by Thought or Braincom, as you have named it. I would like to table my opinion about your suggestion that if Braincom became common place, it would be a boon to humanity. I think nothing could be further from the truth. Already, there is too much information available for the human mind to digest. The case in point: Let us look at the riots that took place at the time of the partition of India. If the newspapers and radio did not exist, I think the rioting and killing would have been much less. As soon as people heard on the radio that Hindus had killed Muslims in such and such locality, the Muslims would take up their spears and move on a Hindu locality and kill equal number of Hindus. And the cycle continued, fed by real or not so real information broadcast by radio and the press.

I look forward to your visit. Do keep us informed.

Regards

Surinder

• • •

The day of Bond & Sons Gala Party has arrived. It is a Sunday. The party starts at 7 P.M. Daddyji has got a new white Sharkskin Suit stitched along with a white Boski shirt and a red tie for contrast. A pair of white shoes is ready with a new coat of White on it. This is his debut at one of the first high level Socials of the movers and shakers of Delhi after the partition of India. Although he is just managing the function on behalf of his employer, he hopes to make some important connections. Kevin Bond has hinted that some senior cabinet ministers may drop by. Daddyji has already made arrangements with Sabua to take him in the Tonga to the hotel, but Sabua insisted on bringing a horse-drawn Victorian Buggy. Daddyji starts getting ready for the party at 3 P.M., and is all dressed up within the hour. Sabua is slated to arrive by 5 P.M.

"You were not this well dressed even on the day of your marriage," Mummyji teases him.

"Tell me Daddyji, what were you wearing on that day," I also join in.

Daddyji thinks hard and says, "I think, I was wearing a dark suit and a tie."

Mummyji carries on teasing him with a smile, "Yes, you are right. Now tell us what color Sari was I wearing?"

He laughs and replies, "Well, all Indian women wear red and gold coloured saris on the day of their marriage."

At 5 P.M. sharp, the bells of the Buggy are ringing, announcing the arrival of 'His Majesty's Chariot', as Mummyji calls it. We all get out to see the well polished and shining 'Chariot' standing on the street. All my friends walk around it to look it over. Daddyji climbs aboard, and the "Chariot" gracefully glides away.

"Mummyji, when I grow up, I would like to have a job like Daddyji's, where I can attend parties."

"Before you can do that, you have to study hard and become educated like your Daddyji. And remember, his work is not attending parties only; he has to do other work also."

As soon as Daddyji reaches the hotel, he gets busy assisting Kevin Bond with overseeing the arrangements. The setting for the party is the front lawn of the hotel, overlooking the Queensway and surrounded by tall palm trees. Large blocks of ice are being placed at the perimeter of the lawn. Pedestal fans are placed behind the ice blocks blowing air at the ice blocks; thereby, cooling the whole of the lawn on this hot sultry day. Tables with white table cloths, chairs draped with silken cloth, and the bearers moving around in red ceremonial uniforms are a sight to behold. The guests start arriving a little after 7 P.M. By about 7:45, the lawn is bustling with the Brown sahibs mixing with the, erstwhile, White sahibs. The reversal of roles is very interesting to watch. The White sahibs are entertaining the Brown sahibs to keep them on their side and win business and other favours from them. Daulat Ram, who seems to know just about everybody present, is going around with David Rankin and Kevin Bond. He is introducing them to the senior Indian Civil Servants and other dignitaries. Ever since Lord Mountbatten has returned to England after the conclusion of his vice regal assignment, the British are feeling a sense of isolation. They feel that the Soviets are trying to grab a dominant role in the Indian political-business spectrum. And that seems to be the reason for Bond & Sons throwing this party. Two guests, who are a surprise to Daddyji, are Hari Nautiyal and his son Veer. Hari Nautiyal is the famous industrialist and philanthropist who he met in Simla. As soon as Daddyji notices him, he goes over to greet him.

"Mr. Nautiyal, I am Surinder Mehra. We met you one day in Simla, last year, on our way up from Annandale. I think you know my elder brother Shyam Nath, Advocate."

Hari Nautiyal narrows his eyes for a few seconds, looking up at the sky, trying to think hard and says, "Yes, of course, I remember that incident in Simla. And your brother has also mentioned you a few times. But young man, what brings you here to this gathering of old men."

"I am the manager of the Delhi office of Bond & Sons."

"Well, this is a surprise—the descendants of the East India Company employing an Indian to be their manager. You must know that Bond brothers pride themselves as the descendants of the East India Company. They must be trying to give an Indian face to their business." And he laughs and carries on, "You know the Bonds are known to be more British than the British. They are known to have the stiffest of the upper lip in the Empire. This is quite an achievement on your part, I must say, old chap." He says, trying to put on an English accent with his chin a bit up—a mocking gesture on his part.

And then he takes Daddyji by his hand and walks over to an aged Political Party leader, in white Khadi attire with a white Gandhi cap, and says to him, "Chandubhai, meet Surinder Mehra. We need educated young men like him to run the country. You old men should now retire. You have served the nation well. Let the next generation carry some load."

Chandubhai Patel extends his hand to Daddyji and says, "Surinder, you should join the Party. We need promising young men like you, especially when you come highly recommended by Hari Nautiyal."

Hari Nautiyal starts discussing politics with the Chandubhai Patel. Daddyji, diplomatically, excuses himself and walks away. Later, he runs into his brother-in-law, Daulat Ram. He starts to point out the different government officials to him.

"See that man with the black rimmed glasses deep in conversation with David Rankin in the far corner; he is the Director of the Delhi Intelligence Bureau."

Daddyji is fascinated just watching the two police officers talk to each other and asks, "Do they know each other? I wonder what a former Commissioner of Police would be talking to the head of the Intelligence Bureau."

"Of course, they know each other. They used to work together before the partition. My guess is that they are talking about the Soviets." Daulat Ram replies.

"The War has been over for three years; what about the Soviets?"

Daulat Ram replies, "They are all worried about the Soviets gaining a foothold in India."

As they are talking, Hari Nautiyal brings, his son, Veer to where Daddyji and Daulat Ram are standing and introduces him.

Hari Nautiyal says, "Surinder, I have told Veer about your accomplishments. Veer has a suggestion. Veer, why don't you two young men have a chat?" And Hari Nautiyal and Daulat Ram move away and start mingling with other guests.

Veer says to Daddyji, "We are starting a post secondary education institute here in Delhi, and we are looking for somebody to be the general manager. My father and I were wondering if you would be interested in joining us. It is still in the planning stages. We are looking for somebody who is an educationist and is also interested in the business side of the teaching profession. As I understand you have both; having worked in Lahore in a private educational institution."

"I am flattered. I would like to think about it. Let us meet again to talk further," Daddyji replies.

Veer takes out his business card and hands it over to Daddyji. Kevin Bond, Daddyji's boss, is standing some distance away. He is talking to one of the guests. He notices Veer and Daddyji talking, and Veer handing over his business card to him. He has a hunch that the Nautiyals are trying to poach his manager.

With the next day being a working day, guests start departing by about 9:30 P.M. The lawn is practically empty by 10:30. The only people left are Kevin

Bond and Daddyji. They both sit down at one of the tables to catch up on who said what, and who should be pursued for new business. After they are finished comparing notes; they both move into the front yard of the hotel and walk towards Kevin Bond's car.

Kevin Bond says, "Come Surinder, I will ask my driver to take you home after he has dropped me off."

Daddyji takes a seat beside him, and they drive away.

27
OCTOBER 1948
ADOPTION

As I enter our Quarter after school, Mummyji is lying down on the bed and talking to Kishi. They are talking about baby Suneeta, the little baby girl at the refugee camp.

"Will we never see her again, Mummyji?" Kishi asks.

"We don't know," she says and gets up to serve us lunch.

After lunch, both Kishi and I go to sleep for a while. After we wake up, we go outside to play with our friends.

Daddyji is home at 6:30 P.M. He always takes a bath as soon as he reaches home from the office. Today, as soon as he reaches home, he puts his bicycle on the side in the verandah and goes inside the Quarter. Both Kishi and I follow him inside. Usually, Mummyji is standing outside waiting for him, but today she is inside doing odd jobs trying to keep herself busy. Something is bothering her.

She takes out fresh clothes for Daddyji and hands them over to him, as he is going for his bath. But he senses some aloofness in her and asks, "Kamla, what is the matter? Are you all right?"

As soon as he says this, she breaks down in a torrent of tears; weeping and talking at the same time. Daddyji says, "Kamla I am not able to make head or tail of what you are saying. Calm down."

He then gets hold of her by her shoulders, makes her sit down on the edge of the bed and says, "Now tell me, what has happened?"

"Sita, the manager of the refugee camp, told me that the camp and the orphanage are going to move to North Delhi near the main refugee camp. This means that we will not be able to see Suneeta. She has become so used to me.

I don't know what she is going to do–poor baby." And she starts weeping again loudly.

After hearing the noise of weeping, Karnail Singh asks loudly from his side of the Quarter, "Surinder, is everything all right? Do you need any help?"

Daddyji replies, "Karnail, thank you. It is just a minor problem, nothing serious."

Both Kishi and I are standing and watching. I am beginning to understand the situation.

I blurt out, "Mummyji, why don't we bring Suneeta home?"

She replies, still sobbing, "We can only bring her home if we adopt her."

I have no idea what adopt means, but I can see Daddyji's colour change as he hears the word 'adopt'.

Kishi asks, "What is that Mummyji?"

She looks at Daddyji, but does not say anything; she can see his stunned face.

We are all quiet for sometime. Daddyji picks up his clothes and goes in for a bath.

When he comes out of the bathroom, he is hoping for the things to have calmed down. On the contrary, Mummyji is lying on the bed with her eyes closed. Daddyji comes into the room and says, "Kamla, can I have a cup of tea?" There is no reaction from Mummyji. She just keeps still as if she has not heard anything. After a while, she slowly gets up from the bed, picks up an envelope lying on the study table, and hands it over to Daddyji. He gets hold of the envelope and finds that it has already been opened. He still blows into it, in his characteristic style, to inflate it; and then takes out the letter, unfolds it, starts to read it and says with excitement in his voice, "Vikram and Kishi, your grandparents are coming to stay with us for the winter. They say it is too cold in Simla in winter. I think they should be here in about two weeks."

It seems that the reason for Mummyji's bad mood is not only that the refugee camp and the orphanage are moving away; it is also that her in-laws are coming to stay with us. It seems Daddyji is in double trouble.

Mummyji finally breaks her silence, "Where are they going to live?"

Daddyji replies, "Right here with us."

She replies with her voice full of irritation, "Where? Are they going to live on my head? Do you see any place anywhere?"

This really sets Daddyji's fuse off, and he fires off his own salvo, "Is this any way to talk about my parents? Have I ever insulted your parents like this?

We will cover the front veranda and convert it into a room. We will manage somehow."

Mummyji replies, "Tell them to rent their own flat nearby until we can find a larger accommodation."

As bickering between my parents is going on, Kishi starts to weep and sits down on the floor and says, "I want baby Suneeta to come to our house."

It appears that Daddyji has had enough of crying from the mother and the son and decides to calm them down. He suddenly holds his head in his hands and says, "Oh, my head is going to burst." And goes and lies down on his bed and says, "Kamla, can you please give a Saridon tablet? I think I am going to faint. I don't know what is happening to me. Everything is going in circles around me."

As usual, as soon as Daddyji has even the slightest health problem, her fear of losing him takes over; she just goes into panic and is ready to do anything. Daddyji knows this very well and has decided to use this weapon to get out of double trouble.

...

By the next morning, things have calmed down, as if nothing happened. I have noticed that the passage of night has a settling effect on both of them—did I tell you that all four of us sleep in the same room? Kishi and I sleep on one bed, and my parents on the other. Early in the morning, as I am still lying in bed with my eyes closed and pretending to be asleep—but able to hear everything; and as the waves of harmony and understanding are flowing between them, Mummyji starts the topic of baby Suneeta and says, "Listen ji, you are the one who suggested on our last night in Lahore that we should think of adopting a baby girl because I would never be able to have another baby. I think baby Suneeta is God sent." As soon as she mentions the name of baby Suneeta, I cringe under the bed sheet waiting for the argument to start again, but nothing of the sort happens.

Daddyji listens to her and just nods his head and says, "Let us see what happens."

After getting permission from our landlord, Karnail Singh, Daddyji engages a carpenter to start work on covering up the verandah, on our side of the Quarter, to convert it into a room where my grandparents can live.

...

As soon the Tonga arrives, both Kishi and I run to them and get our arms around their legs. My grandfather, Pitaji, and grandmother, Beyji, have arrived from Simla; Mummyji also comes out of the Quarter, but does not seem too happy to see them—having had an argument with Daddyji about their living accommodations earlier.

Their room has been furnished with two *Charpoys*—beds with strings of jute strung across a wooden frame—barely fitting in the space. Their belongings, consisting of two steel trunks and a number of bags, are slid under the *Charpoys* to keep some area of the floor free to stand on. A number of nails have been driven into the walls for hanging clothes and towels. A light bulb is hanging from a wire from the ceiling to provide light. In view of the approaching winter, Mummyji already had two quilts made. The cotton for the quilts was fluffed right in our verandah, and the neighbourhood tailor had stitched the quilts. With so many of us living in a confined space, our home looks like the waiting room of a railway station. At night, after our room is bolted shut from inside; there is no way for Pitaji and Beyji to access the bathroom. This creates a problem in the household, so we start sleeping with the doors unlocked. The bath room and toilet is in great demand in the mornings. Some days we have to ask to use our neighbour's toilet when the call of nature demands. Other than the congestion, it is fun to have Pitaji and Beyji around. In the morning, I am the first to leave home for school at 8:45 A.M. The school is now on winter hours—9:30 A.M. to 3:30 P.M. The next to leave house is Daddyji. Two or three times a week, Mummyji and Kishi go to the refugee camp; she teaches there and helps around as a volunteer. The days when Kishi and Mummyji are away, Pitaji and Beyji are left alone part of the day. However, before Mummyji leaves home, she cooks breakfast and lunch for my grandparents.

December is a cold month in Delhi. Everyday, as I am leaving for school, I see Pitaji and Beyji lying on their beds with the quilts draped over like a tent. Sometimes, when they are up early, they are sitting with blankets wrapped around them with cups of hot tea warming their hands and steam rising from the cups. There is talk of renting another accommodation in the same Square or one nearby, but nothing is available at this time. I sense despair on their faces.

One day, I hear them talk to each other. Pitaji says, "Not too long ago we used to have our own house, and now we are sitting shivering in a makeshift accommodation. Instead of becoming Independent, we have become Dependent. God, strange are thy ways!"

THE GOLDEN SPARROW

• • •

The time for the move of the orphanage to North Delhi is fast approaching. One day, when Mummyji comes back from the orphanage, she is hysterical because she has seen preparations for the move being made. Daddyji is not home. She asks Pitaji and Beyji, "We are thinking of adopting a baby girl; what do you think?"

Pitaji is surprised at the question. At first, he is not sure how to respond to a question about adoption from his daughter-law but, after some thought, he replies, "It is a very noble act. All children are Angels. It is when they absorb the world around them that they begin to take different forms."

Beyji has her own ideas, and she says, "One has to be careful and find out the blood line. The blood line of the child is very important."

Pitaji asks, "Kamla, why this sudden interest in adoption?"

Mummyji recites the whole background, and, in the end, says, "I am so attached to baby Suneeta that I love her like Vikram and Kishi. Losing her would be like losing one of them." And she starts to sob, wiping tears with the end of her sari.

Pitaji consoles her by saying, "Many a time in life, one comes across people that one begins to love like one's own. And then, due to circumstances beyond ones control, one has to separate. Flowers blossom through summer, and in autumn they are gone. Night is followed by day. Time keeps moving. It is a great healer. With time one makes new associations, and new relationships are born."

Mummyji replies, "Pitaji, during our journey through life, we come across many destinations that we pass by—never to return to them. But once in our life time, we see the one, and we say to ourselves that we should not let it pass by. This is the one for me. I feel that baby Suneeta is part of me. I want to adopt her as our own. Moreover, I always wanted a baby girl. Beyji, do you remember when Kishi was born; I dressed him up as a girl. Dr. Sandhu told us in Lahore, after Kishi's birth, that I will not be able to become a mother again, so what is the harm in adopting."

Both Pitaji and Beyji are left searching their souls. As Mummyji gets up and leaves their room, Beyji says to Pitaji, "It seems that Kamla must have some connection with baby Suneeta in her previous life."

Pitaji retorts back, "Keep your philosophy to yourself. If Surinder hears about it, he will be upset."

In the evening, when Daddyji is back from work, he senses a cloud of gloom in the Quarter. Only one light is on. Everybody is quite. The usual blanket of smoke is covering the area.

He asks, "Why is everybody so quiet? Has somebody died?"

My grandmother, Beyji, says almost reprimanding him, "Say some thing nice, Surinder. The dusk is the time of prayers and not for saying inauspicious things." And then she signals to him to come to her. She takes him aside in the verandah out of hearing distance of Mummyji and Pitaji and says in almost a whisper, "Listen Surinder... she is harping about adopting that orphaned girl... whatishername... Do not give in to her; otherwise, you will repent all your life. It is a big responsibility; especially a girl... child... you know what I mean... First raising her and then getting her married off. And we don't even know her bloodline... for all we know; she could be a Muslim girl."

For the rest of the evening, there is no talk of adoption. I finish my homework. After that I have a half hour English tutoring from Daddyji–both written and oral. Recently, in addition to English language instruction, he has started getting me interested in general knowledge. He gets hold of the newspaper and shows me what is going on in India and the world. After dinner, we are in bed by 10:30 P.M. As usual, I am pretending to be asleep–actually I am not sleeping. I can hear a discussion going on between my parents about the adoption of baby Suneeta. I have no idea what time it is was when I fell asleep. When we wake up in the morning, Mummyji is cheerful and Daddyji seems happy. As usual, the night seems to dissolve all their problems. I am beginning to understand why God made night: it is to dissolve all the problems, or should I say solve all the problems.

Daddyji announces to us all that they have decided to adopt baby Suneeta, provided the authorities will let us. Kishi and I are very happy; that is what we wanted in the first place. Daddyji has decided that he will take half a day off from work the next day and go to see the manager of the orphanage. As Daddyji is about to leave for work, Beyji corners him again and asks him, "What are you getting into, Surinder?"

He replies, "Beyji, adopting an orphan child is the most pious act–especially adopting a girl. A girl child is the incarnation of Goddess *Lakshmi*; you used to tell us this when we were children. Beyji, my sixth sense tells me that God has sent Suneeta for us. Give us your blessings that we may succeed in the adoption proceedings."

Beyji is quiet for some time. And then she embraces Daddyji and says, "Surinder, I am proud of you. Our blessings are with you."

Mummyji is standing by the door watching all this, with tears of joy flowing down her cheeks.

Then next day, Mummyji and Daddyji go to visit the orphanage. They explain everything to Sita, the manager. She says, "Kamla, are you sure you want to adopt? It is a life long commitment. Moreover, adoption is a long process. You should be prepared that your application may not be accepted. You know, one very important factor the ministry considers is the religion of the child and the religion of the adoptive parents. They have to be the same. I am going to the office of the Rehabilitation Ministry tomorrow. I will find out all the necessary details. Please come back to see me in a few days. And one more thing: You will be happy to learn that the orphanage is not going to be moving to North Delhi for a few more months. So you can continue with your visits."

In a few days, Mummyji and Daddyji go to the orphanage. After they fill all the necessary forms, Sita tells them, "You know, I found out at the office of the Rehabilitation Ministry that they have to publish the name and description of the adoptee child in the Government Gazette before adoption process can proceed. This is to find out if any one of the parents or other guardians are alive or not."

"How long will this process take?" Mummyji asks.

"It will take, at least, three months. And I want to tell you a new development that has taken place. This orphanage is going to be transferred to a private charitable trust—The Nautiyal Galaxy Trust, a division of the Nautiyal Family Trust. This is all owned by the well known Nautiyal family, the owners of Nautiyal Industries."

Daddyji and Mummyji look at each other but do not say anything.

As they are going home in a Tonga, Daddyji says, "Kamla, destiny, repeatedly, keeps bringing us in contact with the Nautiyals—first in Simla, then at the party at the Imperial Hotel, and now at the Galaxy. There must be some message in this."

Mummyji is absorbed in her thoughts. Daddyji looks at her and realizes that she has not heard a thing he has said.

As the Tonga comes to stop in front of our Square, Mummyji blurts out, "I think he was right."

"Who are you talking about, Kamla?"

"Have you forgotten what Swamiji told us, five years ago, at Verinag? He read your palm and told us that we will have a baby girl. This is it. I am sure this is it. It is baby Suneeta."

There is thunder and lightening from the heavens and it begins to pour. Daddyji and Mummyji run inside the Quarter. As they enter, Pitaji asks, "So what happened?"

"It looks that the adoption process is going to take a long time," Daddyji replies.

Pitaji suggests, "You should ask Daulat Ram to help you. With his connections, it should not take that long."

"Well, we don't want the relatives to know about this until it is all finalized; otherwise, they are all going to ask all kinds of questions. You know how it is."

Mummyji says, "Yes, I think you are right. If God has baby Suneeta in store for us, nobody can keep her away from us."

28

DELHI: 1949
THE GALAXY OF STARS

All the employees are gathered for meeting the new management. Mrs. Meera Nautiyal, wife of Hari Nautiyal and the Chairperson of the Nautiyal Galaxy Trust, starts to address the meeting, "As you all know, the government has transferred the orphanage to our Trust. You must have seen the new name. In Hindi we will call it, *Taraun Ki Shalaa*, and in English, Galaxy of Stars. We have plans to expand this facility and make it a permanent institution. We are not going to be moving to North Delhi as was planned before. There are a number of administrative matters that need attention. As some of you know, Sita, your current manager, is a government employee, and she will be moving back to the Ministry of Rehabilitation; therefore, we have to find a replacement. We are fortunate that we have a few possible candidates right here among us, and we will make a decision in the next few weeks."

A week later, the peon brings a note to Mummyji, while she is teaching a class at the Galaxy. After the class, she walks over to Sita's office. Sita and Meera Nautiyal, the Chairperson, are sitting and talking. Mummyji knocks at the door. "Come in Kamla," Sita says pointing to the empty chair and then gets up and leaves the room.

Meera Nautiyal says, "Kamla, Sita has recommended you for the job of the new manager of the Galaxy. Would you be interested? You don't have to give me the answer right now; you may think about it. Oh, and I wanted to ask you something else. Are you related to Surinder Mehra?"

Mummyji says with a smile on her face, "Yes, Mrs. Nautiyal, he is my husband."

"What a coincidence… Will you believe that my husband and son were talking about him a few days ago? Kamla, we would like to invite you and your husband for lunch next Sunday. Are you free?"

"I will ask my husband and let you know tomorrow."

When Mummyji reaches home, she can't wait for Daddyji to come home so that she can give him the two exciting news—the offer of a job of the manager of the Galaxy and the lunch invitation. To be invited to the home of such a high profile family is not a small social accomplishment. Daddyji, when he learns of the good news, is equally excited and says, "Kamla, it seems we are about to move up in the world. You have been offered a job, and, I think, they want to offer me a high position in their organization."

As soon as Mummyji reaches the Galaxy the next day, she goes to see Mrs. Nautiyal." So, Kamla, what have you decided?

"Yes, Mrs. Nautiyal, I accept the job offer and, yes, we are free next Sunday. Is there a special occasion?"

Meera Nautiyal replies, "Well, you could say that. Just you and our family are going to be there; it must be something special. My husband asked me not to invite anybody else. Oh… and, by the way, we will send a car to pick you up and drop you back."

On Sunday, I am outside with some friends. Three of us are sitting at the edge of the open drainage ditch that runs parallel to the road. A car stops just in front of us. The driver blows the horn two times; a tradition of announcing one's arrival both physically and for stature. In the middle class area that we live in, we seldom see cars. As soon as the horn is heard by the residents of the Square, people peep out to look. They are eager to find out who the visiting dignitary is. I know that my parents are expecting a car. The car door opens and the driver, in a white uniform, comes out and walks towards our Quarter. It seems that my parents must be eagerly watching the road. For, as soon as the car driver reaches near our Quarter, my parents walk out—all dressed up for the party. The driver salutes them, says something, leads them to the car, and opens the rear door of the car for my parents to be seated.

As my parents are riding in the car, they are watching the passing landscape from the perspective of being seated in the rear of a Jaguar car rather than a horse drawn Tonga. Daddyji is already dreaming of the future. They are both unusually quiet, but their minds are working overtime. The past, present and the future is floating back and forth in their minds. Being Sunday, the traffic is scant. They are at the Outer Circle of Connaught Place in no time. As the car enters the Inner Circle, Daddyji breaks his silence and points out to Mummyji where his office in located. After a few minutes, the car takes a turn onto Curzon Road and takes another turn into the driveway of the Nautiyal Residence.

They are welcomed by Veer Nautiyal and his wife, Bina, in the portico of their sprawling bungalow. "Surinder and Kamla, we are delighted that you could come." They all go into the house. As they are walking through the entrance area, Daddyji notices pictures on the two side walls. He slows down to look at them. At the same time, Hari Nautiyal joins them and, after the pleasantries, starts to tell them stories behind the pictures. The pictures are mostly about his exploits in various theatres of World War II.

After sitting in the drawing room briefly, they all move outdoors to the lawn in the rear of the house. As light refreshments are being served, men folk are talking politics.

After a while, the women decide to move indoors. As soon as the men are by themselves, Veer asks, "Surinder, which beer would you prefer? We have most of them in stock."

"Thank you for the offer, but I don't drink. I am fine with *Lassi*."

Hari Nautiyal takes beer, and Veer takes freshly squeezed orange juice. After a few sips of the 'golden nectar', Hari Nautiyal is brimming with energy and starts to talk about his organization.

"Surinder, you will recall that we talked briefly the other day at the Imperial Hotel. After that Veer and I have decided to make you a formal offer to join our organization. Now let me first tell you a little more about what we have in mind. Our organization has three Divisions: Manufacturing, Distribution and Civics. As you probably know, we have factories for manufacturing various items. We are stockists of different goods and have distribution centers. The Civics division is relatively new, and this is where we plan to spend all the excess money we earn in the other two divisions."

Daddyji seems a bit confused with the function of the Civics Division. Hari Nautiyal notices the confusion and explains, "The Civics division has been formed so that we may discharge our civic duties in a planned manner. This has acquired a new significance after the Independence of our country. Some may consider it charitable work, but we have decided to look at it differently.

Charity is that one gives from the goodness of one's heart to help those in need. We consider that it is our duty to give, and not a choice. Those who have been blessed much above the others must give back to society without expectation to receive something in return."

Daddyji asks, "Do you mean that people who give charity expect something in return?"

Hari Nautiyal continues, "Not all, but some, I am sure, do. There are two types of returns that the charity giver expects: First, he expects to receive or feel the gratitude of the receiver. Second, he expects to earn *"Punya"*–the grace of God–for having given charity."

Daddyji smiles and says, "Mr. Nautiyal, are you sure you will be completely altruistic? You will have no expectations?"

Hari Nautiyal Replies, "Listen, Surinder, we too are human like the rest of us. We will, certainly, expect to feel satisfied but nothing more" And he continues, "The Civics division will itself be divided into different departments. For now, we have three in mind: Health, Education and Strategic Initiatives. What we will do in the first two is obvious, but the third is probably the most important. Strategy is what gives nations edge over other nations. The British were able to rule over us for two centuries because of a well thought out strategy of Divide and Rule. We also have a strategy in mind; it is to discover the ancient secrets in our scriptures and to use the discoveries to the benefit of our country and mankind. Verinag Ashram is where the research is taking place, and I would like you to get involved in the management of the Ashram."

As soon as he hears the words 'ancient secrets in our scriptures', Daddyji is again reminded of the dream he had on the bus coming back from Verinag about Hitler looking for *Brahmastra*. He is thinking: *May be there is something to the dream I had.* He interrupts again to ask, "If you are talking about the strategy of governing our country, then, I think it, is up to the elected government of the day to form the strategy. Don't you think?"

Hari replies, "Governments have to satisfy many masters; therefore, formation of a long-term strategy for governments is very difficult. And they too need advice from people like us. I have faith in human progress and mankind's ability to create a world of justice and peace. At this time in our history, we have the opportunity. If we seize it, it will lead on to better life for all our countrymen."

Daddyji is rather impressed with the sentiments expressed by Hari Nautiyal and says, "Mr. Nautiyal, I hope you are right. But we should be cautious that we do not start dreaming of a Utopian Society; it works only in the books. Sir

Thomas Moore's novel, Utopia, written in 1516, is very interesting to read but hardly practical."

During lunch, the conversation centers on the enormous task that India faces in creating jobs and housing for millions of displaced people. After lunch is over, menfolk move to a corner of the drawing room, and the women remain seated at the dining table and carry on their conversation.

"Where do you see me fitting in your organization?" Daddyji asks, looking at both Hari Nautiyal and Veer.

Hari Nautiyal replies, "Surinder, as you probably know, Veer is now the Managing Director of Nautiyal Industries. He would like you to work with him as Advisor with the title of Executive Director—Civics Division. In addition, we would like Kamla to be the head of the Galaxy. I have heard that you have already applied for adopting an infant girl. I must say that it is a very noble gesture."

Daddyji smiles and says, "Mr. Nautiyal, are you offering me a job to be my wife's boss? I am sure you can imagine the trouble I can be in." And they all burst into laughter.

Veer says, "Don't worry, Surinder, we all have the same problem. To make life easier for us, my mother will be overseeing all the Galaxy Centers."

"Surinder, how do you find working with Bond & Sons?" Veer asks, as they are still recovering from laughter.

Daddyji replies, "You know, I have mixed feelings. I have told my wife also. Having just become independent from the British, I, for some reason, feel strange reporting to British bosses. Although, I must say that they are very nice to me, but they treat other Indian employees differently and with some arrogance. And the other thing I have noticed is that there is more to Bond & Sons than meets the eye. I have heard Kevin Bond and David Rankin talking to each other and referring to Bond & Sons as 'the Company'—as in the East India Company."

Hari Nautiyal says, "We have suspected for some time that after partition Bond & Sons are expanding their business network in India. They have appointed influential Indian business managers in their offices in Bombay, Calcutta and Madras; and Surinder, you in Delhi because of the influence of, your brother-in-law, Daulat Ram. I think they want to maintain some measure of influence in India after the partition; therefore, it seems, Bond & Sons is being fortified to take over the role of the New East India Company."

Veer has been listening intently to his father and asks, "You mean it can happen again—the New East India Company."

Hari Nautiyal looks at Veer and says, "I don't think so, but we will have to keep an eye on Bond & Sons."

Daddyji has been listening, with interest, what the Nautiyals have been saying. After listening to them, all strange goings on in the office of Bond & Sons begin to make sense. At the spur of the moment, he makes a momentous decision.

He says, "Mr. Nautiyal, I will be pleased to accept your offer but with one caveat. I have another about six months left in my contract with Bond & Sons. I would like to honour that."

In fact, he has no contract with Bond & Sons. He could leave with just 15 days notice. In the next six months, he wants to find out if what is suspected about Bond & Sons is right or not. And the important thing is that he decides not to tell the Nautiyals about it so that they cannot be later implicated in any wrongdoing.

Hari Nautiyal gets up and embraces Daddyji and says, "Welcome to Nautiyal family."

They all move indoors to tell their wives about Surinder's decision to join Nautiyal Industries.

As they are all sitting down for tea and desserts, Surinder asks, "Mr. Nautiyal, how is LESTWEFORGET going?"

Hari Nautiyal Replies, "After August 15, 1947, we have not done much with it. Except that we have a get-together of the membership once a year. After you join us, we will have to think of moving it forward."

Daddyji says, "Mr. Nautiyal, I would like to tell you about a very amusing plan, my friend, Karnail Singh and I hatched to avenge all that the British did to us. We named our plan 'Operation *Vilayat*'. The essential ingredients are as follows.

First: We should beat them in the game of cricket. Nothing would humiliate them more than getting beaten at their own game by the colonials.

Second: We should impregnate the English language by adding Hindi into it, and call it *Hinglish*.

Third: We should flood Britain with Hindus and Muslims and take them over by shear numbers; build Temples, Mosques, Restaurants and Ghettoes for Indians.

Fourth: Food Revenge. Make thousands of Indian Restaurants in Britain; so much so that instead of fish and chips, the British start eating Butter Chicken. Instead of Guinness Beer, they start drinking *Lassi* in their Pubs.

They all burst out in a loud laughter and Hari says, "Surinder, this is the most ingenious scheme I have heard to date. We should put it into action right away." And they go into a fit of laugher again.

29
MOTORCYCLE

At about 7:30 P.M., there is sound of a motorcycle in the distance; nothing unusual we think. A little while later, there are two beeps of the motorcycle's horn. Nothing unusual we think; assuming that somebody in the neighborhood is making his presence felt. There are two more beeps—but long and irritating ones this time. Somebody is being a nuisance, we think. More beeps of the horn…looong, looooong and loooonger. At this instant, my grandfather, Pitaji, picks up his steel pointed stick, gets up and utters a few choicest expletives that he has not had a chance to use since he left Lahore. As he goes out to investigate, he finds Daddyji sitting on a new motorcycle—smiling.

"*Oye*, Surinder whose motorcycle is this?" Pitaji asks.

"Mine, Pitaji, I just bought it."

In the meantime, Mummyji, Beyji, Kishi and I come out to see what is going on. And the rest of the people of the Square are also out crowding around the motorcycle. Nobody in the neighbourhood has a motorcycle. Only a few days back, they had seen a car come by our house and now the motorcycle. It is enough to start the rumor mill. Beyji is concerned about Evil Eye striking. She goes inside and brings an old piece of rope with an old shoe tied to it and says, "Take this, Surinder, and tie it around the handle bars of the motorcycle." Daddyji takes one look at it and is very reluctant to tie the ugly looking contraption around the handle bars of his new motorcycle. However, coming from his mother, and to prevent Evil Eye from striking, he reluctantly follows his mother's advice.

Mummyji walks around the motorcycle, looks at it with pride and declares, "See, we have been blessed with the new motorcycle because Goddess

Lakshmi, the Goddess of wealth, is pleased with us, as we are going to adopt baby Suneeta."

Where to park the motorcycle for the night? That is the question being debated in our household as some of the neighbours have started to disperse. Beyji comes in and says, "Surinder and Kamla, go to the Temple and make an offering of one and quarter rupee, before you go to sleep tonight, to thank God for the motorcycle."

Daddyji says, "Yes Beyji, but before we go, we have to decide where to park the motorcycle at night so that it will not be stolen."

Ultimately, our neighbour, Karnail Singh, comes to the rescue. He says, "Surinder, I think you should park the motorcycle in the rear courtyard. We can bring it through the rear lane."

Daddyji seems very relieved and says, "Oh Karnail Singh, *Yaar*, you are great!"

As Mummyji and Daddyji are getting ready to go to the Temple, they are trying to decide if they should walk or go on the motorcycle. Finally, Beyji makes the decision for them, and she says, "You must also take the motorcycle to the Temple if you want proper blessings to be imparted to it."

Now, this is Mummyji's first ride ever on a motorcycle. Daddyji kick starts the motorcycle, and Mummyji reluctantly sits on the seat behind Daddyji, with both her legs dangling on one side and holding Daddyji by his shoulders. Her face is red, and it appears as if she is just going to die of shame. Her legs are showing below the edge of her sari, and she is holding on to her husband in full view of her in-laws and the neighbours. She is thinking: *Indian women are just not supposed to do that, you stupid Kamla.*

As she is trying to come to terms with her predicament, Daddyji clicks the motorcycle into gear and suddenly lets the clutch go. They lurch forward with Mummyji bumping against Daddyji, and the motorcycle takes off towards the Temple. As they reach the Temple, which is about two minutes ride from our house, a new predicament takes hold. After pulling up the motorcycle on the stand, Daddyji says, "Kamla is it safe to leave the motorcycle here when we go in the Temple?

She replies, "Listen ji, you should stop worrying so much about your motorcycle being stolen. Don't you have insurance? Moreover, you have the key, and we will keep it in our view when we go into the Temple." Daddyji seems convinced. They go into the Temple and present an offering of one and a quarter rupee. The priest asks, "What is the purpose of the offering?"

Mummyji replies, "We have bought a new motorcycle."

The priest recites some Sanskrit hymns with words 'motorcycle' repeated several times within the hymns. Both my parents are satisfied that the priest has done the needful. They respectfully receive the *Prasad* or oblation and one flower garland and depart. As this is all going on, every now and then, Daddyji looks over his shoulder. Through the corner of his eye, he is able to watch the motorcycle standing in the street. As they are moving away, the priest says, "Please tie the flower garland to the handle bars of the motorcycle for blessings to be transferred to it."

When they reach home, Daddyji moves the motorcycle to the rear courtyard and bolts the door shut. After bolting the door, he still does not look satisfied with the 'security arrangements'. Pitaji comes out to see what the problem is and says, "Surinder, strange are the ways of God. When He gives wealth, He also gives some thing to balance it; the fear of losing it. God gave you the means to buy this motorcycle. If He had intended to take it away, He would not have given it to you in the first place; so get the fear out of your mind and go to sleep."

He finally goes to bed, but keeps tossing and turning all night worried about his motorcycle.

Next morning, Daddyji is up bright and early to get his motorcycle ready to take him to work. The first thing he does is take it out of the rear courtyard and roll it to the front yard. The rear courtyard is a busy place in the morning with two families trying to get ready for the day. He decides to call our domestic servant to come and clean the motorcycle and get it ready for the day. Here starts the first conflict. As our domestic servant is cleaning the dust off the motorcycle, there is a shout from inside the Quarter by my grandfather. He is a man of patience, as long as he gets what he wants and when he wants. Today his cup of tea has not reached him by the appointed time—and hence the shout "*Oye*, Chottu, where is my tea?"

Poor Chottu, only 12 years old, tries to keep all his masters happy. He replies, "Coming Pitaji... tea is coming in five minutes."

Outside, Daddyji is not happy with the cleaning that Chottu is doing. "See, Chottu, this speck of dirt... yes, yes... clean... shine this spot... what will people say... I want it to shine on the first day." Then, of course, there is the question of whether or not to remove the 'Evil eye Killer' that Beyji had installed, and what to do with the blessed flowers that the priest at the Temple had given to be tied to the motorcycle. Well, finally, he removes most of the 'artifacts', but decides to leave a trace of both–just in case. He finally kick starts the motorcycle and is off to work.

As he is riding, he feels that everybody on the road is watching him. He has been thinking about it, but has not decided where to park the motorcycle. While he is still thinking about it, he has reached his office. He drives straight to Fauji's cycle stand.

"*Oye*, Surinder ji, I see you have bought a motorcycle. Well done ji. It is always good to move up in the world," Fauji says as soon as he sees Daddyji.

"Fauji *Yaar*, tell me. Is it safe to leave the motorcycle at the stand?"

"Surinder ji, this is Fauji's cycle stand. Nothing moves here without my permission."

Daddyji pulls the motorcycle on the stand, Fauji gives him a receipt, and he goes to the office.

As he enters the office, he is greeted by, Shelly, the receptionist, and she says, "Good morning, sir. How was your ride to work? I hope you have a nice day."

Usually, he says good morning and goes to his office, but today is different.

He stops in front of her desk and tells her, "Shelly, I have bought a motorcycle. I came to work on the motorcycle today."

She smiles and says, "Congratulations, Mr. Mehra."

As he is settling down in his work, the peon brings a note asking him to come to Kevin Bond's office.

As he reaches Kevin Bond's office, there is the usual sound of Shelly giggling and Kevin Bond laughing. He is not sure if he should disturb the boss or not. He decides to knock at the door. There is silence for a while. And then Shelly comes out rearranging her clothes and hair and looks at Daddyji shyly and says, "Mr. Bond will see you now."

As he enters the office, Kevin Bond asks him, "Surinder, what do you think of Shelly? I personally think her shorthand is marvelous."

Daddyji is somewhat taken a back by this comment by Kevin Bond. He does not say any thing out of his mouth but says the following that remains unsaid.

"*Oh Behen Ch…(expletive deleted) Bond, you are fooling around in the office and then you are trying to make a fool of me by talking about shorthand.*"

And then he blurts out, "Mr. Bond, I have never had a chance to use her shorthand capabilities. I usually write in longhand and give it to her for typing. *I think, instead of her shorthand, you fancy her.*" The last sentence is only stuck in his brain; it never comes to his lips.

Bond takes out a paper and pencil from his desk drawer and says, "Let us get back to business, old chap. Things are going to get very busy. Surinder, we have received a flood of inquiries from firms in Britain and other countries to represent them in India. The sad part is that they all have come to the conclusion that the Kashmir conflict is going to go on for a long time and both the newly born countries will need lots of armaments. At this time, armies of both the countries are using material supplied by Britain during World War II. At the time of partition 2/3rd of the materials were retained by India and 1/3rd by Pakistan. As the current stock gets consumed, the replacements will have to come from abroad."

Daddyji asks, "Do you mean the same companies will supply to both sides?"

Bond replies, "It depends on who gets the contracts. Britain is not the only country making armaments. America, Russia and some other European countries will be trying to sell arms to both sides. Arms business has been very slow after World War II. Sometime one wonders..." Bond does not complete the sentence.

But after some thought, Bond continues, "Well, you know what I mean; wars are good for the business of the arms manufacturers. Anyway, let us get back to our own business. We have to create contacts in the Ministry of Defense and the Indian Army. You know, armament purchases are big money items. There will be hefty commissions if we can help our clients get some contracts."

Daddyji asks, "What do these companies want to sell?"

Bond replies, "Automatic weapons, ammunitions, vehicles, tanks, aircraft and host of other material."

Daddyji says, "I have read that all the top military officers of the Indian and Pakistan armies were trained at Royal Military College, Sandhurst, in England. Also there are still many British Generals part of the Indian and Pakistan Armies, so Britain already has an inside track in selling arms to both the armies. Why don't these companies just approach the British government for help?"

Bond replies, "The British government has just left the sub-continent; they do not want to be seen as promoting warfare by helping their companies sell arms to one or both sides."

Daddyji is not happy to participate in the sale and purchase of goods that are going to contribute towards death and destruction. He is not sure how he should respond to Bond. He says, "Mr. Bond. Is it necessary to get involved in the instruments of killing?"

Bond replies, "Surinder, I feel the same way as you do; but if we don't, somebody else will. When war is going on, the governments will try and get armaments wherever they can find them. Moreover, we will become very very rich."

For the time being, Daddyji agrees to go along with what Bond wants, mainly because he wants to find out how the system works.

He is thinking about it on his way home in the evening. At night, he tells Mummyji about what has transpired at the office.

"Kamla, I never thought of War as a business. I must say I learned something new today."

Mummyji says, "It seems to me that politicians create wars to satisfy their egos. The arms merchants make money by selling the armaments. The soldiers are given inspirational speeches by the politicians appealing to their sense of patriotism; soldiers are the ones who give their lives in defense of the motherland. And when things get hot, the planes start raining fire from the sky. The common man pays the price."

"Kamla, it seems that an admirer of the Merchant of Venice is about to become the Merchant of War. I am about to become a Bombwala from Shakespearewala.

With this disturbing thought in his mind, he falls asleep... He has a dream.

Ha, ha, ha... a man who looks like Adolf Hitler is laughing at Daddyji.
Do you remember, Surinder? We met in 1943 in the valley of Kashmir.

I asked you to help me find the ultimate weapon and you gave me a lecture on evils of War. And now you, yourself, are thinking of becoming a Merchant of War. What is the difference between you and me? I ordered the killings of millions and you will, essentially, be doing the same thing; selling weapons that will kill millions.

"No, no... I will not do it. I cannot do it. I don't want to be a Merchant of War." Daddyji is shouting, as Mummyji tries to calm him down.

• • •

In the morning, when he is riding his motorcycle to the office, a cool breeze is rushing across his face blowing his hair and inflating his shirt like a balloon. He has finally made up his mind. He is not going to become a Merchant of War.

When he reaches his office, he finds Kevin Bond entering the office at the same time. "Good morning, Mr. Bond, can I talk to you for a few minutes in your office?" As he is finished saying this, they are right in front of Kevin Bond's office.

He looks at Daddyji and says, "Come right in."

Daddyji walks in behind him, closes the door and sits down, as Kevin Bond is placing his briefcase on his desk. Kevin Bond also sits down and asks, "What can I do for you?"

"Mr. Bond, I have given the matter of my getting involved in arms sales a good deal of thought; I have come to the conclusion that I am not prepared to do it." Daddyji says firmly.

Kevin Bond is quiet, while he rubs his chin trying to compose a suitable response, "Surinder, old chap, you are getting excited for nothing. This is not something we are undertaking tomorrow or the next day. It is going to take a long time to set it up. It is all right; you don't have to get involved if you don't want to. I respect your sentiments."

Daddyji is satisfied and gets up and goes to his office.

In the evening, when he reaches home and is in the process of locking his motor-cycle, he sees Karnail Singh standing outside the Quarter. He remembers that Karnail works at the Ministry of Defense. He asks him, "Karnail, tell me one thing. Is there any arms manufacturing industry in India?"

He replies, "Nothing to speak of. The British made sure of that when the colonial government, under Lord Lytton as Viceroy (1874-1880), enacted the Indian Arms Act, 1878. This Act ensured that no Indian could possess a weapon of any description unless the British masters considered him a loyal subject of the British Empire. The British made sure that all the armaments are imported from Britain under tightly controlled regulations. You know, even Gandhiji writes in his Autobiography: 'Among the many misdeeds of the British rule in India, history will look upon the Act depriving a whole nation of arms as the blackest."

Daddyji says, "So, how will India and Pakistan fight when they run out of ammunitions— with stones, swords and knives?"

Karnail Singh says half jokingly, "Just as well that the British did not permit that any armaments factories be built in India. Now when they run out of ammunition, the fighting will slow down or stop. But do you know what is already happening? We have all the arms manufacturing countries lining up at our doors to sell us arms. And they know we can't afford to pay, so they are all offering easy credit terms. What a world we live in! Sometimes, I feel that the seed for the two nation concept—the partition of India and Pakistan into two countries—was, in fact, sown by some arms manufacturer."

Karnail Singh asks, "Surinder, why this sudden interest in arms and ammunition?"

Daddyji replies, "Bond & Sons is thinking of becoming an agent for arms manufacturers."

30
NEW ARRIVAL

While Mummyji is working at her desk at the Galaxy, a letter from the Ministry of Rehabilitation arrives with the regular post. She starts to open the envelope, and then she stops. It is not common to receive letters from the Ministry. It could be the letter she is waiting for; the letter giving approval for adoption. She closes her eyes with her hands folded and recites *Hanuman Chalisa. Sri Guru Charan Saroj Raj...*" After completing her prayer, she touches her eyes with her hands and then gently starts to open the envelope as if she is opening an expensive gift. When the envelope is opened, she takes the hand written letter out and starts to read it. After she finishes reading, she is stunned, as if struck by lightening. Not in her wildest dreams, she had imagined what she has read. *How is this possible?* She is thinking. *Oh God, I don't want to lose her. Is it possible that those who claim to be her next of kin are imposters?* She has heard of many cases where infants and young children are claimed by gangs who engage in human trade. The letter informs her that the next of kin will visit the Galaxy next week to see baby Suneeta.

The following week, a Tonga stops in front of the Galaxy office at about 11 A.M. One man and one woman get down from the Tonga and come into the office. The man has henna coloured hair. Half his teeth are missing, and the other half are covered with the red residue from eating *Paan*. The woman is wearing a sari and is also chewing *Paan*. The man introduces himself, "I am Deendyal Baluja, and this is my wife Kanandevi. I am second cousin of the late father of baby Suneeta. God give peace to his soul. We are so happy to find her. We have been looking for her for a long time. Finally, God has answered our prayers. We would like to take her home with us today." Mummyji gets up, calls the Gorkha watchman and asks him to stand by the door to her office. She can sense that these people, who claim to be distant relatives of Suneeta, are not genuine.

The man takes out a letter from his pocket. It is written on the letterhead of the Ministry. He shows it to Mummyji. The letter states that, after suitable investigation, it has been determined that Deendyal Baluja is the second cousin of baby Suneeta's father. He should be allowed to take baby Suneeta with him. This does not sound right to Mummyji. She knows that the procedures of adoption are long and arduous. These people could possibly not have obtained permission for adoption so quickly.

She folds the letter, puts it back in the envelope and tells Deendyal, "We will have to do our own investigation. Please come back in two weeks. And before we can start our investigation, we will need some information from you. Please write down your name and address and give us some proof that you are related to baby Suneeta."

After hearing this, Deendyal and his wife become very fidgety and they get up and walk out of the office. Mummyji's suspicion of foul play is coming true. She gets up and goes after them and calls out the Gorkha watchman, "Desh Bahadur, stop them. Don't let them escape."

Desh Bahadur takes out his knife, known as *Khurki,* and goes and stands in their way and says, "Stop, or you will both find the *Khurki* in your stomach."

Both Deendyal and his wife stop. They raise their hands and give up. In the meantime, another male servant comes out, and they are both taken into the warehouse building for detention until the police arrive.

Later investigation, by the Ministry of Rehabilitation, reveals the existence of a gang, who use false documents to abduct orphan infants.

• • •

It is Sunday, May 15, 1949. I am playing in the front verandah of our Quarter with some friends. My grandparents have gone to Simla for the summer. I can see Mummyji walking back from the Galaxy with an envelope in her hand. She sees me from a distance. She is waving the envelope with unusual enthusiasm. I can see she is almost running in her high heels. She is saying something with a smile on her face. I can make out that whatever she is saying is good, but I cannot make out what she is actually saying. As soon as she reaches home, she says, "Vikram and Kishi, can you guess what is in this envelope?" And she gives the answer herself and says, "Baby Suneeta." Kishi and I have no idea what she is saying. How can there be baby Suneeta in the envelope? And then she starts to explain to us that the Ministry has given us the approval for the adoption of baby Suneeta.

"So, when are we bringing her home?" We ask.

"As soon as we can buy a cot and some other baby things, we can bring her home," she replies.

She goes inside the main bedroom and starts to look around for a place for a cot for baby Suneeta. She seems to be eyeing the bed Kishi and I sleep on. There is no other place.

In the evening, the motorcycle announces its arrival from a distance with the characteristic series of one short beep, two long beeps, one short beep and two long beeps... and then comes to a stop with the final two short beeps. But today some thing special happens. After the two short beeps, there is combination of random short and long beeps for a whole minute. Many of our neighbours come out including Chatterjida, an employee of the Indian Post and Telegraph. He comes over and asks, "Surinder, do you know Morse Code?"

"No," Daddyji replies.

"Surinder, in Morse Code, you were beeping the word House, House. Have you bought a house?"

"Well, yes, in a way." And he walks into the Quarter with a brown envelope in hand raised high above his head and asks, "Kamla, can you guess what is in this envelope?"

Mummyji has her own envelope in her hand and also asks, "I will answer your question if you tell me what I have in this envelope in my hand."

There seems to be a deadlock. Both are holding their respective envelopes in their hand and smiling at each other. Daddyji is the first to blink and says in Shakespearean English. "My fair lady, there is a tide in the affair of men. Which, taken at flood, leads on to fortune. I have looked at a piece of land to build a small house for us all."

Mummyji, not to be left behind, says, "My Lord, I hath borne you a daughter that thou hath always wanted."

Daddyji stops in his tracks.

Mummyji carries on, "The house that you are going to build is by baby Suneeta's destiny. We have been given permission to adopt her. All the flood of good fortune that we have been receiving is all due to the blessings of Goddess Lakshmi—our baby Suneeta. I believe baby girls are incarnation of Goddess Lakshmi."

Over the next few days, all necessities required for baby Suneeta are purchased. Baby Suneeta's cot is installed in the main bedroom, and Kishi and I are moved to the small room where my grandparents lived. There is a special religious ceremony being planned for the day when baby Suneeta is going to be brought home. All the relatives are invited. Letters are sent to out of town relatives and to those living in Delhi. Replies are all expressing surprise at not even having an inkling of the adoption process that was going on. Some have called Daddyji at the office to express surprise and offer blessings for Suneeta. Mummyji's parents, who now live in Hushiarpur, have written to confirm that they will attend the ceremony.

One day, Daddyji asks Mummyji, "Kamla, I would like to invite the Nautiyal family and Kevin Bond also to the ceremony."

She starts to think about it with the creases on her forehead deepening with anxiety and says, "Our Quarter is so small. I will be embarrassed. What will they all think of us? They all have such big houses."

Daddyji replies, "Kamla, we know these people well. They are our employers. I think they will feel bad when they find out that they were not invited on such an important occasion. You know, rich people like to socialize with people who are poorer than them. It makes them feel good. What is the use of having money if you can't look down upon somebody?" She gives him a strange look, but he carries on, "My dear, this is not my thinking. This is the way the human nature is. Moreover, we are going to have a nice tent installed in front on the lawn."

Finally, they agree to invite the Nautiyal family and Kevin Bond. And, of course, all the neighbours of the Square are also invited. As Daddyji has moved around in the business circles, he has learned two valuable lessons–both from his brother-in-law, Daulat Ram.

One: the way to influence people is through their pockets. Two: the way to win friends is through their stomachs. So he has decided that while we are at it, we may as well invite and win a few more friends. He decides to invite my Headmaster Atma Ram; Dr.Trivedi, our neighbourhood doctor; the Chopra brothers, the owners of *Kake Da Hotel;* and Mukesh Durrani, the owner of the showroom where he had bought his motorcycle. When Mummyji finds out about it, she asks, "Listen ji, where is the need to invite these strangers? I have never even met these people."

Daddyji replies, "These are very useful people. Imagine if we fall sick and if you know the doctor personally, and if he has eaten your salt, he will certainly look after you ahead of others. And the same way: you know that I frequently go to have lunch at *Kake Da Hotel*. It feels really good when you enter a restaurant, and the owner greets you personally by your name. Other people sitting there look at you, and you just feel good. The education of my children is always uppermost in my mind; and that is where Headmaster Atma Ram comes in. Don't forget, both Vikram and Kishi have yet to go through the hands of Atma Ram at school. Motorcycles always need servicing and that is where, Durrani, the owner of the motorcycle dealership will be useful."

Mummyji says, "Are we having a religious ceremony or a business party?"

Daddyji is in a giddy mood and replies, "My fair lady, we live in a world of contradictions, where introductions are the life-blood of the society. More introductions result in fewer contradictions."

Mummyji feels that he is talking strangely and walks away.

• • •

The big day has arrived. A tent had been installed and the *Hawaii* had set up shop to cook the food the evening before. The guests start arriving by 11 A.M. Both Kishi and I are dressed for the occasion. When Mummyji's brother, Daulat Ram, and his family arrive, he comes out of his car with excitement in his voice, embraces Mummyji and Daddyji and says, "The two of you have done a noble task. God bless you. Where is my newly minted niece?"

Mummyji replies, "*Bhaji,* we still have to bring her from the Galaxy." Daulat Ram looks at her not knowing what Galaxy is. Mummyji clarifies, "The Galaxy is the name of the camp where she is staying. We were wondering if we can bring her home in your car."

"Oh, I am honoured to be asked. It is my privilege to drive her home."

Also accompanying Daulat Ram are Mummyji's parents. As soon as they see Kishi and me, they come and give us kisses and blessings.

As Daddyji, Mummyji and Daulat Ram are walking over to his car, both Kishi and I also tag along. For the past few weeks, as the preparations are being made to welcome baby Suneeta, I am getting the feeling that Kishi and I are being neglected. We all load into the car and drive off to the Galaxy. In two minutes we are there. Baby Suneeta is already dressed up in a pink frock and matching hair clips. The staff at the Galaxy hand her over to Mummyji. As we are getting back into the car, they are all looking on and saying good bye to her. Baby Suneeta is very happy to see us and is smiling at me and Kishi.

In two minutes we are home. As Mummyji is carrying Suneeta to our Quarter, the guests move closer to have a look. All the ladies search their purses for money. They all, one by one, come forward to see baby Suneeta closely and offer a gift of cash. The gift is offered upon seeing the baby for the first time.

A brief religious ceremony starts in which the priest recites hymns in Sanskrit and informs the gathering, "Ladies and Gentlemen, today Surinder and Kamla have taken an oath to adopt baby Suneeta as their daughter. It is an auspicious occasion. It is also Suneeta's birthday today. With the grace of God, she is three years old." There is clapping all around and the brief ceremony is over. After lunch, one by one, the guests start to depart. In the end only the family is left—Mummyji's parents, her brothers, sisters and their families. Daddyji goes over to Mummyji's father and asks, "*Bauji*" as he is addressed by his children, "did you have something to eat?"

Aunty Devika, Mummyji's sister, who is standing nearby says, "No, they have not eaten a thing. In fact, they have not even had a drop of water."

"What? Are you feeling fine, *Bauji and Bibiji*?" says Daddyji expressing his surprise and concern.

Bauji replies, "We are fine. We just had something to eat before coming here."

Aunty Devika says, "They have not eaten anything because they still believe that they should not even touch a speck of food or water at their daughter's home."

Daddyji says, "*Bauji*, we should now leave behind these old Indian customs. India is coming out of the dark. Especially, *Bauaji,* you are an Electrical Contractor dealing with modern scientific inventions everyday. Please have something to eat; otherwise, we will all feel bad."

As Daddyji is talking, Aunty Devika goes and gets two plates full of food for both *Bauji and Biji.*

By late afternoon, everybody departs. The tents are gone and the *Halwaii* has left. From four, we have become a five member family. Both Kishi and I are constantly giving new toys to Suneeta to play with. Mummyji comes in and says, "OK, boys, time for Suneeta's nap. And listen, no noise while she is asleep." Before we had to keep quiet while Daddyji slept, and now we will also have to be quiet while Suneeta is asleep.

After a few days off work, it is time for Mummyji to go back to the Galaxy. She has already made arrangements at the Galaxy for Suneeta to accompany her. Both Kishi and I have started going to school after the summer vacations. Kishi is going in Grade 1, and I am starting Grade 4. During the summer vacations,

I have really shot up in height. In fact, when Aunty Devika saw me during Suneeta's home coming ceremony, she had remarked to Mummyji, "*Nee* Kamla, what do you give Vikram to eat, he is growing like a *Peepal* tree."

And Mummyji had replied, "*Nee* Devika, don't cast Evil Eye on my son." And they had both laughed.

31
GROWING UP

"Vikram, youstupidboy, what are you doing hanging from the door frame?" Mummyji shouts at me.

"I am trying to become tall. I want to be tall like Daddyji and Pitaji. Moreover, there is this girl, Santosh, in our class; she is taller than all the boys. My friend, Suraj, and I have decided to outgrow her."

"You are already tall for your age. See, your pants have already become short; we just had them stitched three months back." Mummyji says while she is hanging my clothes to dry on the clothes line.

Daddyji comes out of the bedroom with my report book in hand and says, "Vikram, you are not doing very well in arithmetic. Instead of hanging from the door frame, you should sit and do some arithmetic sums and exercise your brain. And look here, even Hindi marks are not good. I think I will come and see the headmaster on Monday; I have to see somebody at Gurudwara Road; after that I will come to your school."

I get down from the door frame and say, "Daddyji, I can read what other people are thinking; so reading Hindi or doing arithmetic is child's play for me. First I want to become taller than Santosh."

Mummyji and Daddyji look at each other, but they don't say anything.

Just as the recess has started, I hear the roar of the motorcycle coming up the hill. As soon as Daddyji's motorcycle stops outside my school, he quickly walks over to him. And as soon as Daddyji starts to pull the motorcycle up on the stand, he holds the rear of the motorcycle and helps him put it on the stand. Daddyji looks at him in surprise and gives him a smile. He smiles back and says, "Uncleji, my name is Suraj Rajpal. I am Vikram's class fellow. I know you are

Vikram's father. I really like motorcycles and their sound and the speed. I wish could take a ride on one."

Daddyji looks at him, smiles and walks into the teachers' room. As he enters, he finds Headmaster, Atma Ram, standing there. They shake hands. Daddyji is still thinking about the boy he has just met outside, and, to start small talk with the Headmaster, he says, "Atma Ram ji, I just met one of your students, Suraj. He is quite a smart boy."

Atma Ram replies, "Oh yes, everybody is very impressed with him. He is quite a *chalta Poorza*. And to what do we owe the honour of your visit, professor sahib?"

"Well, let me tell you that I am not a professor anymore; I have taken up a managerial position in a company. I just could not find a suitable position in any college; this job came along, and I accepted. Let us see how things shape up in the future. Atma Ram ji, the purpose of my visit today is this," he says pointing to my report book, "Vikram does not appear to be doing well in class."

"Yes, I have noticed that. You know, ever since Suraj—the boy you met outside—has joined Grade 4, Vikram and him have become very good friends. Many times I see them sitting in the back of the class looking at each other, making eyes at the girls and just not concentrating. But, Suraj is doing very well in his studies. Leave it with me; I will keep an eye on Vikram. Now if you will excuse me, I have to leave. I have to go to Rajouri Garden; we are looking at a plot of land to build a house."

Later that day, near the end of school, we are told that there is going to be a surprise gift for everybody. After a little while, one large red truck pulls up in front of the school. The truck driver, another man in uniform and two *Engrez* girls in red skirt and white blouse alight from the truck. All the students are asked to line up. We are told that we are going to get one free bottle of soda drink and some other gifts. The truck has very large letters of English alphabet written on the sides and the back. None of the students know English, so they really don't know, and actually don't care, what is written on the truck. As usual, Suraj and I are standing at the rear of the line because of our height. We can see everybody getting a bottle of a soda drink, a blotting paper and a miniature bottle as a souvenir. As the line of students keeps shortening, Suraj and I are moving closer to the truck. I know English, having been given daily lessons by Daddyji. I can read the letters as *C...O...L...A*, written in a very stylish way. They don't mean anything to me. By the time our turn comes, most students are preparing to go home. As Suraj and I slowly work our way towards the front of the truck, we find ourselves standing near the driver of the truck. As usual, Suraj starts a conversation with him and says, "Uncleji, you have a very nice truck"

The driver smiles at us and asks, "Which class are you boys in?"

Suraj replies, "In Grade 4."

I ask, "Uncleji, why are you distributing free drinks and gifts?

Suraj gives me a hit with his elbow and says, "Uncleji, all the students are enjoying the drinks. They are very tasty." And then he says, "Uncleji, as there is still a long lineup, can we help you to distribute blotting papers and bottles to the students?"

After a while, we are the only two left. We are given one drink each. We finish it quickly; being thirsty due to having been standing in the queue for about an hour. As we finish our drinks, we tell the driver of the truck, "Uncleji we really enjoyed it. What is the name of this soda?"

He replies, "It is known as Cola. It is from America." The man seems so pleased with us that he gives us one more bottle each to drink, and lots of blotting papers, and a handful of miniature bottles.

After the students have been served the drinks, now comes the turn of the teaching and other staff of the school. As they are being served, both Suraj and I are standing around. The Cola man says to the teachers, "Masterji, we like these two students of yours. They were very helpful to us."

I thought that, between Daulat Ram and Daddyji, I had seen all there was to learn about how to influence people and win friends. But today, two new rules come to light: Help & Praise; they are free. Everybody likes to be helped and likes to receive praise.

It does not take me long to realize that Suraj is a friend worth having.

At night, when Daddyji sits down with me for a lesson in English, he says, "You know, Vikram, I like your friend, Suraj. He seems like an extraordinary boy. If guided properly, he will go far in life. You should make friends with him. Boys who are good both in studies and social conduct are very rare." And then, the Shakespeare in him comes out and he recites a quote.

Friends thou hast, and their adoption tried, grapple them to thy soul with hoops of steel.

Sometimes I feel that Daddyji teaches me English just to remember Shakespeare.

• • •

Daddyji and Mummyji are sitting on the grassy patch in front of our Quarter in the evening. The Sun is setting. He is turning the pages of the newspaper. And then he sets it down on the stool nearby and starts to look at a distance.

"See Kamla," he says, pointing to the setting sun, "for the last few years, whenever I watched the setting sun, there used to be a red blood halo around it. The halo has now become light pink instead; this means that the bloodshed has come to an end. The skies are clearer during the day and the night; less dead bodies are being cremated–hence less smoke."

Mummyji gives him a look and says, "Listen ji, at the time of dusk one should talk of auspicious things. You remember, Beyji told you that once. Why don't you call Vikram and read the newspaper with him. He will learn English and also find out what is going on in the world."

"Vikram," he calls for me, "Let us read the English newspaper together."

"Do I have to read the newspaper, Daddyji? I don't understand all the grownup things" I say, and I run away.

Daddyji is still turning the pages, and he finds something that attracts his attention. He says, "Kamla, there are so many new housing colonies coming up. Headmaster Atma Ram was telling me that he is buying a plot in a colony called Rajouri Garden. I think we should also buy a plot. What do you think?"

"I would love to have our own house," she says.

• • •

The *Dalal's* office is under a torn canvas sheet stretched across with two ends tied to branches of a tree; and the other two are barely kept up by two bamboo poles dug into the ground by the roadside. There are three chairs sitting on the uneven ground. One is occupied by the *Dalal,* one by Daddyji and the third by the man who wants to sell his plot of land before he migrates to Pakistan. The seller is asking two thousand rupees for the 300 square yards plot on the north side of New Rohtak Road; Daddyji is stuck on his offer of one thousand. He knows that the seller has to leave in a few days. The *Dalal* gets up, takes Daddyji outside the office and says, "Mehra sahib, it is a very good deal even at two thousand rupees; I think you should increase your offer by two hundred. I have another client coming in an hour; you should seal the deal before that; otherwise, he might grab it. This land price will be five times by next year."

Daddyji goes in and the deal is signed at one thousand one hundred and fifty rupees. He pays two hundred rupees in cash as deposit, and the balance is to be paid at the time of the registration.

He comes straight home and announces, "Kamla, we are proud owners of a plot of land on Rohtak Road; it is less than ten minutes walk from here. Vikram and Kishi will still attend the same school."

"Listen ji, you should have at least shown me the plot before buying."

"Kamla, there was no time. A Muslim man is migrating to Pakistan and he wants to sell his land in a hurry; the price was so good that I had to decide then and there; otherwise, somebody else would have grabbed it."

"See ever since Suneeta has come into our lives, the fortune has smiled upon our family," Mummyji says picking up Suneeta and cuddling her.

"Kamla, I think you are being overly superstitious."

"Listen ji, believe me or not, every child is born with his or her destiny. Whatever you might say, Suneeta is a lucky child."

I am standing nearby and wondering if the fortune smiled or frowned upon my parents when *I* entered their lives.

I am thinking: *After my birth, Daddyji fell sick, India was partitioned, and we had to move and had to live as refugees with relatives. All in all it seems fortune frowned upon us after my birth. Maybe Mummyji is right; Suneeta has only brought good luck to the family.* But, then, I say to myself: I cannot be held responsible for India's partition, can I?

• • •

"Kamla, I have sent a letter to Pitaji, in Simla, requesting him to look after the construction of the house," Daddyji says as he returns from work.

She says angrily, "Where are they going to live? There is no room."

Daddyji replies, "Don't worry Kamla, I have made temporary arrangements until the house is completed. The tenant in E190 is moving out, and I have made arrangement with the landlord to rent it to us for a few months. He wanted two hundred rupees *Pugri*, but I have settled with him for one hundred rupees, and rent of fifty rupees a month."

She asks with a puzzled look, "Why does he want a *Pugri*? Why does he not buy one himself?"

Daddyji laughs and says, "Oh Kamla, you are confusing this *Pugri* with the *Pugri* one wears on one's head as a head dress. This is just a colloquial term meaning: lump sum payment to secure the accommodation. It is a kind of bribe. In English, it is known as key money."

Mummyji says, "Why do we have to pay bribe? We will be paying the rent."

"Daddyji replies, "This is a price we have to pay to buy advantage over others. Bribe has been used from time immemorial. There are references to it even in Shakespeare's plays such as Julius Caesar; and Romeo and Juliet. But Kamla, don't tell this to Pitaji; otherwise, he will not live in that accommodation. You know that he is against giving bribes."

Mummyji says, "What will happen if we don't pay *Pugri*?"

"In that case, chances are, somebody else will pay *Pugri* and take the Quarter."

Mummyji says, "Why don't we try it and see what happens?"

"Kamla, this is not the time to become a social reformer. If we miss this Quarter, we have no alternative."

Mummyji replies, "I have an alternative. If worst come to worst, Chatterjida has one spare room in his Quarter. I will ask his wife, Babli, to rent it to us. She owes me a favour. So you should tell, Bansal, the owner of E190 that it is illegal for him to ask for *Pugri*. In fact, he is not the owner, the government is. He is just the head tenant."

The next day, Daddyji explains to, his friend and our neighbour, Karnail Singh about the demand for *Pugri* by Bansal and asks him to accompany him to talk to him.

Karnail Singh is furious to hear about it and says, "Surinder there is no way you should pay *Pugri* to Bansal. He has been our neighbour for years. We should help each other rather than rob each other."

As they reach Bansal's Quarter, they see him sitting in the verandah reading a newspaper. He notices their presence, looks up from the newspaper and says, "Well, well, well... look; who is here? Colonel Singh himself," making light of Karnail Singh's name. And he continues, "Tell me, how I may serve you, Karnail ji."

Karnail Singh replies, "Bansal ji, I have heard that you are demanding a hefty *Pugri* from Surinder for renting a room to him for his parents. I hope you realize that it is illegal. You are a government servant, and you can be in trouble."

Bansal's face goes white. He starts to stammer and is at a loss for words. In the end he quickly backs off and says, "Oh Surinder *yaar*, I was just joking with you. I would have never accepted any *Pugri* from you."

They shake hands and the matter is settled.

32
DELHI: 1950
HOUSE BUILDING

As Daddyji reaches home, we can see that there is a roll of large sheets of paper, known as blue prints, tied to the carrier behind the seat of his motorcycle. He lifts his motorcycle on the stand, unties the roll of blue prints and comes in with the roll raised high above his head. He announces loudly, "The plans have been approved by the municipality. We are ready to start construction any day." And then he whispers to Mummyji, "You know, it usually takes six months to get the permit, but I obtained it in just two months. I had to look after the overseer of plans, but it is all part of the game." He nervously looks around to see that his father is not around because if he hears what he just said, he would reprimand him for giving a bribe. He then unties the string around the roll of blue prints and places them flat on the table. He explains to us where the drawing room is, and where the bedrooms are and that the front of the house is a half-round verandah. He tells us, "The architect told me this type of design is called Art Deco. One room will have light blue, the second pink, and the third will have green walls. The floors will all be chips marble of different colors in different rooms. The cupboards will be made of teak wood."

A few days later, our neighbour, Karnail Singh and Daddyji are sitting outside. Karnail Singh asks him, "Surinder *yaar,* I want to talk to you about something. Ever since my wife has heard that you are building your own house, she is after me that we should also have a house of our own. I am a government servant, where am I going to get money to build a house."

Daddyji says, "Well Karnail, this is a very natural reaction on her part. We all aspire to be like our peers."

Karnail asks, "What do you suggest I do?"

Daddyji is somewhat puzzled by the question. He does not know how he should answer it. If fact, he does not really know what Karnail Singh wants from him. In the end, after about a minute or so, he says, "Karnail, it all depends on your financial situation."

Karnail asks, "Surinder, how much money is required to buy the land and build a small house?"

Daddyji says, "About two thousand rupees are required to buy the land, and another about five thousand to build a small house of the size we are planning."

Karnail Singh says, "I cannot even dream of having so much money in my lifetime; unless I get an inheritance from a rich uncle or start accepting bribes from the suppliers of goods and services to the Defense Ministry."

Daddyji says, eyeing him with an amused look on his face, "I thought all government servants have side incomes. In any case, I strongly believe that if you really want something and work for it passionately, nature helps you to get it."

• • •

On a cold December morning, as Daddyji is repeatedly trying to kick-start his motorcycle, Karnail Singh walks out of the Quarter and tells Daddyji, "Surinder, by God, you are a genius. I have been thinking, and thinking, about how to get money and, as you said, nature helped. Today, I received a letter from home that my rich uncle has died and left me all his property. He had no children. Oh *Chacha* Gurdial, may your soul rest in peace!"

Daddyji quietly hears the story, smiles and says nothing.

At night, he tells Mummyji about what Karnail Singh has told him. Mummyji says, "I think Karnail found somebody who greased his palms."

A few days later, Karnail tells Daddyji that he has bought a plot of land in Block 4; our land is in Block 3 of Rohtak Road.

• • •

We are gathered at the occasion of the *Juth* ceremony—the laying of the foundation stone of our new house. We are all seated around the *Havan Kund* with the fire lighted in it. Mummyji is sitting beside Daddyji with Suneeta in her lap. The priest is reciting hymns in Sanskrit. He hands over a coconut to Daddyji and asks him to break it by hitting it on the ground. Daddyji looks around to find a hard surface to hit the coconut on. He points to a few bricks lying around. I run to the spot and bring two bricks. He carefully holds the round bald coconut in his hands and hits it on the bricks. The way he was holding the coconut, it does not break, but his finger gets crushed between the coconut and the bricks. Fortunately, there are just a few scratches but no blood. As he is nursing his finger and looking for somebody to blame, I take the coconut from him and hit it on the bricks and break it open. As the water from the coconut starts to flow, the priest asks me to sprinkle it on the plot of land where our house is to be built. My parents and grandparents look at me with pride. Kishi, who is watching, says, "I want to break a coconut also."

Mummyji tells him, "No, Kishi, we can only break one coconut. You can break this one in small pieces and distribute it to everybody."

The priest, who is looking and relishing the sibling rivalry, asks everybody, "Do you people know why we break coconuts on important occasions?" All our elders look at him with smiles, but nobody comes up with the answer.

The priest explains, "Whenever we undertake work of some magnitude, we feel a sense of pride and begin to feel proud and haughty. The breaking of a coconut symbolizes smashing of one's ego to the ground and complete submission to God. Meaning: God is the only doer."

My elders all nod their heads in agreement, while Kishi, Suneeta and I are playing with the remnants of the 'ego'—the pieces of the coconut.

This concludes the *Juth* ceremony. Mummyji and Daddyji open the boxes of *Mithai*s or sweets and go around distributing it to all present, including a few construction workers who are standing around ready to start.

As the ceremony is winding down, Daddyji goes and touches his father's feet to get his blessings. He embraces him and blesses him with more success in the future.

Daddyji is not able to control his usual habit of bragging and says, "Pitaji, I am the first, out of all my brothers, to own a motorcycle and build my own house."

Mummyji, who is within hearing distance, comes over to where the father and son are standing and says, "Listen ji, the priest just finished explaining the significance of breaking the coconut. Please control your ego. When you show off too much, Evil Eye can strike you." And then she points towards baby Suneeta and says, "Don't forget our Goddess Lakshmi; it is due to her that we are enjoying the good fortune of owning our own house."

I am thinking: *Mummyji tells Daddyji not to brag, but she is herself showing off baby Suneeta as the Goddess Lakshmi; I am afraid that baby Suneeta may be struck by Evil Eye.*

• • •

After the conclusion of the formal ceremony, construction workers start digging the foundation with shovels in their hands. There are white lines on the ground showing the layout of the walls of the house. Daddyji and Mummyji walk the land stopping in each 'room' and talking animatedly to each other. Pitaji is talking to the *Mistry,* who is going to be managing the different suppliers of materials and the labourers. His name is Saudagar Singh. Pitaji and the *Mistry* walk over to where Daddyji and Mummyji are standing and talking to the architect. Pitaji calls over Daddyji and says, "Surinder, Saudagar says that there is a shortage of cement and *Saria,* the steel rods. Even if you have a permit, there may be a few months' wait."

Daddyji asks, "Saudager Singh, what do you suggest we do?"

Saudager Singh replies, "In my opinion, the only alternative is to buy some bags of cement in the black market to complete the foundation work, and by then the permitted materials should hopefully arrive."

In the meantime, a man comes and stands beside them. They all stop talking and turn to look at him. He says, "My name is Vilas Gupta. I own a number of houses in the neighbourhood. I was passing by and thought I will stop and welcome you to the locality. Forgive me, but I just could not help overhearing your conversation about shortage of cement and steel rods. I just want to tell you that I have built four houses in this area, and we have not used any cement in the foundations and the walls."

Pitaji is very eager to say something, while Vilas Gupta is talking. He says, "Gupta ji, I am a retired PWI from the railways. My name is Yodh Raj Mehra. This is my son, Surinder Mehra. I have supervised a lot of construction. I have never seen any construction being done without cement. What do you use as a substitute?"

Vilas Gupta replies, "Mehra ji, I have used a mixture of earth and lime. I reuse the earth that comes from digging the foundation, mix some lime with it, add some water and use it as mortar for brickwork. If you are building a railway bridge, I agree with you. You must use cement but not for a house. Rest is up to you." And he gives a smile and moves on.

It seems that Vilas Gupta has left them in a quandary. The question is: Whether to use cement or not. They decide to ask the architect, who is standing with a smile listening to all the technical conversations.

Daddyji asks the architect, "Kadoo sahib, what do you think about all this?"

He replies, "Surinder, if you want good quality construction for your house, please follow all the specifications on the blue prints. It is very clearly stated therein the amount of cement required and the locations where it is required."

Daddyji says, "That settles it. Let us follow the specifications and buy cement in the black market. What other choice do we have?"

Pitaji asks with anger in his voice, "I would like to find out how cement is finding its way to the black market? Surinder, you know me very well; I am against feeding the black marketers. If everybody stops buying from the black market, that market will cease to exist."

Saudagar Singh says, "I will tell you where the cement in the black market is coming from. They open the gunny bags of cement, take out about half the cement, substitute with sand and sew the bags close. They buy used cement bags, fill them with a mixture of sand and cement and sell them as pure cement. Common person has no way of knowing the difference."

Daddyji remembers that Nautiyal Industries, where he works, own a cement plant. He says without letting anybody on the secret, "I agree with Pitaji. We should not buy anything in the black market. I will go to the cement shop and see what I can find out."

As the discussions are going on, the labourers are working hard digging the ground. There are two men doing the digging. As the dirt piles up beside them, two women fill the containers. As the containers are full, the men help to lift the containers on to the women's heads. The women stand up, carry the containers to the designated areas and drop the dirt on to the ground. One of the women is expecting and is barely able to walk. After a few rounds of moving the dirt, she sits down and cleans perspiration from her face and forehead. One of the men, doing the digging, stops and goes over to comfort her. She is in need of water. He looks around, but there is no water nearby. Mummyji notices it and points it out to Daddyji. They both look at the woman labourer and discuss something with each other. And then Mummyji goes to a nearby house to fetch water. Although, we have always been surrounded by poor people, it is only today that I notice the difference between the haves and have-nots.

As Mummyji is gone in search of water, I am thinking: *Why do we have everything and these labourers have nothing—not even water? Who determines that and why? Will they be like this all their lives, or will they be like us one day? What have we done that they have not, that they are like this; Many questions but no answers.*

Mummyji is back with a brass jug full of water. She goes over to the women labourer to give her water to drink.

Daddyji asks Saudagar Singh, "When are we going to have the water connection? I thought we already had it."

He replies, "Surinder ji, it is the same old story. They all take their own time, unless, of course, you are willing to grease their palms."

Pitaji says with frustration, "I wish their palms would rot with grease."

Daddyji takes Saudagar Singh out of hearing distance of Pitaji, tells him to do the needful to get the water connection and slips some cash in his pocket.

After making sure the money is safely in his pocket, Saudagar Singh says, "Surinder ji, we have to arrange for a watchman for night duty because robberies of construction materials are very common. We are building a hut at the rear of the land to store cement under lock and key."

Daddyji asks, "Where are the labourers going to live?"

Saudager Singh replies, "We are building some huts, on site, for the labourers also. I want all of them to live there. It adds extra security against robberies."

The next day, at the office, Daddyji goes to meet the executive director, who looks after the construction material division of Nautiyal Industries.

He introduces himself, "I am Surinder Mehra." Before Daddyji could say anything further, the man says, "I am Saurav Bannerji. Mr. Nautiyal has told me a lot about you."

They shake hands and Daddyji says, "I have just started construction of my house and…" Before Daddyji can finish the sentence Saurav says, "…and you are having trouble getting cement and steel."

Daddyji asks, "How do you know?"

Saurav Bannerji replies with a smile, "Surinder, remember, I deal with construction materials—cement, steel, wood, bricks and anything else you need for construction. I can give you anything but cement and steel, unless, of course, you have a permit."

Daddyji replies, "I do have a permit for steel and cement."

Saurav Banerjee says, "To stay within the government regulations, we can lend you cement and steel up to a maximum amount equal to what you have the

Permit for. After you receive your quota, you return what you borrowed back to us. This benefit is only for the executives of Nautiyal Industries and must be kept confidential."

Brick by brick, our house starts to take shape

33
THOUGHT PROVOKING

Daddyji is sitting in the verandah going through his office files. Mummyji walks out of the bedroom and asks, "Listen ji, when is our new house going to be ready for occupancy?

"You have seen it; it is almost done. Only some painting and cleanup is remaining. I think we should be ready in another month," Daddyji replies, while he is writing something in one of the files. And then he looks up and says, "I think we should set up a date for the house warming party. I want to invite the Nautiyal family also. I want them to see our new house. And, you know, Kamla, I wish Max Hoffer was here also."

Mummyji, as usual, makes a face; she just does not like Max Hoffer's name. And she goes into the bedroom. Daddyji shakes his head, mutters something and goes back to his files.

A little while later, the postman enters the Square on his routine of dropping letters in the individual postboxes. As soon as he opens our postbox, I run towards him to get our letters. Daddyji looks up and extends his hand, and I handover the stack of letters to him. He quickly flips through them and takes one of them out. He smiles. There are usually only two things that bring smile on his face: One is when he is talking about Shakespeare, and the other is when he is talking about Max Hoffer. By the expression on his face and the breadth and depth of his smile, I can judge that it must be a letter from Max Hoffer.

Daddyji opens the letter by cutting off a corner, blows into it to inflate it and then tears off the edge. As he takes out the one page letter, he calls out, "Kamla, there is a letter from Max Hoffer. What a coincidence! I was just talking about him."

He unfolds the letter and starts to read it:

34 N, 74.8 E

Dear Surinder ji,

I think I am tethered to the Himalayas—especially Kashmir. I am here in Srinagar, as I had written to you earlier, as part of the Canadian Contingent of the United Nations Military Observer Group. We are doing our best to keep peace between India and Pakistan. It seems that I am always tied to some type of conflict whenever I have visited India. I will be in Srinagar during the summer and somewhere warmer in the plains when snow starts to fall. We are treated as guests by the Indian Army, and we are provided with transport and other communications facilities. We will be spending six months with the Indian Army and six months with the Army of Pakistan. Sometime within the next year or so, I will visit Delhi. I hope to see you at that time.

I visited Verinag Ashram and stayed there for three days. I was pleasantly surprised to learn from Swamiji that you will be joining Nautiyal Industries in the near future. You will be pleased to know that a lot of progress has been made in the art and science of Communication by Thought since my last letter. A new theory is emerging: As we know, all things, including human beings, are made of atoms. The atoms are numerous and practically last for ever. Over the centuries, atoms move around from one thing to the other. Each of us has atoms that may have belonged to our ancestors. This may be the reason why you are so fond of Shakespeare, for example! You may contain some atoms that once belonged in Shakespeare's body. The gist of the theory is that human beings, through atoms, have natural bonds with each other; therefore, 'Communication by Thought'— I prefer to call it Braincom, and Swamiji calls it *Divya Drishti* or Celestial Vision—is almost a natural phenomenon. It just needs to be refined. Swamiji should know atoms; he holds a master's degree in particle physics.

As a corollary of the theory of Braincom, it follows that one human being may affect the thinking of another human being, if a sufficient number of atoms are common between the two. For example, you and I have some kind of bond; it may be because we have common atoms that belonged to an ancestor. Is it not thought provoking, eh? Swamiji has named this procedure, *Manoprabhava*; in, English, I call it Mindeffect.

At Verinag Ashram, Swamiji has conducted experiments to prove the existence of *Manoprabhava*. The procedure is conducted by looking intently into the eyes of the subject, while mentally chanting a mantra known as *Mohit Mantra*. Its sound is Shrinnnnnnnngsohummmmmmmmmmmmmmm. The sound is to be mentally internalized for about 30 seconds, while sub-consciously having the thoughts you want to implant in the subject's mind. There is one condition, though; the subject must not be aware that you are practicing this technique on him or her.

I hope I have given you enough food for thought. I do not have any address in Kashmir. I will keep you informed of my program.

Signed
Max Hoffer.

After reading the letter, Daddyji is lost in thoughts. He appears confused with what he has read. The only reference to an Atom he has ever heard of is the Atom Bomb.

He is thinking: *I wasted my time reading Shakespeare, Chaucer and Dickens; instead, only, if I had studied science. The future belongs to science.*

He gets back to his office files, but he is not able to concentrate. As he is struggling to write something, my grand parents, who live in Quarter E190, walk in. Daddyji stands up, moves towards them and touches their feet, a mark of highest respect.

My grandparents, almost in unison, say, "May you have a long life."

Daddyji is very happy to see them; he knows that Pitaji likes to talk about metaphysical matters like Max Hoffer has talked about in his letter.

Pitaji comments, "Surinder, you seem to have something on your mind. I hope we are not disturbing you."

"No, no, Pitaji, it is not that. Just a few minutes ago, I received a letter from Max Hoffer; I was thinking about what he had written." And he hands over the letter to Pitaji.

Pitaji starts to read it. While he is reading, Beyji, my grandmother, goes into bedroom to see Mummyji. After he is finished reading, Pitaji says, "This is quite an achievement. I am glad that the wisdom in our ancient scriptures is being discovered. Surinder, one day the world will beat a path to India to learn these secrets."

34
HOUSE WARMING

Relatives and friends start arriving by about 11 A.M. Uncles, aunts and cousins, who live in Delhi, are all expected to attend the *Griha Pravesh*, a ceremony to receive blessings and celebrate the move to our new house. Mummyji has dressed up baby Suneeta in a pink frock, matching shoes and ribbons and is standing at the front gate telling the guests that we have been blessed with a new home due to Baby Suneeta's destiny.

Daddyji is also standing nearby greeting the guests. I am reading his thoughts. He has not given up his habit of boasting. He does not do it loudly but silently in his thoughts. It seems that repeated nagging by Mummyji, and fear of Evil Eye, has had some effect on him.

He is thinking: *I have built my own house only three years after the partition of India. No other relative has been able to accomplish this—not even Daulat Ram. My elder brother, Shyam Nath, supposedly a top lawyer, has not been able to accomplish as much as I have. He promises to himself that he is not going to brag in front of the relatives.*

After all the guests have arrived, the priest starts the ceremony. Blessings of the Gods are being sought to make sure that no evil befalls the new house. It seems that coconut is present wherever blessings of God are invoked. The priest, Pundit Shankar Dayal Sharma, has brought a coconut along, and he is looking for Daddyji to break it open. Daddyji is wiser by his past experience. He remembers what happened at the time of laying the foundation stone of the house, when he nearly smashed his fingers instead of the coconut. He accepts the coconut from Punditji and looks at me with pride in his eyes, but he does not know that I am reading his thoughts. He is scared to break the coconut. I think

I am a big boy now, and I should share my father's responsibilities. As Daddyji is looking at the coconut wondering what to do, Daulat Ram comes to his rescue and says, "Surinder why don't you let Lalaji do the honours." Daulat Ram addresses my grandfather as Lalaji–a respectful way of addressing an elder of the family. Daddyji feels relieved and gladly hands over the coconut to his father.

Pitaji takes the coconut in his left hand and shows it to everybody by raising it above his head and says pointing to three round marks on top of the coconut, "See, God has given every coconut three eyes. One to look left, one to look right, and the third to look straight down, so that when it is falling from a tree, it will not hit anybody." Everybody laughs. He puts his hand up and signals everybody to be quiet. He then carries on, "God has given us humans, also three eyes; two eyes to see outwards and the third eye to look inwards." Everybody listens to him intently, and then he breaks open the coconut very deftly by hitting it on the floor and collecting the coconut water in a glass. My Friend, Suraj, having worked at his father's fruit shop, comes forward and offers to remove the outer shell and distribute the inner white seed of the coconut to everybody.

After the religious ceremony is over, everybody walks around in the house, admiring the colors of the walls and the floors. The front verandah is half round. Daddyji tells everybody that this type of design is known as Art Deco.

Daddyji is himself showing the house to Uncle SK and Daulat Ram. After the tour is over, Uncle SK says, "Surinder, *yaar,* your house is very nice, but the rooms are small. A house is something one builds once in a lifetime. You should have built the rooms a little larger. What do you think?" Up until now, Daddyji has been at his humble best. Thanking everybody for the compliments he is receiving. And then, Uncle SK shows the red rag to the Bull.

I am reading Daddyji's thoughts, and I can sense anger bubbling inside his brain. I am wondering how to take Uncle SK away. A bright idea flashes in my mind. "Uncle SK, Devika *Massi* is calling you," I say to him.

He walks over to the room where Devika *Massi* is sitting and he asks, "Devika, are you looking for me?"

She makes a face and looks at him telling him without words, "Why would I be looking for you?"

He quietly walks back to the room where Daddyji and Daulat Ram are talking to each other. It seems that Uncle SK is bent upon waking up the sleeping giant of egoism. He is looking at the walls and the floors and says, "Surinder, *yaar,* the colours of the walls and the floors are not matching. I would have preferred if the floors were of neutral colours."

I can sense Daddyji's brain start to bubble again, and then he loses control—well not quite. He tries to control his reaction and says in a controlled but acidic tone, "SK sahib, when you build your own house, you can do what you want. Till then, you will have to be content in your two room house with no kitchen."

Uncle SK is very offended. He strides into the room where Devika *Massi* is sitting, and says to her, "Get up Devika; we are leaving." She can sense that there is something wrong. She slowly gets up and looks at Mummyji, waving with her hand to ask what has happened. By the time Devika *Massi* gets up, Uncle SK is already out of the house.

There is a stir among all present at the house. All the women folk are looking at each other and asking in whispers, "What has happened?" Mummyji goes out running to stop Uncle SK from leaving. "What has happened?" She asks.

Uncle SK replies, "Kamla, money has affected your husband's head. He thinks by building his own house, he has become God. He does not even know how to talk to his guests."

In the meantime, Daulat Ram comes out and tries to calm things down. Mummyji goes in to call Daddyji to come outside to apologize. "I have not done anything wrong. What should I apologize for?" He says.

He really believes that he has not done anything wrong. Mummyji holds him by his hand and takes him outside to talk to Uncle SK. Daddyji goes along, stands in front of Uncle SK with folded hands, with head hung low and says, "Uncleji, please forgive me." He looks so funny, addressing Uncle SK as Uncleji that everybody bursts out laughing.

By late afternoon, everybody leaves except Suraj, who stays behind to play with me. We have just been promoted to Grade 5. Daddyji sees us looking at our new books. He pulls up a chair and sits down beside us.

He says, "Boys, how do you feel moving to Grade 5 and to the big school? Do you realize that the next seven years will determine what you do and how you live for the rest of your life? If you do well in school, you will get admission in engineering or medical colleges and go on to become an engineer or a doctor, and you will be set for a good life. But if you do not get good marks, you will have to settle for admission in non-technical colleges, and end up working as lower division clerks and starve for the rest of your lives."

Suraj says, "Uncleji, I want to build buildings when I grow up."

Daddyji replies, "Even if you want to build buildings, you must have good education. If your building business does not work, you can always go back to your profession. For the foreseeable future, there will be great demand for engineers and doctors in India and the rest of the world. We live in a world where there is shortage of everything. Those of us who are educated will get ahead, others will be left behind."

Suraj says, "Uncleji, it looks like we are in some kind of a race."

Daddyji replies, "Yes, life is a race."

As Daddyji is talking to us, Mummyji walks in holding baby Suneeta's hand and says, "You will see my Suneeta will win the race."

We all laugh, but I am worried about Evil Eye striking Suneeta. I have a premonition.

35
ABDUCTION

At about 10:30 A.M., the door bell rings in our new house. The front door is open. The curtain is swaying in the cool breeze. Kishi runs outside, followed by Suneeta. Mummyji runs behind them. She is always worried about one of us being kidnapped. There have been reports of such incidents in the city. As she pushes the curtain aside and walks into the verandah, she sees a man and a woman standing outside. The woman has picked up Suneeta and is kissing her on her cheeks.

Mummyji takes Suneeta away from the woman and calls for Daddyji, "Listen ji, can you come out? Quick... quick. There are strangers who are going to kidnap Suneeta."

Mummyji is hysterical. Daddyji comes out. He is followed by Pitaji with his steel pointed walking stick in hand raised up ready to pierce a hole in the body of the alleged kidnapper. The man and the woman are startled by the outburst by our family.

The man is well dressed in a light coloured suit and tie. The woman is wearing light blue *Salwaar Kameeze*. They appear to be of the same age group as my parents. The man introduces himself in English, "My name is Munnavar Ali, and this is my wife Salma."

As soon as my elders hear English words coming out of the man's mouth, they calm down. Kishi and I are standing nearby watching the drama. I am looking up reading Daddyji's thoughts.

He is thinking: *The man must be all right, if he can speak English so well.*

I am thinking: *You mean all those who speak in English are all good people?*

But Daddyji looks at me and asks, "Vikram, did you say something?" I shake my head sideways.

I am thinking: *Did he read my thoughts?* I cannot be sure.

Daddyji asks the man, "What can we do for you?"

The man replies, "We have reason to believe that this little baby girl you adopted is our daughter."

Mummyji feels as if the floor has been pulled away from under her feet. She goes and sits down on a chair nearby. Pitaji lifts his steel pointed walking stick and aims at the man, and says, "You *Buzzaat*. Get out of here before I pierce you."

The man takes a step backward.

Daddyji shouts at the man, "Who are you? Is this some kind of joke?"

After listening to the loud noise coming from our house, one of the neighbours also comes into our verandah. He asks, "Surinder, is there any problem?"

Daddyji explains to him what the man had said. The neighbour says, "If you want I can call the police and have these people behind bars in no time. My cousin is the Station House Officer at the Karol Bagh *Thana*."

Daddyji replies, "No. Let us not involve the police yet."

The woman, Salma, says in English, "Please let us explain."

Daddyji looks at Mummyji, and both signal that it is all right. The fact that Salma also speaks English, I think, does the trick. Daddyji invites them to sit down on the chairs in the verandah.

I am sensing all kinds of thoughts emanating from everybody standing around. It is getting confusing for me. A shroud of sadness is descending on me. I am reminded of the dream I had a few days ago where Suneeta was almost left behind.

Daddyji is thinking: *His name tells me that these people are Muslims. But Suneeta is Hindu. How can Suneeta be their daughter? There must be some misunderstanding.*

Munnavar Ali starts to explain, "We remember the day. How can we not? We lost our only child that day. We used to live in Lodi Colony. It was about seven in the evening, September 6, 1947. Nafeesa, our daughter, was about six months old at the time. Salma and I decided to go for a walk in a nearby park leaving Nafeesa with the *ayaya*. While we were strolling in the park, a mob descended on the area and started looting the homes. Some houses were set on fire. We ran towards our home. Unfortunately, ours was one of the houses on fire. We tried to get in to save Nafeesa and the *ayaya*, but the fire was so intense that we could not do anything. When the fire brigade and the Army arrived, the house was all but burned to the ground. We looked through the smoldering ruins and found no sign of any human remains. The Army started evacuating all the

Muslims to the Pak Transfer Office in Connaught Place. About 5,000 or 6,000 people must have moved to Connaught Place. When we reached there, it was utter chaos. We hoped and prayed that our *ayaya,* along with Nafeesa, would be there. There was so much chaos that it was impossible to find anybody. Over the next several days, people were sent by special trains to Pakistan. Since our parents had already moved to Lahore, in July, we also decided to go there; hoping against hope to find Nafeesa along with the *ayaya.* We reached Lahore on September 10 and went to my parents' home. My parents were shocked to hear that we had lost Nafeesa. With the help of relatives and friends, we found out that most people who had moved from Lodi Colony were living in a refugee camp in tents. We spent two weeks going through all the refugee camps. Every time we entered a tent, we would imagine seeing Nafeesa sitting in her *ayaya's* lap. One day, Allah smiled on us ever so briefly."

Both Munnavar and Salma start sobbing. Daddyji goes into the house and asks our servant, Chottu, to bring two glasses of water. Munnavar takes off his glasses and wipes tears and perspiration off his face with his handkerchief. Chottu brings two glasses of water and looks at Daddyji. He points towards Salma and Munnavar.

After taking a few sips of water, Munnavar continues, "One day, as were walking through a refugee camp, we saw a woman at a distance. She briefly appeared in front of a tent and then went inside. Salma looked at me, and I looked at her; questioning: Did you see what I saw? *Ayaya,* we both shouted at the same time and ran towards the tent we had spotted her in. As we were running, my wife, Salma got tripped by the guy rope of one of the tents along the way. She fell on her face, twisted her foot and broke her nose which started bleeding. Many people gathered around. Somebody called the camp doctor. After the first aid was administered, we continued towards the tent where we had seen the *ayaya.* By this time, we were not sure which tent exactly we had seen her in. We entered two tents, but there was nobody inside. As we were moving around, we were praying to Allah to give our Nafeesa back to us. He heard our prayers, but not quite. As we entered the third tent, we saw an old woman lying inside with her face turned away from us. I coughed a little to draw her attention. She turned around ... both Salma and I shouted... *ayaya.* She looked at us in surprise and got up. She said: Munnavar *Mian,* Salma *bibi,* what brings you here? How is Nafeesa baby?"

Both Salma and Munnavar start sobbing again and so does Mummyji. While still sobbing, they continue the rest of the story.

"The last words of our *ayaya* came as a thunderbolt. We told her, we are here to look for Nafeesa. Where is she? She stood there holding her head and uttered: *Hii* Allah. What is going on? Salma held her by the shoulders and shook her and asked, *ayaya* where is Nafeesa? Shaking made her realize what had happened. She began to relate the story:

"When they set the houses on fire, Nafeesa was asleep. I picked her up and ran outside. There was chaos. People were running all over the place. Hindus and Muslims were fighting with each other. I ran to the next street and hid behind a house, with Nafeesa clinging to me and weeping. After about an hour, the army, police, and the fire brigade arrived. That brought some semblance of order. I wanted to go back to our house, but they would not let me. They told me that everything had burned down on our street. I ran in the opposite direction with Nafeesa in my arms. I came across a group of policemen. As soon as they saw me, they shouted at me accusing me of kidnapping the little baby. They thought that, in the chaos, I had grabbed somebody's baby. As I stopped, one of the policemen took away Nafeesa from me and asked me to leave. I pleaded with them to let me take Nafeesa to you. I explained to them that Nafeesa was entrusted to me by you, and I must return your *amaanat* back to you, but they would not listen. Before I left, I told them where you lived and your name. They promised to deliver Nafeesa to you. Many Muslim people were carrying their belongings and walking to somewhere. I started following them. We all reached a place where thousands of people had collected. They put us on buses, took us to the railway station and put us on a train to Lahore. After reaching Lahore, we were brought here."

After Munnavar is finished telling the story, there is silence for a few minutes. Mummyji is sitting with a sullen face with Suneeta clinging to her. From the way she is looking, it appears as if Suneeta understands what is going on.

Daddyji breaks the silence by asking Munnavar, "How did you find us after three years?"

Munnavar replies, "After we came back to Delhi from Lahore, in October 1947, we went to the police, the Home Ministry, the rehabilitation Ministry and many orphanages. We spent a whole year, but nobody could tell us where to find Nafeesa. And then, Allah smiled on us in a different way. We were blessed with another daughter. We named her Aidah—the one who is returning. We began to consider Aidah as a gift from Allah, given to us in place of Nafeesa. We began to feel that Nafeesa had returned. And then about six months ago, as

I was taking out some fruit from a paper bag, I saw an announcement printed on it. It was an announcement in the government gazette about the adoption proceedings for a baby girl. Something in me told me that the announcement was for our Nafeesa. I took the piece of paper and went to the Ministry of Rehabilitation. Nobody was interested in talking to me. After pulling a lot of strings, we found out that the baby girl in the gazette was adopted by you."

As Munnavar is relating the story, I see Mummyji looking at Suneeta and then looking at Salma and Munnavar. I am reading her thoughts. She is trying to find a family resemblance.

After Munnavar finishes talking, Mummyji asks, "But how can you be sure that this is your daughter? So many infants were adopted at that time. Moreover, she is Hindu. The Government would never have let us adopt a Muslim infant. I think you are mistaken."

Salma replies, "I have no proof except the heart of a mother. I can feel it."

Daddyji says with a sharp tone of voice, "So what do you expect us to do; just handover Suneeta to you? Do you know that according to the law we are her legal guardians? Let me tell you this once for all. We sympathize with you, but there is nothing more we can do for you."

Munnavar and Salma quietly get up and leave—she with tears and he with a facial expression: I will be back.

We spend an uneasy day wondering what they will do next. Mummyji is walking around all day with Suneeta in her arms mumbling, "Nobody can take Suneeta away from us."

I keep thinking of the premonition I had about Evil Eye striking baby Suneeta.

• • •

At night, I have a dream. The story in the dream starts from where we had left off the reality in the morning.

The dream:

When Munnavar and Salma are walking out of the house, Daddyji throws a barrage of words at them. As soon as the last word leaves Daddyji's mouth, like an arrow aimed at Salma and Munnavar, I jump off the chair and dive towards them reaching them at the same time as Daddyji's last word. As they are absorbing the impact of caustic words from Daddyji, they reel back as they see me flying through the air towards them. I had aimed my flight towards Munnavar, making full use of the techniques of gymnastics learned in the class of, my Physical Training Instructor, Joginder Singh. As I land on Munnavar, my hands dislodge his spectacles, which fall on the floor with cracks appearing in the glasses. As Daddyji sees what is happening, he gets up to separate me from Munnavar, but he is stopped by Pitaji. In the meantime, I lay a barrage of words on Munnavar that he is likely to remember for the rest of his life. I shout at the top of my voice using expletives that even I did not know I had in my repertoire, "Bastard! How dare you come here to take our sister away? May Goddess Kali have eagles gouge out your one eye?" (I am not sure why I wished only one eye taken out and not both. I guess I was being generous.) I carry on shouting, "Your one leg will fall off, and you will become a leper, and your face will become like melted chocolate, and your brain will be fried and eaten by dogs," After catching my breath, I continue, "and blood will flow out of your body like river Ravi, and your ear drums will beat like a *Tabla*, and your feet will be set on fire when you walk on the road. You will burn in hell to ashes."

After I am finished with my tirade, I cannot believe what starts to happen. Smoke begins to come out of the ears of both Salma and Munnavar—from his left ear and from her right ear. But the smoke smells like coal tar. There is a rumbling sound, as if a road paver is paving the road outside. As the smell becomes more and more pungent, the sound of the road paver becomes louder. I seem to have acquired infinite power. I get hold of Munnavar with my left hand and Salma with my right hand, and I drag them out in front of the paving engine. The big steel roller is moving ever so slowly towards us. I am dragging both of them towards the round roller—the leveler of all sins. I want them to become two dimensional creatures—the residents of the Flat Land and become part of the road in front of our house. That way the bastards can see Suneeta for the rest of their lives, playing and riding her bicycle all over them. As I am dragging them towards the great leveler of sins, they suddenly grab me and push me in front of the great leveler.

As I see myself about to go under the great leveler, Mummyji screams, "Vikram, *beta*, be careful." Before I can move out of the way, the great leveler passes over me relegating me to the world of two dimensions. Munnavar and Salma get away.

And I wake up all shaken up and shouting. Mummyji also gets up at the same time screaming and with perspiration on her forehead, "They got …they got away…" Both of us are shouting. We had the same dream.

Daddyji is up, and Suneeta and Kishi also begin to stir.

Pitaji comes running with his steel pointed stick, "Where are they, the *Buzzat* people, I will pierce them."

I look outside through the window; the Moon is speeding across the sky.

"Swamiji told us that we will have a girl in our future. Suneeta is the one. How can anybody take her away from us?" Mummyji keeps mumbling lying on the bed, with Suneeta sleeping beside her.

Daddyji says, trying to placate her, "You are right Kamla; nobody can take Suneeta away from us."

He does not really mean it. He had gone to see a lawyer after Munnavar and Salma had left. He had come back and not said a word.

He was uneasy all day.

• • •

This day, the postman places his bicycle on the stand just outside the front gate of our new house, walks into the front yard and says, "Namaste *bibiji*," while he is walking to the post box hanging on the wall beside the half-round verandah. Mummyji is sitting with Suneeta in her lap; my grandfather is sitting reading the newspaper with his steel tipped stick sitting in his lap and half-moon glasses perched on his nose. It has been almost month and a half since the incident regarding Suneeeta. Munnavar and Salma have not approached us since their visit. There is a sense of relief.

As the postman is about to place the letters in the mail box, Mummyji looks up. She knows it from the colour of the envelope. She has seen it before at the Galaxy—the letter from the Ministry of Rehabilitation. She says, "Postman ji, give me the letters." He hands over a bunch of letters to Mummyji and walks out. Her heart beat goes up as she picks out the one from the Ministry. *What could it be,* she is thinking. She is used to seeing letters like that at her office at the Galaxy, but the one at home surprises her.

Finally, she opens the envelope and takes the letter out, but does not unfold it. She puts the letter aside and starts to recite Hanuman Chalisa, the hymn of

God Hanuman. After a minute or so, she unfolds the letter, reads a few lines and starts to sob uncontrollably…

My grandfather looks up, looks around and gets hold of his steel tipped stick and asks, "What is the matter, Kamla, why are you weeping?"

She hands over the letter to him.

He is shocked to find out that Mummyji, Daddyji and Suneeta have been ordered to attend a hearing at the Eastern Courts building at the Queensway near Connaught Place.

• • •

About a month later, Daddyji and Mummyji–with Suneeta in her lap–and Munnavar and Salma are seated around a rectangular table in the office of, Suresh Bhaneja, an Under Secretary in the Ministry of Rehabilitation.

He says, "Ladies and gentlemen, we have conducted a thorough investigation into the matter." As soon as he finishes the sentence, there is a knock at the door and a man walks in with a slip of paper. Suresh Bhaneja reads it and says, "Please excuse me, I will be back in a few minutes."

He gets up, leaves the office and goes into an office down the corridor. This is the office of the Secretary of the Ministry of Rehabilitation, the top bureaucrat. The Secretary tells him, "Mr. Bhaneja, I have received a phone call from Mr. Hari Nautiyal, the well known industrialist, about the Baby Suneeta case. He is a good friend of mine; please see to it that matter is settled in a fair and equitable manner."

Suresh Bhaneja asks, "Sir, how is Mr. Nautiyal connected with the case?"

"The Mehra family is known to him, and baby Suneeta used to live at the orphanage that has since been taken over by the Nautiyal Family Trust. He believes that it would be heart breaking for the Mehra family to give up the baby girl at this stage."

Suresh Bhaneja says, "Sir, we have completed our investigation. We have talked to Sita, who used to be the manager at the orphanage before the take over by the Nautiyal Family Trust. We checked the records at the ministry and came to the conclusion that some error was made in recording the particulars of baby Suneeta. The conclusion of the Investigation Tribunal is that baby Suneeta is the daughter of Munnavar and Salma Ali, and the real name of baby Suneeta is Nafeesa Ali."

"Oh, my God," the Secretary says, "I will appreciate if you can handle the matter in a manner that causes minimum anguish to the two families, keeping in mind that the mistake was made by our ministry."

Suresh Bhaneja says, "Sir, I understand the sensitivity of the situation, and I will deal with it accordingly." He gets up and leaves, but, as he reaches the door, he turns back and says, "Sir, there is another alternative."

"What is that?"

"We could offer the Mehras the option to adopt another child from one of the orphanages under our administration."

"Well, I leave it for you to handle the matter."

• • •

When he enters his office, he finds Mummyji, Daddyji, Munnavar Ali and Salma Ali talking to one another, and Suneeta sitting in Salma's lap and playing with her earrings. Suresh Bhaneja is pleasantly surprised and relieved to see the two couples in good spirits. He has been dreading the emotional outbursts that would take place when he announces the Tribunal's decision. As soon as he is seated in his chair, there is silence and Mummyji takes Suneeta back from Salma. A sense of gloom descends on the group as Suresh Bhaneja takes out the papers from the file to read out the decision; Suneeta is sitting in Mummyji's lap playing with the colourful glass bangles on her left arm and oblivious to the goings on.

"Ladies and gentlemen," he says, "The Investigation Tribunal has determined that a mistake was made by our ministry in recoding the vital particulars of baby Suneeta at the time she was brought by the police to the orphanage. We have reason to believe that baby Suneeta is, in fact, baby Nafeesa Ali, the daughter of Munnavar and Salma Ali. Mr. and Mrs. Mehra, there is no precedent in this case that we can fall back upon. You legally adopted baby Suneeta as your daughter; and, therefore, under the law, you are her legal parents. However, Mr. and Mrs. Ali are her real parents. This is the dilemma that the members of the Tribunal faced when rendering their decision. And the decision is..."

Mummyji starts to wipe tears after hearing what has been said. She can guess what the decision of the Tribunal would be.

Before Suresh Bhaneja can finish, Munnavar Ali raises his hand.

"Yes, Mr. Ali, do you want to say something?" Suresh Bhaneja asks.

Munnavar Ali says with his voice choked with tears, "Sir, we are very happy to hear that our Nafeesa or Suneeta, as she is known now, is alive and well. We do not want to hear the decision of the Tribunal, whatever it may be. For we have decided to leave Suneeta with her legal parents, the Mehras. Allah has been kind to us; we are going to be blessed with another child. Suneeta has been living with the Mehra family for almost two years, and we do not want to uproot her. Whatever the decision of the Tribunal, this is our decision."

Both Mummyji and Daddyji break into tears of joy. "Why are you weeping, Mummyji?" Suneeta asks.

Mummyji, with tears still flowing down her cheeks, starts to kiss Suneeta on her cheeks and forehead. Suneeta, not being able to understand what has happened, pulls her face away from Mummyji, touches her own face and says, "Mummyji, you are smearing lipstick on my face!"

After emotions have settled down, Suresh Bhaneja asks, "Ladies and gentlemen, would you not like to hear the decision of the Tribunal?"

There are four voices that say, "No."

"Mr. and Mrs. Ali, does this mean that you are withdrawing your petition?"

"Yes."

36
EPILOGUE

I am tired of punching the keys. My single typing finger wants respite from the worn out keys of my computer keyboard. As I am sitting staring at the jumbled set of keyboard letters, my sixth sense comes alive. I have a feeling as if they are trying to talk to me. I close my eyes and connect to waves emanating from them.

They say, "Sire, we enjoyed the story, but we have a few questions."

"Come on you flibbertibetts," I say, "Let me rest. Can't you see my wrist hurting with repetitive strain, my fingertips swollen, my fingers stiff? Whatever more I have to say, I shall convey by voice and not by punching upon you little tit bits of plastic."

"Sire," they say, alarmed, "Does this mean you have decided to use voice recognition software?"

"Yes, my friends of the keyboard world," I reply, "The old order changeth yielding place to new."

They reply, "Sire, we have stood by you taking all the toil you thrust upon us, and now you abandon us after punching upon us over half a million times. Who shall say that this is fair upon us? We have a few questions. Please tell us by touch, for you know we the inhabitants of the keyboard world cannot hear. Pray, satisfy our curiosity by touch and not by voice."

"All right, my friends, the keyboarders, you may ask me your questions."

The letter, Q, sitting in the left corner of the keyboard asks, "Sire, we are curious. What persuaded Munnavar and Salma to abandon their claim on their daughter, Suneeta, so easily?

I reply, "After the hearing at the Ministry of Rehabilitation, when Daddyji and Mummyji reached home, my grandfather also asked the same question. Both Mummyji and Daddyji claimed credit for saving Suneeta to be taken away from us."

The letter, Q, says, "Sire, we think that the credit should go to Salma and Munnavar. How can your Daddyji and Mummyji claim the credit?"

I reply, "For a whole month before the hearing at the Ministry, Mummyji was keeping fast every Tuesday and visiting the Hanuman Temple and praying, asking mercy to be showered upon our family. She asked forgiveness for all the sins that anybody in our family may have committed, and, in addition, she made an offering for the benefit of the disciples. She believed that her fasting, praying and offerings is the reason why God changed Munnavar and Salma's mind, and they agreed to leave Suneeta with us."

The letter, Q, asks, "Sire, what was your Daddyji's reasoning for claiming credit?"

I reply, "Daddyji claimed that he practiced *Manoprabhava* or Mindeffect, the procedure that his friend, Max Hoffer, had described to him in a letter."

The letter, Q, ask, "Did he explain when and how he did that?"

"He claimed that when the government officer left the room, Daddyji engaged Munnavar and Salma in conversation, practiced *Manoprbhava* and was able to change their mind. And that is the reason why they suddenly agreed to withdraw their claim."

The letter, Q, asks, "Sire, did Mannavar and Salma ever come to see Suneeta after the hearing at the Ministry?'

I reply, "They did come back once, a few months later, to say goodbye before they migrated to Pakistan. At that time, Mummyji asked Salma: What made you change your mind? And she replied: *Allah*."

The keyboarders are quiet for a while, and then the letter, Q, asks, "Sire, we have one more question, if we may."

"And what is that?" I ask.

The letter, Q, asks, "Sire, what happened thereafter? Did everybody live happily?"

And I reply with a laugh, "For that you will have to wait for the rest of the story in my next book."

And the letter Q asks, "Sire, do you promise not to use the voice recognition software for your next book?"

I reply, "We will see."

And now the story ends.

ACKNOWLEDGEMENTS AND MUSINGS

My sincere thanks to all my friends and relatives; for without their help, guidance and good wishes, this book would not have been possible. And, as Barry Padolsky reminded me, the responsibility for any faults in the book rests on my shoulders.

THANK YOU my friends:

Tom Sinclair for putting the idea of a novel in my mind; Yodha Singh for showing me the path to novel writing; Barry Padolsky for reading the early draft and words of encouragement and requesting Boyce Richardson to read it; Boyce Richardson for taking the time to read the first 60 pages and writing the encouraging letter which filliped me to keep writing; Ramesh Sabharwal for periodic review of critical elements of the manuscript; Paul Johannsen for reading several drafts along the way and offering suggestions and ideas; Emilio Granata, my neighbour of 40 years, for reading the drafts late into the night; Desikan for reading the manuscript and encouragement; Tina Bradshaw for insight and help in proofreading and formatting; Professor O.P. Kohli for reading the manuscript and words of encouragement; Jessie and Tony Isenegger for taking the time from their world travels to review the manuscript; Asha Chopra for excellent comments; Asmat and Nancy Malik for refreshing some of my memories of Lahore. Subhash Puri for advice about finer points of publishing.

THANK YOU my family:

Bipin Aurora for reading the drafts twice, in-depth comments and words of wisdom; Rajiv Aurora for facilitating the process;

Malhotras: Anil, Stephanie, Rick and Louise for constant help and encouragement; Romina for reading the drafts several times along the way and offering insightful comments; Rabinder for editorial advice; Subhash for strategic advice and Rajender for critical appreciation of various incidents in the book.

My grandchildren arrived at different times during the planning and writing of the book; it is their inspiration that kept me going.

Last but not least, but above all, my best friend and my wife, Anjou, for sitting by me evening after evening after evening.....a total of 2209 hours, reading one page at a time—hot off the screen—day in and day out over a period of some 4 years, while the Indian TV programs playing on the Asian Television Network were immersing my body and soul in the Spirit of India.

IN MEMORY of:

My father, Late Professor Narinder Nath Malhotra, Vice-Principal and Professor of English literature at S.N. Das Gupta College, Lahore and New Delhi; and my mother, Late Mrs. Shakuntala Malhotra, who was a teacher at *Mahila Maha Vidyalay*, Lahore, in the 1940's before the partition. Inspiration for the characters of Surinder Mehra and Kamla Mehra is based on their lives.

Printed in Great Britain
by Amazon